DuST

A POST-APOCALYPTIC FAIRY TALE

J. R. DEVOE

Dark Tide Publishing

Second Edition: 2024
First Printing: April 2020

Cover by MiblArt

ISBN 978-1-7771231-8-5 (paperback)
ISBN 978-1-7771231-7-8 (eBook)

www.jrdevoe.com

For Rey Selina,
Welcome to Earth

CHAPTER I

NYA

Sunlight glares in my eyes as I scan the desert wastes for my first victim.

I stand tall upon a dune, in plain sight for all to see. The element of surprise is a coward's advantage, after all. That's what they tell me, anyway, those who were caught off guard by my mother's rebellion. But I am not my mother. I am Nya —*Destroyer of Worlds!*

Well, not really. 'Princess of Ash' is the best you'll hear my folk call me. But the ghosts hiding amongst the dunes needn't know that.

I narrow my eyes on the columns standing in disrupted rows. What secrets do those ancient symbols decorating the decayed stone hold? Time has toppled a few, and those that still stand don't have much longer. At least not with me around.

But they are child's play. I need something bigger, a grander display of my power.

And there it is, staring at me from before the Great Pyramid. The great beast looks so regal in his pose, with three massive pyramids standing tall behind him. A hooded headdress hangs behind his ears to his shoulders, flaring wide at the neck, and gives him an air of royalty. With myself being five feet tall, this monarch is at least ten times my height. And that's with him lying down!

But I've crushed greater beasts with my hands.

I stomp over sizzling sand and stop a hundred feet from the forward edge of his paws. Yes, he will do nicely. One of humanity's most enduring creations, soon to become a cloud of dust at my touch.

I spread my arms wide and say, "Greetings, mighty king. I hope you've enjoyed your reign here, for your end has now come."

His limestone eyes stare over me impassively as the statue sits in silence as it has for—judging by its weathered face—thousands of years.

That's okay. I allow him this final moment of ignorance, for once he feels my resonance, he shall tremble. All tremble at my touch.

As I march into the shadow between his outstretched paws, my four translucent wings wrap instinctively around my chest and belly to guard against the chill.

Sizing up the leg resting to either side of me, which stand at nearly twice my height, I can't help but admire the size of this immortal being. But his physique must be a work of fiction. Skeletons I've seen littering the desert tell me the previous masters of this planet were, on average, similar to me in both size and shape. This monument is some sort of strange homage to a megalomaniac.

Exaggeration or not, it's hard not to feel defenseless in my walk between its giant legs. If this figure were alive, he could squash me like a pestering fly.

Well, he could try.

I press a hand against his chest and feel for the frequency range that holds this monument together at the atomic level. Every substance has a song—a silent, harmonic vibration that keeps its structure in solid form—and it's my ability to hear this rhythm that shall be their undoing.

A subtle, earthy vibration greets me. The gentle hum radiates from deep within the limestone, a rhythmic cadence that whispers stories from eons past, the frequency translating to geometric patterns in my mind—intricate fractals that mirror the delicate structures of the limestone's origin.

I close my eyes and allow my body's internal vibration to attune to the patterns. My heart beats faster as I amplify the resonance within the hollows of my chest. I direct this higher frequency through my hands and into the stone.

The megalithic statue above me rumbles in protest. Pebbles rain down upon me.

I smile. That's it... *tremble.*

Raising my vibration, I send a higher resonant frequency and feel the bonds that hold together this monolith's particles strain to maintain their hold. This stress permeates deep into the limestone and moves up the whole carved body, to its cobra-like headdress, and stretches the molecular bonds toward their breaking point. As I amplify my frequency and approach resonance fragmentation, I look up at the king's face and give him a smug look.

Zap! A shock breaks my connection and sends me stumbling backward.

I shake my hand and flex my fingers, which had curled tight against the electric jolt, and give the stone face overhead a suspicious appraisal, though I know it's no spell that causes this resistance.

I spread my fingers wide and examine them in disappointment.

I glare up at the statue. Looks like this giant shall continue its reign for a little longer.

Unless...

I ball both of my hands into fists and spring forward into a double punch, timing a disruptive vibration to shoot through my knuckles when they connect with the stone, to turn this entire monument into a cloud of dust with a single strike.

A bad move.

The energy rebounds and blasts me back through the air and onto the ground, where I'm left rolling around and gasping for breath.

Dust wisps down onto my face, and I shield my eyes to look up in time to see the head of the statue roll forward from its shoulders. Toward me.

No!

Reflexes kick in and I roll onto my belly, then my already-buzzing wings drag me out toward the paws.

A crash behind sends a wave of sand washing over me and tells me I just narrowly escaped.

As the dust settles to reveal the facedown head resting atop its front legs, shame overcomes me. Such works of art do not deserve the fate I bring to them. We should preserve these monuments as a warning to the next species due to inhabit this planet, to remind them that other races had once thrived here. And their disharmony with their home had led to their undoing.

I step close to the decapitated head. Rubbing a hand over the crown of smooth stone, I whisper a silent prayer for forgiveness from its creator.

Why must it be me who is cursed with this ability? *Entropath, chainbreaker, dustmaker...* Those are the nice names they call me.

A low rumble comes in reply and sends a shiver up my spine. But I quickly determine it does not come from the object beneath my touch, nor anything in my immediate vicinity.

I turn in time to see a distant tower near the horizon topple to the ground. I'd surveyed the structure when I first arrived, and deemed the sixteen levels of concrete standing six hundred feet above the surrounding city to be in solid form. Even the antenna spire and latticework casing, with its lotus-shaped upper section of the cylindrical shaft, had survived the ages of neglect with impressive integrity. Pretty much all but the shattered glass, a few pieces of which remained in the upper windows, through which a haunting wind howled.

I watch the tower collapse, a dust cloud rising from where the lower levels first touch the ground near the base, the cloud spreading wide as the higher levels crash to the ground.

A scream rises from the same direction as the dust cloud that blooms into the sky, telling me something is definitely wrong.

I sprint into flight, flying hard toward whoever is in distress.

Most of the cloud has settled by the time I reach the

collapsed tower. In fact, I spot only a single piece of steel in the long berm of dust that lies where the tower had fallen onto its side. I land in the dust dune and pick up the rusted rebar for examination. As my feet sink slowly into the fine powder, I realize it is not dust kicked up from the tower's fall, but the tower itself.

A scream echoes from a cluster of metal towers to the north. I spring once again into flight, but I approach this destination with more caution.

The compound's cylindrical towers are shorter than my previous stop, and the lack of windows suggest they were not designed for occupancy. A network of pipes gives the place a cold, industrial feel.

I land on a platform with ladder access halfway up a tower. Across the site, a figure dangles from a high walkway connecting two cylindrical towers. The walkway explodes above her, dropping her fifty feet to the next walkway, where she grabs a rail and swings away, leaving a cloud of dust in its place. She lands on the ground as another figure does acrobatics above her, swinging from railings to racks to beams. This figure blasts everything she touches with precision timing. Too early and she'd drop to the ground like her companion. Too late and the structure would remain intact.

"I see you using your wings, Doria!" calls the figure on the ground. "You know that's cheating."

Doria. She's the same age as me, but her skill...

She dives headfirst toward a beam, grabs a scaffold tube clamped below it, and catapults herself up fifty feet, leaving a small puff of dust where the tube and beam had been. She does a triple back-flip to the roof of the nearest tower, one of the two that had been connected by the dusted pipe rack and catwalk. She falls through the roof, banging all the way to the ground on the inside.

Her companion backs away as the whole tower rumbles and rattles. Then...

BANG—the tower explodes into a billow of dust.

She emerges from the cloud to join her Entropath sister, laughter from them both filling the air. Crazed laughter that sounds so much like screams. Her companion claps, and Doria gives a mocking bow.

My belly clenches with concern. This isn't right. Ever since my mother's rebellion, the Watchers have forbidden us dust maidens from mingling with each other. We're too much trouble in groups. Too hard to control. Harsh penalties accompany breaking this rule.

I scan the sky warily. Each of us is assigned our own work area and Watcher Overseer, except our Elder. I've heard Ko Skadia has five Watchers, because she can never be left unattended.

Groaning rises from nearby. I see the remaining tower lean, its base buckling without the upper supports.

I gasp and instinctively shout: "Look out!"

My two sisters notice the shadow of the tower sweep toward them. Doria dashes and dives to narrowly make it out, but her companion runs the wrong way, following the length of the falling tower rather than taking a sideways escape. Twisted metal screeches and squeals from the base until the tower slams down onto my sister.

I watch in horror as debris and particles rise from the crash. Only... much like the first tower I'd come to investigate, this one now lies in a pile of fine dust. And from that pile emerges the sister I thought I'd just watched die.

"Woo hoo!" she wails. "See that, Doria?" She lunges and swings her fist in an uppercut, presumably reenacting the technique it took to pulverize the tower as it landed on top of her.

The two black bands on each of her wrists tells me she is less than half my age, but the power she wields puts me to shame. Is that what Doria is doing here with her? Teaching her the ways? And did someone teach Doria before her?

Envy burns inside my chest. No one ever taught me neat tricks like that growing up. But even if they did, I'd never risk my life trying it. I'd be long dead by now if I had. Yet she makes it look so easy. Where does she get the energy?

I know: *Enthusiasm.* You can't fake it like I tried on the statue, even with a simple shift in mindset. But look at them go. I don't get it. They don't stop to look. Don't stop to think and ponder upon the creators and their purpose for these structures, what some of these sites meant to them. It's mindless, reckless destruction with complete disregard for legacy.

Maybe, deep down, they feel like me. They've just tricked themselves to get through the task. Believing is not enough; you have to *feel* it. Their laughter creates the enthusiasm. Or does the enthusiasm create the laughter?

No, there's nothing forced about what I've witnessed here. This is all natural to them.

A faint flutter comes from behind. I turn to see Doria standing face to face with me. She shoves me back against the rail.

"What are you doing here?" she asks.

Her partner appears in my peripheral vision, perched on the rail to my right. With the three of us occupying the same small platform, a sense of alarm rattles me. I've been warned in no uncertain terms: I'm not allowed within five miles of any of my dust maiden sisters.

"I should ask you the same question," I retort, stepping away from the rail and circling Doria to face the two of them. "Quite the racket the *both* of you are making here." I make extra sure to emphasize the 'both' here.

Doria folds her arms and leans back. "At least we're working. What have you been up to? Playing make believe again? Besides, we don't have that psycho Watcher of yours following us around. But now with you here..."

Doria's apprentice gasps and points behind my back. "There she is!"

I scoff. "If you think I'll actually fall for that—"

The alarm spreads to Doria's eyes and sends a shiver up my spine.

I turn south to see a black blot in the blue sky. At first it's only the size of my pinky nail, but it quickly grows until I see a spread of two wings. When I turn back to my sisters, they're nowhere in sight.

I survey the mess around me, piles of dust and debris knocked loose from their antics. It's clear that at least one Entropath has been at work here, but this is not my assigned area, so clearly I'm encroaching on another's.

My heartbeat thumps a dreadful tune on my eardrums. I must distance myself from this place, fast.

CHAPTER 2

NYA

I spring into flight, whizzing west and sidelong away from Doria's site, my heart racing fast as a hummingbird's. I set my bearing on a green tree line that stands between me and the western horizon. That newly grown forest is my only chance for safety.

I fly hard toward that sanctuary, my four wings buzzing twice as fast as my racing heart, which I feel as a throbbing lump in my throat. Cold sweat slicks my skin despite the blazing sun beating down on my back. The last Watcher to catch me messing about threatened to cut off my fingers.

Risking a glance over my shoulder, I see my hunter has already devoured half the distance between us.

I swallow down my heart and return my attention to the trees ahead. In the open sky, my four wings can't compete against the speed of my predator's two large foils, but in the forest I'll gain the advantage of agility.

I put my head down to decrease wind resistance. My hair blows back so hard that its roots threaten to rip from my scalp.

Waves of silky sand roll by underneath me. When it darkens to black earth, I look up to see I'm only a few heartbeats from the nearest trees. I glide through the first rank of redwoods and slow only enough to weave around trunks and branches.

A cluster of two dozen Fori, my tree-tending cousins, lounge on a branch ahead. On appearance alone you'd think we were the same species. Their four iridescent wings are identical to mine, and no doubt their panicked eyes upon noticing my approach resemble my own. But it's our abilities that set us apart. While the hands of these Fori sisters nurture trees to build up the new world, mine tear down the old.

They scatter at my approach. Though, it's not me they fear. They know only one thing can make a dust maiden such as myself move like this.

A crash through the canopy announces the arrival of my predator.

I cut hard left, swerving around tree trunks and tearing through moss curtains. In theory I should be able to outfly my predator down here, but I won't let this offer me a false sense of security. This new advantage has been replaced by a disadvantage, for now my attention is split between avoiding a collision with a tree in the dense foliage and finding a safe place to hide.

Up ahead, a lone Fori clings to a mossy trunk and waves me toward her. She knows these woods better than me, so I respond to her summons. She hovers back from the tree, her clear wings buzzing excitedly, and she points to a hole burrowed under its roots.

I glide to the ground and, seeing her frantic eyes scanning

the forest all around, I can only hope I'm in the clear when I dive under the roots.

My Fori savior pulls a pine bow over the hole and then flies away. Not even the forest's best hiding spot is safe so long as it's anywhere near me, and she knows it.

Light streams through gaps in the covering branches, but the darkness behind me is smothering. My breath shudders and seems to echo into an endless abyss below, so I cover my mouth with both hands and try to breathe as little as possible.

Outside, cheerful birdsongs suddenly die out. Tiny wings flutter away.

My heartbeat pounds hard in my eardrums. Despite the deafening tune, I hear voices whisper from the void behind me. They are the voices of those who my mother had led from the light and doomed to eternal darkness. They demand that I join them.

They aren't real, I remind myself.

This assurance isn't enough. I'm willing to risk a peek outside when the flutter of wings kicks my heart into a frightful dance. I recoil deeper under the tree, where the soil is cold and damp, and I swear I can see my breath puff before me in the faint light. I cover my mouth just to be safe.

The diagonal streaks of sunlight that stream down through the canopy seem to sink unnaturally fast, until the entry points nearly reach the ground. It'll be sunset soon. Darkness is near, and I dare not find myself down here, alone with these voices, when full night takes over. Luckily, I have an idea.

I wrap my wings around my chest and belly, then smear wet soil over my body and rub it into my hair. If it's a Watcher that pursues me, then I can only hope it mistakes me for an Ori. A really tall one, mind you, but it's my surest chance.

I rub some muck into my hair for good measure and then slowly crawl out of my hiding spot.

A quick look around reveals not even a single insect. Everything seems frozen in time, including the leaves. Even the wind dare not trespass upon this place. I see why when I look up.

Legs of copper skin stand like an arched doorway over my burrow.

I gasp and try scrambling back underground, but calloused hands hook under my armpits and hurl me out into the open. My wings react quickly to keep me from hitting the ground, but my attacker springs off the tree and tackles me to the forest floor.

Flipping me onto my back, she straddles me and presses a dagger to my throat. Two blood red wings, shaped like those of a butterfly, rise high above her shoulders. Sweaty strands of scarlet hair hang down from her head over my face.

"You're getting harder to find," Jaleera says. She watches me with unblinking eyes, and the vertical slit in each of those yellow orbs sends a shiver through me.

"You're getting worse at *hide-and-seek*," I say. The movement of my throat against the dagger point pinches my skin.

Jaleera stands and slides her dagger into a sheath hanging from her waist. "This isn't a game, Nya. I checked your work area—you've been here a month and you've not dusted a single thing. Do you remember what happens to those who falter in their duty?"

I sit up and rub my throat. "A delinquent spark goes straight to the Dark," I say.

I shiver at the thought of spending an eternity in that nothingness. Ever since the Watchers agreed to oversee our Penance, they've used a portal to the Dark to keep us in line. That Black Hole is a cold, empty void where you spend forever alone in crushing darkness.

"I'm not honed in yet," I say, resisting the urge to flex my fingers before me, woefully aware of my previous warning. But it's true. I've not yet calibrated to this planet's resonance. I am an instrument out of tune. "This planet's frequency is throwing me off."

Jaleera shakes her head at me. "You're too old to be using that excuse. Whatever resistance you're feeling has nothing to do with Earth." She pokes my forehead. "It's coming from inside that head of yours. You fail because you won't embrace what you are."

"But it's true. It's so dense here—"

Jaleera smacks me upside the head. "Always excuses with you."

My left ear rings, and my temple stings where Jaleera's hand had connected. I lower my head and prod the area to feel a wet spot on my hair, and when I pull my fingers away I see by their glistening tips that her nails had broken the skin. The sight of my own blood makes me lightheaded.

I'm lying down on my back when Jaleera seizes my wrist and launches into upward flight, dragging me up through the treetops with her. The sudden tug nearly rips my arm off, and it takes everything in me to keep pace with her as she hauls me northward over the canopy. Her bearing is set on a mesa that stands high over the forest, its flattened top clear against the orange dusk sky.

My throat tightens. Has she finally had enough of my antics? I once saw a Watcher cut off a Fori's wings before throwing her over a cliff. It was awful. Her tree-tending siblings said it was for being too sick to work, which makes my failings way worse.

My belly roils as we speed toward that plateau. I'm actually going to puke by the way my jaw is quivering, and I now realize illness would have made a better excuse for not getting my work done.

Cowering under the treetops below, Fori watch me with frightened eyes as my Watcher drags me toward a fate that only she knows.

Jaleera's grip tightens around my wrist, her nails biting into my skin, as she picks up speed. Unlike my four narrow wings, her two butterfly-like wings catch more air and moves us so fast that it takes all my strength to keep my arm from popping from its socket.

We arrive at the mesa in record time and rise up its barren slope. That's when the tremors kick in. Though my hand has long since gone numb, it still shakes like a leaf in a hurricane at the sight around me. The new forest stretches in every direction for as far as I can see, making this the perfect place to make an example of me for slacking in my work.

We crest the level peak and fly across its flat top to the western edge. Here, Jaleera dumps me on the ground and hovers in a circle around me.

I rub my wrist and watch her warily.

She points to my feet. "Sit."

My trembling knees collapse into a cross-legged position.

I lock eyes on the sun setting to the west. If that red disk melting into the distant horizon is the last sight these eyes are to see, I suppose I could do worse.

Jaleera looms over me and points her spear down the northern slope. "Look at how busy your cousins have been since they arrived."

I trace her spear tip to an Ori gang hauling a glittering blue net up the mountainside, just above the tree line. The crystalline material attracts the molecules that enrich even the most unforgiving ground.

"The Magister's inspection is in a fortnight, Nya. What do you think he'll have to say about *your* work?"

I keep my shoulders tense to disguise my relief. She wants me to feel guilty for not contributing, but I'm just glad she hasn't brought me here for punishment.

I watch the stout, wingless Ori scramble up and across the incline so eagerly, motivated by purpose as they spread the shimmering blue net that resembles a massive spiderweb, creating conditions that refugee races from other planets shall enjoy for ages to come. That's their legacy. What am I to be remembered for?

A fool's daughter, at best.

But for all their enthusiasm, their tillmaster's shouting suggests they aren't moving fast enough.

I hug myself. Typical. Everyone always gets worked into a frenzy before the Magister's arrival. He comes each year to inspect our progress, and he doesn't take failure lightly.

See, whenever an intelligent species loses their home, it's the Magister's job to find them a new planet. Sometimes that means renewing the home of an extinct race, like this one. *Gaia,* they call her. And she has suffered greatly at the hands of her previous custodians. We have much work to do to heal her, but it's not the first time we've tended her wounds.

My ancestors came here long ago, to reboot the planet after a great catastrophe. Our methods were different then. We worked alongside survivors to restore their habitats. The native folk called us *pixies*. Imagine, *pixy!* What a ridiculous name for a savior of worlds. If anyone ever called me that, they'd get a swift smack on the lips.

Jaleera kneels before me, blocking my view of the sunset, its orange light giving the loose strands of her scarlet hair a fiery glow. She picks flakes of dry blood from my hair, almost tenderly. Almost like she cares about me. *Almost.* But the way she grips her spear with her other hand, squeezing the platinum shaft as if itching to put it to use, betrays her true nature. How many disobedient Servants has she put an end to with its tip?

I hug my knees to my chest and rest my chin on them.

"I loved your mother like a sister," Jaleera says. "It pained me greatly when Jexa sent her life-spark to the Dark. It'd be a shame to lose you, too."

My fingers curl tight around my knees. That name, Jexa, heats my blood. I jerk my head away from Jaleera's hand. She gives up and stands.

Jaleera draws her dagger from its sheath and offers it to me by the blade. "Choose wisely," she says, eying up my fingers.

I gasp and tuck my hands into my armpits.

Jaleera twists her lips at my response, sympathetic but unyielding. "It's the greatest mercy I can offer. Jexa would have your head if she had her way."

As I accept the diamond-crusted handle with a shaking

hand, one of the Watchers' many maxims comes to mind: *'Pain is the great instigator for change.'*

"You've earned the Marshal's ire, Nya. Do you know what that means? It's more than just losing a finger. She wants to take you on as her personal ward."

My heart jumps in my belly. I'd cut off half my fingers right here and now to prevent that from ever happening.

"She believes I'm too soft with you," Jaleera says. "I think she is right. With her as your assigned warden, she'll be able to keep a closer eye on you. If she's not satisfied with your work..." Jaleera shakes her head, then nods toward her knife in my grip. "When I return, I expect the wound to be healed."

You will not delay your self-punishment, is what she is saying. I'm not sure what's worse: having to decide which to sacrifice, or having the decision made for you.

I examine my hands, really taking in each finger, wondering which would have the least effect on my life should I lose it.

"You're leaving?" I ask, suddenly aware of how she's been my only barrier against Jexa's spite. "To go where?"

"I'm needed across the ocean," Jaleera says. "The shadows over there are too vast for even Jexa's light."

I narrow my eyes on Jaleera and note a fresh white scar on the bronze skin of her neck. "Tell me about these *shadows*," I say. "Why have I never come across them in my work?"

Jaleera's cold stare sends a shiver through me, warning me to adjust my tone, reminding me of my place.

She turns her back to me, surveying the spreading forest below in contemplation. "Jexa and I flooded light across this land long before you arrived, that's why. You needn't worry about the patches that still darken distant lands. Concentrate on your own work and leave them to us."

When she looks back to me, any trace of her tenderness has evaporated. "You have one week to clear your first work area. Jexa is coming at the half moon to inspect it herself, and if there's so much as a pottery handle left when she arrives, well, then even I won't be able to save you from her wrath."

I shoot to my feet. Cold sweat runs down my brow. "A week? That's—"

"More leniency than you deserve from the Marshal," says Jaleera with a piercing stare.

I must look quite frightened, because Jaleera's eyes soften —well, they soften as much as a Watcher's are capable of.

"You just need to find your rhythm," Jaleera says. She points northwest. "Head north to the coast, then follow it west through the desert. You'll find just what you need there. It's called a 'drilling rig'. I think you'll have less of an ethical dilemma reducing that eyesore to memory. If you can clear your first work area before week's end, then maybe I can convince Jexa that you need all your fingers. If not—"

"Then I have a difficult decision to make."

I sink back to the ground and watch the half-submerged sun sink deeper into the horizon. How many different stars have I watched set now? How many more will I have to fall in love with, only to eventually see them as an insignificant speck in the night sky of a distant planet?

"Did you hear me, Nya?"

"I heard you, Jaleera."

Jaleera backs away while giving me a wary look-over. She shakes her head, then dives from the cliff edge and flies rapidly west. I watch her shrink toward the horizon until she disappears into red clouds. She's gone before the sun, its light likely guiding her all the way to the shadows of a distant land.

Watchers. They used to be more than just wardens to us. *The Light Ones* is what we called them long ago. *Guardians of Nature.* When the hubris of my ancestors led them to destroy their homeworld, stretching its resources beyond sustainability, sapping the planet's energy to fuel their ambitious designs, the Magister placed upon the Watchers the responsibility of overseeing our atonement. He chose them for their ecological wisdom and terraforming expertise. They were to guide us, mentor us, teach us humility and self-control through service to others. I suppose at one point that's what they did. But now look at them, how they treat us.

I push my toes into the fine dirt in search of the cooler bottom layer, wishing I could burrow away like the Ori. Life would be much easier if I could disappear as easily as my earth-working cousins. My ancestors could actually shrink to conceal themselves, but the Watchers altered our DNA to rob us of that ability. At two to three feet tall, the Ori were allowed to remain small for their underground work. They are minuscule compared to the seven foot, feather-winged Aeri that roam the skies above, far from the Watchers' reach. *Angels,* the ancient folk here called our rain-making cousins. *Egotistical air heads* suits them better. But at five feet tall, myself and the Fori can't slip into hiding among the trees so easily. We are most vulnerable to our wardens' persecution.

Night falls fast in this place. In what feels like a blink, I'm staring at an unfamiliar pattern of white pinholes across a black sky. How many of those stars have warmed my skin from the surface of an orbiting planet? Around which speck of light out there shall I find the next world I call 'home'?

Laughter comes from up high. In the sky directly above me, an Aeri flock swirls water vapor to form clouds that obscure my view of the stars. Thunder rumbles. A raindrop splatters on my nose.

Urgency rises like fear in me. I jump to my feet and sprint to the cliff edge, where I leap into the air and fly west over the forest. Playtime is over. Wet wings will ground me and I'm already facing a tight deadline. Even Ko Skadia, my Entropath Elder and the most senior dust maiden on this planet, would struggle to clear my assigned area in that given time.

My heart quivers. The Watcher Marshal will be less forgiving in her inspection than her second-in-command, so I must hurry.

CHAPTER 3
NYA

My warm-up project appears in the orange light of dawn. Following Jaleera's directions, I'd flown north to the coast, then west past the forest's western edge and into the desert. I'd kept a hard pace all night, bobbing in the breeze over cliffs that separate the sea from the expanse of silvery dunes to my left, before the 'drilling rig', as Jaleera had called it, came into view.

The cube-shaped steel mosquito sits aslant in shallow water, not far from a beach. I don't see an independent means of propulsion, so it must have washed up here in a storm, or was dumped here by those who no longer had use for it.

As I draw closer, I notice brown corrosion has already claimed its place on the tower that looms over the rig's upper platform.

I'm supposed to start from the outside and work my way inward, peeling away the outer layers like skin from rotten fruit, until even the seeds are but a memory to only myself. Instead, I flutter inside the interior compartments to see what this monstrosity is all about.

At the bottom of a stairway, I enter a chamber where a seating apparatus rests behind a large block of furniture. On the floor lies a framed image under broken glass. In it, I examine several wingless alien figures standing on a beach. If they had wings and pointed ears, they'd look just like me. Comparing their height to the palm tree beside them, I'd say we're near the same size. They even smile like me. And in a moment, no one will ever know they existed. The thought makes me ill, so I set the piece down and leave.

Outside, black slime streaks down the tower that looms over the main platform. I dab my finger onto the sticky substance and smell it. It doesn't seem toxic, so I lick it.

Yuck! It's disgusting. The word *petroleum* comes to mind, and this stirs a negative vibration inside my chest. It's enough to get me started. Time to make some dust.

With both hands, I clamp onto a rusted rail at the edge of the structure's main platform. In the shadow of the tower, the metal is cool and damp under my palms. I close my eyes, feeling the trillions of minuscule particles vibrating together at the frequency that holds this steel tube in its solid form. The vibration works its way into my mind, producing a display of intricate, interlocking spirals and coils behind my closed eyelids, telling me this is iron.

My sisters like Doria are unwise to assume what anything is without proper appraisal. Sending resonance into a material like platinum or diamond could have fatal consequences if you get it wrong. The energy rebound can stop your heart or, if you get it really wrong, blow your whole body to dust.

But iron is fairly safe. Its moderate frequency holds only

the occasional spike to watch out for. Nothing to worry about. You got this. It's all a state of mind.

I match the frequency and force a disruptive vibration, echoing the intricate design of the iron's structure through my palms.

A small section of rail crumbles through my fingers. I open my eyes and watch a stream of particles wisp from my hands and sprinkle the water below. I frown at the sinking specks of dust, a rather pitiful amount I must say, dissatisfied. The entire rail and all its supports, all around, should have blown into a hundred trillion pieces, leaving a ringed cloud around the platform. But I know what I'm lacking here:

Inspiration.

I grip the next section of rail and think of my mother, how she abandoned me to start a hopeless war, and how she made me heir to the ashes. This gets my blood simmering. My arm hairs rise from static energy that radiates from inside me, and my fingers tingle with this higher frequency. The anger stirs the energy in my chest, amplifying its frequency.

I discharge this energy as a disruptive pattern through the steel's molecular bonds, interrupting the rhythm that has kept this material defiant against all manner of disaster for who knows how long.

The wave slides into the vibrating field of the iron's molecules, this one stronger than before, triggering a building wave that grows as it spreads outward from my hands, stretching the molecular bonds.

The rail rattles all the way down and around the bend until—*POOF*—it bursts to dust. I watch the fine particles drift away in the breeze and feel a smile grace my face. Destroying this structure conjures far less guilt than the cultural artifacts

I encountered near the pyramids. And there's a small part of me that feels what you could call gratification, with a sliver of enjoyment.

I zip across the platform to the opposite rail and continue my work, breaking the chains that bind its particles, until the entire square tube is dust in the breeze. Then I move to the tower. Starting at the top, I shatter its chain of molecules in chunks from crown to base. It's not the ideal approach, but when I become better practiced, I can stand at the bottom and shatter it all at first touch. If I try that now, though, I might send it toppling into the sea, creating more work for myself. That's just poor handiwork.

By high noon I'm deep in the zone, matching and amplifying frequencies with hardly a thought. Jaleera was right. I just needed to find my rhythm. The bedazzlement of so many resonances mesmerizes me, and I find myself dismantling the structure instinctively. That is, until...

I pulverize a drill pipe, but a chunk of steel survives and falls to the deck. I'm so caught up in my work that I grab the cylinder, capped with a small crown, and squeeze with the vibrational pattern of iron infusing my grip. A mistake.

The energy rebounds up my arm and rattles me so fiercely I'm forced to release the object.

I drop to my knees and gasp for breath. A tremor of residual energy still rocks me, sending a spasm through my heart. It takes me a minute to compose myself.

When I prod the object, I discover it's way more dense and hard than iron. *Tungsten.* Given its original position at the end of the pipe, I conclude it's a drill bit. This oversight, caused by my complacency, had nearly cost me my life. If I'd held on any longer the shock might have stopped my heart. But it could have been even worse than that.

A closer look reveals diamonds embedded into the cutting edge. I once tried to dust a diamond throne, thinking it was glass. That misidentification resulted in a sensation I can only describe as being electrocuted. If I'd used more force than is required for glass, the energy rebound would have blown me into a trillion pieces.

The use of diamond to drill into hard geological formations does not surprise me. I've yet to encounter a material more hard or dense. I'll have to be more mindful when surveying my work areas, to see what's what. As for this particular piece...

I hurl the drill bit from the platform and into the sea. The tide will take care of that while I carry on with my work. No doubt the Watcher Marshal will be stringent in her inspection of my areas, but there's no way she'll go scouring the seabed in search of anything I've missed.

It takes me until mid-afternoon to dust the entire structure. I hover above the patch of unblemished sea where the metal cube recently stood, but any sense of satisfaction I felt earlier has left me. I am born to work this magic, and I do feel a sense of purpose in the moment, but afterwards...

A frown sags my brow. My cousins embrace their roles for the satisfaction of creating conditions that will foster numerous lifeforms: the Fori with their teeming flora, the Ori with their enriched soil, and the Aeri in their bursting clouds... What do I offer by destroying the creations of those who came before the next race to rule this planet? Erasing their love and labor, sweat and blood, only to make room for others to do the same. Will I return to undo their creations as well?

This misery haunts me only briefly. Every bond I break brings me closer to the Final Gateway, the passage that will take me home to my fated mate, Penance served for the crimes of my ancestors. The promise alone makes my heart flutter faster than my wings.

I dive into the water, where endless molecular chains swirl around my skin and wash me clean. I love doing this at night to see the bioluminescence. *Sea sparkle,* the Nixies call it. If I listen closely, I think I can hear the songs of my aquatic cousins echoing from the depths as they work in what I'm told is a universe of its own.

I wade out of the sea onto a sandy beach while wringing salt water from my hair. Wet sand squishes between my toes until I reach dry mounds, which sit before a cliff wall that blocks my view of the desert beyond. Though I'm pressed for time, I'm not going anywhere with wet wings, so I lie on my belly and bury my face in my arms as the sun dries my wings.

I can only hope Jaleera had lied about Jexa coming to inspect my work to scare me into behaving. And what was that about her wanting to become my personal warden? The Marshal of Watchers has no time for such affairs. It's the efforts of the collective that matter most to her. This task is even below her second-in-command, but somehow Jaleera has ended up as my devoted overseer.

I draw Jaleera's knife and examine my reflection in the blade. My attention drifts to my fingers grasping the silver hilt, with its ruby pommel. It would be a shame if something were to happen to this. What if I lost it? How else would Jaleera expect me to cut off my own finger? A finger of my choice, I might add, by the grace of my supportive Watcher. A proper mentor would have provided guidance as to which would be easiest to live without, but I suppose no one is perfect, my benevolent Watcher included.

I close my eyes and see fractals of shimmering, fluid shapes. *Silver*, the whole thing, including the blade. With a smooth, moderate frequency, it's almost as if Jaleera wants me to destroy it. A light squeeze introduces a subtle resistance, a gentle ebb and flow, like swimming against a current. A hard squeeze reduces the knife to dust. Well, most of it, anyway.

The ruby pommel sits on the sand above my hand. I clutch it tight, trying to match its high frequency. Rather than smooth warmth, it's hard and unyielding. When I close my eyes, sharp, brilliant fractals dazzle me. I squeeze the ball of precious gem and send an amplified vibration through it.

A rebound stabs my inner fist with a thousand needles, forcing me to drop the glittering stone. It steams in the sand, but otherwise is unaffected by my attempted destruction.

Diamond. Red, deceptive diamond. Some things resist not just me, but also the likes of Doria and Ko Skadia. Tower fallers and mountain shakers cannot crack this frequency. I've heard tell of a master frequency that can undo anything, but I have my doubts about that. You'd blow yourself to pieces practicing all the different combinations at the intensity required, so unless you cracked it the first try...

I snatch up the stone and fling it into the sea. Hopefully the turning tide will conceal the pesky, stubborn evidence from Jaleera and her fellow Watchers.

I bury my face into my arms once again. The swish of lapping waves and fizzing surf relaxes me, and I'm just dozing off when I hear the sound of pebbles tumbling down the cliffs. I look up in time to see a figure retreat into a nearby crevice in the cliff face.

I'm on my feet in a second. Who'd be way out here in this desolate land? The Ori would have too hard a time working this sand into soil, and the Fori have no business outside a forest. Perhaps a lost Aeri, but why remain down on land? Maybe they're hurt and can't fly. Or it could be a Nixy who wandered from the sea and, in their return, got spooked by the sight of me.

I trot to the cliff and enter the fissure that splits the rock face in half, where black rock stands high to either side of me. The roofless corridor widens the farther I walk from the beach. Slopes of sand from the desert above interrupt the chasm at scattered intervals. A vertical indent in one reveals where someone had recently slid down from the desert above.

A scuffing noise rises from behind a boulder ahead of me. I stop.

"Why do you hide from me?" I say. She must be a Nixy. My sea-dwelling cousins are known to be reclusive, and usually need to be coaxed into interacting with other races. "You've nothing to fear. Come out so I can see you."

A boy with skin the shade of rich earth steps from behind the rock.

My jaw goes slack. A *boy*. It's been so long since I've seen a male counterpart that I've almost forgotten what they look like. Even the face of my own beloved mate has faded from my memory. Only one of a pair must serve the Penance, as separation is punishment enough for us both. Because females wield a higher command of the elements, it's always us who volunteer, for the boys would take too long restoring so many planets. Instead they stay back and maintain our home world, preparing for our return.

The stare of this boy when he locks eyes with me stirs a warm, gentle vibration inside my chest. I don't recall the last time someone looked at me like this before.

A flash of envy hits me. Have the Nixy-folk been allowed to keep their lovers in the sea all this time? Or is he the rare type who commands his element better than his other half? Perhaps he volunteered to do Penance for his partner.

But I assume too much.

"I've not seen you before. Which Hive are you from?" I clap my hands to cut myself off. "Wait, let me guess."

I step closer to examine his spindly frame and wiry muscles, trying to determine which he uses most. He appears to be the same age and development as myself... What strains does his job demand of him? "Let's see..." I say. "You're too big to be an Ori, and I don't see any gills or scales on you. That means you're either a tall Fori, or a short Aeri." I try to walk around him for a look at his back, but he turns to remain facing me, yet not before I make a peculiar observation.

I frown. "Where are your wings?"

His eyes meet mine with a look of surprise, the brownest eyes I've ever seen. In fact, I've never seen such eyes before. And his ears, rounded at the top...

A startling realization sucks the breath from my chest. This *boy* is no cousin of mine.

Rocks crunch above. Pebbles tumble down the crevice face to my left.

I look up and around, my heart racing.

The specimen beside me does the same, his eyes wide in alarm.

Four silhouettes rise from the cliff-top above.

The boy steps in front of me and throws up both arms toward the figures, as if to shield me from an incoming threat, and shouts: "Stop!"

Reflexes break my paralyzed state. I launch into flight, my four wings fluttering furiously to lift me above the crevice. A projectile whistles past my head from the cliff top, and I bank right to narrowly avoid a second bolt. Several more streak past as I rise higher into the sky, until a blow to my chest blasts the wind out of me.

I drop several feet and fall into horizontal flight. My hands go instinctively to my ribs, where I find a length of hardened plastic protruding from my skin. I wrap my fingers around the narrow shaft and turn it to dust. Blood leaks from the wound, sparkling in the sunlight. I cover the hole with one hand and fly hard inland, carrying a burden worse than any physical wound.

We're too early.

CHAPTER 4
DEKA

I should rejoice as I watch the demon fly inland over the desert. One arrow had found its mark in her chest, and though our internal anatomies may differ, I suspect that the wound, coupled with the exertion of flight, will see her falling to her death before she can report our location. Already her flight path bobs up and down as she struggles to stay aloft.

Her kind are the devils who killed my parents, yet my voice is absent from the cheers of my tribes-folk on the surrounding dunes. While they celebrate, I raise a hand to shield the sun from my eyes and squint for a better look at our retreating enemy.

Marlok mounts the dune before me to block my view. Our war chief raises his crossbow high to claim the strike and the honor that comes with it. His crazed eyes lock onto me from behind a veil of locs. He demands my praise. I offer him a slight nod.

Our warriors chant a victory tune as they slide down into the crevice, where I'd been standing during the encounter, and file toward the hidden cave entrance. The crevice had once been a cave, but collapsed from erosion years ago, leaving an open trench. At the inland end, sand has slipped in from the desert, forming a ramp up out of the entrenchment.

Marlok remains above and joins me at the crevice lip. "I'm glad your father wasn't here to see you today," he says. "A man of his worth should never know the shame of seeing his son cower before his prey."

My jaw clenches. "I did not cower. I was unarmed."

"Those demons killed your parents. Any son worthy of their name would have strangled that creature with his bare hands, or died trying."

No doubt Marlok would enjoy watching me die. My father and mother held differing opinions on how to combat the demons, and I have devoted myself to ensuring my mother's strategy endures. We must learn from our enemy. Marlok believes this approach threatens our colony's security. He follows the way of my father. The way of the warrior. Fight the enemy face to face by attacking to kill at first sight. This has led many of our own to their deaths. For this high cost, we have gained so little. If we continue on this path, I will watch everyone I grew up with die. Those like Mali.

She slides down the dune slope to join us. My reflection in each of her round goggle lenses grows larger in her approach.

"Did you see its eyes, Deka?" she asks, her stare snapping back to the shrinking dot in the sky. "Were they all black like the others say?"

Marlok storms over and throws her into a headlock. I lunge at his waist to separate them, but he grabs my arm with his free hand and flings me aside like a piece of tide-plastic.

"I trusted you to watch the entrance," Marlok growls at Mali. "You let Deka out in broad daylight, and now that *thing* knows we're here. If it lives long enough—"

"It won't!" I say as I struggle to rise on the shifting sand.

"Shut up, boy!"

Boy! he calls me. At twenty-one years old, he's got only five years on me. But since we lost all our fighting adults to the sky demons, command of the war party fell to him at age sixteen. He was forty-first in line at the time, but he acts as if Grand Mother's wisdom had declared him chief successor in our prime.

He shoves Mali to the ground beside me and points a condemning finger at her. "You think I'll give you special treatment because you're my sister. Well, it's time you learned a hard lesson. You're off duty until you convince me you can do as you're told."

Mali's brow creases above her green goggles. I'd made these for her coming-of-age five years ago, and I swear I've never seen them anywhere but over her eyes or around her neck.

"That means you'll turn in your weapon," Marlok adds.

Mali's jaw goes slack. She hugs her crossbow to her chest.

Marlok's eyes soften. He shakes his head, his face rife with disappointment. "You two put our colony at risk today."

Neither of us can argue that. We only ever come to the surface at night, to bathe in the sea or to scavenge washed up polymer. That seems to be the only time the sky folk don't come around. Unless it's three days to either side of a full moon. We learned that one the hard way.

"Give me a weapon," I say as I crawl to my feet. If I want another chance to study one of those creatures, I must earn

Marlok's trust. It is he who decides who sees the light of day. He is the gatekeeper I must appease to get my hands on one of those *demons*. "If any of those things come back," I say, "I'll kill them or die trying, if that's what you want."

Marlok's eyes narrow on me. I see he's contemplating. He strokes his chin. "You did get pretty close to it," he says, nodding faintly. "Within striking distance, actually. It even seemed amused by you, if you can compare their expressions to ours. Fine."

He draws a dagger hanging from his waist and offers it to me by the blade. "If that thing comes back, you'll drive this into its heart. Or you'll—"

"Die trying," I say, accepting the knife by its bone handle.

A smile tugs at the corner of Marlok's mouth, as if he's counting on it. "Come, before the sun cooks us into a nice meal for the demons."

As Marlok slides down the path in the crevice's rock face, my eyes remain fixed on the black dot shrinking toward the desert horizon. To get my hands on a specimen such as her would offer great insight into their weaknesses. And much more, maybe. Not only did the thing speak to me, it did so in our language! Usually they come only to kill and then leave without a word. But she was here to make that stranded offshore rig disappear, and then hung around to relax on the beach. If I was quieter, I could have gotten the jump on her. What secrets could I squeeze from it? Enough to give us an edge against her kind, no doubt.

But at that distance I'd never reach her if she fell amongst the dunes. The heat would kill me before I made it even halfway, so I turn to join Mali stomping toward our cave entrance behind the boulder.

I follow the labyrinth of rock passages deep underground. The light from the outside fades until I'm walking in darkness, but I don't need light to conquer this maze. When the first sky demons arrived fifteen years ago, our parents dug this spiderweb of tunnels as a last line of defense. Now it serves as our first. Growing up, we learned to navigate the passages until we could do so in the dark. Should the enemy ever enter our domain, these twisted tunnels will give our lookout a chance to reach the colony in time to issue a proper warning.

The darkness cannot hide Mali's anger, however. She stomps her feet so loud that I know exactly which passage she takes off the main vein, which lets me know the one I should avoid. Her anger is my fault. She needs time to cool down while I find a way to make it up to her. Neither of our tasks will be easy. Usually the youngest warriors are assigned to defend the non-fighters in the escape caverns, ushering the elderly and feeble while the senior warriors form our colony's shield above. At age fifteen, Mali was given this task, which she called *hide-and-go-seek*. She hated every second of it.

So she trained hard, and managed to earn a spot as one of our colony's eight lookouts. A position she held proudly for two years, until today.

"*Everyone should fend for themselves,*" is what she once said to me. "Anyone who cannot is dead weight."

"One day you'll be old," I'd told her, "and you'll be glad for the help."

"No, I won't," was her response.

When I'd asked her which she'd meant—the becoming old or the needing help part—she did not respond.

Normally soft green light would welcome me to the

Grand Gallery, but the unwelcome visit still has the colony in blackout mode. So I feel my way to my alcove, where I light a candle in its entryway. Murmurs rise as my neighbors fuss over the light, the fear still in them, but I know Marlok will not enforce a continued blackout. That risks diminishing his victory.

You are safe with me as your Master of Defense, is all he wants them to know.

I set Marlok's dagger on my desk near the entrance and light another candle. Most think the smell of burning whale fat is not worth the light the waxy cylinder casts, but its illumination helps me design our victory.

The desk drawer squeaks when I pull it out to retrieve my mother's sketchbook. I sit against the rock wall and get to work with a graphite stick, scratching the details of that winged creature while they're still fresh in my memory.

When I finish the contours of her eyes, I examine my work with mild dissatisfaction. It's the irises. The grey graphite does them little justice. Though, would any shade of green capture them? And why do I care? She is my enemy. I'd foolishly risked my safety by permitting her approach, just so I could have a closer look. Never have I seen something so... alluring.

I squeeze the pencil so hard it snaps.

I flip back a few pages, to a similar drawing. My mother had sketched a winged warrior, her side notes suggesting weak spots to aim for. Our fighters back then had landed strikes where the heart should be, yet the beasts continued on without much bother. Come to think of it, the creature today instinctively covered its belly when facing the flurry of arrows.

I return to my own drawing to sketch a target on her soft navel, but when I place the broken pencil's tip to the brittle page, my hand remains firm. For some reason, I am unable to point out this vulnerability, even to myself.

"Always hiding behind your books," comes a voice from behind.

I slam the journal shut and look up to see Mali in the entryway.

"They didn't save your mother when the demons came," she says, as if an orphan needs reminding that his parents are dead.

And my father's spear didn't save him, either, is what I want to say. Instead, I nod to a stack of books beside the doorway. "The words on those pages told my mother how to set up lights for us to see down here. They taught her how to farm the algae that provided oxygen for us to breathe, and plants for food and medicine. Without those books we'd have suffocated in darkness long ago."

Mali crosses her arms and looks around at the rock walls. "Marlok says there is only one book we need down here. It is that book that provides all the light we need."

I bite my lip, knowing a rebuttal will only earn me scorn or worse should she relay my words to her brother. My defense of my mother's methods ring hollow with Mali, and for good reason. My mother is dead. She was our colony's last scholar, and in the end, she reached for a knife to defend herself. Only the fighters survive in this life.

"I'm sorry I got you in trouble," I say.

Mali picks up the knife from my desk and pokes her thumb with the point. "Marlok is using you as bait."

I know this, but I play along with a shrug. "Good thing I have that knife."

"You won't use it."

"You sound so sure about that."

"I am. My brother is, too."

I glance at the knife in Mali's hand. "Then why give it to me?"

"To see if you'll man up when the time comes. Your father was his idol growing up. And your grandfather... Marlok still can't believe the grandson of the last great warlord could choose the path of cowardice."

My shoulders tense. *Cowardice.* That word gets thrown out a lot around here, by warriors who pass their time cradling weapons while staring mindlessly at the sky. Yet I've killed as many enemy as most of them. Even a newborn child has. But those who do not seek the trials of warriorship are considered fat. Not in a physical sense. I've heard Marlok say often the colony should 'trim the fat'. The dead weight. The extra mouths to feed. Mali, concerned for my sake, encouraged me to be harder, stronger. Even a warrior who lives into their elder years is frowned upon, for not having risked enough in defense of our home.

But with me it's different. My grandfather had built an empire from the ruins of the old world. A warlord, yes, for the world at the time knew only the language of violence. But the elegant handwritten notes on the pages of my mother's books do not come from her. His written words reveal a man of science trapped in the wrong age. A feeling I myself know too well. His reign was indisputable, until the sky darkened with the creatures that would shatter his empire, forcing survivors under ground. After my grandfather's demise, my father ruled this sanctuary unchallenged until his death, with the assumption that I would rise to take his place. Marlok didn't try to hide the daggers at his funeral, the target burning red hot on my back. So I shielded myself with books and left the politics to them. To endure, we must study our enemy and learn their ways. Through that we can engineer our victory. Or else this fight will carry on until we are all dead.

"We can learn more from a live specimen than a corpse," I say.

Mali admires the knife with a smirk. "Then I guess you won't be needing this."

"Take it," I say absently as I rub the spine of my mother's journal. Some day I will show my tribe that knowledge is also a weapon. I'd only accepted the knife in a bid for Marlok's trust. Besides, it was my fault Mali lost her crossbow, so I dare not deny her this.

After a few moments, I hear footsteps fading away. I look up to see Mali has left with her brother's dagger.

I tear my mother's drawing from her book and hang it on the wall, then pin mine beside it. I step back, comparing the two. At five feet tall, both figures are the same height, with my mother's appearing slightly older and with sturdier legs and arms. But it's the wings and eyes that suggest they are two different species.

My mother's sketch depicts two black, butterfly-like wings, flat with rounded edges, perhaps once beautiful as a monarch's but now tattered from ages of violence. Her demon holds a spear over its shoulder, and one of its pointed ears is mangled. A warrior. The creature from today had four smaller wings that were so clear I could hardly see them, and it wore the tattoos of a few black bands around each wrist.

Mother's specimen either lacked these, or she failed to capture them.

But it's the eyes that reveal all. Mother's notes describe reptilian eyes—two golden orbs with a vertical slit down the middle of each—all menacing and full of hate. My specimen had eyes like my own, and our encounter drew only a look of curiosity and amusement. If they are of a different breed, and she wishes me no harm, then perhaps she can lead me to the beast who killed my parents. *If* she survives her wound, of course. And *if* she returns. We didn't form a very friendly welcoming party.

A thought occurs to me. What if the winged creatures attack us out of self-defense? If we show them we mean no harm, maybe they'll leave us alone. Or better, become allies.

I stare at my sketch a long while, noting the contours where my shading needs work. Where did you come from? *Demons*, my people call them. Whenever I use that term, it's for lack of a better word. There must be a scientific explanation behind their origin. Genetic engineering? Mutation? Results of an experiment gone wrong? Perhaps they were once like us. Maybe they adapted on their own, separating from us by evolution. And what's the meaning behind those bands around her wrists?

Something whistles past my ear and hits the rock wall. I jump at the *whack* of Marlok's dagger burying between the eyes of my drawing. I whirl around in time to see Mali storm away from the entrance.

CHAPTER 5
NYA

At some point during the evolution of my species, we were hunted by predators higher on our food chain. Though it has been years in the tens of thousands since we faced such threats, the instincts of my ancestors still guide me.

This gift helped me escape that ambush. It's what keeps my heart pounding hard inside my belly and my wings buzzing against my back in my race across the dusk desert.

Their voices cry out over eons, infusing every particle of my physical being with an energy reserved only for near-death situations. They demand that I carry on their legacy.

Keep going! they command by way of my hammering heart. And I obey.

I fly high over the rippled sand sea, wary of another attack, but find myself drifting lower toward silvery dunes as the sky above me darkens into deep night. I've tried my best to ignore the pain in my chest, but the burning spreads like wildfire across my skin, becoming a weight of its own that drags me dangerously low.

But fear rises to the occasion and excites my faltering wings. There are dangers on this land I never thought existed. Shadows of ages past that I must avoid.

My chest throbs, though not from the hole in it. This pain swells from the spark deep within my core, a fire of black flames casting shadows across my mind. In all my cycles reclaiming planets, never have I encountered their previous inhabitants. And for good reason. It's against the rules. The Magister's laws can never be broken, not by anyone. Not even himself.

My people found that out the hard way, many years ago, when they rose too high, stretched our planet's resources to the extreme in the pursuit of more and brought so many down with their fall, including the planet we called our home. Now we must serve Penance to atone for our hubris. And we were lucky to be given the chance.

I'm saved when the full moon rises over the horizon before me. Its surface reflects the sun's rays that give me the energy I need to endure—ultraviolet radiation infusing my weary muscles and battered spirit with renewed life. My body feels lighter, less of a burden to my wings, which now hum away with less effort. As the moon rises high into the night sky, I rise with it.

As my struggle eases and my flight becomes effortless, my heart races with a new feeling. *Excitement.* Finally, something I can help preserve!

I don't know if I've ever felt this rush of purpose before. I can't wait to see the look on everyone's faces. All their toiling away here...all for nothing! The pain in my chest can't even keep the smile from my face.

It's just past midnight when the first hint of moisture

graces the desert air. Not long after, the wavy dunes level to sodden earth. Beyond this expanse of fertile ground, between me and the horizon, glows a dome of soft green light into the night sky.

My tired wings buzz wildly under the bright moon, driving me from the desert toward the forest edge. The smell of wet earth brings tears to my eyes as pity for my Ori cousins swells in me. They've invested so much time and hard work here for nothing.

Beyond the forest edge ahead, a cluster of floating green orbs and faint drumming beckons our roving workers home. But this is no home to me. An outcast has no place to call their own. In fact, my arrival here will have everyone on edge. Entropaths are allowed to visit a Hive only during emergencies. It is said we shatter all things in our path with our reckless nature, including the peace. We're not even allowed within five miles of *each other*. This is something the Watchers monitor closely, as seen yesterday in Giza. It didn't take Jaleera long to come break up the trio of us at Doria's playground.

I can't remember the last time I visited a Hive, but after flying wounded for so many hours over desolate land, the promise of seeing a familiar face gives me comfort.

I glide through the first staggered row of trees that shield the forest border. Water drips onto my skin from the leaves overhead, remnants of my Aeri cousins' work above. What will their reaction be to the fateful news I bring? All their labor here has been for naught. Everyone's toil was a waste, for encroaching on an intelligent race's home will not count toward our Penance.

I shake off my guilt. *Let them feel the ache of*

dissatisfaction for once in their lives, I tell myself. For once, I'll be the one who beams with purpose.

A great tree marks the center of Ko Mirah's Hive. The *Heart Spire,* they call her. She's one of many nodes channeling the planet's energy to support our work, a constant hum for all of her sprouts to hear and rise from darkness toward the light. Glowing orbs hang from her gnarly branches. They cast green light over the bark of her twisted trunk, revealing grooves that spiral from roots to crown and gives her an emerald appearance. She is a beacon in more ways than one.

A Hive's arrival through the portal is chaotic. The transit leaves many disoriented for days or weeks, but everyone knows where to find their new home as sure as migrating birds returning to a nest abandoned at the changing seasons.

Knowing my flight is at an end, my wings give out on me. I slam onto the Spire's giant roots and roll into the crevices between, where all I can do is submit to the embrace of rough bark. Only now, wedged between two immovable tree roots, do I realize how hard I'd been breathing as my chest struggles in this tiny space to draw shallow breaths. Pain rises to remind me of my neglected wound. But the time for rest and recovery have not yet come.

"I guess we didn't make ourselves clear last time you came around," says a voice from up top.

I look up to see two Fori—Squiggs and Sheffa—standing on the root above me. At first glance you'd mistake us for the same race, standing five feet tall with our pointed ears and four wings. But we are not the same, and they're always quick to remind me.

"This Hive is for *makers* only," Squiggs says. She crosses

her arms while a scowl wrinkles her pug face. By the size of her cheeks, I see her sweet tooth for berries still holds her in a tight spell. Her poor wings. It's a wonder she can still fly.

Each of the pair bears the same number of black bands on their forearms—six per side—each a mark for one of the dozen planets they'd helped reclaim. It's only two more than me, yet they speak to me as if I'm a youngling.

Sheffa plants her hands on her hips and nods. "Yeah, ain't no *termites* allowed." Her words whistle through a gap between her front teeth, and her hawkish nose wrinkles as she fakes taking in a foul smell. "Just like the rest of your kind, you got no place here, Nya."

They watch as I claw my way out of the crevice. Sheffa looks like she's going to shove me back down, but when I reach toward a handhold by her feet she stumbles away.

As I stand, my wings wrap around my torso, overlapping thickest on my right ribcage to seal tight over my wound.

I slide down the sloped root to the ground and march around the Spire's base.

Squiggs jumps down after me. "Where do you think you're going?"

"I have a message for Ko Mirah."

She grabs my wrist with both hands and pulls me to a stop. "You can't. She's working."

"This is important."

Squiggs grabs my other wrist and locks me in a stare. "No disruptions."

I forgot Squiggs had appointed herself as Ko Mirah's bodyguard to keep pests away.

"Leave her alone, S-S-Squiggs."

We both look to see Jinny limping toward us. I can always

count on her to stick up for me, though she's the only one. Even with a mangled leg, she's become known as the Hive's anti-bully patrol. If only her body matched the size of her heart.

Squiggs laughs. "What are you gonna do, runt?"

Jinny picks up a stick and holds it out nervously. She limps forward. It was she who'd beckoned me to the hiding spot in the forest yesterday afternoon, when Jaleera had me on the run. No other Fori would stick her neck out for me like that.

To her left, Sheffa swoops down from the high root to intercept her. Jinny flings the stick at her and turns to limp into flight.

This provides enough distraction for me to wrench my wrists free.

Thanks, Jinn, I say to myself as I enter the tree through an acorn-shaped opening in the trunk. No footsteps follow.

Inside the tree, static in the air prickles my skin and lifts the cobwebby hairs on my arms. In the center of a round patch of smooth dirt, surrounded by inner trunk walls, is Ko Mirah.

The Hive Elder sits cross-legged with eyes closed and back straight. Not a single strand of her green hair has survived the ages, leaving her head crowned in grey. She's restored so many planets that her earned stripes cover each forearm from wrist to elbow in one giant, solid black band, with no gap for a single other—one hundred in total. A Penance served. Almost. She's earning her Final Gateway here. The next planet she sees will be the one she calls her home. Or, so it should be.

I freeze in the entryway, terrified to cause a disruption.

And it's not just the dread of letting her know that her journey home to her fated companion will have to wait a little longer. Squiggs was right. It's a great taboo to call one from their inner space, especially an Elder, for it is they who do the grounding work with the planet, exchanging information with the *Mycelium* to ensure our projects flourish. The ancient fungal network is amongst the oldest and wisest organisms on Earth. Its underground threads foster communication between trees and plants, nutrient exchange, and information about environmental stress. It spins the cycles of life and death for the entire ecosystem by breaking down organic matter and recycling nutrients. These were among a few of its purposes before the surface of this planet died. Now it provides the Fori and Ori guidance on what the soil and flora in each area needs to thrive once more. Any efforts must be done in harmony with this information bank that thankfully survived the devastation above. But I've heard these spells can last days on end, and we don't have that much time. We shouldn't even be doing the work that she's grounding.

"We're too early!" I say. My voice booms up into the void above and then cries back to me even louder. I cringe and stumble back toward the green glow of the entrance.

Ko Mirah's eyes slide open. Her brow folds down into a frown until her eyes focus, then raises in surprise as she takes in the sight of me. Her shoulders rise. "Nya, have you not recovered your wits yet? Can't you see I'm busy?"

I rush forward and drop to my knees before her. I lean in, closing the distance between us, and whisper the fateful news. "I saw..." My brow furrows deep as the word eludes me. How do I describe those beings who attacked me? They were so similar to us, yet...different. "I saw *Others*."

I close my eyes and wince, expecting the wrath delivered upon carriers of ill messages. Instead, I feel cold hands enclosing mine. I open my eyes to see Ko Mirah's nurturing smile.

"You have the imagination of your mother," she says, almost wistfully. "Just don't let Klora's folly lead you to darkness as well."

Hearing my mother's acts referred to as folly by an Elder stings me with shame. We are the remnants of our parents' deeds. I am a fool's legacy. An Elder's confirmation of this burns away all delusions of anything else, much like how the sun burns away a morning fog.

But my errand here is not that of a fool.

I stand and open my wings. A patch sticks to my wound, stinging as my inner flap peels from my right ribcage. My four wings spread wide. Their instinct to curl inward at their ends to return to my wound is stopped only by my conscious effort.

Ko Mirah leans forward to examine the sticky hole in my chest. Her brow sags in concern, her lips twisting in anger. "Where did this happen?"

"Why does that matter?" My wings flap shut around my chest and once again suck tight to my wound. "We shouldn't be here. It's against the rules. This is their home."

Ko Mirah, Elder of this Hive and Keeper of the Sacred Laws, sinks back and waves a hand dismissively. "Forget what you think you saw. The Light Ones have studied them and made their appraisal. They know what's best for an ecosystem. And what is not. It's better to see them as ghosts from a species long dead—mindless beasts cowering in caves."

"*Shadows*," I say, finally realizing what Jaleera had meant by that word.

Angst grips my heart. I suppose deep down I always knew that's what she meant, but to hear an Elder of mine speak of this so casually sits heavy on my heart. The time for my ignorance has passed. I've seen that these shadows have faces. "Does the Magister know about this?"

Ko Mirah shows me the black bands on her arms. "I'd have about as many marks as you if we just up and left every planet we found survivors on."

This hits me like a punch to the gut. She can't be serious!

Ko Mirah closes her eyes and takes a deep breath. "You had a traumatic experience, Nya. Rest here until you're ready to get back to work. Let the Light Ones take care of these *Others*."

I step back and study my Elder in disbelief. Her indifference toward this discovery strikes me harder than that arrow to my chest, and drives deeper than any weapon ever could. My belly clenches, but I compose myself. "What will the Watchers do with them?"

"Their time here is done. The *Light Ones* will bring them to a new home. We must prepare this planet for a new race—one that will take better care of this gift. Now, go. Rest."

"But..."

Ko Mirah frowns. "Must I summon *The Hammer* to come set you straight?"

My throat tightens as if a hand just clamped around it. My Entropath siblings make me uneasy, for they enjoy our destructive work too much, which you'd expect considering our ability to destroy evolved from our nature. But our leader, Ko Skadia, is on a whole other level. They say when she fought against the Watchers in my mother's rebellion, *The Hammer* used our skill to turn her opponents to dust. Living flesh—*POOF*—gone! Jexa let her live because only she can control the unruly dust maidens without killing us. But to prevent us from causing trouble, we're not allowed to associate with each other. Lucky for us, we happen to be loners by nature as well.

I storm outside, my head swirling like the strings of particles that form the clouds of a hurricane. This can't be right. We're *reclaimers*, not *invaders*. We clean up the mess; we don't make it. And she's wrong about them being mindless beasts. I saw awareness in that boy's eyes. *Concern*, even, when his people attacked me.

But Ko Mirah is right about one thing: I must rest. Right now I'm wobbling on my feet and at risk of falling over. A weary body weaves a cloudy mind.

I find myself a cradle of latticed branches near the top of the Heart Spire. A poultice of grey leaf and *singa* root cool my wound, courtesy of Ko Mirah, a gesture to remind me she has a heart. But it's only for the pain. The Spire's healing energy pulses through me. A cool tingling spreads wide across my chest, soothing the burning and lifting the heaviness. But it is not this physical wound that requires attention.

Despite the Spire's uplifting energy, my heart grows heavier with each beat. That *mindless beast* tried to save me. I saw the alarm in his eyes. He was afraid for me, and even tried to shield me from the attack. We have no right to force him from his home. I know too well the feeling of being taken from the place of your heart's center.

I cast a stern gaze at the Moon. Yes, the same celestial body that gave me the strength to reach this haven still sparks my ire. For it is that thing that imprisons me here. Somewhere on its cratered surface stands a tower, and from that tower spreads a frequency that ensnares the essence of the departed, barring their disembodied Spark from returning home. The invisible net casts a stranglehold over Earth, preventing the release or ascension of departed souls. Or perhaps it acts more like a vacuum, drawing the Spark to a central point on the Moon. Much of the mechanics behind this 'Soul Recycler' remain a mystery to me.

Yet, the intricacies matter less than the consequences. The fact that it spits you out through the Great Pyramid in the same body you left with, minus your Marks, is what matters most. Not only are you reborn in the same form to endure this place again, possibly under the watchful eye of your executioner, but you'll have erased all proof of prior service. A complete reset. It's the worst thing that can happen to you, aside from getting sent to the Dark.

I hold both of my forearms together. How many of the five black rings circling each wrist have I earned from unknowingly displacing a struggling species? I'm required to earn ninety more before I can cross the Final Gateway. Both forearms will be black to my elbows when I'm reunited with my beloved, a constant reminder of the many who lost their own homes so I could see mine.

I sigh. If only I could make the best of my time here like the others do.

Chanting resonates from the surrounding forest. Fori

cohorts shout and taunt each other in lively banter, occasionally engaging in light-hearted theft for sport and enticing others into playful pursuits. Yelps and laughter interrupt the spirited shouts, and I am reminded of how much I've missed the vibrant energy of a Hive.

In my mother's younger years, before my time, we Entropaths had a Hive of our own. After the rebellion, Jexa disbanded the dust maiden collective and forbade us from interacting with each other. They've even reduced the number of us on each planet, increasing the workload for each of us. I've heard we are forty on Earth at most. With work areas spread thin as they are, there is no reason nor excuse to overlap. Which is fine by me. The way my kin revel in their violent nature makes me uneasy. Give me a slapped-together nest at the foot of a dune after a hard day's work, and I'll have the best sleep of my life.

But sometimes, after I've arrived on a new planet, I'll make my way to the outer edges of a nearby Hive when I'm feeling lost and alone. I remain far enough away so they don't know I'm there. So they won't get in trouble for hosting me. Hearing them from a distance gives me comfort as I shiver alone on the cold dunes. But this is a rare solace I seek. And it's always just a matter of time before someone discovers me encroaching.

And so lounging in the comfort of a Hive is a rare luxury for me. Ko Mirah's invitation has granted me sanctuary, and I intend to use it. She even had this poultice sent up to me. Yet, it doesn't stop the stares.

I don't have to look below to know there are eyes watching me. Squiggs and Sheffa have surely spread word of my arrival. My mother, Klora the Fool, ignited a rebellion that drew the wrath of the Watchers upon all of our kind. No doubt some think I spoil this sacred tree with my touch. Still, I hear them skitter and maneuver below, looking playful in my peripheral vision.

Finally, one braves an approach. She climbs up the branches and leaps across the gaps to close the distance between us. A face smeared with dirt and mud-caked hair marks her for an Ori. It's not like the soil tenders to venture so high from the ground. The wrinkles across her skin suggests she may be a leader.

"Careful, Mora," warns a harsh whisper from the group huddled below.

Mora. That name rings a bell. She'd be an Elder now if she hadn't tended my mother's wounded during the rebellion.

Mora climbs onto the main branch supporting my cradle, but she keeps her distance.

"We heard you were attacked," she says.

My hand drifts instinctively to the poultice bulging from my rib.

"Don't worry," Mora says in a shaky voice. "The Light Ones will flush them out. Perhaps they'd even let you join to get your revenge."

"*Revenge?*" I look to Mora curiously. This word I've not heard before.

Mora inches closer. "Sure. Your attackers are going to die anyway. Better by your hand to level the scales."

The poultice throbs and burns in my chest. I give Mora a curious look. Why has she come to me? She takes a great risk by interacting with my kind.

I stand and Mora shrinks away, poised to leap back to the

safety of her kin waiting below. Her reaction takes me off guard. Sometimes I forget how others see me. To some I'm not just a nuisance or outcast. To some, I'm a wrecking ball with wings, an ardent destroyer of civilizations. But I have no quarrel with the Ori. And I realize it's not even me who has her on edge.

I trace her stare to the sky, where thirteen winged figures fly in arrow formation below the full moon. Spear tips glint in the silver light as they sweep west toward the desert.

"Word travels fast," Mora says.

My heart pounds like a drum in both of my ears. It plays a song of death. I heard Watchers can smell a drop of blood a hundred miles away. They'll follow the trail of mine back to my work area, to those *Others*.

I leap from my branch, four wings fluttering hard to carry me up into the night sky. I'm dimly aware of the burning in my chest. This pain can wait. I have an extermination to stop.

CHAPTER 6
NYA

Hard as I try, I cannot keep pace with the thirteen Watchers ahead. I can't even hold the same altitude. As they fly high in the night sky, maintaining a perfect arrowhead formation, I drift lower until the treetops are only an arm's reach beneath me.

As the night drags on, I sink lower. I'm barely skimming the forest canopy when the moon disappears under the horizon ahead and the first sign of pink lines the eastern sky to my rear. But worse than that, in the absence of moonlight I've lost sight of the Watcher hit team. They've outrun me. They're probably already there, commencing the slaughter.

Tears blur my vision. I've failed. They will find the remnants of this race and send them into extinction. And it will be one hundred percent my fault. Everything I set my eyes upon turns to dust. That is my curse. I should listen to Jaleera and accept what I am.

A grid appears across my blurry vision. It's like a spider web, only—

My heart races and my throat tightens. Before I can change course I'm crashing into it...no, *it* is crashing into *me!*

Sticky fabric wraps me from head to toe, sealing my arms and wings to my sides. I try grabbing a loose strand to undo its bonds, but my palms are pressed tight to my skin. Any vibration I send will be forced into myself.

I fall.

I close my eyes and cringe as I brace for impact. I crash through the upper level of tree branches, but that's as far as my fall takes me. A tugging at my feet suggests this netting is anchored above. I come to rest upside down and swing like a pendulum under the canopy of leaves. My heart slides down my throat as I rock back and forth, my head narrowly missing tree branches. But a whack to the head is the least of my concerns.

To what predator does this entrapment belong? I've not been warned about creatures on this planet's food chain that threaten my kind while in flight.

I wriggle and thrash, swinging my head and hips, but it's no use. Panic rises from deep within. My chest heaves as I resist the urge to wail out in despair. I'd been so afraid to see my discoveries die, when it was I who was at risk the whole time!

"Why are you following us?" croaks a voice from below.

I freeze. Over the blood rushing in my ears and the creaking branch bearing my weight, I hear the flutter of wings draw near.

A Watcher rises and hovers so that her face is level with mine. Pointed teeth and four arms tell me this freak is Bercidia the Butcher. A black ponytail sprouts from the top of her head like a hairy fountain, its base wrapped by the eye socket of a fragmented skull from some disobedient Ori. Two vertical slits in each of her yellow eyes lock onto me as we observe each other's upside expressions. Mine must be a mix of relief and lingering terror. Hers is cold as stone.

"I..." I'm at a loss for words. In my haste, I hadn't thought of what to say should I catch the hunters I was hunting.

Two more Watchers rise behind her. I hear the fluttering wings of several more behind me.

"Well?" says Bercidia. She squeezes her platinum spear shaft, which holds a serrated blade of gold at each end.

Their blood is hot for the hunt, and I sense they have no time to waste on me. They will likely leave me here and finish their job. This is my only chance.

"I want 'revenge'," I say. This word sounds strange rolling off my tongue. Though I don't know what it means, Bercidia's eyes light up in understanding.

"It was you they attacked," she concludes.

I wince and nod.

"Cut her down," orders Bercidia.

With astonishing precision, a Watcher swipes a spear tip down from my toe tips to my throat, somehow slicing open the sticky net without nicking my skin. I fall briefly, my feet flipping backward toward the ground, but two Watchers snatch my arms and keep me from falling farther. I try flexing my wings, but they remain stuck. Bercidia is not done with me.

"Return to your work," she says. "Leave this cleanup to us."

"I can lead you to their hive," I say.

Bercidia raises her broad chin and looks down her nose at me. "This work isn't suited for your kind. Besides," she flashes a wide smile and slides a forked tongue across her pointed teeth, "we enjoy a good hunt."

"You missed them in all your other sweeps," I point out.

Bercidia's smile levels and her nostrils flare. "Whatever your work is, *Servant*, I suggest you stick to it."

To a Watcher, a Fori and Entropath probably look the same.

"Destroying is my work," I say, and I force a weak smile.

If I didn't know any better, I'd swear Bercidia just flinched. But it was too brief, a fraction of a heartbeat, so I can't be sure.

"A dust maiden," she says to the Watchers who weren't close enough to hear.

"We're not like the others who serve," I remind her. "I've obliterated the remnants of a dozen civilizations."

"And you think taking life is the same," Bercidia says with an amused rise of an eyebrow. She exchanges a look with her team, who simper and sneer at my naivety.

I feel my face burn red hot. "At least let me watch," I insist. "I'll sleep easier knowing they're gone."

The laughter fades, and finally, Bercidia gives a mocking bow. "If you insist. Just make sure to stay out of our way."

I break free of my captors' hold, my wings now moving freely, and whiz up into the sky to take the lead before Bercidia can change her mind. "Follow me," I say.

What soon becomes clear to me is that Watchers aren't accustomed to following anyone below their rank in the chain. Their bickering about the flight path toward the coast nearly comes to blows until Bercidia threatens to skewer the whole lot.

It's mid-morning when the glittering ocean comes into

view. The way the Watchers grip their weapons behind me and scan the rippled dune sea below suggests they're eager for a fight, so they follow me without much fuss.

I lead them to a beach, far up the coast from where I'd encountered my assailants, where a high cave darkens the cliff face. I land in wet sand before the tall entrance. Several feet squish onto the sand behind me. Bercidia lands in front of us all, towering at almost twice my height.

I point a shaky finger toward the dark cave. "They came from in there."

Bercidia nods for her warriors to advance. "Stay behind us," she tells me.

I hold my rib wound anxiously and force tears to glaze my eyes. Though, with the memory of my near plummet into darkness fresh in my mind, the tears don't need much coaxing to come.

"Having second thoughts?" Bercidia says.

I look to my feet in shame.

"Stay here," she says, then leads her sortie into the cave.

I approach the entrance and place my hand on the damp stone mouth. I have no idea how deep the cave runs, so I don't know how much time I have.

Closing my eyes, I tune out one world and dial into another. Layers of vibrating webs brighten the darkness behind my eyelids, particles of solid mass held together by a common frequency. My heartbeat matches the rhythm, generating a pulse of energy that pushes through my arm, to the rough surface beneath my palm.

The bonds between particles flex.

My heart flutters. *Almost there.*

My heartbeat increases, dialing in on the rhythm, producing a frequency that vibrates out my hand until...

I hear a burst and then stone crumbling to the ground. When I open my eyes and step back, I see a cloud of dust rise from a pile of rocks sealing shut the cave entrance.

For a moment all I can do is stare in shock at my betrayal. Then I snap out of it. I place an ear against a fallen boulder and hear muffled shouts of rage from beyond. At least they're alive. That loosens the tightness in my chest. But it's not too late. I can dig them out and claim it all an accident. My nerves got the best of me and a rogue vibration slipped out. That's what I should do.

No. My primary duty is to uphold the Sacred Laws, among which is the protection of intelligent life. If my elders have lost sight of that in pursuit of their own freedom, I will remind them.

My stomach churns as Ko Mirah's words slip into my mind. *"I'd have about as many marks as you if we just up and left every planet we found survivors on."*

But I can't really blame her for tipping off the Watchers. My discovery jeopardizes our progress on this planet, and with her being so close to her Final Gateway, I can't fault her for that response. And so she leaves me no choice. I must go above her, all the way to the top. All the way to the Magister himself. His inspection is in less than a fortnight. If I can find a way to reach him, I can let him know what's happening here. It's his duty to protect races like that.

The image of the Magister executing a Watcher for mistreatment on our last planet leaves me with no doubt as to how seriously he takes his rules. The survival of races such as these Others are what he is divinely dedicated to, and he will not let this transgression slide easily.

I sprint west and take flight. First I'll warn the *Others*, then come back and dig out the Watchers. I'll say it was an accident. That something spooked me and my nerves got the best of me. Adding some scrapes and cuts to my arms and head will give the impression I was buried, as defenceless as I was in their web.

Yes, that could work. It's only a slim chance, but I can't back out now. How could I live with all those deaths on my conscience? I won't.

As I fly onward, a feeling of doom rises in me, telling me I've just sealed my fate.

CHAPTER 7
DEKA

Every night the dream is the same. Shouts and ringing steel echo down the cavern as my mother lowers me into our escape tunnel. I sink into her sister's waiting arms and allow my auntie to pull me back into the passage, to make room for my mother. Instead, mother slides her desk in front of the hole.

Through a crack in the desk's backing, I see my mother turn away from me with a dagger in hand. Her other holds a rattling oil lamp.

A shadow rises on the rough cavern wall before her, two arches growing high until black wings come into view. My eyes fix on the dagger in my mother's shaking hand. So futile. Then my auntie covers my eyes and all I know is the voice that sang me to sleep every night screaming for her life.

This is why I wake ready to fight when feet scuff toward me. It's too dark to see, but I hear the rattle of crossbows as our war party slinks past my alcove in single file. When the last warrior passes, I grab Marlok's knife and pull a fishing net from behind my desk, then slip into the passageway to follow.

A hand grabs my wrist through the dark and pulls me down a side passage.

"This way," Mali whispers.

She drags me down toward the fisherman's gate, her hand clamped around my wrist so tight my fingers tingle. We travel blind until a white dot lights up the darkness ahead. Rock turns to wet sand beneath my feet. The tide is out.

"What's happening?" I say.

"It's back," says Mali over her shoulder.

My heart races. "The same one? You're sure?"

"Huxley sent a runner from the lookout post to tell Marlok. Said it did three passes already. So yea, I'm sure. And he said it's alone."

Cold sweat slicks my skin. Though the creature from yesterday looked nothing like those that slayed my mother, I hear their spells can deceive our eyes. Some of us see angels. Others encounter devils. But yesterday, I'm not sure what I saw. And something about the look in its eyes tells me it wasn't sure about me, either.

I grab Mali's wrist with my free hand and try pulling her to a stop. "Then we shouldn't be down here," I hiss. This entrance is used for sea excursions during high tide, and only at night. It'll be another three hours before the tide line creeps high enough to cover our tracks.

"That thing is back to finish you off, Deka. It's got your scent. You know what that means? It'll sniff you out, wherever you are. We need to get you away from the others so they'll be safe below. And *you* won't be safe until that thing is rotting in the sand," she says, and drags me along.

This is a bad idea. Our tribal warriors are headed for the inland crevice access, which will bring them out on the high ground among the sand dunes. It's the entrance Mali sat watch over yesterday. The same one she sometimes lets me sneak out through for a bit of sunlight and fresh air. That tunnel isn't as risky to compromise. Its walls and roof are braced with shoring. If an enemy discovers it and ventures inside, we need only to pull the jacks. The collapsing rock will kill them while sealing off the entry. This fisherman's tunnel, however, is our colony's main entrance. There is no collapsing it. An enemy discovers this entry and there's no stopping the flood of steel and blood.

At the cave mouth, Mali releases my arm and risks a peek outside, to the cliffs above. It's here that I see she's carrying two crossbows—one on her back and the other in her hands. She must have stolen them from the armory, or had them hidden away for a time such as this.

She gasps and jumps back, bumping into me.

A shadow glides across the wet sand outside the entrance. It sweeps out toward the sea, then darts back toward the cliffs. A flurry of arrows arch down from the dunes and pepper the beach.

Mali unslings the bow from her back and offers it to me. "I need you to reload for me," she says, shoving the weapon into my chest.

She steps outside with her crossbow aimed straight up. Staying close to the rock face, she makes her way down to the crevice entrance, where yesterday I stood face to face with our enemy.

I follow Mali, fumbling with her backup bow and its quiver of arrows. As we turn into the crevice, a shadow ripples across the sand between us and up the cliff face beside me.

THWAP!

An arrow launches up from Mali's bow at an angle, but the figure is long gone.

Mali keeps her eyes trained on the sky directly above as she hands me her crossbow. Only now do I realize I've not loaded the second weapon. She sees this and huffs with impatience, then rips it from me and drops its head to the sand. She pulls up on the string with both hands until it locks in place, then slides an arrow into the flight groove.

She raises the bow just in time for the next pass and looses with a *THWAP*. The demon twirls and narrowly avoids the bolt. Mali cusses.

"We need to get to high ground," she says, then runs deeper into the crevice.

Normally I'd protest this move against an aerial enemy, but it does seem to be alone, and judging by the arrows peppering the beach from above, Marlok's warriors are already up there in force.

I follow Mali deeper into the crevice, my eyes to the sky in fascination as the flying intruder zips back and forth, avoiding arrows that whiz from every direction.

Sand slides from under my feet as I follow Mali up the slope at the crevice end.

We emerge among the dunes, where fifty of our warriors have spread out for better angles on their target.

My belly lurches. This sky demon has effectively split us up, with only two groups of two in sight. Mali should be below, marshalling the non-fighters in case they need to escape.

Instead, she races up a dune just a stone's throw from me and drops to a knee.

Marlok's voice rises from a distance. "Ready!"

He wants a volley, which is smart. It'll be harder for their target to dodge fifty bolts at once.

Those with loaded bows take aim while the rest hurry to reload. As I watch my tribe-mates prepare their weapons, I squint for a better look at their target, and I confirm it is indeed the same creature from yesterday.

"Stop!" shouts a voice from above. The intruder sounds so much like a human girl. It was this, and her appearance, that kept me from retreating from her approach in the crevice yesterday. "I'm here to talk! Please, listen!"

And as with yesterday, today she comes unarmed.

I'm about to point this out when Marlok's voice cuts me off.

"Loose!"

Arrows arch from every direction in a dome around the sky creature. Our target dives and swirls and somehow manages to avoid every bolt. As fifty crossbow heads hit the sand for reloading, I open my mouth to alert them to the fact that the demon isn't here to harm us, but something different stops me this time.

The demon veers south, then makes a sharp turn back and falls into a course dead set on Mali.

Mali rushes to reload, but seeing the demon bearing down on her sends her into a panic. She drops her bow and breaks into a sprint toward me. In doing so she has become the prey to a much faster predator. She'll never make it.

Her wild eyes fall on me and my crossbow. They plead for me to shoot.

I drop my bow head to the sand. The string creaks and the bow's polymer limbs groan as I haul on the string to lock it in place. *Click.* I slide in an arrow and raise the butt to my shoulder.

Time seems to slow as I center the winged attacker in my V-sight. The demon is so close I can see strands of her brown hair waving against the blue sky. It thinks we have all loosed our bolts and is sweeping in for an easy kill.

Not today. Not my Mali.

My finger feathers the trigger. The demon's face sharpens into view, so close. So...innocent. Up close, her soft features don't look menacing at all. Without the wings and pointed ears, I'd think it was a human girl no older than myself. And those eyes, how they sparkle like gems in the sunlight...

I can't keep my weapon from shaking. Sweat burns my eyes, so I squint to focus on my target. I'm dimly aware that, to my left, Marlok has tossed his crossbow aside and is racing for mine. Instinctively I jerk it to the right, away from his reaching hands, and in doing so accidentally pull the trigger.

THWAP!

No! My breath catches as the bolt zooms wide, but in a stroke of luck the demon banks in the same direction. The arrow doesn't make it past her, piercing her belly.

Mali slides to a stop beside me. Together we watch the demon crash into a dune only an evening shadow's length away. Mali's hand squeezes my shoulder, her fingernails digging into my skin enough to draw blood as a plume of sand rises from the crest where she'd just been shooting from.

All around, sand swishes under feet as my tribes-folk

converge on our fallen enemy. They form a semi-circle atop the dunes to either side of me.

I check the ground behind for my net. I must have dropped it on the beach or in the crevice, because it's nowhere in sight.

Marlok falls in beside Mali and I, his eyes locked on the settling sand cloud. Mali grabs the dagger from my belt and forces it into my hand. An urgent smile graces her face as she shoves me forward. "Confirm your kill, Deka, before someone else does."

Goosebumps ripple my skin. Mali doesn't trust her brother's ambition any more than I do. And if the kill is mine, I decide what happens to the body.

Sand swishes as more of my tribesmen arrive.

"Give me the knife, Deka." Marlok stands only a few feet away, his hand extended toward me, impatience and angst in his eyes.

I ignore him and step forward, the whale bone handle cold in my clammy hands.

All around me, my tribesmen level their crossbows and spear tips on the demon to finish her at the slightest twitch.

I swallow hard and press forward. Swishing sand announces my approach. I cringe at every step toward the fallen girl—

No, not a girl. It is some form of witchery that gives this demon her benevolent appearance, and I will not be fooled.

Drawing closer, I see the demon that looks so much like a girl curled on its side in the fetal position. The swish of sand under my feet is so deafening that it almost drowns out my thumping heart. I stop a few feet away.

At this proximity I see faint breathing, her—I mean, *IT's*

—iridescent wings rising and falling only slightly. A sliver of pity seeps into me. It looks so innocent, her cheeks flush from heat or exertion.

I push this feeling away and crouch beside it, but the sand scorches my bare knees and I shoot upright. That's when I see the arrow shaft clasped tight in the demon's delicate hands, its tip inches from her belly.

She springs to her feet with an eruption of sand. I turn to run but, as usual, I'm not fast enough. She wraps her arms around my waist and before I know it my feet are off the ground. I'm flying.

I'm *flying!*

But my captor carries me with little grace. It grunts in its struggle to bear my weight. My toes skim the tops of the dunes as she turns me toward my tribe to use me as a shield. If she only knew how quickly they'd do away with me.

A few arrows whistle past. A few too many.

I kick my feet and flail my arms to disrupt her flight while all sorts of ghastly images invade my mind. While my tribes-folk no doubt see her dragging me off to a fiery underworld, my imagination goes elsewhere, to a hidden lair where her kind conduct experiments on their adversaries. Mali was right. She marked me yesterday in the crevice, and she won't return to her lair without me. I am fighting for my life.

When we cross the cliff edge over the beach, my weight becomes too much for her. We fall.

My feet hit dry sand and I crash forward onto my face. She tumbles forward and recovers as I rise to my knees. She leaps and clings to my back and lifts me again, dragging me toward the water.

In my thrashing, my foot catches wet sand, sinking deep

enough to create sufficient drag to break her hold. I keep my footing this time and stumble to a stop on the beach beneath her.

The demon swerves left in a half circle and lands to face me. We square off and I see by her gaping mouth that she is speechless, just as amazed at the sight of me as I am of her. The look in her eyes is pure curiosity. No evil that I can see. A clever spell, perhaps.

Faint shouts call from a distance, alerting me to how far we've traveled in that harried flight. Two dozen of my tribe's warriors line the clifftop, while others search for a safe way down. But they are too far to help me, well beyond crossbow range. This thing has carried me at least a mile, much to my surprise and dismay.

I widen my stance and raise my fists. "Stay back," I say. "I'm stronger than I look."

Her head cocks to the side. "What do looks have to do with strength?"

Everything in me wants to cover my ears to block out any spell that may be laced into her words. Instead, I listen.

"Why do you not hate me like the rest of your kind?" she says while studying me with her green eyes.

I'm aware of my fists loosening and my hands lowering as I size her up in return. She'd be a foot shorter than me if not for her wings, which sunlight passes through like still water. Her slight movements filter the light, making the clear veins shimmer with every color of the rainbow, like sunlight through mist. So different than the ragged black wings of the creature that killed my mother.

"You look different than the others," I say.

"Others?"

I frown, feeling a tide of sorrow rise up in me. "The demons that killed my parents."

"Parents?" she says, as if playing with an unfamiliar word.

"My mother and father."

Her jaw drops and her eyebrows arch high. When she notices me studying her wings, she wraps them around her torso and hugs herself with her arms while looking awkwardly at her feet.

Shouts echo from afar, yet closer than before. She joins me in looking at the silhouettes lining the cliff.

"Those 'demons'," she says, calling my attention back to her, "they're coming back to finish you off. You need to keep your heads down. Stay out of sight, and do *not* try to fight them."

We cannot stay below indefinitely, I'm tempted to say. We must surface for sunlight. But I dare not reveal anything about my colony's routine that may put us at risk.

"You wish to help us?" I say, and I cringe at the tone of hope in my voice. I must sound like a fool. To remind myself of what I'm dealing with, I summon the memory of the last time I saw my mother. How she begged for her life. "For all I know, you're trying to keep us here for when more of your friends come."

"I wouldn't!" she says defensively. "I'm different than them."

I see a hint of truth in this, just on physical appearance alone. My mother's notes and my own memories have noted the slight differences between this being and those who attacked our colony all those years ago.

"We cannot hide forever," I say.

She steps closer. "It'll only be for a little while. I have a plan."

"Why would you help us?"

She bites her lip and looks away. "Your peril is...it's my fault. I brought this danger to you." She locks eyes with me. "But I can make it better."

A demon with a conscience. My people will never believe this.

Rocks crumble down the cliff. The girl demon's pointed ears twitch, and we both turn to watch Marlok lead a descent down a diagonal cleft.

A hand grabs my wrist, soft and gentle.

"My plan will work," she tells me, "but you have to trust—"

Without warning, her eyes roll back and she wobbles. Her hand goes instinctively to cover a wound in her ribs, from where clear fluid leaks. And then I remember the shot Marlok had landed yesterday.

Her head tilts backward and she stumbles to the side, all her muscles going slack as she falls to the ground.

For some reason I may never understand, I rush to catch her before she hits the sand. I end up on my knees with her head on my lap and a terrible dread overcoming me as I'm painfully aware of how gently I hold her for all of my tribe's warriors to see.

Fool! Marlok will never let me live this down.

CHAPTER 8
NYA

Waves of light lure my mind from the depths of nothingness. Heat warms my face, and my eyelids flicker to the glow of an orange light, like that of a flame. Like a fire.

Fire!

My eyelids snap open and my body jolts upright in panic, a panic made worse by my restricted motion. I'm stuck.

I look up in terror at my hands, which are spread wide and chained to a rock ceiling. I test my bonds and find they offer no give. The cool air has me shivering, suggesting that I'm deep underground, far from any help.

The fatigue and stress from my wound must have caught up with me on the beach. The urgency of my mission to warn the Others had kept me going, and once my message had been delivered, my body must have shut down. Too bad it couldn't have lasted long enough to get me away to safety—wherever that would be. Perhaps I'm safer down here. That all depends on the status of the Butcher party.

"Deka says you speak our language," says a voice from behind me.

I look over my shoulder to see an elder woman with dark skin that's wrinkled, though not with age. The ripples on her cheeks resemble burnt flesh. Her long grey hair is fashioned into numerous braids that hang from her head in thick strands, like furry serpents. Her hunched back and gnarly fingers suggest a good many years stuck in this lifetime. How old is 'old' to these people?

Six males with spears flank her. The solid oval masks covering their faces fail to conceal the fear in their eyes.

I pull again on the chains and gain no more freedom than with my previous attempt. My shoulders ache from the outward stretching of my arms, but it's faint compared to where the manacles dig into my wrists.

"Well, creature?" says the elder. "Can you speak?"

I open my mouth to reply, but the world spins and stirs my belly. It takes all my fortitude not to retch.

Orange light glows from a lamp on the floor between us. It stinks of burning fish, which further upsets my stomach. The wavering flame casts light across the matriarch's face, emphasizing the ripples on her cheeks as they deepen with impatience. She looks to the spearman to her right. "Give it a poke. See what noise comes out."

"Yes," I say, my jaw quivering, before the spearman can obey. "I speak your language."

The elder lifts her chin and narrows her eyes on me. "How?"

I take a moment to measure my words, but not too long, for my captors have grown impatient with me. "When I arrived, I inherited the words of every native tongue that ever inhabited this planet." I won't pretend to know the details about how this works. All I know is that, upon crossing through the Gate to this planet, everything I need to know to orient me to this world is uploaded into my consciousness through the portal's membrane. See, a planet has a memory, just like intelligent races do, but something about these people suggest they're not in tune with it. The Magister infused us with this knowledge in the event we ever encounter survivors, so we could communicate with them. If they pass the intelligence and reasoning test, then we're to report their existence to him, which is exactly what I'm going to do, with or without the help of my immediate superiors.

"And you just walk around speaking our native tongue?" says the elder, genuinely curious.

Here comes the tricky part. We call the phenomenon *Enchantment*, but I'm reluctant to use that word with these people, for their minds may receive it differently, and interpret something forced about it. In reality, I'm not entirely sure how it works. I just know that all of us, the Fori, Ori, Aeri, my sisters, different cohorts... we each speak different languages, but we all hear but one. It's said our minds even distort the speaker's mouth, to shape the words for seamless interaction. It's how we evolved to work coherently with other races. Now that I'm forced to think about it, it's quite amazing. But I always assumed it was the receiver, the *listener*, who did the processing. These people understanding me proves the effect comes from the speaker's voice. Almost like a spell. I sense this concept will not sit well with these folk. Besides, I don't have time to enlighten these folk on the intricacies of my existence. It's theirs that matters most now.

"Did..." What did she say his name was? Deka? Yes, that sounds about right. "Did Deka also say I came here to warn you? That I'm a friend?"

"We have no friends among your kind."

I glance to the shackles above my head and wonder why that's so, but their healthy suspicion brings me comfort. Perhaps they'll stand a chance at eluding the Watchers long enough for me to seek out the Magister. The Protector of Light and Life will not be pleased to see how the Watchers have been treating these people.

"Let me prove we're not all the same," I say. "Just hear me out."

"Your kind killed half the people I ever knew," the elder says, "maybe even half of what remained of our race. Why would I trust anything you say?" Her words are caustic, full of venom. Yet, despite her animosity, I know she ordered them to keep me alive for a reason.

"You could have killed me already," I say, "and I could kill you all right now." *For I am Nya - Destroyer of...* No, that talk will get me nowhere here. I rattle the shackles above my head. "Yet here I remain."

My audience laughs. The elder points a shaky finger at me. "You are in no position to make threats, young demon."

There it is, that word again. If they want superstition, then I'll not deny them any longer. "Enough games."

I squeeze my hands into fists. The manacles binding my wrists explode to dust.

Everyone watches the chains disappear in awe. One guard quickly gathers his wits and thrusts a spear at my belly. I spin to the side, grab the polymer shaft, and then *WHOOSH*—it explodes to dust.

The five remaining guards level their spear tips at me. I eye each up and know I can't take them all on if they charge at once, which I believe they will. I'm cornered.

I raise both hands with my palms facing my aggressors, hoping this will keep them at bay. It does seem to inspire some hesitation.

The elder sinks back through the semi-circle. Her voice rises from the shadows behind. "This witch requires a different manner of death."

In response to her call, orange light glows from the depths of a tunnel to her rear. It intensifies until six flickering orbs emerge around a bend. They grow larger with the approaching footsteps until I see they are flames dancing from arrowheads loaded into crossbows.

My heart almost bursts inside my belly. Even at a distance, the flames draw sweat from my skin despite the cold air. By the time the archers join the enclosure of spearmen, my whole body is slick. I shrivel back despite my best efforts to remain firm. Hard rock halts my retreat.

"Aim!" orders a male voice, and the bowmen raise their weapons.

Six waving flames taunt me through the tears blurring my eyes. But I won't go down without a fight.

I grit my teeth, clench my fists, and march forward.

"Stop! Everyone!"

The boy they call 'Deka' shoves through the line of his kinsmen and stands before me, spreading his arms wide as if to shield me.

The elder narrows her eyes on Deka. "So, it's true what they say. You've developed an unnatural affection for this creature."

A crossbow archer takes aim at Deka. "Just give the word, Grand Mother."

I slip in front of Deka and extend my hands out wide to appear non-threatening. As I advance, the line of wary fighters shuffle back, their fingers on the release mechanisms of their weapons, but they dare not retreat behind their elder.

"I can only help you if you accept that my intentions are pure," I tell the warriors. If I can't get through to that hag, perhaps I can influence her followers. "If I found you, others will. They will come in great numbers and they will not fall so easily as me."

The elder's eyes remain cold in defiance, her skepticism clear. "Why would you betray your kind?"

"It's complicated," is all I can offer for now. There is little time to explain the nature of our work and the rules that accompany it. But once the Magister learns of this tribe's existence, he'll declare their planet off-limits. For it is races like this he is sworn to protect. Luckily, he's coming to inspect our work in less than a fortnight. They just need to stay out of sight until his arrival, when I can safely reveal their sanctuary.

A distant voice echoes down the tunnel: "They're here!"

The dozen guards keep their weapons aimed at me while their heads swivel toward the voice.

My hair stands on end as their panic prickles my skin like static electricity.

One warrior points to me while looking to his companion. "Watch her, Huxley."

The big boy called Huxley aims a crossbow at me while his warrior kin peel away and scramble down the tunnel.

Even the elder makes toward the danger, leaving only Huxley and Deka as my company.

Deka drifts to Huxley's side and, crossing his arms, joins him in staring me down.

"How many are up there?" Deka asks me. I detect a hint of cunning in his eyes, his words containing more than just a question. There's an invitation there.

"At least a dozen," I say. "But their leader could count for twenty on her own. She's vicious."

Huxley shifts nervously and spares a glance over his shoulder, up the tunnel. Deka nods for me to continue.

"They can smell fear across open air," I announce, "but so long as your people stay underground, away from any openings, you'll be okay."

Huxley returns his attention to me. He forces a smile and says, "Good thing we don't feel fear, then."

"Yes, you do," I say. "I can smell yours right now." Although *smell* isn't the right word. For me, it's a frequency he's giving off that makes my hair rise on end. Like a static charge.

Deka leans close to Huxley. "You know Marlok has everyone at the crevice entrance."

Sweat trickles down Huxley's forehead as he squeezes his crossbow tight. He keeps it trained on me while he risks a longer look up the dark tunnel.

"If we clash and one gets away," Deka says, "they'll bring more." He returns his attention to me. "How many are out there?"

"Thousands," I say.

Huxley's grip on the crossbow tightens until the polymer groans.

"You need to warn them," Deka says.

"You go," snaps Huxley.

"They won't believe me. Besides, I'm the colony's biggest coward. If I go anywhere near the surface then my fear will give us all away."

Huxley's gaze shifts to Deka, and the look in his eyes suggests he agrees with Deka's claim. But I sense the lie. Deka isn't scared at all. Not in the way his companion is, anyway. Deka, I'm learning, does not fear for his own life.

"It's true," I tell Huxley. "I can hardly sense your fear because Deka's is nearly suffocating me."

"I'll watch her," Deka says. He holds out his hands for Huxley's weapon. "I shot her once already. I'll have no problem doing it again."

Huxley's eyes narrow on Deka. A long moment passes, with several glances between me and Deka, before he hands over his crossbow.

"I'll be right back," Huxley says, then he shoots me a sharp glare. "And if you still have a soft spot for this creature," he says to Deka, "just remember what her kind did to your parents."

Deka aims the crossbow at my chest, his finger curled around the release mechanism. Huxley remains, studying Deka's expression and stance with great skepticism. I'm sure he's about to change his mind, but then he reluctantly sets off up the tunnel.

When his running footsteps disappear into darkness, Deka sets the crossbow down and grabs my arm to drag me into a side passage. I follow without protest.

CHAPTER 9

NYA

As we descend into the abyss of twisting tunnels, my hand slips into Deka's and our grips lock tight in the blackness. My breath shudders into the void around us, and it takes all my strength to keep from unraveling. Deka, on the other hand, is calm and steady.

How can he see where we're going? My wonder actually distracts from my panic.

"You're afraid of the dark?" he whispers.

My quivering breath is all the answer I can manage.

"It's not much farther," he says. "I know a way for you to escape, but we need to cut through the main colony. How many are actually up there?"

"Thirteen at most." It all depends how many of the Butcher party made it out of the cave unscathed. "They'll be tracking me now." *For revenge.* My belly churns. Part of my plan involved returning to rescue them while banging myself up, too. This scheme is already off to a bad start. "They won't expect that I've taken refuge amongst your kind, so they'll do a quick sweep over the area and then move on. So long as everyone lays low, your people will be fine."

From the darkness ahead, a mint green glow gives shape to Deka's silhouette. When my arm comes into view before me, I release our hold.

Hushed talking grows louder the deeper we travel. Like the green light, it comes from a gateway that opens up to a great cavern.

Deka guides me to an alcove and motions for me to sit. "I need to get you a disguise," he says. "Wait here."

I crouch and hug my knees to my chest. As he proceeds through the gateway, I study the stone pillars to either side, which support a crown of flames that looms fifteen feet over me. Each column bears the carving of a sky serpent spiralling up the polished stone.

These statues stir memories of similar creatures I've seen on other planets. Those abominations have a tendency of accidentally jumping between dimensions and causing all sorts of havoc on unsuspecting worlds. In one case, it took the Watchers nearly two turns of that planet's moon to clear out a nest of them hidden deep inside a volcano. It was Jexa's first campaign as Marshal. She even managed to tame one, which she kept as a pet.

Despite the clear differences noted between the beasts I've seen, Hive Elders claim they all came from the same place at some point near the beginning of time. Eventually they started having these mishaps of crossing dimensions—an inherent ability they had without much awareness nor control over. They spread out across the Universe, each evolving to adapt to various and ever changing planetary conditions.

Perhaps that's what happened on this planet, to Deka's ancestors: wiped out by an invasion of fire-breathing sky serpents.

Sweat beads my brow at the thought, but the source of the mint green light suddenly steals my attention. I leave my alcove and step into the archway, where I look up to see a glass lantern full of liquid bioluminescence.

Mindless beasts, Ko Mirah had called them. Yeah right! Would you call harnessing *sea sparkle* for underground lights the work of clueless animals? Though this on its own is no particular feat, getting it to stay glowing is a true wonder. I've only seen these organisms flash for a second or two at a time.

This innovation holds my attention only briefly, however. Beyond the doorway, the cavern opens up into a massive downward pit, the outer edge of which houses levels of dwellings and diagonal stairways connecting them, all illuminated by a faint green glow. For a while, all I can do is stare in amazement at the beauty of this subterranean sanctuary. It also gives me hope that other *extinct* races have survived on the planets we've left behind. They may have even made peace with their new co-habitants.

"Demon!" cries a voice from within the cavern.

A steel mechanism clicks above and triggers the downward release of the gate. I spring back just in time to avoid getting crushed.

The lantern hangs on the inside of the door, so I'm suddenly left in darkness.

NO! The walls are closing in on me, going to crush me, so I swing my fists through the dark to keep them away. My wits abandon me and I unleash a guttural scream.

Footsteps rush toward me in the dark. Green light grows brighter from a side tunnel, pushing shadows into nooks and cracks in the stone wall. Deka arrives carrying a glowing glass jar.

I rush to meet him and grab the lantern. It's cool in my hands and helps me breathe easier. Soon I'm back to normal.

"Are you okay?" Deka asks. "That was quite the scream."

"It was nothing."

He gives me an appraising look. I realize how I must appear to him, with my heavy breathing and rattled eyes.

"Why do you fear the dark so much?" he asks.

A lump swells in my throat. If he only knew the things that lingered in the darkest depths, he'd be afraid too. I need to change the subject.

"Someone saw me," I say, recalling how the gate almost crushed me.

"I told them you chased some children down the east passage. Come, in here."

I follow him while examining the sparkling liquid inside the lantern.

"Where did you get this?" I say, fearing its glow will die out any second like the flash of sea plankton.

"It's bacteria from an octopus."

"Octo-what?"

"Creatures of the sea."

I hug the bioluminescent lantern close to my chest. The flicker of an idea flashes in my mind.

"What do you call your people?" I ask. The information I'd received when arriving on this planet is limited to what pertains to my purpose here, and since my job was to erase any signs of their existence, even the name of their species was to die out. We do learn their languages in the event we encounter survivors, so we can communicate to help them while assessing their self-awareness, but this possibility was considered so remote I'd never given it serious thought.

"There were many names," Deka says while stroking his chin, "but my mother's books call us *homo sapiens*."

"*Sapiens*," I repeat, admiring the way the word rolls from my tongue. "What is your mother's books?"

The faintest hint of a smile tugs at Deka's mouth. "Here, put this on and follow me."

He hands me a large piece of woven fabric and shows me how to wear it so it covers my head and body, with my wings tucked against me. Then he leads me down a side passage that circumvents the main gate. We emerge at the top edge of the grand gallery, its ringed concourses resembling those of open-pit mines. We take a stone stairway down to the second terrace that circles the edge of the pit. Rectangular holes darken the wall all around this concourse.

"There're two guards watching the other entrance," Deka says. "We have to wait until they're stood down or called away. Come, in here."

He ushers me through a rectangular doorway in the outer wall.

Green lantern light radiates from my hands to paint the walls and illuminate crafted furnishings.

Inside the entryway, Deka picks up a rectangular block from a stack of similar pieces. It groans as he hinges it open to reveal its girth is made up of hundreds of thinner rectangular sheets, all stacked together. As he flips through them, I see each contains a unique set of scripture and illustrations.

I gasp in wonder. What a way to pass down knowledge! It's so much more efficient than constructing massive monuments or megalithic sites, and more reliable than spoken word.

I set the lantern down and pick up the next book in the pile, sitting cross-legged to flip through its sheets. There's such craftsmanship in these drawings, and I even come across an image of a seafaring vessel with swaths of fabric that harness the wind, similar to how the Aeri use their wings to glide effortlessly over long distances.

The idea that had flashed in my mind moments ago does so again, this time clearer.

"You were travelers before we arrived?" I say.

"We were many things not so long ago," he says solemnly, rubbing the book cover in his hands. "My people came from the south. Harsh conditions pushed everyone away from the Equator in search of food and water. We were preparing to cross the sea when the demons—I mean, *your people*, arrived. Suddenly we became the hunted. We've been stuck here ever since."

I close the book. "Those who hunt you think you're mindless animals." I trace the words on the cover with my finger. "This proves you're not," I say with hope, but I bite my lip as doubt drops in to squash my optimism. This collection of writings could easily be dismissed as remnants of a civilization past. I need something more tangible. Something living and breathing. A being that speaks and can explain how they survived so long. "It could work," I muse, trying to work out the details in my mind.

"What are you thinking?" Deka says, hope clashing with

caution in his eyes. No one could deny that fire. Not even Ko Mirah. These people have life-sparks of their own.

"The Magister is coming to this planet at the next New Moon," I say.

"Who?"

Right. These people have been cut off from the cosmic consciousness. "He is the Guardian of Light and Life. The Custodian of Cosmic Harmony. The Arbiter of Interstellar Refuge. The divine representative within the physical realms. The Supreme Gate Master a.k.a the Master of Cycles. All that and much, much more. If he heard you speak, he'll order that we stop our work here and move on to the next planet."

Deka sits up straight. "You're saying I must travel to meet him?"

I smile and nod. "In doing so, you'll act as an emissary for your people."

His head drops and his shoulders slump. "They'll never allow it."

"Are you their servant?"

He frowns. "It's not like that. We are a family. I can't just leave them without permission. Besides, we don't have enough fresh water for me to go wandering the desert. Our well-spring here is almost dry."

I suddenly notice his cracked lips and dry skin. "It's only desert for a little way. The forest edge is only half a day's flight."

Deka perks up. "Forest?"

"Sure. There's plenty of fresh water there."

"And food?"

"Of course! All kinds of nuts and berries."

"Do you know which are poisonous?"

I frown at this question.

Seeing my confusion, Deka pats his belly. "The wrong plant may kill me. Have you never gotten sick after eating something?"

I shake my head. "I don't eat. We get our energy from the Sun."

Plenty of Fori and Ori indulge on berries because they like the taste, with some even fermenting them to drink during celebrations. But they don't *need* to eat to survive. We'd evolved past that long ago. Now it's just something they do for fun or for spiritual practice. Plus, they created that ecosystem, so they'd know what's harmful to them. Deka, on the other hand...

That forest was designed to host the incoming race. Their biological makeup determines the profile of all the resources the Ori and Fori have created. There's no telling what an edible plant for them may do to a creature outside those specifications. This is a problem.

"Must you eat often?" I say.

Deka ignores me as he uses a stick to scribble something in his book. He flips back through the sheets, scanning rows of written words. "Energy from the Sun," he says, more to himself than to me. "That's why the demons only travel during the day and near full moon." His eyes open wide with a realization. "The moon reflects the Sun's rays."

"Right!" I say, my hope for this race rising. They are far wiser than Ko Mirah gave them credit for.

But a sinking feeling rocks my gut. How many races like this have we swept from their homes? Conquered and driven into extinction to make room for the next?

I swat the horrible images from my mind before they can form fully. I didn't know what we were up to then, but now I do. We can do this if we work together. It's never too late to do the right thing. That's what the Watchers told my ancestors after they destroyed their home, when they convinced us to enter the Pact and serve Penance for retribution.

Deka's frantic flipping of his pages expels a loose sheet. The sketched image of Jexa sucks the breath right out of me, and I find myself backing away until I hit a wall. I've only ever seen her once, from a distance, so over the years she has been little more than a threatening name to me.

Deka takes great interest in my reaction. He picks up the drawing. "You know this creature?"

I nod, feeling my throat for the invisible hand choking me. "That's Jexa, the Marshal of Watchers. She's been here before?"

"She killed my mother."

My jaw drops. Something we have in common. "She killed mine, too."

Deka's eyes flash open wide, and if I didn't know better, I see the corner of his mouth twitch with a relieved smile. "You can lead me to her?"

"You want revenge," I say. This feeling has been growing in me lately, too. "Well, if we shine a light onto her ways, the Magister will save us the trouble. See, we're not even allowed to be here. Those who hunt you are actually supposed to mind the work that my folk do. They're to maintain order and keep us safe from predators, but we're breaking the Magister's rules by pushing you out. He won't stand for it."

Deka stares longingly at the drawing. "Then I will do what I must to go with you."

"So your problem is food," I say.

"Maybe not." He closes his book and jumps to his feet. "Follow me."

We exit the dwelling and emerge onto the second level concourse, where Deka motions for me to step to the edge. Below, a brook trickles across the bottom level in the faint green light. I crouch for a closer look, my toes curling around the curved concourse lip. Many of Deka's folk are still carrying their belongings to the lower levels via the spiral terrace that rings the pit, to settle in for an indeterminate amount of time.

Deka points over my shoulder, to a metal drum at the waterway's entrance. "Back when the river flowed strong, that turbine powered our artificial lighting system," he explains. "The dry rock bed was once a flourishing valley where we grew plants so high they touched the ceiling. We feasted on corn and potatoes, fed chickens from grain which gave us eggs in return. But we've not had a drop of rain in five years. Now we can barely scoop enough to quench our thirst. Our days here are numbered."

Even without the drought he'd be right. With the expanding forest edge, it's only a matter of time before the Ori discover this sanctuary. This realization relieves a bit of my guilt. Better that I came across these *sapiens* when I did than to have the Ori report them directly to the Watchers.

"My mother had a plan to extend our time here," Deka says, "by harvesting food from the sea. She ordered we make boats and set out with nets and lines. My father volunteered to go first. Everyone thought he was crazy until he returned with a boat full of fish—every kind of sea creature you could think of to kill our hunger. We were saved."

My belly roils at the idea of having to eat other living things to survive. But I keep my disgust to myself. There is much about their existence I do not understand, and I can't have Deka doubting his means of survival should he undertake my proposed endeavor.

"We feasted for many turns of the moon," he says, his voice growing heavy, "until people started getting sick."

"Why?"

"Pollutants. Mercury. Who knows? Your people killed my mother before she could investigate the sickness more."

I reach out to touch his arm, but he waves me away. He composes himself remarkably fast.

"G-Ma, our elder, forbids us from using the boats or fishing gear," he says, "but we still have them stored away. If I travel some of the distance by sea, I can survive long enough off of fish without having to raid our colony's stores. But I'll have nowhere to hide during the day. Even if the tides and the weather permit me to come ashore safely, I may not find anywhere to conceal me and my boat."

I'm tempted to offer myself up as a guide, but Jaleera has this talent for finding me. Even now, as my assigned Watcher, she's no doubt already sniffing out my trail. Deka wouldn't get far in the open with me nearby. Even without me around, so long as the Watchers roam the sky...

Wait, of course! That might be an option. "Can you sail in the rain?"

Deka shrugs. "It poured down during my first voyage. Others say it's dangerous, but I found it refreshing."

I clap excitedly. "Good. Now, all you have to do is sail to

the forest edge." Deka will be easier to hide in the forest. That's our domain.

"How do I find it?" he says.

"Can't you smell it?"

Deka sniffs, then shrugs.

I'd not considered he wouldn't be able to sense the forest. I always smell which direction it's in, like fresh rain from an approaching storm.

"There must be some way for me to show you where to meet," I say, frustration creeping in over my excitement.

Deka raises a hand, as if telling me to hang onto my thought. He hurries to his dwelling and returns with a square chart, which he spreads across the floor.

"A map," he says, tracing a squiggly line with his finger. "This is the coast. Which way do I have to go?"

It takes me a few seconds to orient myself to the drawing. When I do, I use the pyramids as a reference point and trace my finger west, while he indicates our current location on the northern edge of the continent. I tap an inlet near where I think the forest edge should be. "We'll meet here. Can you make it that far on your own?"

He hugs himself, a wary expression plaguing his face. "It's a lot farther than any of our fishing crews ever traveled. Though I guess they never had much reason for venturing so far." He nods. "I think I can do it."

"How long?"

"Five days," he says, but his tone sounds more like a question than an answer. He has no idea.

"I'll give you seven without any Watchers. Make sure you reach the forest before the eighth morning."

Above us, atop the stairs over Deka's dwelling, the large

gate creaks open. A warrior enters and shouts down into the pit: "All clear!"

The downward movement of *sapiens* halts and reverses back toward the upper levels. This exercise seems well-rehearsed. If they survived this many Watcher encounters, then I may have enough time to save them.

Deka grabs my arm and leads me around the concourse and into a tunnel. As we slink deeper into darkness, a salty breeze blows stronger on my face. When faint daylight comes into view, Deka stops.

"This is the Fisherman's Gate," he explains. "It'll bring you out onto the beach."

I nod my appreciation. "Hit the sea as soon as you see my signal," I tell him.

"What will I be looking for?"

I pause and consider how best to convey my signal while keeping the surprise to myself. I love a good surprise. "Look to the heavens, and when nature's blessing falls from above, then you'll know."

I turn to leave.

"What is your name?" he says.

I stop. A smile tugs at the corner of my mouth. He sees me as more than a demon. "They call me 'Nya'."

He grabs my hand and squeezes it while giving it a shake. I don't resist, I simply watch this custom curiously. When an appropriate amount of time passes, he releases me.

"I'll wait at the forest edge in case you arrive early," I say. "From there, you'll be safe with me watching over you."

"Okay," Deka says. "I'll do as you say and await your signal."

I race to the cave entrance and hope those aren't the last

words I ever hear from him. I wish I could stay and guide him the entire way, but the Watchers wouldn't take long tracking me down at the pace he'll be moving over water, especially now that the Butcher party is on the loose and looking for me. The next few days will be perilous for us both, but our efforts will be worth it. For once Deka meets the Magister, the era of Jexa's terror will be but a dark memory.

CHAPTER 10

NYA

Keeping Deka alive long enough to reach the Magister will be the hardest thing I've ever done, but the reward will be worth it. If the Magister is pleased by my efforts, he'll award me the *Magister's Mark*. It's a rune over the third eye that allows its bearer to navigate the gateways to any world. I'll be able to use it to find my home planet without the Councilry's help or the Watchers' approval.

My heart flutters at the prospect. But this is a perilous task, to say the least.

The existence of survivors such as Deka not only threatens Jexa's reputation, but once the Magister finds out the Watchers have been exterminating races like those he's sworn to protect, he'll send *her* and her minions to the Dark. Somehow the *sapiens* escaped her campaign to clear this land of *shadows* before we started our reclamation of this planet, and she will not take that slip-up lightly. Every breath these *sapiens* take whittles away at her wicked name and threatens her very life. So she will not rest until they are bones in the sand. She may already be leading a large company here to clear them out herself.

Luckily, a storm is brewing to the east. And one thing the Watchers and I have in common is our vulnerability to rain.

I follow the coast toward black clouds swirling over grey water. At the edge of the storm, where the first drops of rain spatter my face, I turn north over the sea. Before I can stray too far from the safety of land, an Aeri swoops down to meet me. Wind from her massive feathered wings blasts my hair.

"You plan on going for a swim?" she warns with an arrogant smirk and a nod to my translucent wings. Already I feel mist gathering on the flimsy membranes, which has them buzzing faster to dispel the build up of moisture. The expansive wings of the Aeri can overcome most of the challenges that ground my kind, and even the Watchers — rain, gales, and even gravitational anomalies.

"Your work here must wait," I say, feeling my throat tighten.

The Aeri leader frowns at me.

I swallow hard to loosen up for the lie. Recalling how I've heard senior Servants speak, I muster my best grown-up voice and say, "I bring a message from Ko Mirah. They need rain for a special project—one of great importance to the Councilry."

The Aeri leader's frown deepens to a look of suspicion. She hovers back away from me for a better appraisal.

"I've heard nothing of this project," she says.

My heart swells into my throat. I see Fori messengers delivering instructions to Aeri flocks all the time. Are they always met with such contention? An ecosystem evolves fast under the hands of my cousins. Sometimes predictions and projected growths are faulty and require correction. I'm just not sure what wording is used to convey these remedial orders.

"It's an emergency trial," I say, "for the Magister's inspection. Something bad happened to the last planet we regenerated and they're blaming your work. They say you fouled the soil with toxic rain."

The Aeri's eyes flash wide, her hands going to her throat as if she's choking. Then her eyes narrow on me with accusation. Though her skepticism is rightly placed, she should have little reason to suspect anyone other than an Ori of trickery. Our earth-working cousins almost went to war once with the Aeri over the claim that the Aeri, in their rush, failed to scrub toxins from the upper atmosphere. They countered that it was poor artisanship by the Ori that had tainted the soil. But I see this flock leader is not convinced by me. I see she wants to go discuss the matter with Ko Mirah. I can't let that happen.

"Right now I'm on my way to deliver a message to the Grand Councilry," I say. "I'll be speaking with them before day's end. Shall I pass on your refusal to do their bidding?"

The Aeri's eyebrows rise while I keep my face hard as stone. She clenches her fists and crosses her arms, her shoulders hunching as her gaze drifts to grey clouds swirling over the eastern forest. Over Ko Mirah's Hive.

"Where is this project?" she says.

I twirl to face west, so that my back is to the Aeri when I release a sigh of relief. Pointing to where the north coast curves south, I say, "There. Make it rain for the next seven nights. Then you may return to your work up here."

"We can get started," the Aeri says, then nods to the east,

"but we won't make decent rainfall for another day. Had to send half my flock east to put out a Hive fire."

"Hive fire?" It's all I manage to say before an invisible hand squeezes my throat. Horrible images flash in my mind's eye as I connect some dreadful dots: Watchers digging their way out of a cave, led by a four-armed freak, then taking flight in fewer numbers than they'd set out with... Revenge hot on their minds... Them knowing the Hive that welcomed the local dust maiden... Revenge on their minds...

Revenge!

I shoot like a bolt of lightning away from the Aeri leader without another word. I fly hard east over desert toward the green horizon, where the swirling grey clouds over Ko Mirah's Hive have already thickened to black. Only, as I get closer, I see that it is not the molecular bonds formed by the Aeri that give the clouds their black shade, but a plume of smoke billowing up from below.

I clutch my belly as I feel a storm swell up within me. I'm going to be sick. If a few of those Hivers had managed to hold out on resenting me for this long, they'll have no reason to not swarm me if I drove Bercidia the Butcher to burn out their home.

It's worse than I thought. Much, much worse.

I cling to a tree and allow cold rain to pelt my skin and soak my wings. Below, wisps of grey smoke rise from smoldering ash piles, where only a few hours ago there stood trees... where there once stood the closest thing to a Hive I ever knew.

Hundreds of crows swirl above in a hurricane of black feathers. Their raving caws are enough to drive me mad. A murder crying murder.

"It was Jexa herself," Mora says from the branch beside me. "The Watcher Marshal has gone mad, deaf to the pleas of even a Ko Elder."

Ko Mirah. Tears swell behind my eyelids. I have no doubt she lies where a dozen Fori have gathered beside the Heart Spire's charred stump.

The rain batters me so hard I can no longer sustain my grip on the tree. I slide down the mossy trunk and come to rest in a cradle of roots.

A shuddering sob rises from around the trunk. I risk a peek and see Sheffa kneeling over Squiggs, whose eyes are closed, with her hands folded over her navel.

When Sheffa looks up and notices me watching, her puffy eyes flash wide with fury. "Ya wasn't satisfied with just makin' dust, was ya! Had to go turnin' everything to ash, too!"

I clutch my heart. I can see why she thinks this is my fault, and for a milder punishment she'd be right. But looking around at the bodies strewn among heaps of ash, it's clear Jexa overreacted. Yes, by offering me sanctuary they'd have been breaking the law...under *normal* circumstances. But I was wounded and in distress. It was an *emergency!*

I feel the poultice in my rib, the one Ko Mirah had made for me. The simple act of generosity that drew Jexa's wrath is nothing to my delinquencies over the years, and I have Jaleera to thank for that. Having her for my Watcher has shielded me from the realities my cousins have faced.

"Nya," says a voice from behind. It's harsh, yet fully defeated.

I turn to see Vera, Ko Mirah's primary understudy, standing between us. Her soot-covered cheeks are streaked with tears.

"Ko Mirah left you a final message."

My heart squirms in my belly.

"She wants the violence to end here," Vera says. "I know you're not in the habit of following orders, but you will grant our Elder her last wish."

My heart quivers. *Last wish.* Her choice of words hits me like a punch to the gut.

"Did you hear me?" Vera says. "You won't fight Jexa."

Fight Jexa? Does she think me crazy? Though, I suppose if she heard that I was willing to trap a few Watchers in a cave then I might be mad enough to challenge their leader.

I nod.

"Say it!" growls Vera through clenched teeth. Her two shaking fists suggests she wants to hit me.

"I swear it," I say. "I won't fight Jexa." Fighting is a Watcher's game, anyway. I will do more than that. I shall seek justice with my words. Although the Watcher Marshal may cast punishment in minor cases, she cannot commit a mass execution based on the actions of a single ward. Her actions here are downright criminal.

Vera turns to join the cluster of Fori and Ori whispering the passage rites around Ko Mirah's body. They must know it's all for nothing. She defied Jexa and now her spark is doomed to the Dark. It doesn't take long for Mora to confirm this.

"Jexa said you trapped the Butcher party," says Mora from behind. "She knew you'd been here and that Ko Mirah offered you sanctuary. Jexa pressed her for your whereabouts.

When Ko Mirah said you were recovering in the dunes nearby, Jexa called her a liar and took her Spark."

I feel the poultice in my ribs, medicine crafted by Ko Mirah's skillful hands only hours ago. My heart aches. It seems showing a dust maiden any kindness is among the worst of crimes.

Wailing and sobs rise loud over the rain. They are stricken with grief and need someone to blame, and I am an easy target. But this is all on Jexa. And Jexa has given me an opportunity to shine a light onto her methods. I can't undo death, but I can see that she answers for at least this crime.

"I'll tell the Grand Councilry what happened here," I say, but my choked words are only a whisper. Over the pattering rain and sobs, they are nothing. But they will bring down Jexa. This Hive has served faithfully since my mother's rebellion.

Rather than await the Magister's arrival at the next New Moon, Jexa has given the Councilry cause to summon him at once. This may all be settled before Deka even reaches the forest.

I nod with resolve and wipe the tears from my eyes. It looks like I'll be meeting the protector of Light and Life earlier than planned.

CHAPTER 11
DEKA

The sea had claimed fifteen of our colony's bravest souls in the one year we were allowed to fish. I know that's why Marlok assigned me to fishing duty at my turning of eight. Two months of night sailing with a mentor was all the training I had when they gave me my own boat. Whether I returned empty-handed or with a bountiful catch in my net, the look on Marlok's face was always the same: disappointment. He didn't even try to hide it. From my first solo venture I knew the only thing that would please him was for me to not return.

Today, I'll grant him that wish.

I lift the chest lid and flinch at its groaning hinges. The noise seems to echo all the way to the Grand Gallery, so I must be quick. I rummage through the trunk of stored fishing gear and gather two cans full of fishhooks. Setting them aside, I continue my search until I find a spool of fishing wire. That's all I need from here, so I ease the lid shut and slip out into the passageway.

I slink down the dark tunnel toward the fisherman's gate. It's night, so there's no circle of light to guide me to the end, but the salty breeze blowing on my face grows stronger with every step and assures me of my direction.

The cans of fishhooks rattle in my shaking hands, so I hold them tight to my chest. My shuddering breath rises to replace the clamor.

"*Jexa.*" I whisper that name into the dark. *Jexa...* The killer of my mother; the killer of many mothers. Saying the beast's name aloud gives me a measure of power I've not known until now, for I no longer seek a nameless enemy. I now have a clear target and an absolute means to its end. I will save my colony and, with any luck, return with that creature's head. Only then may we begin our climb out of darkness.

I emerge onto the beach under a sky full of stars. The spattering of white dots across the black ceiling that covers our world never fails to inspire me. Even now, in my rush, I take the time to crane my neck back to admire the bulging seam of white that stretches from horizon to horizon.

Jexa, echoes the voice in my head. *Magister.* Two factors in an equation that equal *Justice.* Hope rises in me, but it is not without its doubt. What variables stand in my way? This is unknown territory I venture into, even if my ancestors had once charted every rock. This is not the same world. The Earth of Man died a long time ago.

Despite this, my heart beats with a thrill I've suppressed for so long. It's possible I've explored the world through words more than anyone who still lives. It's time for an adventure of a more immersive nature. It's time for me to expand our understanding of this planet. All I need is Nya's signal to embark on this epic journey of discovery. I'm now wishing I'd pressed her more to tell me what to watch for.

I follow the cliff face in the opposite direction of the crevice. My polymer boat rests where I left it, upside down and buried in enough sand to resemble a dune. The commotion of the evacuation's reversal had provided me a narrow window to slip into the mariner's hold and drag it outside, though I'm never sure who may be lurking in the dark. That doubt has plagued me all afternoon, but it's clear now that I've made a clean escape.

I scoop away the sand with both hands. My heart beats faster with each handful removed, from both exertion and excitement. If anyone knew what I was up to, they'd surely think me crazed just from the smile on my face.

"Halt," orders a voice from behind.

My heart obeys, holding still for at least three beats before resuming its frantic race. I turn to see Mali with her crossbow half raised.

"You know G-Ma ordered we keep those locked away," she reminds me.

"I know that and more," I'm quick to say. I'd spent my free time rehearsing a variety of excuses should a sentry find me, but none will work on the person who knows me best. "I know that if we stick to our ways, I will bury you all and watch our race fade into darkness. As the last survivor, I will bear a pain greater than any human to have ever lived." My dreams have warned me of this fate on many a night. I shake my head at Mali and say, "That I cannot do. I'd sooner risk dying with a sliver of hope in my heart."

Mali lowers her crossbow, but keeps it at the ready. "How?"

"Nya—"

Mali squeezes her crossbow and growls.

I continue. "*Nya* knows of a great authority that can save us."

"You believe her?" Mali says, her mouth agape, as if it's the most ludicrous thing she's ever heard.

"She lost her mother to the same creature that took ours."

"So she says."

I shrug. "It is only my life I risk in this. I will give it gladly for this chance, however small that turns out to be."

Mali hugs her crossbow and turns away, kicking rocks as she shakes her head and mutters to herself. I carry on brushing sand away from my boat.

"You're really willing to bet your life on this?" Mali says.

I nod without hesitation. Even if something stops us from making it all the way to see this Magister, there's much I can learn from a bit more time with Nya.

"I always hated when Marlok called you a coward," Mali says, kicking a rock out to sea. "Doing this proves you're either really brave, or just stupid beyond any level I've ever heard of." She huffs and releases a nervous laugh. "Okay. We'll need more weapons, and more fresh water than you have there. I'm not much of a mariner, but you know my company and singing are second to none."

I want to laugh with relief. Instead, I step forward and take Mali's hand. "There's no one else I'd rather have at my side in this, but I must go alone. The colony needs its finest warrior guarding our gates while I'm gone."

Mali pokes my chest. "You need someone watching your

back." She grits her teeth. "Especially with that *Nya* creature around. I don't trust it even the slightest."

I know Mali well enough to know she won't let me leave without her, and her estimation is true. I've not smuggled enough water for both of us. Even under strict ration, I'll be lucky to get two days out of it. Only now do I realize I've abandoned part of my scientific reason in hopes of a miracle.

Mali backs away toward the cave entrance. "I won't be long. Huxley is on lookout tonight. If anyone asks what I'm doing, I'll say he asked me to fetch him some provisions to cover my watch."

Considering Huxley's affection for Mali, I myself would never question why he'd fill in the gaps left by her removal from the sentry rotations. So I nod and send her on her way.

I flip the boat onto its keel and rub sand from the gunwale. As I do this, I can't deny my heart now beats a little easier. Mali will indeed offer great company, and she isn't too bad with a crossbow either. Plus, she has the eyes of a hawk. On the sea this quality will prove invaluable.

This thought brings a great oversight to my attention. The sea can be many things, and *blinding* is one of them. I'll be sailing in daylight without goggles. Having Mali's will allow us to take turns between watching and sleeping.

The sea. Its salty breeze has misted my nostrils for so long that I can now sense a change in the air. This sudden shift is strange, yet not entirely unfamiliar. I'm stepping toward the tide line to investigate when Marlok's voice stops me dead.

"Don't put up a fight, Deka."

I whirl around to face a dozen warriors marching out from the fisherman's gate.

And Mali walks behind her brother.

I shoot her a rueful glare. This betrayal cuts so deep I can't even find words to throw at her. I doubt there's even a word in my mother's dictionary for how I feel right now.

"It's for your own good," she says, but she can't even look at me when she says it. She did this to regain trust with Marlok. To make up for letting me outside during her sentry watch that led to our discovery. By reeling me in, she's hoping for redemption. She doesn't realize she just doomed us all.

They escort me below, Huxley leading the way, with six warriors following close behind me. They tap their spear butts on the ground every few steps, to remind me that they're armed. To intimidate me. This solid, unified pounding eventually disintegrates to a rattle.

Rather than throw me straight into the 'pit', they take me to the chamber where earlier in the day they held Nya. Marlok reminds Mali that she's been suspended from her warrior duties, so she remains outside.

I'm forced to my knees before G-Ma. Despite the shadows concealing her eyes in the candlelight, I feel the heat from her glare. Normally I'd bow my head until she permits me to raise it, but there is no time for our old ways. Nya's signal may come any second. We can't afford to miss it.

"You were going to defy my sea ban?" G-Ma says. It's a question, not an accusation. She's offering me a way out. I can avoid punishment, but none of us will be safe if I follow the easy route.

I give a single nod.

Her eyes narrow and her nostrils flare. "What madness has gotten into you, boy?"

"It's that sky devil," Marlok spits. "She's luring him away so she can squeeze information from him."

"I didn't ask you," G-Ma says to Marlok. "I want to hear the words from Deka, to see what manner of spell that creature has woven in his mind."

Spell, she calls it. I'd call it logic, reason, sense. "The sky demons think we're mindless animals," I say. "Watching the way you've acted around them, I can see why."

G-Ma flashes her teeth, but then catches herself. I feel static from the anger of those behind me.

"They'll come back in greater numbers," I say, "and this time they won't stop until we're all dead. But we are not without hope. I'm going to meet their highest authority, to show them we're of intelligent design. Nya says—"

G-Ma's face twists with revolt. She raises a hand to silence me. "You will not speak that devil's name in my presence, you hear?"

Anger swells up in me. I swallow it down. "You risk only losing *me* if this plan fails," I say. "But if it works, the demons will leave this planet for good. They've already seen us. They know where we live. But my journey could lure them away. If I'm seen far enough away, it could throw them off. You chance nothing by letting me go, but wager everything by keeping me here."

Marlok scoffs from behind. He steps up to my side and points a condemning finger at me. "We've heard those words before, from his mother's mouth. That's the argument she used to gain permission to go fishing. I needn't remind you of the loss we suffered over that."

G-Ma nods her head in ominous reverie.

"Now this fool is walking into a trap," Marlok says. "That demon couldn't kidnap him with us around, so it's leading him away. He will betray our secrets to those devils and bring about our end. His final breaths will signal the end of ours."

"She is not like those who killed my mother," I say, my cheeks burning red hot. "She is different."

"Listen to him! *She*, he calls it. As if it's a human girl. He has fallen under its spell and become its agent. They infiltrate our colony through him."

Rage boils in me, along with a sliver of doubt that keeps me from lashing out. Is what Marlok says true? If Nya really does play tricks on my mind, I'd never know it. After all, what son would defend a being that so much resembles the beasts that took both of his parents? In this light, Marlok's suspicion seems warranted. Yet something inside me—my intuition— assures me this is the right path. This reminds me of a quote in one of mother's books: *Intuition is the highest form of intelligence.*

"What information has this beast offered you?" G-Ma says.

I see in her eyes she cannot hide her curiosity. I indulge her. "Those *demons* have come from another planet, and are here to make this world livable for new owners, because they think us all dead or mindless. But this is our rightful home. The authority I'm seeking is responsible for protecting races like us. We're wasting time here. I have to watch for her signal."

"What signal?" she asks.

"A..." I draw a blank. What did she say? *Look to the sky...*

Frustration swells inside me as my audience shifts from curious to impatient.

I close my eyes and summon forth her voice from that last memory of us together. "Look to the heavens," I say aloud, calling forth her words and courage, "and when nature's blessing falls from above, then you'll know."

Marlok scoffs. "*Nature's blessing...* to a demon that probably means fire and brimstone."

I ignore him and look to G-Ma.

She closes her eyes and rocks her head in contemplation. She does this for some time, giving my words deep thought. When she opens her eyes again, she says, "A clever story." Her eyes soften. "You have a good heart, Deka. I see how you were fooled. I'll show you some leniency for that. You'll serve only three days in the Pit, to let the darkness clear your mind of any spells that creature tangled in you."

She nods to Marlok, whose large hands were already moving to seize both of my arms.

"Wait!" I shout as I kick and thrash. Huxley and two warriors grab my legs.

"*Easy, Deka!*" Huxley hisses. "You'll hurt someone."

Marlok pulls my arms together in front of me so his partner can clamp rusted manacles around my wrists. The snapping of metal locking injects a shot of panic through me. I scream and try head-butting Marlok, but he pins my shoulders to the floor.

This commotion should be the loudest thing underground right now. But for all my kicking and thrashing and yelling, it's not enough to cover someone else's shouting down the tunnels.

Marlok stiffens and cocks his head to listen. The others

follow suit, with even G-Ma rising to her feet, a deep frown sagging her brow.

Footsteps race down the tunnel toward us. Mali bursts through the entryway without permission, a huge no-no even during regular times. But no one berates her, for she is covered in sweat and her cheeks smeared in tears so much that every part of her skin gleams in the candlelight. She's panting and can hardly catch her breath, her eyes wide and wild. I've not seen her so worked up since the death of our parents.

Then it hits me—the smell of her. It's the same scent I picked up on the beach before Marlok detained me, but now I know what it is without a doubt. It only took me so long because I've not smelled freshly fallen water since my childhood.

"You have to come see this!" she says, still gasping.

When she turns to leave, Huxley and every warrior but Marlok race from the council chamber, with G-Ma almost knocking me over in her hurry to join them. I've never seen our elder move so fast.

Marlok drags me by my chain to follow. As we approach the lower concourse, I hear a sound I'd nearly forgotten. It's been five years since we've heard more than a trickle through our water vein, so that when I hear the rushing sound, my first thought is that it must be my imagination. When we emerge onto the lower concourse, however, my eyes confirm what my eyes and nose have claimed.

Our water vein has swelled to a gushing artery.

I wedge between Marlok and Mali to watch a flood rush over rocks below, which grows in force and volume by the second. We stand at the concourse edge, staring in awe at the swelling river until its force is enough to send mist up to the lower rings of the Grand Gallery. Fresh, saltless moisture wets my nostrils. Suddenly I'm aware of how much my breathing had become a chore over the years. Everyone's hair and skin are soaked within minutes. Before we know it, the upper concourse is hard to see in the mist.

My breath catches. *Nya's signal - Nature's Blessing!* Life flowing back into our sanctuary, compliments of a 'conniving demon'. It takes everything in me to refrain from jabbing a gloating finger in all of their faces.

The miracles don't stop there. A bit of my mother returns to life when, for the first time in five years, the lights above flicker. Explosions of blinding light pulsate erratically overhead. Like the lightning storms of my childhood, light and dark struggle for dominance over our sanctuary, until those lamps we'd forgotten about flash on and stay that way. At first the steady glow is dim, but it quickly grows bright, so much that we must cover our eyes and shirk back into the shadows.

It takes me a few moments to notice that everyone from the council is now watching me. Some are stunned, like Marlok. Others, like Mali, cannot keep the wonder from their eyes. I know many are wondering if they should consider this a gift or a curse. G-Ma is giving me a long, appraising look. If I didn't know any better, I'd say that's the hint of a smile gracing her face.

"You understand the risk you take by leaving?" she asks. She has to yell over the rushing water.

I nod, my heart racing with excitement. Never in the rest of our days would I have bet on gaining the colony's approval to seek out Nya's council. But never in that long would I have expected to see water flow like this again.

G-Ma knows it, too. It's clear now in her eyes. Even with such a shield of distrust, she cannot deny this gift. In Nya, she is willing to believe we have found a worthy ally.

In this moment, humanity's future looks a whole lot brighter.

CHAPTER 12

NYA

A green glow near the horizon guides me through the night toward my destination.

Summon the Magister, I say to myself in frantic flight. That has become my mantra, and I shall repeat it until I say those words to the Councilry and demand that they do just that. I will say it to them until they set the Capstone atop the Great Pyramid, open the portal, and perform the ceremony to call upon our savior.

Summon the Magister, and all of our problems will be solved. Jexa will be held accountable for her crimes, and Deka's people will be saved.

Summon the Magister. Don't think about Ko Mirah.

Oh, Ko Mirah! How could I not think of her? Jexa has stolen her spark and will cast it into the Dark if I fail.

I couldn't imagine being stuck in the quantum vacuum Jexa holds in her grasp, knowing at any moment you'll be sent onward to the Dark. For that reason, the spear she wields is a terror for more than just its pointed ends. The quantum device uses opposing interdimensional forces to disembody a

Spark, the very essence of your immortal being, encapsulating it in a extradimensional container until we leave this planet for the next, when Jexa uses the gate to open a wormhole to a satellite that orbits the edge of a Black Hole. That is where your journey of existence ends. What goes into the Dark does not come out. Until then, a dizzying, crushing vortex within Jexa's grasp is all you know.

I suppose after that, the quiet stillness of the Dark might seem a welcome reprieve. And that's what frightens me most. What a fate that would be, driven mad enough to beg for the mercy of a Black Hole's crushing depths, alone and ionized until only thought and awareness remain for eternity.

I shiver at the thought. Do some of those souls actually come to wish for that release, knowing where it will end? Not even a Watcher deserves such a fate. So I must succeed for Ko Mirah's sake. The Magister will get her spark back and cast his judgment upon the Watchers. Murder is not their mandate. And I know he will grant justice. I once saw him punish a Watcher during one of his inspections. The Consul I now seek had reported her mistreatments, and we were all invited to watch when he put her in a cage and dunked her into a lake.

"The reward for those who abuse their power," he declared as she struggled for air. Her golden reptilian eyes bulged in fear as her death dragged on. But death would not find her there. It was then that we saw drowning is not how you kill a Watcher.

When the Magister got his message across to Jexa and her remaining warriors, he pulled her from the water. She struggled on her hands and knees, still gasping for air and spitting water from her flooded lungs, when Jexa took the

Watcher's sword at the Magister's command. She struck true and swift, lopping off her sister-in-arms' head with her own blade. Jexa appeared stoic in her duty, but her cold gaze revealed her disdain for the forced act.

I fly harder than I ever have until the source of the green glow comes into view and halts me in my flight. Few structures survive in my memory that could rival this beauty.

Carved into a mountain slope, the three-story temple boasts two dozen columns across its upper level, with even more spaced across the terrace below. A long ramp rises from the ground to the lower terrace, and then another leads to the upper level. This construct seems redundant for a winged being like myself, which leads me to believe this complex was created by Deka's folk.

I land on lime green grass a good distance before the lower ramp. Though I've never held audience with the Councilry—I have no idea what they even look like—instinct warns me that to fly into their presence may be taken as a great disrespect.

The grass is soft and cool beneath my feet as I march to the ramp. I stop at the bottom of the sloped stone and ponder what I'm about to do. Those of my stature are only allowed to set eyes upon the council for judgment. But I have no one else to turn to. They are the only of my kind on this planet who exceed Jexa in rank. I must report.

I proceed up the lower ramp, and though I'm moving upward, my legs feel as if I'm going down. In fact, my entire body somehow feels lighter. Like I'm shedding pounds with every step. The stiffness in my chest where the wound had tightened my muscles loosens the higher up the ramp I walk. There's a cool, tingling sensation atop the red blotch of the hole that sits deep in my chest. The enchanting air refreshes me. With each breath I feel the release of physical pain and mental darkness these past days have wrought upon me. I walk toward those emerald-tinted pillars with a spring in my step, emboldened and invigorated by the energies of wise masters and their environment.

At the top of the upper ramp, I'm greeted by statues of giants with chin hair that hangs down to their folded arms. Their grandeur casts a shadow of unworthiness over me. Between the pillars flanking them, the glowing green orbs that had guided me here turn to indigo blue. An overwhelming sense of welcome draws me inside. I enter without hesitation, almost in a trance. In the entry hall, I admire walls decorated with murals of colorful hieroglyphs and compare this work to the rugged cave walls of Deka's home. My, how far his species has fallen.

I emerge into an open-air courtyard and am immediately drawn to a golden pyramidion that gleams orange in torch light. The *Capstone*, key to the gateway of this planet's portal, stands thirty feet high under the night sky. Fifteen years ago, it sat high upon the Great Pyramid and focused the energy stream that tore through the fabric of space-time, opening the path for our arrival. Also functioning as a lens, it's what allows the Consul to see the way between worlds. Wherever a pyramid has been constructed over an energy node, it can generate enough power to open a portal, so we call them gates. The Capstone is the key that funnels the energy through its apex, concentrating enough power to open a portal to any other gate, no matter how far that other gate is. The bounds of space-time have no limits. What is near is far, and what's far is near.

Only two beings on Earth are permitted to use this Capstone, each a priestess ordained by a cosmic order of ascended masters, a representative of both Watchers and Servants alike, to ensure the proper serving of our Penance. It's the Priestess Darxa who approves our stripes before we exit the planet through the gateway. Only she and her Watcher counterpart can build a stable connection between distant gates. They are the Magister's representatives on this world and personal heralds. A tether between realms. What power.

But to ensure a safe opening and stable connection, it must be done during the proper celestial Alignment, when the heavens are arranged in a certain way known only to the Consuls and their master. The Magister arranges his inspections around these Alignments.

I approach the gate key in wonder, but stop when my reflection sharpens in the golden face. A Watcher stands on guard at each point, an upright spear gripped tight with both hands, their eyes fixed ahead in a lifeless stare. Their wings hug their torsos, fitting tight like pliable armor.

My mother once stood guard over a capstone like this, ten planets ago. Before the rebellion, the honor of Consul bodyguard was shared between two servants and two Watchers. Each Watcher stood next in line for Marshal, while the second served as deputy when the time came.

But these four Watcher guards are not what keep me from venturing in for a closer look.

The internal chains that bind sacred structures such as this were set by masters possessing skill beyond any who now wander the physical planes. Before ascending back into the higher dimensions, they set the bonds as unbreakable, and so unbreakable they are. For one like myself, a breaker of chains, to even touch such an object risks unbinding my own physical being.

I'd rather not explode into a cloud of dust and light, so I carry on around the Capstone toward the far end of the courtyard, where a shifting green light lures me through a door in the base of the mountain.

I'd been expecting a challenge from the guards before meeting the council, but seeing the Grand Councilry in person is enough to halt me in the doorway.

In the center of a sunken chamber, the most senior representative to either the Watchers or my kind—it's too hard to tell which from here—sits before a golden bowl that bears a green flame. I'm lucky to have never encountered her outside of this temple. I'd certainly get myself into trouble by questioning her status because, unlike our Ko Elders—whose wrinkled skin and colorless hair reveals their age and wisdom—the figure before me has the appearance of a human child.

From here she appears to be wingless. I heard this is to prevent bias against councillors of my kind. In the Councilry there is no division. They are to be respected by all—Watchers and Servants alike—as mutual guardians of the Pact. And because her eyes are closed, I cannot tell if she's my kind or a Watcher. There are supposed to be two. So where is the other? I'd prefer to report Jexa's crime to the Priestess Darxa, but I can't be sure this is her. Though Councilry members are wise and unbiased, I feel Ko Mirah's Hive would garner more sympathy from one of our own.

I pause inside the doorway, unsure how I should interrupt her meditation. This work to support all our efforts is of utmost importance—*would* be, I should say, if we were allowed to be performing a reclamation of this planet in the first place.

Her gaze suddenly locks onto me. At this angle and distance, her eyes remain shrouded in shadow, but I feel her stare pierce through me.

She spreads both arms wide in greeting. "Come, child. Sit."

Such strange words coming from a being who appears years younger than myself, but her tone commands a respect no youngling ever could.

I accept the invitation and sit cross-legged across the brazier from her. A chill comes from the green flame dancing between us. By the color of her green eyes and round pupils, I see she is Darxa, High Priestess and Consul of my kind. I allow myself to relax in relief.

"You join us with a troubled heart," she says, her voice soft and empathetic. "More trouble than usual, I feel."

Fearing that at any moment guards will rush in from deeper chambers to haul me away, I waste no time.

"Jexa destroyed Ko Mirah's Hive. She killed many loyal Servants, including Ko Mirah herself."

Darxa responds to this news with a grave and knowing nod. All innocence abandons her young face. "Jexa takes interferences in her affairs very seriously."

"But to do *that*? Ko Mirah took me in, it's true, but I was gravely injured. There's no excuse!"

Darxa shuts her eyes tight. When she opens them again, much to my dreadful surprise, they are yellow with a vertical slit in each. These reptilian eyes, a manifestation of another entity within the same host, take in my presence with less warmth. I'm guessing this new emergence is the Sage of Faes—Watcher Consul of this planet.

A shiver freezes my spine.

"That stunt of yours severely injured two Light Ones," she says, sounding very much like a brat with her tone. "They'll be lucky to ever fly again."

Two less Watchers in the sky is nothing to cry about, is what I want to say, but I keep it to myself. Such talk will gain me no support here.

The vessel before me blinks, and then I'm looking into Darxa's eyes again.

I try my best to conceal my angst. No wonder we're not allowed to converse with this being. I'd never considered they inhabited a single body—two minds to form a single Consul. As a youngling, I'd sometimes dreamt of becoming the Consul of my kind. But the idea of sharing a body with a Watcher is just plain horrifying. I'd almost take the vortex of Jexa's spear shaft over that. *Almost.*

"Why did you interfere in the Light Ones' work, anyway?" Darxa says, her green eyes replacing the reptilian orbs in a single blink.

This pair of supremely wise elders seem more concerned with my delay of the genocide than for the genocide itself. What are we, if not invaders and murderers?

"The owners of this planet are still here," I say. "I saw them, and... I saw how the Watchers kill them."

"They killed themselves," snaps the Sage of Faes, "a long time ago. They almost took this planet with them. Now we are restoring it for those who will take better care of it. If a few stragglers remain, well..."

My Priestess, Darxa, returns and places a comforting hand on my leg. "The Light Ones are just speeding up the inevitable. Much like how the Ori draw in the right combination of nutrients in the soil, or the Aeri stir particles in the atmosphere to call upon the rain. All these processes are natural, much like the certain death of those survivors who cling to life. Consider it a mercy."

The words of this council sit heavy on my heart. They confirm that everything I ever knew about our work to be a lie. Worse, an *invasion*. Oh, Darkness! We're not repenters! We're invaders! I feel helpless and at the same time complicit in these deeds. "But...*killing*...It's..."

"Nature," the Sage of Faes says sternly. "You've not seen the behavior of this species in their prime. Even at their best, they were very much accustomed to self-inflicted brutality, and far worse than that which we offer. Now, go and do your work like an obedient Servant. And forget not your place again."

So that's it? I'm supposed to just go tear down the accomplishments of this race and act like they're not being driven to extinction by my masters?

The Consul closes her eyes, and I feel much of the tension evaporate from the chamber. I've used up all my time with the Sage of Faes. When the host speaks again, it is all Darxa, her voice heavy with defeat.

"So long has it been since the Pact came to be, that the generations of new have forgotten why the Light Ones were appointed to oversee our Penance in the first place. Forget not their wisdom, young dustmaker. They are far more qualified to distinguish between that which makes an ecosystem thrive, and the rot that must be cut away to survive." Darxa looks to the doorway. "Now, go. We have much work to do before the Magister's inspection."

I suddenly feel abandoned. And worse, vulnerable to retaliation from forces outside these walls. Forces that drove me here in the first place. We've gotten sidetracked with talk of Deka's folk, but my visit here wasn't even about them.

"What of Jexa's atrocities against your own kind? Are you just going to ignore that?"

Darxa closes her eyes. Her face is startlingly serene, with a hint of... satisfaction? "We do not take this transgression lightly. We've already summoned Jexa to report to us at once. She will stand trial and face our judgment. This will be settled well before the Magister arrives."

"Does *he* know about the...the..."

"*Humans*, they're called. And their existence is of no concern to him. If we halted our work on every planet that still harbored survivors, we'd never fulfill our Penance. You worry too much for others, when it is your own life at stake. Be grateful for our leniency with you. If there were more of your kind, you'd be long dead. But our tolerance stops here and now. Your next transgression will end with you in darkness. That is why we permitted your visit tonight, to deliver you that message. Nothing else. Now, you've wasted enough of this council's time. Leave us."

I want to stand, but my knees remain locked in a cross-legged position. I didn't come all this way to be shooed away like a pestering fly.

Though, what else can I say? This seems to be the way of it. Everyone on this planet conspires to fulfill our Penance at any cost. But the Magister would not stand for it. Heads would roll if he knew these were intelligent races we condemn to extinction.

And it's not only humans the Watchers must answer for. My people have also suffered at the hands of our wardens, and it's whispered there'll come a time when the Magister is made aware of all the names lost to the Watchers' brutality. *The Reckoning*, some call it. I could never understand why our Elders never exercised this option, but now, feeling powerless in the presence of the Consul, I do. Any who the Watchers suspect may speak up are condemned to the Dark. How many Ori and Fori have been sent there to keep their testimony from reaching the Magister? They wish to silence me, but a dust maiden cannot disappear so easily. If they didn't need me to fulfill their work, they'd have let Jexa do away with me years ago. It's this reality that I must adapt to, not change. That's what the Grand Councilry is telling me. The complicity of all our Elders tells me the same. They know this game better than I. Resistance to what has become the way is futile and intolerable. Yet I feel like I can do this task no easier than my destructive dust making.

I now sit across from a breathing body, but I know I am alone. So I take my leave.

In the courtyard, I give my reflection in the Capstone a hard look-over. Ignorance allows me to forgive myself for going along with these crimes before now. But now that I know, I'd be no better than those spilling the blood if I continue to do what I'm told.

No. I won't let it happen. I have ten nights to keep Deka alive and arrange audience with the Magister when he arrives.

I stride past the Capstone with great urgency. Outside,

on the upper terrace, the night air cools me. I stare at the waning gibbous moon, wondering if its three quarter surface will provide me enough energy to last in my flight until daybreak. I must reach Deka's meeting point without delay, for I do not know at what speed he can reach the pyramids for the Magister's arrival.

"I thought I smelled Servant blood nearby."

The voice creeps up like a serpent's slither and makes me squirm. I look down to see an ivory figure climbing the ramp. Pointed ears of the palest white protrude from the blackest hair I've ever seen. Black as the Dark I so fear. Ragged wings of the same color, flat rounded membranes shaped like those of a butterfly, bespeak lifetimes of violence, and the black lips of her wicked grin have issued commands of unspeakable terror.

My heart races. It takes everything for me to remain in place, to keep my feet from retreating into the temple in search of the Councilry's protection.

Jexa joins me on the upper terrace and walks a circle around me, sniffing me as she does so. "You reek of fear, girl. And... something else."

She leans close and takes a whiff of my hair. My skin feels as if it's lifting from my bones.

"Smoke and burnt skin," she concludes. Her voice is softer than I'd imagined. Almost pleasant. But there is no telling what atrocities that black tongue of hers has ordered. Perhaps the burning of my Hive will serve to save many others from her harsh retributions.

"You made good timing for your trial," I say, and cringe at the quiver in my voice.

Jexa gives a mocking bow. "The masters speak and the servant obeys."

"You crossed the line," I say, my anger flaring. "The Councilry will make you pay for your crimes."

She raises an eyebrow in amusement. "Don't threaten me with a good time. I'd invite you to come watch, but I know you have more pressing affairs to attend."

Is she referring to my work in serving? Or does she know of Deka's plight? The smile on her face is hard to interpret. As is the amusement in her yellow, reptilian eyes, with their black slits.

She continues on into the courtyard. Two of the Capstone guards greet her with shackles, rattling them tauntingly, their short swords drawn and ready. Their two companions wait behind, their spears at the ready. I wonder which will have their turn at command next. Whoever it may be will have to wait for the next planet. For continuity, Jaleera will assume command for the remainder of our time on Earth, until a new Marshal and deputy are appointed.

Part of me wants to take Jexa up on her offer to attend her tribunal, but I cannot waste time. Who knows how long such a proceeding will take.

When she's disappeared inside, I bound down the ramp, race across the grass, and then leap into the air to take flight.

Jexa's ill fate offers me little comfort. Should the Councilry strip her of her command, someone else will take her place. Perhaps someone worse, a Watcher keen to make an even more malicious name for herself.

At least justice will be served for my Hive. In the meantime, I'll need a distraction for Deka's voyage to the pyramids.

An idea springs to mind, and I know it's a good one because my heart flutters at the thought of it. The idea swiftly blooms into a series of images...

I'll return to Ko Mirah's Hive to order they feign unrest. At first nothing serious, just enough to put the Watchers on edge, to have their eyes away from Deka and me. Then, when the Consul arrives at the Great Pyramid to perform the gateway ceremony, they will draw the Watchers away with a great ruckus. Black smoke and cheering songs of forbidden times. Songs of dissent. Celestial alignment for the portal opening is key, so the Consul will go ahead with opening it, regardless of what's happening in distant forests. With any luck, the Watchers will respond in full force, and I do think they will, to quell any signs of disturbance before the Magister's arrival.

A smile tugs at my mouth. Yes. This could work.

CHAPTER 13
NYA

I find Ko Mirah's Hive where I left them. They are in a much different mood now.

Two Fori fly out to intercept me over the desert, not far from the forest edge. They escort me to a grove some distance away from the charred remains of their Hive. "Wait here for Ko Vera."

Ko Vera... Ko Mirah's understudy has already taken her place. Just like that, life goes on for them.

The new Elder arrives with the rest of her Hive. They perch themselves in the surrounding trees while she squares off with me. "You've got a lot of nerve coming here."

"I bring no quarrel with me," I say, my hands raised. "I've come to help."

Ko Vera's face twists in revolt. "You are trouble with wings. Destruction incarnate. The only way you can *help* is to steer far clear of any Hive you happen across."

A few Fori hold sharpened sticks. Their rueful glares suggest they might be willing to use them on me—whether for revenge or to show the Watchers they'll not make the same mistake as their dead Elder, I do not know. Either way, I don't have much time with them.

"By now I'm sure you've all heard of the *sapiens*. They are an intelligent race, the exact type the Magister is sworn to protect, and we are pushing them from their rightful home."

I see in the eyes of many their glares soften in realization. Others furrow their brows deeply, trying to absorb the meaning. Perhaps trying to deny the implications of my words. But there is no denying the truth here. On this planet, we are invaders.

Mora steps forward. "Does the Consul know of this?"

"She just came from the Consul," says Ko Vera.

My face burns red hot. I can't tell if it's from anger at being followed, or shame for not knowing it. It seems she's kept eyes on me to ensure I will honor Ko Mirah's last wish. And I fully intend to.

"The Consul will not help us." She is corrupted, is what I'd like to say. "But we don't need them. It's the Magister who will sort this out, and he's coming in a week."

"You plan to meet with him?" Ko Vera scoffs. "And say what? That Jexa burnt our Hive and killed our Elder for breaking the law by taking you in? Because let me tell you: If there's one thing he doesn't tolerate, it's disorder. He's likely to reassign a Marshal with a bit more restraint, and that's all that will come of that."

"We've heard enough from this termite," says a Fori. She squeezes the shaft of a sharpened stick. "Send her away."

Many murmurs rise in agreement. They don't care about Deka's people. Not in the way I do. To appeal to them, it must be more personal.

"It's time for The Reckoning," I say.

I see in their eyes this is not what they want to be hearing. That all the years of talks for justice was just that — talk. Even Mora, who supported my mother in her rebellion, shirks back and avoids my stare. This crowd is made up of bluffers.

Ko Vera clenches her fists and steps up to me. "What did you just call us?"

My pulse pounds hard on my eardrums. *Oops.* Did I say all of that out loud?

Even if I did, it doesn't matter. This is no time for lies and deceit. Anyone who lies in a parley such as this is an enemy. And lines are about to be drawn.

I clench my fists and stand tall, staring Ko Vera in the eyes and talking loud for all to hear. "You heard me. You've all lost your spine, it's a wonder you can still stand upright."

Ko Vera sneers. "You say you seek justice. But I see rebellion in your eyes."

My throat tightens. The very words make many shiver and huddle together. Many have seen this look of rebellion before, and many more are not here to tell of it.

I clear my throat and step back from Ko Vera, to address my wider audience. "My mother grabbed the snake by its tail and got bit. This time we'll go straight for the head. Then... we'll bash it in with a hammer."

Ko Vera folds her arms and raises her chin. "And this proverbial hammer will come in the form of what, exactly?"

"Names," I say, and the word hangs heavy in the air. The Reckoning. Justice.

Ko Vera lifts her chin and stares down her nose at me. "The Magister is great, true, and that's why you'll not get within ten thousand cubits of him. Every Watcher on the planet will be there to make sure of it. We've all seen the ceremony. When the Consul opens the gate, they'll be present in full force, standing before the pyramid in their neat ranks."

I purse my lips to contain my rage. Ten thousand cubits isn't even that far. Especially when you have wings!

"Draw them away," I say. "No need to fight them." Fighting is the last thing I want them to do. "Just give them a chase. Then I'll get to the Magister."

Whispers rustle through the crowd like a breeze through autumn leaves. They're growing impatient with me.

"The Reckoning is upon us," I say, "whether you like it or not."

"The Reckoning was a dream," hisses Ko Vera. "Words to console us in our grief. Even if the Magister was willing to upset the order of things for a few Servant names, the Watchers are too cunning. He sees what they want him to see. They will label our lost ones as dissidents, the Magister will dismiss us like pestering flies, and when he leaves, the Watchers will drop the hammer on us."

Many around Ko Vera nod their heads in agreement. Until a voice rises from the trees behind.

"Sataria the Oakbender!"

Everyone turns to look upon the speaker, Jinny. She stands tall upon a high stump, shaking in anger. "They took her in the night," she says, her voice cracking, "two full moons ago."

Ko Vera bristles. "For what crime?"

"For smelling roses." Jinny's lips quiver, but her eyes beam with rage. "We teamed up to tackle a stubborn pocket of bushland that kept turning to swamp in the east-fold. She stopped for a short break, just when a Watcher happened to be flying by. She hauled Sataria away and broke my leg when I tried to follow. Sataria had forty rings on her wrists, for forty planets revived. She was the finest tree-tender I ever knew." Jinny's eyes glaze with tears. "She was my friend."

"We all know the rules," Ko Vera says sharply. Callously. "When the sun is up, we toil."

"Kelifa the Daisymaker," says another voice, this one closer. Mora steps forward to reveal herself. "She disappeared a year ago, carrying a message between Hives."

"Tell us the nature of her message," presses Ko Vera.

Mora looks to her feet. "She was bringing a friendly warning, that the Watchers were headed that way for a random inspection."

Ko Vera opens her mouth to speak, but another voice cuts her off.

"Allis Deeproot!" This comes from someone in the back. "For sleeping during work."

Ko Vera again opens her mouth to speak, but once again someone pipes in to cut her off. "Allis worked five days straight without rest. She covered my area because I was sick. And that's the reward she got. They slit her throat right in front of me. I still hear the gurgles of her last breath in my sleep."

A squeal of despair rises from another Fori, seemingly at the same or similar memory, and it rips my heart in two.

More names come from the crowd. Many voices have several names to speak, from planets and assignments long past. So many. Too many. Others just rhyme off numbers, for whole Hives lost or displaced.

The crowd draws closer around Ko Vera and me. They

shout names of the taken and jab fingers at Ko Vera, berating her for excusing the Watchers' crimes.

The faces around me blur. I rub my eyes and feel they are wet with tears.

"Ko Mirah." My voice is soft when I say her name, but it's enough to quell the ruckus. Everyone watches me in silence, their anger softened as they join me in despair. "Ko Mirah, for showing me kindness during my darkest night." I press my fingers to the sunken skin between my ribs, where Ko Mirah's poultice had fused a few days ago. "Ninety-nine planets she has helped revived. How many names could she add to our list?"

"And we are but one Hive," says Mora. "How many could our sister Hives add?"

My fists and jaw clench tight. I jump high onto a stump and stand tall, emotions of despair and anger surging through me. "Who here has been forced into service?" I say. "None. Each of us has volunteered to serve our Penance under the Law of Free Will. That is proof enough for me of the Magister's benevolence. Anything else is against his ways. So is the systemic extermination of an intelligent race. The Watchers' treatment of us is a story unto itself. In saving the humans, we'll also be helping ourselves by revealing the Light Ones' dark side. By doing this, you will save people like Sataria the Oakbender from lifetimes of cruelty."

The faces around me beam with hope. Even Ko Vera's expression has softened as she nods in contemplation.

"You've all shown me something very profound here today," the new Elder says.

My heart swells with satisfaction.

"You've all shown me the need for strong leadership," Ko

Vera says. "Because it's obvious that each of you lacks the foresight to assess the consequences of your actions."

The swell in my heart deflates.

A Fori with thirty bands to each wrist shoves her way forward. "Anyone who's ever talked about telling the Magister has disappeared. You all know this. So ask yourselves, why are The Watchers so desperate to keep word of their deeds from reaching him. It would be their downfall, that's why. And they know it."

"If we succeed in revealing Jexa's crimes to the Magister," Ko Vera explains, "he will remove her from her post. Of that I have no doubt. But who will rise to take her place? Someone worse? Someone like... The Butcher?"

Everyone around me shudders. I, too, feel a shiver creep up my spine. But no, they assume the worst.

"Jexa's second-in-command will take her place," I point out.

"Immediately following her removal, yes. But when we move on to the next planet, the Magister will appoint a permanent replacement."

"If we do exceptional work under her," I say, "the Magister will have no reason to appoint another."

"And who's to say Jaleera will be any better? At least we know what triggers Jexa. We hadn't seen her near our Hive until you came around."

My shoulders tense. I have to turn this conversation around, fast. "As most of you know, Jaleera is my personal Watcher. She has shown me great kindness over the years, more than I deserve."

Someone scoffs. "I wonder why."

Her sarcasm draws a curious stare from me. Others join in.

"Jaleera killed Nya's mother," declares the Fori.

"*Jexa* killed Klora," reminds Jinny.

"You were there?" counters the Fori. "I know I was. I saw Klora's fall with my own eyes."

"You?" mocks another Fori. "The one who cut off her own finger while dicing *singa* root? You have the eyes of a blind mole rat."

"This happened ten planets ago, remember? My vision worked plenty fine back then."

I look to Mora, whom I know participated in my mother's rebellion.

She shrugs and raises her hands. "I was busy tending the wounded. I didn't see the duel for myself."

I turn my gaze to the crowd. "Who else witnessed this?"

"There was only a handful of us," says the Fori with the vision of a mole rat. "I am the only one who still lives."

"How convenient," I say.

"Convenient indeed. Of the twelve of us, eight have succumbed to *accidents*, while three were sent to the Dark for disobedience. As for me, well, I'd been blinded during the fight. I never saw it was Jaleera who stabbed your mother in the back. That's what I told Jexa, anyway."

Anger burns inside my chest. This blind Fori's penchant for trickery threatens our cause. And to lie about such a thing... What would it be like to dust someone's bones while leaving their skin intact?

The wretched thought churns my guts. To even consider using my ability on a living thing brings me nearly to tears.

Ko Vera sees my anger and interjects: "The past is done.

Klora is dead. So is Ko Mirah, along with many others. The question now is what do we do about it."

Her choice in words dampens my anger. Hope rises in its place. I step close and place a hand on her shoulder. "We will do this without violence."

She shrugs my hand away and steps back. "A distraction is what you need?"

"Yes. It will start with general unrest the morning of the gate opening. When the Consul arrives at the pyramid, we'll need a disturbance big enough to draw a majority, if not all, of the Watchers away."

"We could celebrate Klora's rebellion," suggests Mora.

Gasps rise loud from the crowd. To utter such a thing in normal times would risk certain death if the Watchers found out. But Mora's suggestion is perfect, and the others will soon realize they must curve their thinking to succeed.

Ko Vera nods. "That could work. I doubt the Magister even knows about the rebellion. Jexa will want to silence our songs before his arrival, to keep it that way."

This surprises me. How could he not know?

"Yes," agrees Mora. "The Watchers will have certainly kept that from him."

Their words get me thinking. *Of course.* Rebellion would look bad on the Watchers, threatening their reputation as wise overseers of the Pact. We entered into it willingly, so not only would it undermine their authority, it would prompt an inquiry from the Magister. He'd ask questions. Questions like... Why would the Servants revolt? What caused their discontent? It would shine a light onto their mistreatment of us. After all, it's easy for us to forget how they started out as our mentors and guides, benevolent arbitrators of the

Penance. They were to help us, not oppress. To show us back to the light. Hence their name: *The Light Ones*.

Ko Vera sighs and straightens. "Alright then, it's settled. We'll spread word to the other Hives. With any luck, we can have a real party going when the portal opens."

My heart thunders inside my belly. Not only is my idea catching on, but they intend to use my mother's deeds as the ruse. Imagine that. They intend to celebrate my mother. Even if it's a joke, it feels better than hearing her labeled a fool.

I conceal my smile. With that out of the way, I can concentrate on my other plan.

CHAPTER 14

DEKA

The wailing of young children on the open beach rattles my nerves. So loud. They cling to their parents nearby, who have come to see me off. Whole families venturing to surface to witness this fateful moment. My departure shall bring salvation or death. The most pivotal moment in our colony's memory. No pressure at all.

I scan the grey sky from the shoreline, wary. How far do these cries travel over the water? The dunes? Do our enemy scouts take note, or do we have time? How far can I possibly expect to make it in the open? This is a fool's endeavor. I am leading my species into—

A hand smacks my face. My own, coming to rescue me from my self-destructive thoughts. We've come past the point of doubt. There is no looking back from here; only forward. Besides, my embarkation aside, this is no regular day.

Standing on the beach, with dozens from my colony spilling out from the crevice to witness my departure, the falling rain soaks everyone from head to toe. This may be what upsets many of the children. Or it may be the wind. Or the wide-open space. Many have never been above ground, and are not prepared for the occasion. A few retreat back to the safety of our caves.

Though the downpour from earlier has eased to a gentle shower, there's no sign of it stopping anytime soon. It's grey sky for as far east as I can see. This gift of Nya's, I'm guessing, is twofold. Not only has it breathed life back into our sanctuary, but I suspect rain acts as a deterrent for the kind who hunt us. It will keep Jexa off my back until I reach Nya in the forest. It must.

Marlok escorts me to the water line, where my boat awaits. He picks up one of the oars from inside and offers it to me.

"We wish you fair winds on your voyage, Deka." It's all ceremony. This is his way to secure support should I succeed, without having to do any real work.

Mali breaks through the crowd and dashes across the beach to join us. She carries a canvas pack with an antique shotgun strapped across the top, which she tosses into my vessel.

"A gift," she says. "For your coming birthday."

My whole body tenses at the lightness in her voice. She'd almost robbed us of this chance at salvation, and now she acts like nothing happened. Some may even praise the generosity of her offering. But this may be the last time we ever see each other, so I offer her a slight nod of gratitude.

Marlok takes her arm to usher her back, but she resists.

"He is my oldest friend," Mali tells him. Her lips tighten and tears glaze her eyes. "I may never see him again, so at least allow me to see him out."

Marlok keeps a firm grip on her arm, sizing me up as if

I've planned something deceitful. But he must see the anger I still hold for her betrayal, so he releases her.

I grab the bowsprit, putting the boat's nose into a headlock. Mali takes up the rear and helps me carry our colony's vessel of salvation into the sea.

My first few steps into the water are shocking. This fresh rainfall comes from cooler skies, and passes on its chill to the sea. By the time I'm up to my knees, my teeth are chattering.

My training kicks in. I jump into my boat and use the momentum to send me into a glide. An incredible rush accompanies these first few inches of my monumental journey. The fate of everyone behind me relies on everything I do in the face of the challenges ahead.

Mali's help with launching me into the sea wasn't unusual. She'd often helped me during my fishing days. This was before she'd been assigned to the warrior cadre, when she had nothing better to do. That's what made this launch feel so smooth. Except for one thing.

Normally when I jump aboard, the bow dips forward under my weight. That didn't happen this time. This phenomenon warrants a check over my shoulder to confirm my fear.

Mali sinks back at the stern. She gives me a nervous smile and scrambles to raise the mainsail.

"You think this'll make up for what you did?" I say.

"I'd say it's a good start," she replies with a grunt as she hauls on the main halyard. I must not look convinced, because she adds, "Don't worry, Deka. By the end of this voyage, I'll have made up for it a hundred times over."

"Mali!" shouts Marlok. He's already waist deep in water.

The irritation in his voice suggests he's more

disappointed at his own benevolence than her disobedience. He doesn't think she'll make it far. He shouts orders for the war party to fetch a few fishing vessels and pursue.

I join Mali in raising the sail and, by the time it reaches the masthead, we have two dozen warriors sliding two boats into the sea behind us.

I trim the sail so that the triangular canvas bulges full of wind and drags us at a nice cruising pace. All we have to do is outlast them. The wind isn't much, but it's enough to propel us forward with minimal effort on my part.

But still...

"Set the oars into the outriggers," I tell Mali. We may need more than wind to make our escape.

She quickly obeys, fumbling to set the polymer paddles into their grooves. She's no skilled mariner, but I'd be lying if I said I wasn't relieved to have some company on this adventure. Whether we succeed or fail, they'll be telling stories about this moment until humanity's last breath.

CHAPTER 15
NYA

Mist sprays me at the forest edge, limiting my line of vision to a short stretch up the barren coast. Somewhere out there, Deka is piloting a watercraft to meet me. And I can't wait to see the look on his face when he sees this forest. Have his eyes ever spied such splendor? Having seen his current living conditions, I'm guessing not.

I shift my weight on the tree branch. I've been sitting in this spot for three days already. How much longer must I wait? The first day had offered a much needed rest, but this has long since gotten old. I *hate* just sitting around doing nothing. But our reunion must be near. He could emerge from that mist at any moment, so I dare not leave for even a blink.

Only, those clouds to the north have been growing darker. The sky there is almost black as night. That's the Aeri trying to impress the Magister. No doubt the Watchers are seething over this deviation from the work plan, especially so close to the Magister's inspection, but there's nothing they can do. Only the Aeri, with their large feathered wings, can fly in such weather and at such heights. Not even Jexa could venture into those clouds. Her butterfly-like wings are too flimsy, much like ours. Not that she could now anyway. The Consul has surely detained her ahead of the Magister's arrival. We can't have a Watcher Marshal causing all sorts of havoc, like burning hives and slaughtering elders, so close to inspection. This aligns well with my plan. Except...

Will the storm be too much for Deka? Suddenly I feel helpless just sitting here. And guilty. His arrival here will be only the beginning.

Pity rises in me for my brave *sapien*. This journey must be such an ordeal for him, and when he reaches the forest he may think the hardship to be over. He may expect to rest. But we don't have time for that. To avoid detection from the Fori, we'll need to avoid areas of the forest still under development. That means taking wide detours. Sure, they're all aware of his existence now, but the fewer who know of his exact whereabouts, the better. My trust in the Fori and Ori is not enough to assure me none will squeal in hopes of gaining favor from the Watchers. It will only take one set of loose lips to doom our endeavor.

A chill blows through me. The hair on the back of my neck stands on end and I'm on my feet just as fast. I know this feeling too well, so when I whirl around in the tree canopy, it's with both fists raised and ready to fight.

Jaleera is perched on a branch overlooking me. Her scarlet hair appears more auburn in the absence of sunlight.

"You look tense," she says, almost too lightly. She and Jexa must have the most pleasant conversations together.

I keep my hands raised in defense mode. Does she know the full extent of what I've been up to? As Jexa's second-in-command, I'd expected her new role as Interim Marshall to keep her too occupied to check in on me.

My legs are wound tight like springs, ready to leap into the air in escape. It takes everything for me to avoid stealing a glance back at the sea. If she sees Deka arriving, I'll have to attack her before she can make a move.

Jaleera holds out her hands and shows me her palms. "I come unarmed."

I leap across branches in a circle around her to confirm her claim. Then I scan the sky all around to ensure she has come alone, but it's too misty to tell.

"What do you want?" I say.

"I bring you ill tidings," she says.

"I know about my Hive."

"Not that," Jaleera says. She tucks her hands under her armpits, lowers her head, and shifts uneasily. "Jexa has done much worse since then."

My hands squeeze into fists at the sound of my grinding teeth. How could Jexa do worse than killing innocent Servants? And from the confines of a holding cell at that? Before I can press her, Jaleera acknowledges my anger and speaks.

"Jexa has stolen the Capstone."

A flash of heat warms my body despite the storm's chill. "Impossible," I say. "The Council—"

"Is dead," Jaleera says, her voice tight.

I laugh at Jaleera's audacity. Only a fool would buy this news. I saw the Consul only a few days ago, and Jexa...she... she was there to...

I grab a branch to steady myself as I nearly faint. *Oh, Darkness!* I was the second-to-last person to see the

Councilry host alive! Our lifeline on this planet has been cut!

The realization drives me to my knees. This changes everything. Without the council's protection and the key to this planet in Jexa's control, we are completely at her mercy.

A tsunami of grief rises over my mental horizon, but I have the luxury of shock keeping me calm for the time being. I use this numb state to press Jaleera before I'm too overwhelmed to function.

"How?"

"The Consul allowed it to happen. Millenia on Earth starved the good from her. Her nature is, by design, a ticking time-bomb. The only way to diffuse it was a benevolent force created by humanity, something they could not achieve. The Priestess Darxa had done her best to keep the light alive inside the Consul, but Earth had done her in. It was a rare task for a Gatekeeper to endure such long ages of turmoil. Many ends comes swift. She was the strongest of your kind, but the negative forces against her were insurmountable. The burden of salvation should not have been hers to bear alone."

My throat tightens as I process Jaleera's words. The Consul allowed herself to be taken by darkness because her hope and goodwill had been destroyed by Deka's ancestors. Over the years, her resistance to darkness faded as Darxa's voice lost sway. This would be hard to envision had I not just met with them and saw their form for myself—two minds to a single body. But... for Jexa to kill the Consul is madness. Without her we cannot safely open the gate. If she accidentally opens it near a Black Hole, or inside the depths of a burning star, that would be the end. Or even if she did manage to open a gate, the traveller may end up anywhere.

They could get stuck in limbo. Purgatory. The Consul keeps the coherence of space-time. When you reach into the unknown, there's no telling what you might pull out.

My throat is too tight to form such a long string of words. All I can manage is: "Jexa... why?"

Jaleera sits beside me and looks to the clouds darkening above. The storm is spreading to encompass us.

"There is a force that exists beyond the farthest reaches of the Universe," Jaleera says, "where darkness is not simply the absence of light. It was the nothingness that existed before even empty space came to be. The birth of this Universe brought chaos into that silent void. So fast and violent did it arrive, that it sparked awareness into the darkness.

"Since then, from the beginning of time, the expanding Universe has encroached upon it, ever pushing away its borders. The resistance formed by the void against the infringing light develops evermore awareness in it, even to this day. But not all of the nothing is displaced to the outer reaches. Left behind are threads of this dark life force. And it cannot rest, not until the sound of life is silenced."

Jaleera places her hand on my shoulder. A fuzzy, static sound pervades my mind as her touch tunes my head to the frequency of the cosmic background radiation left behind after the explosive start to the Universe, using my mind like an antenna.

I squirm from her touch. Having to hear that noise all the time with no escape would drive even the sanest person mad.

"Now, that darkness begins its fight to restore the silence that it lost. Jexa encountered it in the hollowness of her heart, where she stared deep into the nothing, and from that nothing, something stared back. Dark tendrils laced through her mind, weaving tales and lies that would see the end of all light, a primordial being driven by eternal torment."

The mere memory of that noise prickles my skin. I shudder, fearing that to have heard it once would be enough to hear it forever. That such a brief glimpse into the mind of madness is all the initiation needed to join the cause as Jexa has.

"In her," Jaleera says, "the Primordial Darkness has blossomed. Through her it walks the realms of life, seeking a means to Omega — the collapse of the Universe, and with it the end of all life. Until then, together they suffer. To find peace, Jexa must aid her master in his task, to drain the Universe of all that is good and light. But they are not alone.

"This trait, the *susceptibility*, is not unique to her. Others need only hear her words to awaken the corruption that lies dormant within them. She will use them to silence the noise of life, to drown all light in darkness."

I laugh in disbelief. "And here I thought you were all benevolent overseers of the Pact."

"At one time that was true. From what I can tell, the factions overseeing other planets have remained unblemished by the corruption that has seized Jexa."

This hits like a stone dropped onto my gut. I'd assumed my kind on other planets had been suffering the same mistreatment as us. But if the Watchers there did not follow the path Jexa has chosen, then perhaps they've maintained the integrity of the Pact. I'd assumed their deviation had gone back farther than her. This makes my journey to the Magister all the more important.

My heart drums out a hopeful rhythm. With this new

insight, I truly believe we can overthrow the Watcher tyranny here. Together, with Deka's people, we can restore harmony.

"We've all seen how you've changed," I say, feeling emboldened by these new revelations. "You are not the race you once were, and soon the Magister will see it too."

"This has been a concern of mine for some time," Jaleera concedes. "We would indeed suffer the Magister's wrath if he learned of the wicked deeds and liberties my kin have taken in their duty. I have the voice of a lone few who have opposed this path. But resisting the evolution of an entire species is too grand a task for so few. In truth, I fear what we have become. And worse yet, what will become of us. The path we tread now... we have lost our way. It would be less a tragedy if we dragged only ourselves into darkness. But Jexa's plan will affect all life, not just here, but everywhere."

"Well it's a good thing she is not the supreme authority here," I say, trying not to feel bad for Jaleera. The Protector of Light and Life will come down hard on her regardless of her sympathies, but her kind have rightfully lost their place in his design. Their time in his grace has ended. "The Consul was corruptible by nature. You will not be so lucky with the Magister."

Jaleera's face remains hard as granite. If I didn't know any better, I'd say that is sorrow in her eyes. But not for herself.

"Our force on Gaia is a splinter of a much greater formation," she explains. "Now that Jexa controls the gate that connects all life-bearing worlds, she can call upon every Watcher to rally on one planet. It's been foretold, a long time ago. They called it the *Black Tide*."

My whole body trembles at the energy behind those two words.

But wait... "You said the Watchers on other planets have not been corrupted. Why would they respond to such a call?"

"They wouldn't. But a distress call in response to a Servant rebellion... that would draw quite the crowd. Reinforcements will come from the farthest reaches of the universe to restore order. They will not ask questions. They will neutralize anyone wielding a weapon. Anyone Jexa has declared hostile. And once they stomp out all traces of your existence, they will fall victim to Jexa's wicked tongue. Her ideology will spread back to the farthest reaches like a parasite. Her initiates will see the light in all life as something to be extinguished. 'All Sparks to the Dark'. And without the parity between dark and light, her darkness will collapse in on itself, leaving nothing behind, not even *time* itself. By sending all that light into the Dark, she will end the Universe."

I jump to my feet and loom over Jaleera, who remains seated with her palms on her thighs. "You're lying," I say. My elbows lock stiff and my fists squeeze to numbness.

"I wish that were so," Jaleera says. And for the first time in all the lives I've known her, she lowers her gaze to the ground in defeat.

I sink to my knees and join her.

"Was this because of me?" I say, knowing I may regret asking this question.

Jaleera chews her lip. All the answer I need. "Jexa has been planning this for ages," she says. "You simply gave her the opening she needed to follow through. The defensive energy around the Councilry's temple kept even the Marshal of Watchers out. No one on this planet could enter without invitation, or—"

"A summons to trial," I say, confirming that this *is* my fault.

Jaleera gives me a grave nod.

My belly clenches. Though, this can't be. "If that's so, then how did I get in?"

"The Priestess Darxa must have sensed your approach. No doubt she saw the opportunity to set you straight. Rather than send me to end your life, she did you both a service by sparing one of her rare dust maidens."

I vaguely recall Darxa saying something to that effect. At the time, my mind was so busy processing her more consequential revelations, mainly her excuses for genocide, that it didn't properly sink in.

"And in return I brought her death." My belly roils like the swells of an ocean storm. "But Jexa could have killed off a hive anytime she wanted to earn a trial, no excuse required. Why now?"

"You forced her hand. Your strength is rising, Nya. Along with your boldness. She had to put her plan into action before you become too strong to stomp out. She has seen the wildfire a single spark can ignite."

I'd like to protest her reasoning, to claim she's exaggerating my potential, but the words of my recent assembly come to mind, where I persuaded a hive who hated me to defy the Watchers for the Magister's arrival.

"Why are you telling me all of this?" I ask. Jaleera should be clapping me in irons and taking me to her master.

"Jexa crossed the line this time."

"But murdering a Ko Elder was fine?"

"This is on a different scale, Nya. There is far more at stake."

All this news swirls in my head, making me dizzy. I lay back on my branch, cover my eyes, and hope to wake from this nightmare.

Jaleera pries my hand away. Her face hovers over mine. "This is one duty you cannot hide from."

I sit up so fast I nearly smash my face into Jaleera's. "Duty?! What duty? What can I possibly do against Jexa and you Watchers?"

Jaleera lifts her chin toward the east, to the forest that grows out across the great sand sea.

"Word of Ko Mirah's Hive has spread," she says. "Many Fori are rallying in the east. I've spied their ranks, overheard their plans. You told them to raise a ruckus and nothing more, but since you left, others have had their say. They're arming themselves to fight. They've seen Jexa's slaves wither under the Capstone's weight. That she is stuck on the desert sand. They believe Jexa doesn't think them a threat. That they have the element of surprise. But ears loyal to Jexa have heard much of the same, and she does see a threat growing among the forest folk.

"Plus, she requires more slaves. The Capstone is heavy and will take a mighty effort to reach the pyramids. By luring the rebels into a trap, she'll stomp out the first sparks of unrest while rounding up enough to seat the Capstone atop the Great Pyramid. Because getting it there will be the easy part. The steps up the pyramid face are steep and the levels many. She will need every able body she can capture. Those strong enough to think they can defeat her in battle will serve her well in this task."

My heart thumps so hard that it draws Jaleera's gaze to my belly.

I stand. "I have to warn them."

I bend my knees to launch into flight, but Jaleera grabs my wrist to anchor me.

"A simple warning will not do."

I watch her expectantly, demanding elaboration.

Jaleera stands and holds a palm to each of my cheeks. "*Nya - the Evening Star -* that's what your mother called you at your birth. Your arrival was a time of immense joy and pain for her. Too late in her life did you arrive, for the sparks of rebellion were already drifting over the deadfall. The flames of war were inevitable."

Jaleera's lips twist in discontent. "But her fight did not die with her. No. You must finish what your mother started. Your kin gathering in the forest need the blood of Klora to lead them once more. Only, right now, they are too few. You must gather more before you face Jexa in battle."

I step back, shaking my head in disbelief, and nearly fall from my branch. Jaleera has either lost her mind or is pushing me toward a trap, trying to trick me into slipping up for Jexa to send me to the Dark.

Yet...if what she says of Jexa is true, then the Watcher Marshal is beyond the days of requiring reason for her actions. But what is Jaleera's motivation for siding with me?

"Why do you conspire against your own to help us?" I ask.

"For the sake of our salvation. As I've said before, we have lost our way. There is nothing I can do on my own, but with your help, we can set things right. Together, we shall restore harmony to the Pact."

And for your reward, the Magister will promote you to Watcher Marshal.

"You'd use us as pawns for your own gain," I say.

"Should my efforts be recognized by the Magister, I will make it my purpose to undo the wrongs my kind have wrought upon you. We shall once again become teachers, not oppressors. Wardens instead of Warlords. I will make good the promises made in the name of light."

Jaleera's eagerness to sacrifice us for her own ambition makes me wonder if she and Klora had a similar conversation before the last rebellion. *Face Jexa in battle*, she tells me. That's a far cry from my original intent to cause a harmless disturbance. She'd turn our peaceful protest into a full-blown riot. "My people still endure the consequences of my mother's foolishness," I say. "I'll not bring more suffering upon them. We've learned our lesson: Jexa cannot be defeated in battle. If my mother could speak to us now, she'd tell us the same thing."

Jaleera sighs and hangs her head. "There is much you don't know about the fight between your mother and Jexa."

My face burns red hot as the words of the blind Fori return to me. Mischief and mind games are fine during times of peace, but making claims like hers during times like this is playing with fire. "I know who won and who lost. That's enough for me."

"Your mother didn't lose, Nya. At least, not in the way that you think."

I stare Jaleera down. What game is she playing?

A hint of shame softens Jaleera's eyes. She can't even look at me.

"In the final minutes of the war," she says, "your mother faced Jexa in single combat." Jaleera closes her eyes and takes a deep breath, as if picturing the scene on the back of her eyelids.

"Everyone thought Klora would turn Jexa's weapon to dust and finish her off, but we quickly saw that wasn't necessary. It turns out Jexa was no match for your mother's skill. Klora disarmed her with ease, and when she knocked Jexa onto her back and held a spear tip to her throat, some Light Ones even fled, because we'd just realized we were sorely outnumbered, and suddenly numbers mattered more than fear."

"Then my mother fell for some form of trickery...Jexa outwitted her...or..."

Jaleera opens her eyes to lock me in a stare. Much to my surprise, tears glisten in her eyes. Until now, I thought Watchers lacked the biological means to feel sorrow, let alone express it. "Nya, before your mother could deliver the fatal blow, I . . . I shoved my sword between her shoulder blades."

Jaleera's face blurs as tears well in my eyes.

"No," I say, shaking my head. "Jexa the Mighty slayed Klora the Fool. That's the story. Everyone knows it."

Everyone except those who actually saw it.

"A lie Jexa made every witness swear to tell. Betraying her secret promised death and eternal darkness. But all who stood on the battlefield that day saw that it was I, not Jexa, who slayed your mother. You must understand, I—"

I swing wide and hard, so that when my open palm connects with Jaleera's face, it produces a deafening smack. I recoil at my own defiance, shocked at what I've done. Striking a Watcher is certain death.

I watch for Jaleera's reaction. My life now rests in her hands.

She rubs her cheek and smiles. A deep sadness remains in her eyes where there should be fury. "You cannot deny your nature. Your mother's fire burns too bright in you."

"I am not my mother," I say, "and you will not trick me into bringing more misery upon my people. If what you say is true about their plans, I will order them to stand down. They will back away from this fight and they will live."

I at least owe them that. Besides, my plan is still salvageable. All I need is to persuade the belligerents to delay action until the day of the Magister's arrival, to lay low and be discrete in the meantime, and discourage violence when they do take action. If they are unarmed and the Watchers come down hard on them during the Magister's arrival, even killing some, it will serve our cause even better. To be armed, however, will justify any harsh response from the Watchers.

Yes. This could work.

With that, I dive below the canopy. All I can do is hope I return in time to greet Deka when he arrives at the forest. For if I do not stop what Jaleera claims is happening, there may not be a forest for much longer.

CHAPTER 16

NYA

Jaleera is a liar. She must be.

That's all I can think during the entire flight between columns of tree trunks. Too many wild claims. She must have flown headfirst into a tree and knocked her sense loose. *Lead* my people? They hate me! Besides, who is there to lead? Every decent fighter foolish enough to rise against the Watchers died during my mother's rebellion.

As I venture deeper toward the heart of the forest, weaving between staggered ranks of tree trunks and mossy curtains, I see I am not alone. Figures buzz to my left and to my right. I catch glimpses of them whizzing between trees, moving in the same direction as me.

This place has long been finished and is ready for the Magister's inspection, so they're likely Fori at play or traveling to a distant work area.

"Hey, Leeta!" echoes a voice from my left. "Look, it's Nya!"

I stop mid-flight and almost sink to the forest floor in shock. If I didn't know any better, I'd say by her tone she is actually pleased to see me. Not just pleased, even, but... excited? Relieved? No, I am mistaken.

Ahead, a Fori breaks her flight and loops back toward me. Her wide eyes are intense and have trouble focusing on me as they rattle side to side.

"Are you here to fight with us, Evening Star?" this one called *Leeta* says. Her wings buzz faster than is necessary to keep her aloft.

"I've come to warn you."

It turns out the Fori I'd seen flying at my flanks were only a tiny part of an entire migrating Hive. As I hover before Leeta, many of her kin materialize from the surrounding green and gather around me. They carry spears of wood and axes with heads of sharpened ore. I wait for the stragglers to join before making my plea.

The Fori who'd announced my presence shoves through the group to fall in beside Leeta. Rippled skin covers half her body, even her head, making a ragged border of purple hair that divides her scalp. A quick glance around me reveals most of this cohort bears similar scars. *Fire Divers.* Of course they'd be first into the fray.

"See, Leeta, I told you," says the newcomer. "A few of us mobilize and the rest will join. Even the dust maidens!"

"You forget how to count, Kassini?" says Leeta with a sharp, sideways nod toward me. "I see only *one* duster here."

Kassini's frazzled eyes scan the forest behind me, presumably in search of my sisters, but it's only more of her cohort drawing up to join us.

The cause behind the pair's erratic behavior becomes apparent when Leeta seizes Kassini's wrist and pries loose a handful of brown beans, which she shoves into her mouth.

Kassini's wild eyes fall on her sister, and when her lips curl up in a threatening growl, she reveals brown-stained teeth. This, and the rate of their buzzing wings, tells me they're hopped up on java seeds. Pacifying this lot won't be easy.

"Where is your Elder?" I say.

Leeta spreads her arms and looks around with flabbergasted eyes, as if it should be obvious. "'Tis I."

I look to her cohort expecting to see mischievous grins on their faces. Instead, I get nods of agreement. But that can't be. Leeta's arms bear the same number of stripes as my own. She's not much older than a youngling.

Noticing my skepticism, Kassini says, "We don't last long in these bodies, doing what we do. I'd say Leeta earned her Final Passage twice-times over already."

Her cohort crowds close around me. Their dilated pupils tell me they deal with the dangers of quelling fires by seeking the effects of psychedelic plants. And they do not take kindly to me questioning their leader's status. Come to think of it, Leeta had called me *Evening Star*. My mother called me that at my birth. It's the meaning of my name in our home language. This leads me to believe she was close to mother during the rebellion.

A wave of goosebumps ripples my skin. I suppress a shiver as a tide of frigid grief rises from deep within me. Could she tell me things about my mother that don't include the words *fool* or *folly*? I'll have to quiz her on the details of their relationship later.

Leeta crosses her arms and gives me a haughty glare. "You're no Fori, but you are an outcast. For that, I'll let you fight alongside us."

"I didn't come here to fight," I say. "I come to you as a messenger."

"Well, tell the others," Leeta says, then motions for everyone to continue on with their flight.

They obey, and I'm dragged along by the wind of a hundred wings. The deafening flutter drowns out my protest. Soon we are joined from all directions, and not just by Fori cohorts. A mismatch of beings who you'd never see together outside of this moment—particularly Ori gangs and Aeri flocks—move toward the forest center. Aeri wings rarely glide beneath the treetops, save for the rare stray feather, which the Fori fight over to wear as decorations in their hair. It's their presence that must embolden them. Some Fori actually see our air-swirling cousins as deities.

But even god skin can burn in the heat of dragon's breath. Though this gathering is an inspiring sight, I must smack them with reality before more sparks become prisoners to Jexa's spear shaft.

I'm about to shout the order for them to halt when the forward flyers glide to a stop. They come to rest in a small meadow and in trees surrounding the open field, where a few hundred more have already gathered. Normally I'd have heard such a large group long before coming across them, but here their chatter is drowned by the croaking of a thousand frogs. It's near deafening.

The armaments of those gathered confirm Jaleera's claim. They've all come to fight the Watchers. Yet I don't see a single Fori from Ko Vera's Hive. Surely she spread word about causing a ruckus, but others have seen the opportunity for more. This could actually work if timed better, but the Magister may jump to conclusions at the violence and side with the Watchers. At least those who fancy themselves warriors are still clustered into separate factions, lacking a single leader. They'll be easier to influence like this.

I land at the center of the meadow. I will follow Jaleera's advice, though I will lead this group in a different direction.

"Listen to me carefully, cousins," I say.

"Silence!" shouts Leeta. "Let's hear what news the Evening Star brings us."

All chatter dies off, leaving only the croaking frogs.

I nod my appreciation toward Leeta, then I say, "Jexa knows—"

Sudden silence cuts me off. All at once, the frogs have stopped croaking. I see on the stricken faces around me that this is cause for concern.

"Watcher!" cries a Fori. "Over there!"

All heads whirl toward the Fori's pointing, to a tree behind me.

"A scout!" someone observes.

"Catch her!"

Before I can utter another word, anyone with wings is leaping into crisscrossing flight patterns in pursuit. The canopy rocks as leaves swish from the disturbance of the simultaneous take-off of several hundred Fori and Aeri.

"It's a trap!" I shout, but it's only the wind of pounding wings that hears my warning.

Jaleera had told me that Jexa's scouts already heard the Servants' plan, and my visit here confirms that claim. Which means her spies are only seen when they wish it so, which lends further credibility to her claim about Jexa's plot to capture more slaves.

Bile creeps up into my throat. I swallow the bitter taste

and spring off a tree trunk in pursuit. I fall in at the rear of the pack of Servants weaving through redwood forest.

A chill blasts through me. It's not the eerie kind, either. The air has actually turned cold to the point I see my breath puff before me. This change is too sudden, and sends a chill of a deeper kind through me.

I shiver at the sight of my sisters disappearing into a wall of white mist ahead. Shouts and cries echo loud from beyond the fog screen. Some lingering in the rear recoil and hang back. The dauntless charge forward, and those who've hung back rush to join them. I can't help but admire their bravery and press on ahead, though not so fast as to lead the way.

The fog is so thick around me that I feel as if I'm alone. Cries of fear and distress soon dispel this illusion. I proceed cautiously, moving from tree to tree, using thick trunks as cover until a horrifying sight takes shape in the mist.

Ahead, a wall of Fori and Aeri stretch across my vision as far as I can see to either side. They hang in mid-air, frozen in various splayed out positions, their upside down and sideways arrangements most unnatural.

An Aeri flies into the invisible barrier at top speed. The impact rocks the whole lot outward, then springs back and forth several times before coming to a stop. She hangs upside down as one more fly of hundreds caught in a web.

I land on a tree branch a stone's throw from the net, where I survey the chaos. Those who'd managed to veer away in time to avoid the web rush to help their stuck companions. Their efforts only further the disaster. Pulling and prying leads to many would-be saviors becoming dragged into the sticky wall. And like trying to save a drowning person, frantic captives latch onto any rescuer within reach and hold them tight in panic.

I look above for the spiders. Where the fog does not conceal, the canopy does. This is a well-laid trap. A quick assessment reveals that two thirds of our force is stuck to the web, with the rest trying to free them.

Less than twenty in my sight remain free flying. They move on to the web's anchor points woven around large tree trunks, where they hack at the wood. A few lose their weapons when they accidentally hit the webbing.

Part of me wants to grab the net and shatter its bonds, but I resist the urge. My previous encounter with this material, when the Butcher party snared me, did not fare well for me. But this isn't exactly the same. Back then I'd been forced into an anatomically disabling position, with my hands pinned to my sides, palms to thighs. Here the material presents a different challenge. Sometimes a springy material, stretched out and taut, can resist my resonant charm more than the densest metals. Sending a vibration up the web and back in an endless loop not only risks hurting those tangled above, but would at least jar my senses, and perhaps tangle my hand to claim me as well. Just thinking about the eye-rattling reverberation makes me nauseous.

"Nya! Down here!"

I look below, to a cluster of Ori gathered around the base of a massive tree.

"Hurry!" Mora says.

Looking up the redwood, I see all web strands connect up the length of its great trunk. The center anchor pole.

I glide to the ground at the base of the net wall.

"Quickly, girl," Mora urges as she watches the canopy warily.

Hearing the havoc above is all the coaxing I need. But when I place my hands on the rust-colored trunk and feel the life force from within, I hesitate. I've used my ability to destroy the legacies of the dead. That is one thing. To end a living being, though...

I once dusted a daisy, reducing it to powder in my palm. That was the first time I saw my ability for a curse. I saw in that moment the monster I could become.

Screeches and howling rise from above. They turn my blood cold. Before I can look up to see the cause behind the eruption of despair, a Fori slams onto the ground beside me.

The cracking of her bones sends my stomach into backflips. Her eyes remain open, locked on the canopy above, but she does not blink. Nor does her chest move.

A battle rages above. No, not a battle. A slaughter. Watchers swoop down from the treetops and pick off the Fori who aren't trapped in the web with swipes of their spears before disappearing back up into the canopy. Their sweeping runs separate the free clusters of Servant prey, who, in their panic, scatter into easier targets. This I can see from here, but it may not be so obvious to those in the ambush above.

"Nya!"

Mora's voice rattles me. I don't need to be told again. My kin will be greatly outnumbered until I untangle those in the web, so I press my both hands to the tree and feel its life force breathing out through me, concentric rings expanding and contracting in sync with my breath, the tree's essence resonating with my own. I don't even need to close my eyes to see this. But when I do, another force reveals itself from slightly beyond, spiraling fractals that threaten to spring at the slightest push. The web.

"I'm sorry," I whisper. A shriek from a falling Fori rattles me as I send a vibrational shock through my palms.

A dust cloud blasts me like the winds of a hurricane, blinding and choking me. As I cough furiously to clear my lungs, I don't need to see to know that not a splinter survived the chain break.

Dozens of Fori hit the ground all around. Many are quick to recover and spring into flight. Others catch themselves before hitting the forest floor.

I watch the sight in wonder. I'd been expecting everyone to fall in a tangled sticky pile, but somehow my blast had disintegrated the entire web as well.

Great breaking ions! If I didn't know better, I'd say the tree helped conduct my vibration to free the Fori who'd nurtured it from birth. Or perhaps the Fori shriek had jolted a force through me that sent more of an instant shock than a prolonged wavy vibration. Or... was it something else?

Mora pats my back. "Nice work, dust-maker. Now, let's join the fight."

Fight? I promised *not* to fight the Watchers. It was Ko Mirah's dying wish.

A wounded Watcher hits the ground nearby, and a dozen Ori swarm her with clubs to ensure she stays there.

I'm watching the clubbing in shock when an Ori shoves a branch at my chest. "For you," she says with a wide, hopeful grin.

I accept the smooth shaft and realize it's a spear. All around me, Ori and a few grounded Fori are fashioning weapons to replace those lost in the fray above. They whittle slender branches into spears, hack fallen trunks into clubs, and bend boughs into bows. When an Aeri falls dead to the ground, they pluck feathers from her wings to fletch their arrows.

Every few seconds a Fori swoops down for a replacement spear. Their Watcher chasers attract volleys of Ori arrows that find more wood than flesh, but the effort keeps the ground free of attack. The wounded are safe to rest here.

My heart flutters at the inspiring sight. I see why so many followed my mother. She needed only to show them they had the smallest sliver of a chance to win. A glimmer of light in the dark.

That one dead Watcher on the ground nearby is all it takes for me.

Through the thinning dust cloud above, where Fori and Aeri clash with Watchers, I see an opportunity. The blast has created enough confusion that we might use it to repel our enemy. After all, the world beneath the canopy is a Fori domain. Only trickery managed to catch the forest folk off guard.

I leap into the air and fly straight up the column of swirling dust, where a massive trunk stood only moments ago. If I can take the life of a harmless, life-giving tree, then I can kill a murderous Watcher.

Beneath the canopy is chaos among a cloud of buzzing wings. Wood clacks on wood, groans and cries add to the clamor, and screams of terror from the falling wounded tear at my nerves.

I cling to a tree and search for a target to ambush. This leaves my head spinning. Watchers whiz by and cut down the Fori before they even know they're near, with weapons far superior to our crude Ori craft. Blades fashioned from the metals and gems of distant planets slice through Fori bone like it's made of water.

It's too much for most. The Fori and Aeri retreat to the cover of trees, desperately using branches for concealment. Some aren't lucky enough to remain hidden when the Watchers swoop by and pick them off in coordinated runs. The Watchers at first had not been so organized. They'd expected a quick nab and dash with their newly collected slaves, and had come unprepared for much resistance, let alone battle. But these lords of war adapt quickly.

I watch the slaughter with frustration. We outnumber the Watchers, but our force is scattered across many trees, each choosing a different branch. Each alone and vulnerable.

We need to rally.

A nearby oak tree with five mighty branches provides cover for three dozen Fori and a few Aeri. That's where I start.

I fly to where Leeta glares up at the canopy. She spots me in the open, and when I motion for her to join me, she remains firm. Her attention shifts from me, to where an Aeri thrusts a spear at an unarmed Watcher. The Watcher swats the spear aside and grabs the shaft midway, then pulls the Aeri in close. She wraps her legs around the Aeri's waist, then drops back into a somersault, releasing the Aeri a few feet above the ground. The Watcher rises in flight as the disoriented Aeri goes crunch on the forest floor.

I see other Watchers use this maneuver on unsuspecting Fori as well. Leg-lock and drop, somersault and release. The disoriented victims are left with no time to stop the crash as their assailants whiz away.

A tornado of anger swirls inside my chest. The Watchers are playing with us now. It's been a while since they've had a good fight, and it will be long again before they see another. They laugh and applaud, showing off in their kills.

Fury heats my face and swells into my fists. It is one thing to kill in your duty, but to do so with such revelry... It is the deepest disrespect.

I scan the area all around me. There's something I've been wanting to try, preferably without an audience, but I don't have that luxury. Most of our force huddles in the trees, watching all around for Watchers. Any movement in the open draws all eyes. I find myself doing this as well, clinging to a tree, watching all around. But I am on the hunt.

My opportunity comes when a Watcher swoops down from the canopy, her course set on a Fori hiding on a branch below me. I wait until she's about to pass the trunk to jump out and whack her with my spear.

I've timed it just right. She's whizzing just below me when I leap into the open and swing my spear downward. But a second before making contact—*WHOOSH*—my weapon bursts into a trillion pieces.

I watch in terror as the particles slip through my fingers from a rogue vibration. My hands feel so empty as the Watcher passes underneath. She spots me, the only lone Servant now in the wide open, and abandons her original target, banking upward to loop back toward me.

"Nya!"

I turn to see Mora clinging to the adjacent tree trunk, which she'd scaled from the ground. She tosses me a spear. When I catch it I notice it's heavier than my last, courtesy of a core of iron ore.

When the Watcher rises high and then takes a forty-five degree dive at me, I point my spear at her and brace for the collision.

Her eyes narrow tighter the closer she comes. I am the only thing that matters to her. Just before smashing into me, she bares her teeth and growls.

At the last second I dart left and shove my spear across her path. She bats my shaft away with her own, and at the moment of contact—

Crack! Both turn to dust.

She glides on past and, when she whirls around to face me, she can't hide her surprise.

This isn't exactly what I'd set out to do. My attempt to transmit a vibration from my weapon into hers, to knock it from her hold, worked better than expected, destroying her weapon entirely. But it's rendered me unarmed as well.

Her expression quickly hardens as she draws an axe.

I force my wings to freeze and allow myself to fall backward, flipping head first into a nosedive toward the forest floor. Tears glaze my eyes from the increasing speed. The ground grows dangerously close, but the warning of an Ori scout informs me that the Watcher is still on me.

As the ground comes within a hundred feet, my wings start fluttering in an act of self-preservation. My fall angles into a glide and, as I bank around a tree, an Ori tosses me a spear. I catch it and immediately swing wide around to my rear. I shoot a sharp pulse of vibration up the shaft, timing it to exactly when the end quarter hits my pursuer's axe blade. The strike obliterates the top half of my spear, along with her entire axe.

We both stop in flight to square off. She reaches for a

short sword while I try to muster the courage to charge in and finish her with my splintered spear shaft. But before either of us can move, a Fori drops from above and lands on the Watcher's back.

They fall and slam onto the ground, where the Fori—Leeta—rolls off the Watcher, and several Ori quickly pounce in to finish our fallen enemy.

I swoop down and grab the Watcher's sword, then fly upward. The make of the weapon is tempered platinum, cool and smooth, more resistant to my disruptive vibration. A better conductor for my war magic.

As I rise toward the canopy, a Watcher swoops down and circles me. She swings a metal spear, a smug smile on her face. I block it with the sword, timing a vibration that travels from the handle gripped in my palms and up the blade, increasing toward the tip.

CRACK!

I watch in relief as her metal weapon disappears like a puff of winter breath, and with it her smile. I don't need to finish the job. Two Fori grab her legs and drag her to the ground, where the Ori mob awaits with clubs.

I continue my rise upward, smashing Watcher weapons to dust and watching my Fori cousins swoop in to finish them off. I don't get every vibration right. But a violent resonance is enough to jar a weapon from a Watcher's hold, their hands not as accustomed to the shocking vibrations as I am.

Before I know it, I'm at the canopy. Some of the bolder Fori, including Kassini, join me until we are a dozen. I meet the Watcher attacks with my sword, banging their weapons to dust or clanging them from their hands, which grants the Fori the openings they need to vanquish their superior opponents. I'm fully aware of how risky this is for me. Sure, my ability allows me to disarm my enemies, but I have no combat training. One bad parry and a Watcher could clip off my fingers. And losing my fingers might be the least of my worries.

"Nya, behind you!"

I whirl around with my sword gripped in both hands, swinging with all the force of a tornado. But instead of the satisfying pop of exploding particles, I feel as if I've hit a steel wall.

My resonance shoots back down my arm to my elbow, rattling me so hard I drop my weapon. I hear the ringing steel fade all the way to the ground. The violent clang stops everyone in the skirmish, even those mid swing. Suddenly my foe and I are the center of attention.

It takes everything in me to remain firm at the sight of Jexa hovering before me. The black shaft of her diamond spear lacks even a scratch where my sword edge had connected. Flecks of gold dot the onyx finish.

Her black lips curl into a wicked grin. She circles me, ignoring the Fori and their shaking weapons, confident they won't attack her.

I spin to remain facing her. I'm so jarred by her presence that I don't even know where the spear in my hands came from, though it must have been a Fori or Aeri who tossed it to me after my sword fell.

"I knew someone who fought like you," Jexa says, her voice soft and soothing. Almost sweet. So much so that it rattles me further. "Never could hack a fair fight. But I found a weakness in her tactics."

Jexa holds her spear out to offer me a better look at the golden flecks inside its shaft. "Do you see them in there?"

My chest tightens. I do see them, the sparks of her vanquished, souls doomed to suffer in the quantum confines of her spear until she no longer needs it and tosses it into the Dark. They whirl in a vortex, an inter-dimensional prison completely within her grip.

I swallow hard. Until now I'd thought the stories about her weapon were only lore. A story crafted to frighten us serving folk. But I feel pain and terror radiating from the shaft. I swear I can hear their cries of despair echo in my head. They beg me to free them.

Jexa stares wistfully at the swirling flecks. "I don't even remember how many are in there, but I'd trade them all for one." She stops short of saying my mother's name. Her eyes lift to meet mine. "I suppose I'll have to settle for yours."

I grip my spear shaft so tight my fingers go numb. That fate terrifies me so bad it paralyzes me with fear. I'd surely drop if not for the automatic movement of my wings.

"Don't worry," Jexa says as she steals a glance at the Fori in the trees, "your time has not yet come. You still have a purpose to serve. Word of your victory here will spread. Many will flock to your cause. And when you've gathered your strength, I will stomp you all out like the ants you are. By the end of this little revolt, my staff will glow brighter than a supernova. And you'll be with them. They'll blame you, Nya, daughter of Klora. Did you hear how she begged for her life? Squealed like a pathetic little—"

Rage flashes in me, evaporating any reason and turning my wooden spear to dust. I lunge at Jexa with both hands out, hoping to snatch the spear from her. Of course that's exactly what she wants.

She recoils and unleashes a scream, but I notice the flicker of a smile when she does so. She retreats up through the canopy, and an explosion of rustling leaves announces her escape into the sky.

Cheers erupt from below. I shiver as Fori and Aeri rise to embrace me, the smell of sweat and blood overwhelming.

I shove them away.

"Listen to me!" I say. "This is no victory. Jexa was only..."

Their chanting smothers my voice so that I can't even hear my own words. Already they've broken off into groups to recount the deeds of their comrades.

I drift below with them, watching for a leader to emerge among the rabble. Someone who has proven themselves, someone I can reason with. Leeta, perhaps.

We join the wounded on the ground, where a few tend to the dead, but even the loss of life cannot stifle the celebration.

I find Leeta lying on her side. She looks unnaturally innocent there with her eyes closed. Almost peaceful, like she's having a nap. But it's clear the fall had killed her.

"You should have seen her," Kassini tells a few others in astonishment. "She was so brave!"

Kassini is in shock. When she realizes her Elder friend is not coming back, she'll regret her reaction here. But right now, that revelation seems a long way off. Not just for her. But for everyone.

Before I know it, stringed instruments and flutes bellow music into the dusk air. Fires burn bright, around which many dance. Their shock will wear off, they will realize the finality of their losses, and then they will mourn.

But, looking around, I find I am also guilty of strange behavior. A few days ago the sight of my own blood would make me lightheaded. Yet now there's blood everywhere, smeared on bark and dripping from leaves, and here I sit with a calm belly and a steady head.

I must be in shock. Though, that doesn't explain my actions during the battle. It's one thing to fight back when you're attacked, but to go on the offensive like I did... What got into me?

Madness, clearly. Or maybe it was something else. My mind was clear when my hands swung those measured strokes. It was as if the violence had woken a dormant trait in me, a genetic wiring that's been inside me all along, driving me to act out as my mother had years ago. And as with her, many were quick to follow me. That memory sends a flutter through my heart.

I shake my head and swat this rousing feeling away before I can revel in it. We got lucky here. Next time I'll be leading them all to their deaths. And I do feel the truth behind that fear. Because as I survey the scattered bodies, I'm struck with the feeling that they were the lucky ones. Those who now celebrate may have worse fates awaiting them in the coming days.

While the celebration intensifies, Jexa's words hang heavy in my mind. *Word of your victory here will spread. Many will flock to your cause. And when you've gathered your strength, I will stomp you all out like the ants you are.*

Mora claps my shoulder. "You're in it now, girl."

I bristle at her touch. "Jexa told me this is part of her plan. They won't listen."

"Maybe Jexa's plan is to throw you off. She's just as likely to try to disguise her defeat as victory."

I don't believe that. The look in the Marshal's eyes told me otherwise. She's seen how this ends, a long time ago with my mother. Sure, it was Jaleera who'd shut down the rebellion by stabbing my mother in the back. But for Jexa to have killed the Consul, she'd have defeated her four guards first, each the best of their kind. Each a contender to become the next Watcher Marshal. A role once held by mother, back when it was permitted. And I am not my mother in many regards, combat in particular. Against this improved Jexa, I'd rather not even consider the outcome.

CHAPTER 17

DEKA

"They're gaining on us," Mali says from the bow.

I look over my shoulder to confirm her claim. We'd lost sight of the fishing boat packed with warriors a few hours ago, when the storm hit, and I'd been hoping Marlok had turned around like the other boat he'd ordered back earlier. But the wind has since picked up to a fierce gale, bringing the swell up with it. Any attempt to turn around now would see them capsized. There was a point early on when they nearly caught up to us, and I'd have been tempted to toss Mali overboard to end the chase if I didn't need her. And it turns out I really do need her.

The clouds overhead are so dark I can't tell if it's night or day, and rain hits the water so hard it bounces back up. The constant pelting on my skin is starting to hurt, but that is minor compared to the rising water level in our boat. My shins are half submerged, and that's with Mali bailing as fast as she can with a plastic jug. Even if we had another, I'm too occupied trimming the sail to keep us going in this constantly shifting wind. If I'd undertaken this voyage alone as intended, I'd already be sunk.

"How many days of rain did she promise?" says Mali as she pauses for a rest.

"Seven."

She hangs her head and continues scooping water from our tiny boat that grows heavier with each second. We'll have to switch soon, and Mali won't be able to adjust the sail as skillfully as me. It is this that gives Marlok the advantage. They have many bailers and free hands to spare. Their boat remains light while mine is near sinking.

"They're going to catch us," I tell Mali, preparing her so she can accept her fate.

The words haven't even left my mouth when the wind and rain suddenly die off. The sail luffs as we bob aimlessly over the swells. With only the creaking stays that hold up the mast and water sloshing against our hull, it's eerily quiet.

My heart drops like an anchor. This is where I'd normally start paddling, but Marlok and his warriors will outrow us in no time.

"Now they're definitely going to catch us," I say. *It's over.*

Mali squints back at her brother's pursuit. "I count twelve of them weighing down that boat, and only two of us in ours."

"They have six paddles," I point out. The defeat in my voice makes me cringe.

"*Had* six paddles," she says as she slides in beside the starboard oar. She grabs the handle with a devious grin on her face. "I'm no scholar, so you'll have to help me on this one: what's six minus the four I hid on the beach?"

I stand up in the knee-deep water and squint to better see

Marlok's boat. A single oar reaches out from each side, both dipping into the water, out of unison. The uncoordinated effort propels the boat to the right.

If I wasn't in a rocking boat I'd jump for joy. Even if Marlok's rowers synchronize their paddling, the drag created by their weight will slow them enough for us to maintain our lead.

I could kiss Mali for this forethought. Instead I plop down beside her, grab the port side oar, and together we start rowing. Without rain adding to the flood water at our feet, our bailing can wait. Right now we need to get as much of a lead as we can.

CHAPTER 18

NYA

The first group of recruits arrive before midnight. The mixed lot march up to our bonfire in two neat ranks. They'd started their journey in the south, gathering numbers in their northward travel. Their faces, painted with red and black paint, are hard and intense in the orange glow, and suggest this is not the first time they've marched together.

"Caught wind of the skirmish from our Nest," says their leader, an Aeri Elder. *Ko Tora*, the whispers around me call her. She's stout and broad, and at five feet tall, she's built more like a grand-sized Ori than an Aeri. A thick braid of silver hair hangs between her powder-blue feathered wings.

I give the rest of the group a look-over and see their leader's unusual size is not unique to her. Some Ori stand taller than me, and rather than feathered wings, a few Aeri have clear wings like mine. A quick inspection reveals the only thing consistent about this group is their inconsistencies. *Mutts*, the whole lot of them. Their skills vary depending on which genes they inherit most, but in many cases they aren't effective enough to master any element. If they can't display a command of some natural force as a youngling, the Watchers kill them. I'm surprised to see so many have survived into adulthood.

"Who's in command of this rabble?" Ko Tora bellows through her barrel chest.

Every eye that witnessed the battle looks my way.

"Nya rallied us and led the charge against Jexa," says Kassini.

Ko Tora's eyes narrow on me. She nods faintly in acknowledgment. "Are you the same Nya they call the spawn of Klora?"

I raise my chin, unsure if this connection is meant as an insult or an honor.

Ko Tora turns her back to me and addresses everyone else. "We saw Jexa gathering a swarm of Watchers to the south. She was preparing a counter-attack and had gathered enough to come stomp you into the ground, but," she puffs out her chest and says, "the sight of my force sent them scattering."

I roll my eyes. There's that classic Aeri ego at work. Judging by the spaces between the bands on her arms, she is a newly-minted Elder, and likely earned her position through some sycophantic act that's left her with a self-appraisal above her worth.

"It's a ploy," I tell her. "She wants to gather us all in one place to crush us with one swat. Her own words."

Ko Tora scoffs. "Jexa is a proud warrior. I find it hard to believe she'd sacrifice her reputation by feigning a loss in battle. Not her style."

"So she'd have you think," I say, my face burning in anger and frustration.

"Whether what you say is true or not no longer matters," Ko Tora says. "Your actions here have made us all enemies of the Marshal. If she gets the Capstone to the pyramids, then every Servant on Earth will drown in the Black Tide."

I can't argue that. And as the treetops shake with the arrival of more Fori and Aeri, I see a bond forming that words alone cannot break. But I must try.

"Only a small number of us stood against her today," I point out. "The rest of you can still save yourselves. Whatever Jexa's plan is, she'll still need Servants in her future. Stand down, and she will spare you."

"Your mother said something similar," snaps Ko Tora. "She prevented us from uniting and instead chose to face Jexa with a smaller force. We all know how that ended. A leader must bring together all our assets, or we will *all* fall." She gives me a smug look. "This is no task for a chain breaker."

My gaze lowers to my feet. Shame has this way of subduing even the strongest of us if it strikes at the right moment. And though the daughter of Klora can be many things to many people, *shameless* is not one of them.

"What's your plan?" I ask. There are few things an Elder does without great reflection, and going to war is the least of them. She wouldn't have come here on a whim.

Ko Tora looks to the rebels gathered around. "We'll attack Jexa before she gets anywhere near the pyramids, reclaim the Capstone, and hide it where she'll never find it." Her painted warriors slam their spear butts to the ground twice in unison, in some sort of acknowledgment. "But first, we will nest here for two nights, to allow time for the outlying Hives to join us. Any who have already come to this fight are in it until the end. We can't have anyone falling into enemy hands with valuable information about our force and our intent. Tell every newcomer when they arrive: anyone caught leaving will be buried to their heads in desert sand and left for the vultures."

This threat doesn't kill the mood. Quite the opposite. Newly-branded warriors—still hot from the battle behind us—whistle and cheer. If this Ko is willing to lead so many to their deaths through a direct attack on the Watchers, then so be it. At least this failure won't have my name attached to it. This was supposed to be a Reckoning, not a rebellion.

As Ko Tora assigns sentries to guard the perimeter, I find a perch in the canopy to watch for a way out. I need to get Deka into hiding for when this gathering storm wreaks havoc across the forest.

It doesn't take long to see this won't be easy. Even before this, I see Ko Tora had a militant way about running her flock. The half-breed sentries stick to their posts and keep their heads on a swivel. Maybe this gives the others a sense of confidence in her leadership, but she doesn't fool me. They've not seen our enemy do battle like I have. Some who fought alongside me earlier claim the Watchers numbered in the hundreds, but that was an illusion. Their swift, confusing movements simply gave that impression. They were a dozen against hundreds of us, and we killed only four of them. Jexa will bring much more to the next encounter.

As the night drags on, however, it becomes obvious the extent that the Watchers have used systemic separation to weaken us. Hives arrive in numbers greater than I'd ever known to exist, hundreds from all over the continent, with the prediction of more coming from across the great seas once word of Jexa's defeat reaches them. And though this gathering is exactly what the Marshal claimed to desire, I can't help but marvel at the sheer numbers of our swarms, which black out the night sky in their arrival. Word of the Reckoning to the other Hives has brought more than just lists of their taken kin and the agreement to sing against injustice during the Magister's arrival. Saying the names of our taken aloud, as I'd experienced myself, has inspired resentment and revolt. The whole canopy rustles with life, with defiance. Ori and Fori and Aeri, all banded together against our common enemy.

When a gang of a thousand Ori arrive over land, breathless under an Elder named Ko Zola, who hails from the deep, *deep* south, I realize there is no stopping this. The hurricane has gained too much momentum.

The corner of my mouth twitches with a smile. We are the rain and the wind, the thunder and the lightning.

Yet war is not our practice. It was luck that thwarted Jexa's ambush earlier. If there'd been more Watchers, or if I'd been killed before I could destroy the net, there'd have been a much different outcome. We'll need more than luck the next time we meet. And even if we can recapture the Capstone, hiding it away will only cause endless war between us and the Watchers here on Gaia, and eventually Jexa will get her hands on someone who knows wherever we end up hiding it.

And Deka. *Oh, poor Deka!* My heart sinks to my feet. He has risked everything to come to this forest, which I assured him was safe. Now all of Jexa's focus is on the storm gathering in the trees. I must get him to safety, or divert the Watchers' attention. But how?

I watch my novice warrior kin dance and laugh around a

great bonfire, cheering and learning the ways of foreign cohorts, or reminiscing with reunited siblings of lives past. This camaraderie is a good start, but it's only that.

I join them at the central fire, but I do not dance.

"Yes, go on!" I say. "Dance and be merry! Let your own death songs rise loud through the night."

Three thousand sets of eyes fall on me in the firelight. They stare me down from every branch, some angered by my damning words, others curious. Every furious and curious eye on me. Good.

"You may call today's success a victory," I explain, "yet wars have many battles. And today we gave Jexa something of great value: she now knows how we fight. She's seen our strengths and our weaknesses, and she knows what to expect when we clash again."

"Then we'll show her what a hundred times your numbers earlier can do," says Ko Tora, and she beats a fist against her chest. Bold, unrestrained words for an Elder. Emotion has too great an influence over her judgment.

"We can muster a *thousand* times what we have now," I say, "and Jexa will eventually find a way to outwit us. What we need is an ally more powerful than any army. While Jexa breaks sacred laws, we fight to uphold them. The Magister will see this clearly."

"True!" says Ko Tora. "But what you propose is to steal the Capstone from Jexa, then transport it to the Great Pyramid, *then* drag it up the steep stone face, all while repelling swarms of desperate Watchers. They'll whittle us down to nothing!"

"No," I say with a grave shake of my head. I dread my next words, but it is the only way to stop the Black Tide from flooding this planet and spreading across the Universe. "I say we forget the Capstone altogether. It's true that without it we will not be able to summon him, but he is coming regardless. All we need do is await his arrival."

My words inspire a lot of confused faces. They are unsure of the workings of the gates and portals. Even Ko Tora is uncertain, though she tries to hide it and is reluctant to say anything. I suppose none of them have had a Watcher like Jaleera, a mentor open to imparting such knowledge to her underlings—

No. We are not their underlings. That's how it was supposed to be, them teaching and mentoring, for the Pact. They were to guide us. Not oppress or oppose us.

"The gate opening is all ceremony," I explain. "The Magister can come when he wishes. A door need only be unlocked from one side. When the Consul fails to open the gate during the Alignment, he will realize something is amiss and open the portal from his side."

"So you propose we set up a defensive perimeter around the pyramid to await the Magister's arrival," says Ko Tora, eager to not lose her voice in the discussion.

"Those pyramids are in the wide open!" someone says.

"And they're on sacred ground," Ko Tora points out. "Spilling blood near a celestial gate would be blasphemy."

I raise a hand to demand silence. Much to my surprise, I get it. "To take land from the rightful custodians is a blasphemy even worse than that, great Elder. Yet how long have you directed your followers to break this sacred law?" There's no way any Ko Elder has been doing this for so long without knowing this dark secret.

My accusation draws skeptical glares from Ko Tora's followers.

Ko Tora steps toe-to-toe with me. "Careful, dust maiden. There is much you don't understand."

"All I need to understand is that, right now, this planet's rightful inhabitants are fighting Jexa against extinction. When we make this clear to the Magister, he will condemn her and her followers to the Dark."

Mutters and whispers ripple through the crowd as many lean into groups for deliberation. Some can't believe my claim. Others piece together strange happenings of times past, to which this explanation would solve many a mystery.

"Let us not forget about the Anomaly," says Ko Tora, desperate to sway everyone from my plan.

I was hoping no one would think of this. The area surrounding every planet's gate, which often comes in the form of a massive stone pyramid, contains a gravitational phenomenon that prevents all but the Aeri from flying over. Their large feathered wings generate enough lift for them to defy the Anomaly's pull. The thin membranes that make up a Fori and Entropath's are a different story, and not just for us.

"Our wings won't work near the Great Pyramid, it's true. But the Watchers will suffer the same disadvantage. Only the feathered wings of our Aeri cousins can defy the gravitational phenomenon. The Watchers will be forced to attack over ground. With Aeri air support, Ori entrenchments, and Fori-built barriers, we can craft a formidable defense."

I see by the many furrowed brows and eyes in deep thought that they are working out my plan in their heads. A few nod slightly. Whispers profess my plan holds more merit than madness.

"If we rally at the pyramids first," I say, "we can secure the high ground and fortify our position."

Ko Tora crosses her arms and gives me an appraising look. "All fine ideas in word. But your plan requires giving up our most important advantage—the element of surprise. She'll not expect a direct attack on the Capstone. At the pyramids, we'll be on full display, giving her a chance to study our position and devise a means to overcome us. If we catch her off guard, however, she'll not have time to adapt. If the Watchers are there in force, we shall swarm them with superior numbers and be done with all this. Fear is the chain that binds us, children. The only path to freedom is to overcome it."

Anger swirls in my chest. My fists throb with it. Their disregard for Jexa's expertise will cost us dearly. "She is a Master of War! Who knows what tactics she's learned in her lifetimes exterminating races? She's luring us into a trap."

"Jexa fought *one* war. Against your mother! We'd have won, too, if Klora had given us time to muster our strength. But no. She couldn't wait. Hard as I tried to rally a formidable force, it wasn't quick enough for her. Her impulsiveness doomed us all."

"You mean she tried to seize the element of surprise?" I say. "Remind us all how that worked out for her."

Ko Tora's nostrils flare and her eyes go wide.

My tone draws uneasy looks from our onlookers. It's one thing to question an elder; another thing entirely to speak against them. But to throw their own words back in their face... But I see now that growing old does not necessarily make someone wise.

Ko Tora composes herself quickly and says, "That was different. Look around. We have the numbers now, with more arriving by the hour. But let's pretend what you say is true. If we plant ourselves in the open like that, we'll be leaving the initiative in the hands of a *Master of War*. It's too risky. We can't let her anywhere near the gate with that key."

"The Watchers will have to get through us to reach the apex," I say, "while dragging the Capstone up all those levels. Fighting the Watchers there is the best way to ensure the battle is fought on our terms." Our presence there will also keep Jexa's eyes far away from Deka. He'll be safe in the forest until the Magister arrives.

Many more heads now nod their approval of my idea. This is good.

"Jexa may have already dispatched a company to guard the pyramids," Ko Zola points out.

"Unlikely," says a senior Fori Elder. I'm guessing by her age and frailty she is Ko Rantha, the oldest Servant on this planet. "If she's been expecting a turnout like this, she'd not weaken her grip on the Capstone by dividing her force. As it stands, we outnumber the Watchers three to one. That number is sure to grow through the night. The New Moon is a week away. That's seven days of defending both the pyramids and the Capstone. Even a *master of war* cannot stretch her numbers to guarantee success in both areas."

Ko Tora closes her eyes and rocks her head side to side. Then, as if someone had declared her Rebel Marshal, she nods her approval. "All right, then. We fly at first light to the pyramids. Get some rest, children. You will need it for the trials ahead."

In quick response, Fori loyal to Ko Tora kick dirt over the fire and stomp out the coals.

A strange feeling rises in me while I watch the party die out, as the growing army obeys Ko Tora's command without question and retires to make their nests for the night. I rallied us during the battle, turned the tide of attack in our favor, squared off with Jexa without backing down. They should be looking to *me* for direction.

And yet... none have defied a single command from me, for I have not issued one. I'd told Jaleera I don't want that responsibility. My mind reassures me that I'd spoken true in that, but my heart says otherwise.

A walk around the growing perimeter reveals more sentries on watch. A majority of their eyes look inward more than out. I'm not going anywhere without Ko Tora's approval, but I am not without options. While the lookouts have keen eyes for the skies and the trees, they cannot see what happens underground.

I find Mora sleeping among her cohort, entangled in two dozen sets of arms and legs. As their leader, her position in the middle makes her hard to reach. Many stir at my fluttering wings as I hover low overhead. When I grab Mora's shoulder, she wakes with a sour expression, which softens upon seeing me. She looks to her sleeping juniors warily, so I nod for her to join me off to the side.

We meet up under the stringy curtain of a willow tree.

"I need your help with something very important," I say.

Mora nods. "My Ori are yours to command."

A tingle of pride touches my heart.

"I need you and a few others to head back west."

"West? The battle lies east, where we'll need every sword

swinger we can find. What sort of trouble are you sending us to?"

"An envoy from the surviving species is set to arrive at the western forest edge. He may already be there."

Mora shifts uneasily.

"Consider it a favor," I say. "I'll focus on Jexa better if I know he's safe with you watching over him. We need him alive for the Magister's arrival."

I suppose anyone from his tribe could do, but he is the only one who's not acted like a caveman around me. The Magister will not respond well to being shot at on sight. Deka's refined demeanor will take no time convincing the Magister of his intelligence.

Mora looks around warily and fidgets with her forging apron.

I take both of her hands in mine. "*Please*, Mora."

She glances at the breathing mounds of nests covering the forest floor. "You're becoming more like your mother with every breath." She sighs and rolls her eyes. "Fine, we'll watch over it."

I place my hands onto her shoulders. "Thank you. And *its* name is Deka."

When I watch the last of Mora's four workers-turned-guardians burrow underground, I breathe a sigh of relief. I'd love nothing more than to go see Deka myself, but my place is here. And it's not only Ko Tora's orders that keep me. If we don't meet the Magister upon his arrival, Deka's people and mine will all die at the hands of the Watchers. Jexa has no choice in the matter. Her plan is in action now. By killing the Consul and seizing the Capstone, she has done too much to brush this off. She must carry through with summoning the Black Tide.

I find a cradle between two large roots, where I curl up on my side. Two Fori join me and wrap their arms around me. They smell of smoke and the tang of blood. They fought the battle with me earlier. In the dark I recognize Kassini's purple hair, but I'm not sure about the other.

I'm slipping off to sleep when whispers drag me back from oblivion. Heated words waft through the smoke of the dead bonfire, the intensity of them drawing me to sit up on my side. I'm rubbing the sleep from my eyes when I hear my name. There is venom and fire in the voice that hisses it.

I slide from between my sleeping companions and tiptoe toward the voices, taking cover from tree to tree until three figures come into view. They're huddled close in the haze, perhaps to smother their words, but the heat of the conversation blazes too hot to contain it completely.

Crouching behind a tree trunk, I listen.

"It's our surest chance," Ko Tora says. "Leaving the initiative in Jexa's hands will end with our defeat."

"There must be another way," says Ko Zola of the Ori, but her words lack the conviction of Ko Tora's.

"None that guarantees us victory. You both know this. We must get Nya to disable the Gate the first chance we get."

Cold sweat covers my skin. She can't be serious!

"Doing so will trap us on this planet," Ko Zola says gravely.

"You think I haven't considered that? But with the force we've rallied here, we'll be able to carve out a piece of land that no surviving Watcher would be foolish enough to trespass upon."

"Klora's Dream," one of the others says. By the rattle in her voice, she is an Elder proper. Ko Rantha.

The mention of my mother's name by a senior Elder gives me goosebumps. Though, I've never heard her name spoken with a word other than *folly* or *fool* before. What is this dream of which they speak?

I move closer, crawling from around the tree and staying low among the ferns.

"You know what destroying the pyramid will do to the young dust maiden," says Ko Zola.

I freeze in my crawling, desperate to hear Ko Tora's response. Though I don't need to hear the words. The first rule I learned about dusting was that breaking a sacred bond comes at the cost of undoing my own. I got a taste of this as a youngling, when I tried dusting a diamond throne. It felt like I was getting electrocuted! The mere memory has me shaking like a leaf in a hurricane.

"I know just as well as you," Ko Tora spits, "but we're at war. A war *she* started. If she must sacrifice her life to end it, then we'll see she's given all the honors and remembrance she deserves. Besides, there'll be no place in our new paradise for her destructive nature."

My throat tightens as if a hand is choking me. So much so that I rub my neck to ensure this is not the case. My heartbeat drums so loud in my ears that it muffles the following words, but I've already heard enough. Too much, actually. They intend to sacrifice me to stop Jexa.

I scramble back to the glade and look to the treetops. I'm searching for the widest gap between sentries through which to make my escape, pondering places to hide so the Elders cannot use my powers to strand us on this planet, when squealing stops me.

At the base of the tree where I'd left her, Kassini cries in her sleep, no doubt haunted by images of the recent violence and the loss of her dear sister Leeta.

I lay beside the pair and wrap my arms around them both. Kassini squeezes my hand and stops fussing. Did they join me because I make them feel safe? Can I abandon them now in the uncertain hours to come?

No, I dare not. Besides, the Elders cannot force me to use my ability. Once everyone rallies at the pyramids, I'll see they're put straight to work building defenses.

I've never known the comfort of a Hive's nest. The warmth of my companions and their rhythmic breathing soothes me, and is enough to smother my woes and ease me to sleep.

CHAPTER 19

NYA

I wake to wood clacking and the rhythmic ringing of steel. I sit up and find myself alone among the roots, my two nesting companions nowhere in sight.

It's still an hour before sunrise, but the forest is alive with activity.

A quick look around reveals Fori and Ori practicing melee drills with spears and axes. A few seniors drift between sparring pairs, offering tips and playing coach as if they have a clue. The Aeri must think they're already good enough and above coaching the others, because they watch in amusement from the canopy.

Those not practicing gather dry wood to feed the dozen blazes that roar from stone forges spread all around, their flames burning bright beneath the indigo sky. Steel hitting steel rings loud from Ori hammers as they beat glowing orange pieces into spear tips and axe heads. But it's not just weapons they craft.

My cousins study our fallen dead, taking note of their wounds. In the calm of dawn, it's clear the Watchers did not go for the easier target of the heart. Instead, a Fori lifts the pale limp arm of her dead sister to show a gash through her armpit. It's the only wound on her body, but they say she was dead before she hit the ground. Others note where forearm tendons had been sliced with precision, disabling the Fori and forcing them to drop their weapons. They relay the location of these weak spots and others to the Ori smiths working the hearths, where they bend glowing steel into shoulder guards and chest plates, and curl shin greaves and arm sleeves that cover from elbow to wrist.

A familiar voice draws my attention to a lineup of Fori waiting for weapons at a forge.

"I hurt it in the battle," Jinny says insistently. She is the first Fori from Ko Mirah's Hive I've seen since I convinced them to spread word about the Reckoning. Of course she'd be the first to come fight. 'Runt,' her Fori sisters call her. But her heart is bigger than all of theirs combined. She wears a cow skull she's painted blue as a helmet, and when one of her antagonists flips it off her head, I see she's shaved the sides of her hair, leaving a wide strip of green hair atop her head and down the back.

Those gathered around her laugh as she bends awkwardly to pick up her helmet. One Fori limps in a circle to mock her while another crouches in for a closer look at her mangled leg.

"I don't see any marks," notes her observer.

"Get out of here," says another Fori to Jinny. "These weapons are for fighters only."

Jinny holds her helmet to her chest, and I can see she's about to burst into tears. The bullies at her Hive had stopped bothering her years ago, because she'd later find them on their own and pester them relentlessly, day and night, until she actually drove one crazy. That Fori tried to hide her sleeping spot, but Jinny always found her, dripping water on her forehead all through each night, denying her sleep until she lost her mind. These Fori haven't learned that yet.

I storm toward the group lined up at the forging hearth.

When Jinny sees me coming, her eyes light up. "Nya!"

She limps my way to welcome me with a hug, but stops herself short. She realizes I'd just heard her lie about being wounded in the battle. "I was just telling them…" Her breathing speeds up and her eyes well with tears. "I was telling them…"

"How you dragged that Watcher down to her death, all by yourself?" I close the distance between us and throw an arm around her. "I thought for sure that fall had killed you. How are you even standing right now? You must have bones of steel."

The expressions from those around me lower in shame.

"I'm glad you're still kicking," I add. "We'll need you on those pyramid steps." I pretend to notice her taunters for the first time. "Who are your friends? Did they fight with us yesterday?"

A few hug themselves and turn away in search of better conversation. Others offer Jinny a shoulder squeeze or a pat on the back.

Jinny ignores them and wraps both arms around my waist.

"It's nice to see you," I whisper in her ear, "you little devil."

She squeezes me tighter.

I scan the crowd for more of Ko Mirah's Fori. "Did you come alone?"

Jinny releases me. "Ko Vera forbade us from fighting, on account of Ko Mirah's last wish, but a few of us snuck away. We're going to make Jexa pay for all she's done."

"Nya."

I turn to see Kassini approach wearing armor. The ornate curves and swirling patterns make it the most beautiful attire I've ever seen. "We got up extra early to make you this. You look about my size, but they'll adjust it to fit you better if needed. You like?"

I walk around Kassini, admiring the elegant yet practical design, the work of proud artisans. "It's wonderful."

"Next time you face Jexa, you can get close enough to stab her right in the eye!" Kassini says, thrusting an axe in imitation.

My belly lurches at the idea of facing Jexa again. The feeling, however, vaporizes when I remember how many allies fill the forest around me. Even now, word drifts through the pre-dawn air, claiming outrageous numbers.

"Lots more arrived during the night," Kassini says. "They say we're five thousand strong, with more on the way."

Her eyes dart erratically back and forth as she bounces on her toes, barely able to contain herself.

"You're sure?" I say.

"Fly as far as you can in any direction and you'll not see the end of our lines. Go on, do it."

"It's true," Jinny says.

"I believe you," I say. Perhaps Jexa really was trying to deflate my confidence. Maybe she knows we stand a chance. Jaleera did tell me the Marshal sees us as a threat. Either way, if the estimates are anywhere near true, we'll make an impressive turnout at the pyramids.

"Fall in with your cohorts!" bellows Ko Tora's voice.

Ferns rustle and feet pound the ground as hundreds of Servants race in every direction in search of their workmates. Party leaders call out names to rally their people, while Ko Elders try shouting some order into the chaos.

I watch the stampede with concern. Even during the calm of a peaceful morning, it's a difficult task keeping control of this 'army'. Battle will be absolute mayhem. But that's a worry for another time.

Jinny grabs my wrist and hauls me to the few defiant fighters from Ko Mirah's Hive, who have formed a mixed group with three smaller hives. *Rag-Tags*, some call us. The name quickly gains popularity.

Ko Tora walks the lines with Ko Zola and Ko Rantha, assigning each group their place in the flying order. Aeri flocks will scout from high up. Fori cohorts will make up the vanguard, with Ori gangs moving over land in reserve. She shouts each assignment for all to hear, flexing her authority, showing everyone who it is that commands this great legion.

When she arrives at my cohort, she spares me not even the slightest glance. I am a peasant to her.

"Rear guard," she says, then moves on.

Tension deflates from my group of forty. Some from relief, others from disappointment.

The Aeri scouts take to the sky before the flying order is decided in full. Squadrons of six fly out in eight directions to cover our advance. It seems they've learned a thing or two about warfare from my mother's rebellion. I commend Ko Tora for this move. At least she is not overly secure in our numbers. I suspect she's studied at length my mother's shortcomings in preparation for her own moment to shine.

A long while passes, everyone shifting nervously, while Ko Tora continues on with her spectacle.

"Have you seen Sheffa?" I ask Jinny.

She gives me a curious look. "You didn't hear? She wanted to get Squiggs' spark back, so she went to Jexa to turn you in. That's the last anyone has seen of her. I'd say Jexa put her to work moving the Capstone."

Ko Tora flies overhead while shouting, "Rise, children! Rise! To victory!"

A horn blows loud from nearby. Several more answer in the distance.

The *WHOOSH* of four thousand sets of wings lifts off from the ground, leaving the wingless Ori to move over ground. Branches snap as cohorts explode through the canopy into the open sky. It's here that I see our force in its entirety for the first time. It stops me mid-flight. Never before have I witnessed so many of our kind moving toward a common task, with work parties now flying boldly as battle squadrons. It is magnificent.

"Nya, keep up!"

Ahead, Jinny checks over her shoulder for me. I dart ahead to join her.

My heart drums a victorious tune. There must be a Servant to cover every stone of the Great Pyramid's exterior. We will stop Jexa, or our blood running down the steps will give her one hell of a climb.

Ko Tora peels away from the head of the force and hovers to the side, watching us parade past. A twelve-point antler crown sits high on her head. This adornment sickens me.

When she spots me in the line, she snatches my arm and hauls me from the stream.

"We have a special assignment for you," she says. "To guarantee our victory over Jexa, we'll need the dust maidens at our side. Deliver my summons to your kin. Tell Ko Skadia to round up her Entropaths and join us at the pyramids."

This order wipes the smile from my face. My kin number less than fifty on this planet—a sliver of the force strung across the sky before us. There is only one reason she wants the dust maidens. She doesn't care about appealing to the Magister. She'd sooner destroy the gate at Giza and any backups we may know of, sealing us here for good. She'd use my sisters to claim dominion over Earth. And I know a few who would happily accept the challenge.

Well, I'll see that the Magister puts her in her place.

"I'll fetch them at once," I say, placing a hand on my belly and bowing slightly, as much as my armor allows.

Ko Tora gives a smug, satisfied smile. "Then go. And be quick about it. I want them at the pyramids in three days."

She doesn't spare me a second look as she whirls around and falls in with the stream of black dots stretching toward the eastern horizon.

I shake my head. She doesn't understand the forces she commands. She can't boss Entropaths around like the other Servants. Even the Watchers and Ko Skadia have trouble scaring us into submission. And if I've allowed myself to be seen as different in that regard, well, that's about to change.

CHAPTER 20
DEKA

I'll never forget the first time I saw the color green. Mother had taken me deep under the Grand Gallery, where leaks in the riverbed above provided enough water for her algae blooms. When she showed me the source of our colony's oxygen, floating in thick layers across the top of plastic water basins, I failed to see through to the true beauty of this biological wonder. All I could do was marvel at its unfamiliar color.

Mother had forbidden me from showing Mali. This lab was to remain hidden away from everyone, even Father. She assured me the secret was necessary, because our leaders thought all of our breathing air came from the surface. But in the early days, the slow effects of hypoxia afflicted our densely-populated colony, especially in the deeper caverns, where ventilation was restricted. Our leaders never had to live down there. They never suffered the effects of prolonged oxygen deficiency. They'd see those tanks as a wasteful use of water and decommission the project. In doing so, many would suffocate. After Mali's betrayal a few days ago, I'm glad I managed to keep my mouth shut all those years. Even if it meant denying her a glimpse of this exotic sight.

After Mother died, I maintained the vats as best I could. Her meticulous notes served me well — to a point. I was too young, and lacked her skill to adapt the process. Not that it mattered. The drought eventually left us in darkness, with no power for artificial light. The blooms died, but the loss was mine to bear alone. We'd lost half of our colony the night my mother and father died in the attack. The reduced population allowed the dwellers below to move up from the depths, needing only to return below briefly during drills.

Only I felt the loss of the beauty below. To let something so vibrant and life-giving perish was a silent tragedy I endured on my own. In this barren world beauty is purpose enough. All I could do was savor the memory of something else lost to time.

Since those days in the deep, I thought that's all there was to it. Just that one shade of green. I'd accepted that assumption as truth until a few days ago.

It was the color of Nya's eyes that had locked me in her spell. I'd risked my safety by permitting her approach, just so I could have a closer look. A life underground makes you desperate for new things, so when those glittering orbs fell on me, it was like staring at jewels from a distant planet. There is no telling the wonders those eyes have seen. And despite that, the sight of me seemed to intrigue her.

Nya's arrival had brought a new opportunity to show Mali this wonderful color, yet she was the first to fire a bolt at her heart.

Since that moment, I was sure *green* couldn't possibly show me any more surprises. But the forest now sitting above the coast beyond my bow leaves me in stunned silence. The spectrum—every shade from dark to light, dull to bright—is pure majesty. No, that's not the right word. Because there is no word.

Mali leans far over the prow. She hasn't spared me the slightest hint of acknowledgment since spotting the first treetops an hour ago. The storm is behind us, with only a hint of mist in the air here, and with the forest in clear view, it's enough to make her laugh with crazed joy.

Her reaction pulls my attention away from the magical forest, to within the confines of my ugly plastic boat. Just as rare as the forest before us is that sound coming from my oldest friend. I've seen her smile for a variety of reasons—mischief, threat, sarcasm. Never joy.

"It's a spell!" Marlok shouts from his boat to our rear. "They lure us into their domain to make us easy targets. Turn around, Deka! *Please!*"

Marlok's desperation sends a shiver through me. So does heat from the sun breaking through the thinning clouds overhead.

The majesty fades as fear kicks my heart into an ominous rhythm. Nya had promised seven nights of rain to keep the demons from the sky. It's been only five. Something went wrong, and we need to find cover. I grab both oars and start rowing.

Mali slides back and grabs my right arm to stop me. "What if Marlok is right? What if it's a trap?"

"Look behind you," I say, nodding toward the western horizon. "We've been easy targets since we left home. If Nya meant us harm, we'd be resting on the seabed by now."

Mali doesn't look convinced. She watches Marlok's overloaded boat struggling to keep up with us.

"You can go back with him," I say. "Me, I'm going all the way. I'd sooner risk the unknown ahead than go back to that familiar misery."

Mali folds her arms and sinks low at the bow. Good. I can't let her go, anyway. I need to get everyone off the water and into cover, and she is the only reason Marlok will lead his warriors into that forest.

It takes longer than I'd guessed to close on the shore. As the afternoon sun beats down on me, I wish we'd kept some of that rain water we'd been so eager to toss overboard. My mouth is so dry I'd drink my own blood if it could quench my thirst. This doesn't slow my rowing, though. All will be well when we reach the forest. Trees require water. Lots of it, actually, in order to look as green as they do now in the orange light of the lowering sun.

We just have to make it to the shade of that forest. Those trees that seem to stretch away from us, teasing and taunting.

I row harder.

Get to the forest. Get to Nya.

I run us aground and jump straight onto the rocky beach. There's no time for hesitation. We've been in the open for too long, so I ignore Mali's warning and race to the broken wall of trees guarding the forest border at the shoreline.

Hissing rises from the trees and halts me. It's as if the trees warn me to stay back. But as I stand on the shore before these giant sentinels, I see it is not a sound of warning or threat, but the rustling of leaves in the breeze.

I enter their domain without further delay.

Shade provides a welcome respite from the sun's heat, along with the psychological comfort of cover. I collapse on the soft ground and hope I'm not alone for long.

Lying back, I feel tiny blades of grass tickle my skin. Grass! I can't believe it.

Streams of sunlight break through the forest ceiling, treating my eyes to a splendor of the darkest green in the shadows, to the brightest moss that covers the trees, which stand tall like towers, rising higher into the sky than I ever thought possible.

"Deka?"

I sit up and see Mali standing on the beach beyond the trees. She pulls down her goggles and stares into the forest with a high level of caution.

"Over here," I shout with a wave of my hand.

"Mali!" shouts Marlok. "Get away from there!"

Mali turns back toward her brother, then darts away from him and into the forest. As she stumbles toward me, I spring to my feet and carry on deeper through the trees. Low shrubs tickle and scratch my legs as I run, causing me to jump in fright at first, then in delight.

Trickling water lures me to a glade. Here, a pool sits at the far edge. The water is so clear that I see the stones at the bottom perfectly, which makes me question if it really is water. No mud or murk at all. Ignoring my better sense, I stick my hand in and laugh at its refreshing coolness. I splash some onto my face and feel tears bulge in my eyes. Tears of relief.

"Deka!" hisses Mali from behind.

I turn to see her crouching beside a tree with her crossbow aimed straight up. Marlok and six warriors fall in around her. They all aim at the canopy, where winged creatures dart from tree to tree.

"Fire!" orders Marlok.

Seven bolts whiz upward.

"Wait!" I shout as they reload.

Marlok raises his bow for another shot, but I race over and slap it down.

"Listen," I say.

He does, with everyone else also falling silent to the chirping above.

"Birds," I say.

A few crossbows hit the ground as the alarm in my kin's eyes softens to wonder. *"Birds,"* Huxley mutters absently in his fixation. He sits cross-legged and stares up at the tiny creatures flitting between branches, his mouth agape.

We've seen birds before, of course, but these are different than the rowdy gulls and ragged sea eagles. The cheerful banter here is a welcome chorus from a hospitable environment.

Marlok keeps his crossbow at the ready and scouts the perimeter. Any punishment he has planned for us can wait. Security is priority.

For the most part, my warrior kin fall quickly to this glade's charms. They watch the birds above, or feel the grass and small plants at their feet, with Mali even digging into a tree and finding insects we'd never before seen.

Even the air here is sweet. I breathe deeply through my

nose, inviting fresh moisture through my nostrils and down into my lungs.

I smile. This is not the dark land of demons. This is a garden of love and care.

When Marlok's sweep fails to detect any danger, everyone claims a soft piece of shaded land on which to rest, for rest is well needed. Even Marlok lets his guard down a bit. He leans against a tree with his crossbow on his lap, watching the birds warily. And if it were anyone other than my war chief, I'd swear that was a smile twitching at the corner of his mouth. I can tell he's torn. Duty compels him to return home at once, but he's not eager to get back on the water.

I slide into the spring and shiver in the cool water. The chill wakes all sorts of indescribable sensations in me, which piques Mali's curiosity. She joins me in bathing in this seemingly endless water source, her teeth chattering loudly. I close my eyes and try relaxing my weary muscles. Nya will find us soon, and we must be ready to travel at once.

We don't last long in the cold. When we've had enough, we lay on the forest floor and stare at green leaves of all shapes flutter around patches of blue sky. Descriptions in stories never completely captured the beauty our ancestors destroyed.

We lounge like this for hours, watching streams of golden light shift across rows of mossy trees, these invading rays lowering westward with the sinking sun. It's hard to believe creatures like those that took my parents oversee the creation of such divine elegance.

By the time the sun sinks below the horizon, I'm sure I've seen the most beauty the human eye is capable of processing. Then I am treated to another surprise. As twilight darkens, platforms of fungus bloom from tree trunks like small balconies. Each ledge glows with a magical green light.

When Mali leans in close to one, the glow paints her face emerald green. Even she can't keep the wonder from her eyes.

As I watch glowing green insects float through the air, I swear there's nothing more on this earth that can catch my breath. Until someone says four words that make my heart flutter.

"Your demon is here."

I turn to see Nya standing beside a large tree. I jump up to go meet her, though not too eagerly. My relationship with this ally of ours has already caused me much strain among my folk.

Marlok leans on a spear at the center of the glade, watching Nya, though it's clear he's not expecting a fight.

Before I reach her, she turns to lead me away. I glance back and see Marlok starting to follow, so I nod for him to remain behind.

"I thought you'd come alone," she says. She's hugging herself despite the balmy air, and her shoulders are hunched with tension.

"I tried."

Something is different about her. Though she avoids looking at me directly, she can't hide the darkness in her eyes. I've seen this loss of innocence haunt my own people.

"You've seen death," I say.

Nya hugs herself tighter and nods to the right. "There's fighting to the east. It's not safe for you there yet, so you have to stay here for a little while."

I survey the trees with their spiral staircases of glowing

mushrooms. "I don't think my people will protest this order."

Nya locks eyes with me and tilts her head as if studying my expression. Then she joins me in admiring the canopy.

"Come," she says. "There's something I'd like to show you."

She leads me to the largest tree in sight and rubs her hand over its rough skin. It's so massive that, to hug its base, it would take two dozen members of my tribe holding hands to encircle it. Looking up, I see its point rises above all its surrounding neighbors. I'd read trees take hundreds to thousands of years to grow this large. Nya's folk must have methods to accelerate the process.

"Can you climb?" she says.

My head spins at the mere thought of rising so high. To someone who has lived a life underground and never stood higher than the edge of a cliff, this activity seems unnatural. But I don't think she'd suggest I do something that may cause me harm.

I climb onto the lowest branch. My hands and feet feel strange on the rough bark, and for some reason I feel the urge to apologize to the tree. Yet to think such a grand being would be bothered by my presence seems arrogant. So I continue on, branch to branch, rising higher until I risk a glance below. This glance draws out into a gaping stare. The ground is so far away!

I hug the tree tight. The width of my outstretched arms offers me little comfort, with my fingers curling into cracks in the bark for purchase.

Nya flies into my peripheral vision. "Don't worry," she says, "I'll catch you if you fall. Keep climbing. *Rise.*"

I obey, and Nya is never more than an arm's reach away.

Whether she can slow my fall, I'm not sure, but that doesn't matter. Something tells me she'd die trying. For me, this is enough.

I keep my eyes on the bark before me, but I know I've risen above the forest canopy when a breeze hits my skin. My arms shake and burn from exertion, but I dare not loosen my grip for even half a breath. Not unless I risk being blown away by a rogue gust of wind.

"This is high enough," Nya says.

The branch beside me creaks and sinks to bear her weight as she takes her place beside me. When I muster the courage to look away from the tree trunk, the danger of my height no longer concerns me. For if I died now, I would do so with eyes that have seen more wonders than any human in over five hundred years.

To our left, the black sea glitters under moonlight, much calmer now than the tempest that brought us from the desert behind us. I dare not waste my time turning to see what that wasteland looks like from this vantage point. Every morsel of my attention belongs forward, where the green paradise stretches as far as my human eyes can see. Maybe words to describe such beauty existed in times past, but they have long since fallen from use.

"Do you approve?" Nya asks.

I give her a sidelong look and see a smile lifting the corner of her mouth.

"Yes," I say, for whatever my approval is worth.

"This will all be yours soon."

My heart flutters, though this promise seems too good to be true. "Your people created this place. I find it hard to believe they'd just abandon it."

"To us, this planet is only a temporary lover." Nya looks upward, longingly, to the pinholes of light that make up the bulging seam across the black sky. "My home is my true love," she says wistfully. "Some of my kind wish to trap us here, on Gaia, but I'll die before that happens."

"Why?" *Is this place so bad you'd choose death over it?* Her folk could turn this entire planet into paradise with enough time.

"The survival of our race depends on our reunion with our mates," she explains. "My kind are rare enough as it is."

Her answer stings me for some reason. "Your mate..."

"Is someone I try not to talk about." She looks away, her face glowing red. A warning to change the subject.

I survey the sky, where an impossible amount of stars stretch from horizon to horizon. "Where is it? Your home."

"It's too far to see with your eyes."

I feel a deepening crease in my brow as I try to make sense of her claim. Is she saying there are stars beyond what we see from here? Or that my human eyes are incapable of seeing that far.

Seeing my confusion, she says, "We were celebrated architects of our own world once. God-like creators. We built the most wondrous ecosystems you could ever fathom, crafted paradise for ourselves and all who wished to join us. Races came from all over the galaxy to bask in our glorious creations. My ancestors tailored the most ideal conditions and experiences for the civilizations they took in. It was..." Nya frowns and twists her lips in search of the right word.

"Heaven," I offer.

Her eyes brighten. "Yes. But the hubris of my ancestors led them to overreach. They became complacent in their methods and stretched the resources of our planet to create a utopia that was unsustainable. When the inevitable catastrophe destroyed our planet and killed off all the lifeforms under our dominion—some of them the rarest known to the Magister's List—my ancestors earned his scorn.

"In the last moments, they predicted the imminent collapse and escaped the devastation. Many outsiders saw our survival as an insult. Others considered it a hostile act. And so the Magister stripped us of our free will. The only way to earn it back was through service, to races like those we condemned, to learn humility and control. This fate has been passed down to all their descendants. We must carry the burden until the balance is restored."

"And the Watchers enforce this agreement on behalf of the Magister?"

"They foretold our demise, long before anyone else. The Watchers are an ancient race once revered for their ecological wisdom and terraforming expertise. *Guardians of Nature.* They warned my people about their ways, but they wouldn't listen. So the Watchers appealed to the Magister, urging him to intervene. But the Magister refused to break the Law of Free Will. The consequences were regrettable, more dire than even he had predicted.

"To atone for the devastation, my ancestors entered into the Pact. The Watchers' council had earned the Magister's confidence. His trust in their abilities and intentions inspired him to assign them as Wardens of the Pact. They were to mentor and guide us back toward the light. That's when they started calling themselves *The Light Ones.* Their ability to assess the planetary needs of refugees resettled, combined with our abilities, made us the perfect match for the Magister's design. We could physically harness the forces of nature far greater than they could. In return, the Light Ones provided assessment and planning, structure and guidance. And when it came to it, disciplinary measures."

This does not sound like the race who now oversee Nya's folk. "It seems they've lost their way."

"Yes. The universe is undergoing a period of upheaval. From the chaos, servants of Darkness and Light are emerging. To some, being a guardian now requires a more active approach. They see saving life sometimes requires taking it. Like removing parasites from blood, or rot from flesh."

"And so now they fight for Darkness."

Nya turns quickly to face me. She takes my hand and squeezes it. "Only Jexa and the Watchers on Earth have succumbed to it. They've taken their power too far. Watchers on other planets have maintained the balance and honored the Pact. When the Magister learns she is lost, he will send her to where she belongs."

"You mean, he'll kill her?" I wonder if he'll let us watch. I wonder if that will bring me peace.

"She will be reformed."

"As in... imprisoned?" That mild punishment stirs disappointment in me.

"In a way. It is said that those who mistreat others will come back in the form of the mistreated. One of the Magister's Principle Promises."

"Come back?"

"After the disembodiment," she says matter-of-factly.

Seeing my confusion, Nya says, "Where do you think you go when your body expires?"

"I go with my body. Either into the ground, or burned to ash. And that's it."

Nya almost laughs. "If only it were so easy."

"You believe in life after death?"

"Hard not to. I'm living it. You don't?"

"Most of my people do. My mother taught me to believe only what I can see and measure."

Nya leans forward on her branch. "Have you heard of radiation? Gamma rays? Ultraviolet light?"

I nod. Radiation is what killed most of our race.

"Can you see and measure that?" she asks.

"We did have ways. And even without instruments, we saw the effects of it." The awful, terrible effects. "But there's been no proof of what you suggest. So I'll have to take your word for it."

"Well, maybe a sapien scholar would have discovered it... if your race survived long enough."

I have a hard time accepting a claim without evidence. Too many of my kind do. Someone needs to remain skeptical.

Nya closes her eyes and takes a deep breath.

"What are you doing?" I ask.

"Tuning in to the frequency."

Nya opens her eyes and looks over my shoulder, then above my head. I look up and around to see what's caught her attention.

"You really don't see them?" she says.

I focus my attention in the direction of her gaze, but see nothing beyond the obvious.

"They're *everywhere*," she says in wonder, her eyes glistening at some mystical sight I am denied. And then, through the glaze in her eyes, I see it. At first it's just a white spot over my shoulder in the reflection of her eyes. Then... several—white, yellow, blue.

My breath catches. But judging by her unrestrained wonder, this is just a glimpse of what she is seeing.

I allow her a few moments to enjoy whatever mystical experience she's having.

"Is that why you risk fighting them?" I say, breaking her trance. "If your body dies, will you be free again?"

Her smile flattens and her expression turns solemn. Nya narrows her eyes on the sky directly overhead, in an effort to see something that obviously eludes her. Something that brings a frown to her face.

"Like all things," she says, "our sparks vibrate at a defined frequency. The Watchers have an ethereal capsule around the planet, like a net, tuned to a frequency that snares a rising spark. If we die in our service, our spark will try to return to our home. But that net..." Anger rises in her voice. "It creates a stranglehold on every planet we work on. The only way to freedom is to earn it by reclaiming one hundred planets."

She extends an arm in front to show me the five black bands tattooed to her wrist. "Only *then* will they release us. But if I lose this body, I'll have no way to prove my contribution. I'll join them on the next planet in a new body, all signs of my previous work erased."

Forced reincarnation. If there was ever a religion my mother spoke fairly of, it was those of the East. Soul recycling does sound like an effective punishment, as evidenced by Nya's predicament. "So all of you who fight...if you lose, you...will you just...start over?"

Nya cringes and rubs her belly. "There's a different punishment for that. Those who misbehave are sent to the

Dark, forever. It's the only real form of death, because there's no coming back. Light goes in and never comes out. It's crushing eternal darkness."

Awful as this sounds, I have trouble picturing it. "The Dark?"

"The Watchers have a portal that opens at the edge of a Black Hole. They force all the delinquent sparks through its gate. I saw them take a Fori once. No one ever saw her again." Tears streak down Nya's cheeks. She wipes them and sniffles. "But she visits me in my dreams. She screams my name, begs me to save her. When she grabs me it feels like it's for real."

I shiver. I'm glad there are those like Nya among her people. "You're very brave for fighting your masters."

"We have no choice. If Jexa opens the gateway and patches into the network of all life-bearing planets, the Watcher army she musters will sweep across the Universe, slaying all beings of light and drowning everything in muted darkness."

Cold sweat slides down my brow.

The light returns to Nya's eyes, hope brimming through the tears. She gives my leg a tender squeeze. "But it won't come to that."

"You are slaves fighting an army of skilled warriors," I say. "Do you think you can win?"

"We have the numbers," Nya says with an optimistic nod. "Enough to hold the gate until the Magister's arrival. Then you'll get to keep your home, and maybe I'll see mine."

"The Magister will reward you? He'll free you from the Pact?"

"He could give me his Mark. It's a rune over the third eye that allows the bearer to navigate the portals, giving them free range without help from the Watchers or Consul. He gives it for exemplary service, and saving your people might qualify me."

"So you're helping us for a reward."

"I'm helping you because it's the right thing to do. But... yes, I'd do anything to see my home again. If I help you keep yours in the process, well..." she cracks a smile, "then that's a bonus, I suppose. You deserve better than dark caves. Unless, of course, you miss them."

"No. Those caves are a tomb. This forest is a gift."

She squeezes my hand. "Make sure you take care of it when we're gone."

A lump swells in my throat. Even with the enemy expelled and our planet reclaimed, an ally like Nya would make our return to the world at large so much easier. There is no telling what dangers or disorder will arise upon their departure. "So you'll leave forever? I'll not see you again?"

Nya looks me in the eyes. "No one can ever know the answer to that."

A long silence settles between us. Chirping insects fill the void. Leaves rustle as a warm sea breeze blows Nya's hair in the midnight air.

"At the next New Moon," she says, "keep your eyes to the east. If you're lucky, you'll get to see the portal open."

"You're leaving?" I cringe at the despair in my tone.

"I have friends on their way to watch over you. This is their domain. If danger approaches, you'll have plenty of warning. So long as you're among the trees, you're among friends."

I appreciate Nya's intent, but I've already seen she doesn't have firm control over the elements she thinks she commands. "Your rain cover stopped earlier than you predicted."

"The Aeri left to join us in the fight."

I must appear nervous, because she places a comforting hand on mine. "So long as you're here, you are safe. My Ori cousins will be your devout guardians. You can trust them. You can trust me."

My gaze drifts east.

"Say it," Nya says, her tone heavy and serious. "Say that you trust me, and that you'll stay here."

"I trust you."

"And...?"

"We'll stay here until you come get us."

She gives me a satisfied smile. "Good."

The journey down the tree is a lot faster than the climb up. Wrapped in Nya's arms, we drift gently toward the forest floor, though I feel by her labored breathing that she bears my weight with difficulty.

We land on a flat patch of luminous grass. Though we're on solid ground, I keep my hold around her. She glances at my arms, confused, but remains in my embrace for a little longer.

"The leader of your guardians is called Mora," she says. "So long as you're under her watch, you'll be safe."

Okay, I think with a measure of relief. I'll gladly bet my life on her claim, because what other choice do I have? If she meant me any harm, I'd be dead by now. Our fates are entwined. Though, Marlok may need some convincing.

CHAPTER 21
NYA

Arrival at a dreaded destination always comes faster than when traveling to a place of desire. I'm sure a race somewhere has named and studied this psychological phenomenon, and I very well may have sent the records of their findings—the books, inscriptions, carvings, or however else they communicate their thoughts and observations—into the void of eternity. Anyway, it's what I experience when leaving Deka's sanctuary for the pyramids.

My belly winds into knots the entire flight until the megalithic site comes into view. On their own, the three gigantic pyramids are enough to halt me in my flight. Add to that some five thousand of my kin gathered on the levels of the left-most, grandest pyramid of the three, and I'm left with a heart bursting with pride.

But I am returning empty-handed.

Sure, I should have gathered my sisters. And I would have if I didn't know what Ko Tora intended to use them for. She'd have all forty of us destroy the pyramid, or at least damage it beyond repair. Then she'd move us on to any backup gates they may know of and destroy those as well, cutting the planet off from the Black Tide, and from the Magister too. And with that, separated from our mates, my race would go extinct. The Fori, Ori and Aeri might endure, due to their vast numbers. But Entropaths are rare as it is. Perhaps it's that rarity that drives me to reunite with my beloved. A biological instinct to propagate the species.

I'll admit, Ko Tora's plan would save us the trouble of fighting Jexa over the pyramid. With the gates disabled she would have no use for the Capstone. But we'd be trapped on Earth with the Watchers for eternity, a nightmare I dare not entertain for long. Besides, with trouble stirring, my sisters will be under close observation by their Watchers. Ko Skadia on a normal day has five assigned to her. Officially, anyway. Sometimes they venture away and check in occasionally, or leave just one or two, or switch out. Whatever the case, there's no way I'm getting anywhere near her with rebellion brewing. Even the Entropaths with one warden will now have at least a doubled and permanent presence. I'm only allowed to roam freely because Jaleera is partial to our cause. I'll not press my luck by seeking out places where I know Watchers to roam.

I fly hard to the eastern forest edge and then over barren earth toward the greatest, left-most pyramid, the one with the missing apex. The key that opens the gates between planets was removed shortly after our arrival to this world. It was to stay that way until the Magister's upcoming inspection. These check-ins are scheduled every ten years for the next seventy, when we're due to finish our work and move on to clean up the next mess.

That's the worst part about our work—spending

decades constructing paradise, living in it and falling in love with every tree's leaf and beach's grain of sand, and then being forced to move on to the next carcass of a planet, to bring it back from the dead, fall in love, rinse and repeat.

At least, that's how it was until a few days ago. While Jexa possesses the golden pyramidion that connects us to the network of all known life-bearing planets, she can send a distress signal and summon reinforcements to stomp us out, then spread her wicked word back to those other worlds, brainwashing more to her cause.

She has this power for now. But to set the Capstone key atop the Great Pyramid, she must get through us, and the sight before me promises this will be no easy task. Because, as I fly closer, I see the call to arms has traveled farther in my absence.

Beyond the pyramids, an Ori leader blasts orders through a horn in a strange accent. Her workers are digging a trench from the great river to encircle the Great Pyramid. Seeing this defense mechanism brings the word 'moat' to mind. Anywhere else and this measure would be preposterous against our flying enemies, but in the Anomaly the Watchers will be forced to attack on foot. Out of all of us—Fori, Entropath, Watchers—only the Aeri's large feathered wings can overcome the gravitational phenomenon that surrounds the gate. Dozens of them now fly in a halo pattern high above the apex, either as lookouts or as a flaunt to Jexa and the Watchers, I do not know. The remaining hundreds occupy the pyramid's upper levels.

Inside the moat, around the Great Pyramid's lowest level, Fori workers plant wooden stakes at outward angles. Their bickering seems derived from their lack of familiarity with each others' dialect and working style.

If I were to guess that these new arrivals have doubled our numbers overnight, I couldn't be far off.

I smile at the hardship awaiting Jexa. Even if she manages to get that mass of gold across the moat and through the picket line under a flurry of stones and arrows, her force will have to fight through a legion of rebels occupying every level of that great stone slope. It would take the Black Tide itself to wash us from that pyramid, and Jexa cannot summon those waves of darkness until she knocks every last one of us from those stone levels.

In my fixation with the activity ahead I've completely forgotten the power of this sacred ground, and the extent to which it reaches. That is, until I'm falling.

My wings flutter erratically, desperate to stop my three hundred foot drop, but they catch no air. It's like trying to fly in the vacuum of space, with no atmosphere to push down against. The energy that sits under this place does not allow it. The Anomaly sends me diving headfirst toward the base of the Great Pyramid.

I shriek and shield my face with both arms, bracing for impact. This is going to hurt.

Splash! Instead of hard ground, I plunge into water.

The moat!

When I emerge from the warm river water, I'm greeted by two dozen spear tips glinting in the afternoon light, their points all aimed at my face.

"It worked!" declares an Ori among them.

"Spaced it just right, I did," claims another.

"No way!" shouts the first Ori. She points back across the

moat, toward the forest. "You wanted to dig it there. Then the Watchers would land right inside our perimeter."

"Nah-ah! *You* wanted to put it there. Not me!"

Both drop their spears and one tackles the other to the ground. Dust rises from the scuffle, and the Ori trenchers turn their backs to me to cheer for their favored wrestler.

The butt of a spear shaft taps my shoulder from behind.

"Always know how to make an entrance, don't you."

I grab hold of Ko Zola's spear and allow the senior Ori to pull me to the moat's outer wall, where a temporary ladder of handholds rises from the water surface. I climb from the flooded trench with a sense of joy and relief. Our people have really come together on this. We actually have the odds on our side.

This elation, however, evaporates in an instant.

I'm joining Ko Zola on the outer bank, shaking the water from my wings, when an arrowhead of Watchers swoops in from the great river behind the pyramids.

I gasp in terror. I've seen this formation before, when I led Bercidia the Butcher's squadron astray to buy Deka's tribe time.

"Incoming!" I shout, and it takes everything in me to resist diving back into the moat for cover.

The wrestling Ori and working Fori all stop and give me perplexed looks. What are they doing? They must prepare to face the attack!

"Relax," Ko Zola says, pulling my arm down. "They're ours."

I squint for a better look and see she's right. It's not two large, butterfly wings that propels each figure in the sky, but four narrower wings. Like those of a dragonfly. Those of my serving kin, Servants no more. The object of their chase, however, is a different story.

My heart skips a beat at the copper skin and scarlet hair waving in the breeze.

"Jaleera came here unarmed," Ko Zola says. "Ko Tora insisted we take her hostage, but I stuffed that idea."

"Jaleera..." I say absently as I watch her zoom around the Anomaly's boundary with my kin in pursuit.

"They're playing 'Chase the Watcher'," Ko Zola adds. Then she scoffs. "Never thought those words would ever pass these lips. Interesting times."

Interesting times indeed. I'd been spectator to a few games of '*Escape* the Watcher', back when the very mention of that game carried harsh consequences. Back then, you couldn't even suggest defying our wardens. Now we train to kill them.

"She's teaching the Aeri and Fori leaders to fly in formation," Ko Zola explains, "should we need to meet the Watchers in the sky."

I'd seen the effectiveness of the Watcher strategy to separate us during battle, using havoc and chaos to disorient us. I'm amazed and comforted at the strict formation above. We must make the most of our numbers in the coming fight, and Jexa may find a way to lure us from the safety of our defenses and into the sky. I'm glad we're preparing for that.

Jaleera banks right. A few Fori miss the cue to follow and stray away from the group. Jaleera scolds them in her flight. In battle this will make them easy targets while weakening their squadron strength. And here we must be mindful of other dangers. As I'd just learned myself.

I cringe as the three stray Fori enter the Anomaly and

tumble toward the ground. The first, Kassini, splashes into the moat, which incites riotous cheers among the Ori canal diggers. However, the two behind her crash into sand and draw a collective gasp.

Shouts of pain rise from the fallen Fori. As Ko Zola rushes to render aid, a set of feet land on the sand behind me. I turn to see Jaleera smiling at me.

"I'm relieved to see you, Nya."

"Worried you'd have to come find me?" I say.

Her smile levels. "I'd never drag you into war. That's one decision I left entirely to you."

I see why she's here. She wants to be on our side when the Magister arrives and distributes justice. I'll admit, accepting my mother's killer doesn't sit well with me, but right now we can't be picky with our allies. And I do believe her in her motivation to restore their role as benevolent Wardens of the Pact. Plus, having heard of the harsh treatments the Fori and Ori receive from their Watchers, the fact that I'm still alive after all of my antics shows the pains Jaleera must have undertaken to cover for my slacking. A testament to her benevolence. Any desire for revenge must be reserved for Jexa. For the sake of my people, I cannot allow a personal vendetta to blind me. Jaleera's desperation to return to the Magister's grace is all the assurance I need.

Ko Tora swoops down and lands beside us. "Well? What news?"

"Ko Skadia won't commit the dust maidens to fight," I say, avoiding Jaleera's stare, knowing she may sense my lie and give me away.

Ko Tora's eyes flare wide and her nostrils flare. She grits her teeth and clenches her fists, but before she can say anything rash, she notices Jaleera give her a subtle look of caution. She is my Watcher, yes, and guardian, too.

Ko Tora backs off and launches into flight.

"It's too bad about the dust maidens," Jaleera says slyly. "At least we have you."

"Well someone has to disable the Gate, right?"

A sly smile spreads across Jaleera's face. "I know you better than that, Nya. You'd never risk not seeing your home again. It's the only thing that's kept you in line for so long. What was his name again?"

My cheeks burn red hot, and my heart flutters shamefully. I'll not dignify her barb with a response.

I hold a hand over my eyes and squint at the flat pyramid top. From this angle it seems so far away.

"How long do we have?" I say.

"I checked the moon last night. We're five days from Alignment. When the gate fails to open at the designated time, the Magister will quickly realize something is wrong."

"Five days," I repeat absently, wondering what mayhem Jexa can unleash in that time. Will she lay low until the last minute? Or try to scatter our force? At least with Jaleera here advising us, we'll not be easily fooled. No one knows Jexa's methods better than her.

"I hear you squared off with her," says Jaleera, pulling me back to her presence. "Got your mother's spirit, I'll give you that."

My mouth twitches with a smile as I recall how Jexa issued her threat before feigning fear and taking flight, ending the skirmish at the web and granting us our first victory. "Jexa couldn't fly away faster."

"A trick."

"I know. She even told me so."

"Another trick."

"I assumed as much."

Jaleera grabs my wrist, squeezing hard, and gives me a warning look. "You won't be so lucky next time."

"Now that you're here, I don't suppose it's Jexa I need to worry about."

Jaleera's face glows red. She looks to the ground. "I've made my choice by coming here," she says. "This is the side I'm forced to stand with, to whatever destiny we create. Our fates are entwined now." She shakes her head, at me or herself, I cannot tell. "I witnessed your birth, Nya. It would pain me greatly to witness your death as well. When you do battle again, you must avoid Jexa at all cost. Leave her to me."

This order I will not protest. Though Jaleera's confession to killing my mother eats away at me, I cannot deny having her at my side reassures me. Sure, I should suspect her of spying for Jexa, but there is little to gain from this close look. Whatever Jexa needs to know, she can see from a distance with her own eyes. Besides, I believe Jaleera when she says Jexa crossed the line by stealing the Capstone. I also believe she regrets her role in snuffing out my mother's rebellion. Jaleera was amongst the first to be swayed by Jexa's wicked tongue. She clued in too late to the corruption. Too late for my mother, anyway. But not for us. The same ambition that drove her to kill my mother will keep her loyal to our cause. Only by displacing Jexa will Jaleera rise to Marshal. Only then can she restore her people to grace.

Jaleera folds her arms and watches Fori squadrons practice flying in formation above.

"Jexa could kill every Servant on this planet, but it'll

never satisfy the hunger I cursed her with. Klora is the one that got away. The one she can never get back. But I've seen the way she perks up when I mention your name, how much interest she's invested in your growth. How much time she's pondered the reports she receives about you. She obsesses over the day she lost. I swear she'd trade every victory for a single drop of Klora's blood, so much that she'd settle for yours."

"She's had all these years to make her move. Why wait so long?" Why am I still alive?

"She has wanted to kill you since I denied her the chance of killing your mother. Her reputation suffered greatly by my intervention. It is common knowledge amongst our kind, though none dare speak of it. But to kill a spawn, or even a junior dust maiden under her watch, would not have the effect required to restore her image. For that, she needs a worthy opponent. A respected rival to kill in front of everyone, in spectacular fashion. Another Rebel Marshal."

My throat dries as my belly sinks to my feet. "So this is all setting the stage for a duel."

"That's the personal side of it. She needed you to start this war, for her larger design. All she needed was to provoke you at the right time, when your powers started to blossom. Now, when she summons reinforcements from the other planets, they will respond heavily and without hesitation. They will see a swarm of Servants defying the Pact and drop the hammer on them, hard. No questions asked. No mercy."

The world feels as if it's closing in around me. My heart slams against my navel, trying to punch its way out of this cursed body of mine.

"I will try my best to protect you," Jaleera says, "but

battle is chaos. It will take only a single blink to lose sight of you, so you must be prepared to hold her off until backup can reach you."

The possibility of dueling against Jexa with both sides watching makes me ill. I might actually puke right now. If I don't have the stomach for even the thought of it, I doubt I'll fare well in the actual situation. Sure, I clashed with her once before. But she wasn't trying to win then. She was using me as a pawn to rally all the disobedient Servants. But I cannot run when the time comes. That would destroy morale and reverse our momentum. It could even reverse the tide of a battle we're winning.

Looking Jaleera in the eyes with all the intensity I can muster, I say, "Teach me your fighting arts. At least enough to hold Jexa off. Then you can do what you do best, and when she least sees it coming, you can swoop in and drive that spear through her back."

Jaleera's cheeks glow red. I hope it's with shame. "I think that's the best you can hope for. Here."

She offers me her spear. I accept the weapon warily, unsure what dark energies may have attached to this cruel device. But instead of negative vibrations, there's a tingle of familiarity that prickles up my spine. Its shaft is smooth like polished stone, solid, yet light as a feather. I admire the carvings in what appears to be mahogany wood, but is actually some foreign metal I've not encountered on any recent planet. The designs of swirling knots mesmerize me.

"Learn to use it properly," Jaleera says, "and you'll give Jexa the fight she's been looking for."

Holding the weapon by its center, I feel a considerable imbalance. The pointed end is much heavier than the bulbed bottom end. When I give it a swing, the shaft slides in my hand, with the tip shooting away from me until my hand chokes the swollen end. As I do this, I notice the center of the shaft part slightly. When I swing again, this time with more force, the shaft parts enough to reveal a spring at the spear's core.

I swing again and again, even twirling the spear around my back and shooting it forward. The snapping back of the spring produces a loud *ting* each time. It doesn't take long before my movements becomes smoother, more refined. The *spring* and *ting* become the rhythm of my deathly dance, emboldening me more with each thrust.

"Nya the Evening Star," Jaleera says while nodding her approval. "I think your mother was wrong. I think you arrived just when you were supposed to."

NYA

Jaleera must hate me. In the orange glow of the sinking sun, that's all I can think as she presses her attack.

I raise up my spear to block her swipe. She bats it away with her tip, then whacks my shoulder with the blunt end, which forces me to drop my own. The pain is blinding.

Why else would she be doing this if not out of hate?

"Pain is the ultimate motivator," Jaleera taunts, as if she actually believes crippling me will make me a better fighter. "It decides the difference between survival and extinction among all physical lifeforms. You'd not be here if it wasn't for the pain of your ancestors."

I bend to pick up my spear from the grass while warily watching Jaleera for a cheap shot. As my fingers curl around the spear shaft, I can't help but wonder why the Watchers use such primitive tools for their dirty work.

"I think ballistic weaponry would make us much more efficient at our task," I say to Jaleera. I've handled all manner of firearm in my work, turning countless designs of range weapons and their munitions to dust. "Why do you Light Ones choose such a crude means of death?"

"We are not indiscriminate killers, Nya. To ensure the beings we neutralize are not a protected race, we must face our targets up close. Proper identification is imperative. But not only that... To take a life with honor is a deliberate, personal act. One you must experience with the full awareness of your being. Not the flick of a switch or pull of a trigger."

"How noble of you."

Jaleera nods absently as she examines her spear, missing my sarcasm. "These weapons are sacred artifacts, forged and blessed in the name of Light. Each death leaves a mark, a sliver of the damned essence, forever binding the wielder to the slain. After each campaign, our weapons are reviewed in a ceremony by a Sage, who examines each death against our commandments. A sanctified termination is one that serves the ultimate well-being for all life. From that, reputation is awarded. Reputation comes with promotion and elevated status."

"What about punishment for wrongful deaths?"

Jaleera smirks, catching my meaning this time. "Like I said, we are very deliberate in our work. We do not make mistakes."

"You mean, the Priestess who reviews your kills has a high tolerance for miscalculations."

Jaleera raises her chin to my slight. "Have you forgotten my stance in this fight? I agree that a Reckoning is due. That we have lost our way. But all will be made well soon."

All across the barren circle of land that surrounds the pyramids, wood clacks on wood and steel clinks on steel as battle groups hone their skills. Their choppy, uncoordinated movements do not inspire much confidence. Do they think the same of me? Many eyes watched my practice with Jaleera in our early hours, so I had her move us into the forest. But still, a few Fori now watch us from the trees.

"I think you have an admirer," Jaleera says, nodding to one Fori hiding behind a stump.

It's Jinny. She's been watching us since we started, hardly blinking when Jaleera offered me corrections on my technique, but it's not me she's interested in.

The obsession started yesterday morning. Jaleera had gathered all the top-tier fighters—relying mainly on rumor—and taught them close-quarter combat drills, one movement at a time. As the combination of swinging, blocking and thrusting increased in complexity, those who could not keep up were eliminated until only fifty remained. Their names went to Ko Tora to approve as battle group leaders. Then Jaleera ran them through grueling drills all through the night —stabbing, thrusting, swiping—allowing for failure in these rounds until they were good enough to smoothly parry back and forth. When satisfied that they'd gripped these essentials, she sent them to train their followers.

Jinny had been eliminated from the first round because she wasn't fast enough on her feet. But she'd lingered to the side, practicing the skills on her own, swinging a crude short sword of rippled iron through the air until the new battle commanders were dispersed. Now she watches us to learn from Jaleera. Everything Jaleera does, Jinny is quick to practice. Even down to the way she walks with her back rigidly straight and her chin held high.

I'll be the first to admit that if I'd been in that try-out group, I'd have not made it past the first round.

"I don't think my fighting skills are going to inspire many," I say, swinging my spear through the air in a crisscross pattern. This weapon belongs in the hands of someone who will put it to good use. It's clearly designed for a skilled warrior, perhaps a master of an old fighting art, but in my hands the split shaft jars around clumsily.

"Your skills are meant to keep you alive," Jaleera says. "That's it. You just concentrate on your spear and Jexa's."

"Because that worked out so well for my mother," I say, injecting a bit of venom into my reminder.

Jaleera's face sets into a frown.

Now it's my turn to go on the offensive. "Klora must have fought well to have risen to Consul Guard." Before the Rebellion, it was common for the Guard to consist of two Watchers alongside two elite Servants — equal representation for a Council of equal arbiters. "Some say Jexa even made Klora her right hand," I add, taking another stab. For Jaleera, a rising star destined to serve as Deputy Marshal, it must have stung severely to watch a Servant steal her place as Jexa's second-in-command. A Servant had never been allowed to hold such a position. And never would again.

Jaleera takes my jabs with a smile. "There was no shame in being bested by your mother. Any who saw her fight would tell you that."

"Who trained her? Was it Jexa herself?"

Jaleera smiles, but the corner of her mouth quivers. "Klora had a fascination with the races we hunted. She led a double life, studying their combat arts in secret. She'd train with them until the inevitable day that our hit squadrons tracked them down."

This hits me like a blow to the gut, knocking the air from my lungs. "She learned what you were doing, but... instead of igniting revolt right away, she plotted and prepared. For years and lifetimes, it seems. And still... look where that got her."

Jaleera's awkward smile fades. "Klora's rebellion was poorly timed. The Magister's inspection wasn't for another five years. There's no way she could have fought us off for that long. We had time to adapt to her strategies. But fear not. Here, we have both time and numbers on our side."

Something feels off about this revelation. "If she was so sympathetic to these survivors, and knew Jexa's plans, why not warn them of the attacks?"

"She did. Many times she helped them evade capture. But these warrior races, with their pride and resilience, would not tolerate a sustained retreat from their homes. A final stand was always inevitable."

"So she had no choice but to sit back and watch the slaughter."

"Those people lived on through her. She carried their legacy, ensured their funeral rites were honored. There was no greater help she could have given them. And they returned to life every time she took up her spear."

Jaleera's eyes soften as she stares off in reverie. "I'd never seen anyone fight like her. It was the Bo'reni style she'd adopted as the base of her art. And it truly was an art. It took only a dozen of that race to wipe out a whole company of us, so when Klora later employed their techniques in her duel with Jexa, the esteemed Marshal never stood a chance. Her style was so effective that Jexa still spends all her free time meditating over it, reliving the greatest fight of her life, learning from the only being to have bested her."

"Too bad the Bo'reni didn't teach her much about strategy," I say, "like when to start a war."

"Wars rarely start at the ideal time for both sides, no matter how prepared they thought they were. Your mother wished more than anything to give you a better life, one free of the evils spreading from the Dark through Jexa. And things were about to get a lot darker." Jaleera squeezes her spear shaft and lowers her voice. "Jexa had just learned to control her dragon, and she was eager to use it. You've heard of the sky serpent called *Raxor?*"

I nod.

"That beast fed off the sparks of a dozen civilizations before your mother killed it," Jaleera says. Even this mighty Watcher before me cannot suppress her shiver. "Those tortured souls trying to escape the darkness of its innards are what gave the beast its soul-searing fire. The flames from its furnace lungs grew hotter with every vanquished race." She stares at my spear with great intensity. "When a group of Fori refused to cover up a massacre before the Magister's Inspection, Jexa turned the serpent on them. Burned them all in their forest kingdom, three thousand Servants vaporized with a single blazing breath, and their sparks immediately siphoned up in the following inhale."

My people still talk about that day. *The Scorch.*

"When your mother heard of this, it was the first time I'd seen her cry. They were black tears of bubbling rage. Blinding, terrible anger so intense that I dared not stand in her way, even though I knew what she might do. You see, for all her greatness, Klora had the most wicked temper I ever did see. She broke my arm when we were younglings. Never apologized for it."

It sounds like The Scorch drove my mother *Berserk*. It's a spell that afflicts my dust maiden kin, a murderous rage directed at who or whatever triggers it. The only way to break the spell is to destroy the object of their scorn.

"Anyway," Jaleera continues, "when the beast retired to slumber that night, Klora crept into its cave and drove that spear," Jaleera nods at my weapon, "straight through its eye. And with a mighty pulse she turned his head inside out."

My breath catches. I hold the spear out in front of me and study the shaft's carvings.

"After the rebellion, Jexa gave me your mother's spear as a trophy," says Jaleera, solemnly.

Suddenly the design of twisted knots are images, clear to me now. Its spade tip of wavy red steel—forged from the ore of my home planet—seems to glint brighter in the afternoon light.

I press my cheek to the wood-like metal and close my eyes. To hold and feel something my mother once touched threatens to bring tears to my eyes.

"Your mother didn't start that war, Nya, but she took the reins. She steered your people toward hope. So long as that serpent roamed the skies, any resistance was doomed to ash. And if you think your treatment by us has been unfair, you cannot imagine what your people endured before the rebellion. Klora's uprising was too close for Jexa, and that fear remains in her. She's taken great effort to avoid stirring the embers too much. But your intervention left her with no choice. Retribution had to be dealt swift and heavy. At least, that's what she'd have everyone here believe as she sets up the pieces to her crafted war."

I take a deep breath. All this time I'd thought my mother's legacy was a fool's warning. It seems I've inherited a rebellion that's been smoldering in the ashes all along. That's why so many were quick to answer the call to arms. This has been my fate all along. Is that the real reason they call me Princess of Ash? Is it more than just a dig at me and my mother's failure?

My spine tingles. I twirl the spear with both hands. An energy—my mother's fire—burns inside the warm metal of our home. It spreads through me, and suddenly I'm surging with her strength.

I take a deep breath and step back from Jaleera. Gripping the spear in both hands, I smile and say, "Let's fight for blood."

Jaleera gives me a devious grin. She adopts a fighting stance, but before either of us can make a move, wails of despair rise from the pyramids. She snaps to attention and looks straight up.

The treetops sway westward as flocks of Aeri fly past. Hundreds, perhaps all of them, race away from the pyramids.

I crane my head back to watch the migration with great fascination. Strange, because Jaleera had convinced Ko Tora not to send scouts. Jexa would only capture them and squeeze them for information or ransom.

"Wait!" shouts a Fori in pursuit.

"Come back!" pleads another.

Kassini, whose fighting skills had earned her command of one of our fifty battle groups, finds us at the forest edge. She appears on the verge of tears.

"What happened?" I ask.

"Ko Kraal, Grand Chief of all the Aeri flocks, made an agreement with Jexa," Kassini says, breathless, her frazzled eyes darting all about. "She'll forgive them for turning on her if they sit out the fight."

"I guess they weren't confident in our chances," says Jaleera, her tone placid and unsurprised.

Sweat slicks my palms. I have to squeeze my spear tighter to maintain my grip. Was it the offer for leniency that drove the Aeri away? Or did they see something from up high that we have not? Maybe they were never really in it with us. They'd likely taken our side for lack of options.

Damn that Jexa... And damn those spineless air heads!

"Come," Jaleera tells me. "We need to revise our defense plan."

Back at the Great Pyramid, Fori and Ori occupy the bottom third of the structure. They are restless. Despite the loss of our feather-winged Aeri, most remain confident in our defenses and are prepared to fight. It was just the shock of three hundred Aeri leaving at once that had caused the panic. The dust has since settled, and we see clearly that the odds remain in our favor. The only who hasn't accepted Jexa's offer for amnesty is Ko Tora, who Jexa has declared an enemy of the Marshal.

I walk the causeway across the moat toward the Great Pyramid with Jaleera at my side.

"You think she'll order the Aeri to fight?" I ask. Having

the whole lot of them against us would present our greatest challenge. Our finest archers are mediocre at best.

"I'm expecting her to do anything. So should you."

As we enter the perimeter of the moat, a Fori on the pyramid's fifth tier points her spear toward the western sky. "Incoming!"

I turn to see a black dot growing larger over the forest. The winged traveler's course lines up with the causeway on which I stand.

Jaleera steps before me and shields her eyes with a hand to see better. Whatever it is, it's bad, because her shoulders tense. She instinctively takes a step back and walks right into me.

"What is it?" I say, stepping around her to see.

"Jexa."

I swear the hair on my head must be standing straight up.

Jaleera plants the butt of her spear onto the ground by her foot. "Stay behind me."

"To arms!" bellows Ko Tora from behind.

Thousands of feet patter over the stone causeway to our rear. Fori and Ori race across the moat and fan out to either side of the walkway, where they form three ranks on the outer bank.

But while they are preparing to fight, I'm expecting trouble of a more subtle nature. Why does Jexa come here alone?

Ko Tora appears between me and Jaleera, but not half a step ahead. And she's conveniently forgotten her antler crown.

All eyes lock onto the Watcher Marshal nearing the Anomaly's boundary. Like me, they're eager to see her crash to the ground. Maybe she'll land near our battle lines, where some Fori or Ori will get the pounce on her.

We are not so lucky.

Jexa enters the Anomaly and glides to the foot of the causeway, landing in a forward march as if she's practiced this arrival a thousand times. She makes straight toward us, all the confidence of her victories pushing her forward without restraint.

Even with our outrageous numerical advantage, many in our forward battle line instinctively shuffle back in hopes of fading into the rear ranks.

As Jexa draws near, however, I see she is unarmed. This doesn't fool the ranks of Servants into lowering their weapons.

Is she bold enough to believe she can come scout our defenses unchallenged? Maybe she is testing our reaction time.

Or maybe she's here for me. Has the hour of our duel arrived?

My stomach lurches. What if Jexa does challenge me to a duel, with the loser's side forfeiting the pyramid? That would spare a lot of bloodshed, though I doubt my side would allow it, as they know for certain who would win.

My angst must be visible, because Jaleera places a steadying hand on my shoulder. "Stand your ground, Nya. I've seen numerous races accept weakness, but none are kind to cowards."

I raise my chin and keep my face as neutral as possible.

Jexa stops a stone's throw from me. I'm expecting her to address Jaleera, to call her out for her betrayal, but she doesn't spare her former right hand even the slightest glance.

Instead, she assesses the ranks of Fori and Ori to either side of us.

She points to someone standing in line to my right. "I see you."

The Ori quavers back.

Jexa points at a Fori to my left. "And I see you."

The Fori tries to stand firm, but her arms shake so bad her spear rattles.

Jexa continues pointing out Fori and Ori, seemingly at random. "I see *you*. I see *you*, and I see *you*." She points a sweeping finger across our ranks. "I see *all* of you. But my line of sight does not stop here. No," she says, shaking her head. "*Watchers*, you call us. And watching we are. I have eyes on every one of your Hives right now. Many of you left benevolent siblings behind. If you do not return to them by first light tomorrow, every one of them will die. Their blood will be on your hands and the suffering of their souls will haunt you until time's end."

A wave of unrest ripples down the ranks to either side of me.

"You can spare them that fate," Jexa says. "Throw down your weapons and abandon this sacred site, and I'll forget you ever stood against me."

Harsh whispers rise from our ranks, suggesting that a few are shaken by Jexa's threat. The Marshal is peeling away the layers of our defenses, one group at a time. Though many Hives have traveled here in their entirety, we cannot afford to lose those who've left their pacifist kin behind. The fact that none have shot an arrow or hurled a spear at her is a testament to the sway Jexa holds over their mentality.

I step forward. Jaleera grabs my wrist, but I twist it free. Jexa locks eyes with me and smirks.

My intent in coming forward was to accuse her of deceit, but now that I'm front and center, I see my words are better directed elsewhere.

I turn my back to her. Many an eye flare wide at this act of disrespect toward the Watcher Marshal. I point behind me, where I know she is watching, fuming at my insolence.

"She is the mother of trickery," I say. "See the lies laced in her every word. She would not spread her forces out like that, not with the Alignment so close. And for what? To harm the only obedient slaves she has left? What strategic gain would that give her? Think about it. To move against your Hives will only drive more fighters here. But if you leave, you'll not only soften our defenses, but you'll leave yourselves vulnerable to her nets. She will throw you right back into chains and force you to move the Capstone against us."

I look over my shoulder to see she is watching, her eyes narrowed, lips curled in disdain.

I give her a smile and return my attention to the ranks of Fori and Ori stretched out to my left and right. "This is the only chance you will ever get to make a stand. What you face by leaving is far worse than the fate you risk by staying. Dying here in an act of defiance is better than an eternity of servitude. And make no mistake, cousins, that's the best she will ever offer you. She will unleash the Black Tide if given the chance, and you will be the first to drown in its darkness."

"I heard similar words before," says Jexa from behind, "from a dust maiden who looked just like you, a long time ago. You all know what happened to her and the fools she led against me. How many of these good Servants will you lead to their deaths, daughter of Klora?"

My fists clench and my ears burn. I keep my face hard and my chin held high.

Thousands of heads in the ranks before me turn slowly leftward, tracking Jexa as she paces behind me. Many are armed with bows and arrows, but none ready them. I see in their eyes they remain Servants in their minds.

"You all heard the extent of my mercy after that rebellion," Jexa says, "and how I reward loyalty. Until recently, I, too, was a slave, forced to do the Council's bidding. Now that I've freed myself of their control, I have the power to grant each of you your greatest desire. That's right... for your cooperation, I will gift you your Final Gateway. All you must do is step aside. Return to your Hives, sing your songs, and await my invitation to return to your true home."

This offer has many an eye before me opening wide in surprise. Some quickly acknowledge the lie, but a good many seem eager to delude themselves into thinking Jexa will keep this absurd promise.

"Sit back and let me guide you to freedom," Jexa says with outstretched arms, "or follow the fool's heir to eternal darkness."

Thunder rumbles in the east and to the west. Then in the south. A clap to the north, over the sea, almost makes me jump.

"You have until midnight to decide," Jexa says. "Any who remain should spend their final hours taking in the scenery. After I usher the cooperative cohorts through the Final Gateway, I will *nebulize* the entire planet."

I've not heard this word before, but coming from Jexa, I don't like the sound of it. I look to Jaleera for clarification.

"*She'll open a portal,*" Jaleera says flatly under her breath, "to a nebula."

"Searing gas will boil your lungs and eyes," says Jexa. "Nothing will survive, only your tortured souls stuck on this dead world until I decide you've had enough. You will give anything to come back to this moment, to join those who'll now bask in the sunlight of your homeworld. You will beg me for the Dark. Then, and only then, will I show you mercy. I will open a gate to the center of the Dark itself. And you will thank me for that end."

I turn to see Jexa take flight. When I about-face to look upon my fighting force, the three neat ranks are already collapsing into groups as cohorts huddle for discussion.

"Everyone, across the moat!" shouts Ko Tora. She's desperate to keep everyone contained, but none are quick to respond. "Group leaders, on me!"

Only a few peel away from their cohorts to join her.

"This is not good," says Jaleera. She scans the murmuring clusters of Fori and Ori. "You've already lost some, I see it in their eyes."

"Then they were never really here to begin with," I say, thinking of the Aeri. "They'll only weaken the chain in our defense."

Jaleera gives me an impressed smirk. "A refreshing point of view."

We don't have to wait long to see the first takers of Jexa's offer. She is still a dot over the forest horizon when the first dozen Fori flee to the safety of the trees. They leave without announcement and fly low, hoping to slip away without anyone noticing, but their departure draws boos and scolding shouts from the remaining defenders.

At the same time, some remaining Fori hug themselves and shrink away, plagued by inner conflict.

Black clouds close in on us from the northern sea and the forested south. I smell moisture in the air. Lots of it. Soon we'll be shivering in the rain, cut off from the sun's energizing rays, our wings wet and useless even beyond the Anomaly's grip.

The group disappearing into the forest will not be the first to leave. The question is: how many more will abandon us?

I watch nervously from the bridge as a lone Fori paces the picket line, her head hung low as she mutters in self-debate, while most of the others huddle in heated counsel.

"We need the dust maidens," says Jaleera.

"I told you already: they won't join us."

"Did you tell them what's at stake?"

I suspect Jaleera knows I'm lying about trying to recruit my Entropath siblings, and that she means to drive home the consequences of our failure. As if I don't already know.

"Our assured destruction?" I say. "You know who you're talking about? They're not like me. The idea of destroying everything excites them. They'll level this pyramid to the ground if Ko Tora tells them to, laughing while they do it."

"We need only a handful of your sisters to turn the tide in

our favor. Jexa knows the strength of your kind too well. It's why she keeps you all separated."

"Then go get them," I say, my voice ablaze.

"I'm a Light One. They'll never trust me."

"You stand a better chance than me. Ko Skadia was lucky to escape punishment for following my mother." Anger burns inside my chest as tears of frustration blur my vision. "Jexa will not spare her a second time if we fail. Besides, they have it good now. It's in their best interest to keep Jexa in power. It doesn't matter which one of us goes to talk to them; they won't risk losing what they have for an uncertain future."

Jaleera grabs my shoulder. "You have to try, Nya."

I face Jaleera and stare her down. "You don't think we can win," I say. "Admit it. You only want them here to destroy the pyramid."

Jaleera gives me a grave look. "We need a backup plan."

"No, we don't. We need to keep the Watchers from climbing this pyramid until the Magister arrives. We do that or we die trying. There's no other option."

Shouts of outrage and wails of despair rise from within the moat as a group numbering in the dozens—maybe even a hundred—peels away from the line. They fly low toward the trees.

"Cowards!" I shout, my disappointment flashing to rage.

As they disappear into the western forest, I have no doubt we'll lose many more in the cover of night.

CHAPTER 23
DEKA

"A couple of ground rules." Mora addresses us from atop a stump. "Don't go anywhere alone. There's plenty of shade and fresh water here, so no need to go wandering. Always stay in sight of one of us."

"Are there predators we should be aware of?" Marlok cradles his crossbow, eager to use it.

"You would know better than us," Mora replies. "I heard they've been hunting you since we arrived. But the canopy here will provide adequate cover. So long as we're not making a ruckus, we'll be safe."

"Not them," Marlok says. "I mean wild game. *Beasts.*"

"You need not fear the animals here."

"What kind roam these woods?" Huxley asks. "Any antelope?"

"I've never tasted antelope," says Mali, almost salivating.

Mora's expression turns cross. She points a threatening finger at us. "You'll not harm a living thing in these woods, you hear?"

Marlok stands tall. "We are low on provisions. Some of us haven't eaten in days."

"You let us worry about that. Rest assured, all your needs will be met under our watch."

Marlok and Huxley exchange impatient looks. I see trouble brewing in their eyes. They're eager for a hunt. I'll have to keep an eye on them, to make sure they don't do anything to anger our hosts.

Mora sighs in frustration and jumps off the log. She stomps over to Marlok, grabs his wrist, then kneels on the mossy ground, pulling Marlok down with her. He frowns and gives us a wild look, unsure what to do. He's not accustomed to people invading his personal space. It's usually him doing the invading.

We all watch curiously as Mora buries her free hand into the dirt. She keeps Marlok's wrist gripped tight in her other hand while she digs to her elbow, forcing Marlok to crouch lower beside her.

I lean close to the nearest Ori, who is perched on a branch. "What's she doing?"

"Connecting with the Mycelium," whispers the Ori.

This word I am not familiar with.

"It's a thready network of fungus that reaches for hundreds of miles. It is the oldest and wisest organism on the planet. We work with it to ensure our work takes hold and thrives."

I'm surprised my mother never mentioned this network. She must not have known of it.

Marlok squirms and fusses in his awkward position, his frown deepening. I'm sure he's about to tear himself free when his eyes open wide in alarm. He gasps and looks ahead, his mouth agape and stare a hundred miles away. But it's not fear that seizes him.

Elation fills his watering eyes. It's the first time I've seen him without a frown or scowl, so the expression appears awkward to me.

He drops his crossbow and sits into a cross-legged position.

"They're exchanging information," says the Ori in my ear, "to see what your biological composition requires. So we don't poison you by accident. The world has changed since your people thrived. The soil, the air. Even your bodies."

After some time, Mora withdraws her hand from the earth. The Ori beside me slides from the branch and gathers close with the others to hear Mora's message. "There's good forage to the east. Mushrooms, nuts, berries, anything of the like. An apple tree grows not far from here. Start there."

"And bananas?" asks an Ori. "I've seen bunches on the way here."

"Yes," Mora says. "Bananas will do fine."

"Race ya!" says the Ori who'd taught me about the Mycelium to her partner.

Both Ori sprint off into the deep forest.

"You'll be well nourished soon enough," Mora assures us.

Marlok remains cross-legged, staring at the trees in wonder, his gaze softened from the information exchange. He doesn't notice when I steal his crossbow and hide it in a tree trunk.

"I saw you in the tree with your new friend last night," Mali says from behind me.

I jump up straight, my heart racing with fright. I didn't realize she'd been watching me.

"You two looked pretty cozy up there. Don't tell me you're falling for that creature."

Mali only calls them by such names because they are so similar to us that it frightens her. She ascribes a name to separate us. Only our differences matter to her. "We were just talking."

"Her presence in this world is unnatural. Look how that little creature, *Mora*, just subdued my brother. You tell me that's not a spell? All it took was a touch."

My cheeks and neck burn with unease. I'd say Marlok is experiencing a flicker of enlightenment for the first time in his life. Nothing to be concerned about. "You trusted Nya enough to accompany me here."

Mali flashes a grin and draws a knife, the one Marlok had given me back when we first encountered Nya. "Soon she will lead us to our true enemy, and all will be made right."

My throat tightens at the crazed look in Mali's eyes. Is that why she accompanied me? To assassinate the Magister?

"He is not the enemy, Mali."

"He sent them here to kill us."

"He doesn't know what they're doing. He protects people like us."

"Then he failed. For that, he will pay." She offers me the knife. "Revenge for your parents. They won't be at peace until all those responsible are dead."

I accept the knife and fling it aside.

Mali's nostrils flare. "So you continue to walk the coward's path."

I grab Mali's shoulders and look her deep in the eyes. "One day you will see it's 'reason' that drives me."

She shoves me back and jabs a finger in my face. "If you won't do what's right when the time comes, I will."

I watch as she recovers the knife and storms off.

"I do not envy you," says Huxley. He approaches from my left.

"Keep an eye on her," I say. "Make sure she doesn't stray beyond the boundary."

Huxley walks past in pursuit of Mali. "I'm on it. As for you, I'd keep your distance for now."

He doesn't need to tell me twice. There are fewer things I fear more in this world than a scorned Mali.

CHAPTER 24

NYA

The rain holds off until exactly midnight. Not a single drop slips through to warn of the imminent cloudburst so that, when it dumps on us, the ice-cold water shocks me. It pounds down so hard and heavy that it feels like I'm standing under a waterfall.

Deserters use the downpour and the dark to slip away, but we see them in the flashes of lightning, their backs to us in their dash toward the forest. Ko Tora had posted her most loyal followers to guard the causeway in hopes of keeping everyone contained within the moat, to enclose any would-be deserters from escape, but in no time the deluge has raised the moat's water level high enough for those who can swim to cross. Others pull up wooden stakes and cling to them while paddling their way to freedom.

Jinny and Kassini cling to me at the base of the Great Pyramid, shivering in the icy rain, desperate to share body heat. The deafening rattle of rain on steel had forced me to remove my armor. Teeth chatter, sniffles rise, but I don't so much as let my jaw quiver. Instead, I hold my companions tight, because I know they must be tempted to retreat to the forest where they can find dry wood to start a fire, and maybe safety from the real storm that's coming.

The rain doesn't let up for even a blink. The mud at our feet disappears under rising water, which floods in from the river through the moat's canal until we're forced to climb onto the pyramid's bottom level. As the dark hours drag on, I hear whispers of doubt rise louder down the line.

"Jexa forgave nearly everyone who followed Klora," one voice says.

"If Jexa opens this gate, ain't no one gonna be around to need forgivin'," counters another.

Her partner hugs herself and looks to her feet, but I see she's not convinced. I see she'd rather risk fleeing to safety, to take Jexa up on her offer.

To my left, another pleads her case. "Four more days of this? Even if we last that long, we won't be able to fight when the time comes. Those backstabbing Aeri are gonna soften us up too much."

"Shut up," hisses her friend. "You try to leave and I'll gut ya me-self."

Many see what Jexa is doing. More see it than don't, but some do not care. All I can do is hope those who have stayed this long have done so from an unwavering dedication to our cause.

Ko Tora makes a round, identifying the fledgling soldiers and forcing them higher up the pyramid to perform lookout duties, where they themselves can be more easily watched.

Somehow the pounding rain can't keep my body from shutting down on me. Travel and stress have worn me out beyond the point of caring, not to mention the clouds blocking out the sun, so sleep creeps in and takes me without a fight.

I wake to a sight that makes my heart feel like it's being ripped right out of my belly.

Kassini sits cross-legged to my right, hunched over with her eyes locked on the forest through a veil of drenched hair, her nostrils flaring as she fumes. Jinny is nowhere in sight.

"I'll gut that little weasel," Kassini says, "and you can wear her innards as a necklace."

I rub the sleep from my eyes and lean forward to better see down the line, confirming Jinny really did leave during the night.

I pull my knees to my chest and rest my forehead on them. I hadn't really considered whether my closest companions here would abandon the cause. Jinny is stout and hearty, yes, but a defender of innocent as well. Jexa's threat against her Hive must have put a hacking on her heart strings.

When dawn lightens the black clouds to gray, it brightens no one's spirit. All I can do is stare at the dark patch of forest before me, seething and cursing the cowards who followed us here, only to leave us to the enemy without a fight. Jaleera was right. The world has no pity for cowards, and I will see they get theirs if I live through this storm.

But Jinny...how could she? Her desertion makes me sick, though I know I shouldn't judge her too harshly. She defied Ko Mirah's dying wish to come make a stand, and she returned home to preserve what remains of her Hive.

When it's clear the rising sun will provide little more

than a gray tint to the clouds, Ko Tora orders every cohort to form up for a headcount. Normally we'd do this on the ground before the moat, but that area is flooded halfway to the forest, so we stand on the pyramid's steps.

My knees have locked stiff from the cold. It takes a bit of crawling to rise and some walking along the base level to loosen up. When we fall into our lines, we are a pitiful sight. Everyone's wings are wrapped tight around their bodies for warmth, except for the wingless Ori, who hug their neighbors for body heat.

Kassini shivers beside me and looks to her feet. She deliberately avoids even a glance down the defense line. I know she shares my fear. Do we still have enough to put up a fight? Sure, on our side of the pyramid we stand shoulder to shoulder to occupy the three lowest courses from corner to corner, but we're the side that faces the causeway and the nearest forest edge. I'm assuming this is the pyramid face that the bulk of our force have naturally gathered on, to avoid missing anything important.

It takes four attempts to come up with an official count. "Nine hundred and ninety-five cowards have left us!" Ko Tora shouts from seven steps above us, almost victoriously.

I think about this figure. That's only a tenth of our force. Though, with the Aeri gone, we've lost a huge advantage.

Before we can lament too much at our losses, I pick up my spear and whack Kassini's shoulder with the butt end. She gives me a wild look, eyes wide and teeth clenched in a growl, ready to slash me back with her axe. Then she sees from my taunting smile the invitation.

She swings wide, her axe blade turned around so the flat back side would strike me should she make contact. I back away and block her strike. The clatter draws everyone's eyes to us. I shuffle back as Kassini presses her attack, fully aware she's garnered a champion's name for melee skill. The perfect person for my demonstration.

When I reach a shorter stone stacked to my right, I climb up onto the next course. Her axe smacks the block below. From above I easily jab my spear butt into her chest, knocking her down a level.

Jeers rise down the line.

Kassini quickly recovers and looks to a Fori below her. "What are you laughing at?"

She kicks the Fori down to the next level, showing how mighty an advantage we still hold by fighting from the high ground. And with that, a game to practice our skills and lift our spirits is born.

Ko Tora orders the remainder of the idle Fori to pair up with sparring partners and run through drills to warm up. Meanwhile, she sends every Ori out digging canals to drain the floodwaters.

"Ko Tora should dispatch teams to bring those cowards back for trial," Kassini says. "I'll skin that Jinny alive if I ever see her again."

"Don't talk about her like that," I say.

The words slip out without forethought. They draw a disappointed look from Kassini, who shakes her head at me and walks away to find a new sparring partner.

I shake off her spurn and climb the courses in search of Jaleera among the scattered trainees. By the time I reach the twelfth level, above all the sparring, I'm lying on my side and gasping for breath. When I look up toward the apex, my heart quivers. How many courses of stacked blocks did they say there are? Over two hundred?! That explains why only a handful of Fori have bothered making the climb. They came back exhausted and warned everyone else to save their energy.

I scan the levels below for Jaleera's scarlet hair. She is the only fighter who can prepare me well enough to face Jexa. She's nowhere in sight on this side, but this vantage point offers me a view that dramatically raises my confidence in our chances.

Spread out across the lower ten courses, with everyone warming up from movement, our force looks better than half bad. Partners take turns fighting from higher and lower levels, demonstrating just how difficult it is for those fighting from below, as I'd done with Kassini. With us commanding the high ground, we possess a priceless advantage.

The rain tapers to mist by mid-morning. Our Aeri cousins can't dump like that indefinitely and on such short notice. Last night was overkill, and now we have a window to regain ground. Literally.

The Ori work wonders on the land around the pyramids. My initial reaction was to seek out Ko Zola to halt their canal digging, to preserve the new mud flats, to give Jexa another challenge with the Capstone. But Jexa has surely considered the consequences of the rain and saw the moat for a formidable obstacle. I don't suppose it would be too hard to construct a barge or raft capable of traversing the mud.

By midday, the Ori have diverted enough floodwater away to reveal the ground and give us back our moat. They return to the Great Pyramid in high spirits and to much praise from the cheerful Fori. Those who've remained are steadfast in our cause. We see that the threat of the Black

Tide overshadows any perceived threat against our pacifist kin.

I am less successful in my endeavor. Despite an exhaustive search, I cannot find Jaleera on any of the pyramid's four sides, so I'm forced to seek out Ko Tora. I find her crouched over a map sketched in the face of the thirteenth level. Her feathered wings are arched in a dome over her lowered head.

"Have you seen Jaleera?" I say.

Ko Tora's focus remains on her map. "She left last night. The lookouts spotted her heading north, but it was too late to stop her."

My heart drops like a meteor. Was there a secret meaning in Jexa's words yesterday, meant for Jaleera, offering her amnesty?

"You could've gone after her," I say. *She knows our plans!* Ko Tora's Aeri wings can fly higher and faster, even in the Anomaly.

The back of Ko Tora's neck turns red. "She told the lookouts she was leaving under my orders. By the time I learned of it, she was long gone. Besides, it could have been a trap to lure me out. She's a Watcher, after all. It's what they do. Sneak, infiltrate, deceive. Our cause cannot afford to lose me to Jexa, especially now. I'm too valuable."

Her pompous self-perception boils my blood.

To my own surprise, it doesn't take me long to forget about the loss of Jaleera. The drive to stay warm has motivated everyone on the pyramid to move faster and work harder, and the desire to avoid pain sharpens their movements. The clumsy smacking of wood on skin that plagued recent sessions has slowly turned into steady clacking as our fighters learn to block from experience, rather than by relying solely on following instructions.

And watching the Ori spar in the mud below, I see Jexa has created another obstacle for herself. In the soft ground, the Ori move easily, but the Watchers will not be so agile in those conditions. And the Ori's low center of gravity makes them phenomenal wrestlers.

I allow myself a smile. Those we lost through the night were the fat, soft links that would only weaken our defense lines. Those who remain are the real fighters. The muscle.

"Incoming!"

On the outskirts of our defenses, the Ori sparring in the mud stop and point to a Fori flying in from the forest.

The Fori newcomer reaches the Anomaly and lands clumsily in the mud.

"Where's Nya?" she shouts. "Nya! Where are you?"

Despite the distress in her voice, my heart flutters with pride. They seek me out before Ko Tora or any other Elder. She likely fought with me in our first clash against Jexa.

I raise my hand from the twelfth tier. "Up here!"

The messenger notices me and dashes across the causeway toward the pyramid base. I slide down the stone courses to meet her at the bottom level. Her arrival draws a crowd of curious defenders. Running takes its toll on my kind, so when she reaches me she doubles over to catch her breath.

I allow her a few seconds, then say, "What is it, cousin?"

She stands straight, and I recognize her as a roving scout. "Our sentries snared a Fori approaching the pyramids. She claims she was a slave who's been moving the Capstone for

Jexa. She says she escaped Jexa's guards and knows where she's holding the gate key."

Gasps ripple out through the surrounding crowd as the news spreads.

"Escaped?" I say, toying with this word. Is it escape if your captor allows you to flee? "We'll see about that."

"You think she's a spy?" asks Kassini, squeezing her axe handle so tight it groans.

"She might be," I say, "whether she knows it or not. Bring her in."

The Fori who allegedly escaped Jexa is one I know too well, and her reaction upon seeing me raises my suspicion further.

Sheffa is too weak to stand, so when the scouts bring her before me she collapses to her knees. But her eyes light up upon seeing me. "Nya!"

She lunges to my feet and hugs my legs. Her grip is loose and shaky.

I crouch to eye level with her and offer her an amaryllis stem of water. She gulps it back and reaches her free hand out to demand more. Someone offers her another stem. She finishes that and reaches for another, but I seize her wrist.

Sheffa's haggard eyes meet mine.

"Tell us a story," I say. "What have you been up to this whole time?"

Sheffa winces and looks away. She wipes the water from her chin. "It was awful," she says. "When I went to Jexa to..." Her eyes flare wide as she catches herself.

I finish for her. "To turn me in. You went to Jexa to turn me in." Best to show everyone who they're listening to. I see a few onlookers narrow their eyes on Sheffa and rub their chins in contemplation.

Sheffa hangs her head. "That was a mistake. I shouldn't a done that. I was mad coz Squiggs was dead and I thought it was all your fault, but now I know the truth." She looks to the audience around us. "Jexa just needed an excuse to attack. She was gonna take the Capstone anyway. But having Nya to blame... that divided us. It gived Jexa an advantage. I'm proof of that. I's sorry, Nya. But listen, I knows things about the Watchers."

"Things Jexa wants you to know," I say.

"Let the girl speak," says Ko Tora, who'd just shoved her way through the crowd. "Can't you see she's risked her life to bring us this information? We owe her our ears."

Sheffa stands and wobbles, giving Ko Tora a grateful nod. "I knows where the Capstone is. I helped move it there."

My skepticism must be obvious, because tears glaze Sheffa's eyes and she jabs a finger at me. "It's true! We lost many a good Fori and Ori moving that block. They's dead now, some lost to the Dark, and I come to see Jexa pays for it."

Ko Tora slides between Sheffa and me. Much to my surprise, the half-breed Elder wraps her arms around Sheffa and hugs her.

"There there, sweet child. You're safe now."

I'm expecting Sheffa to look stunned, but instead she buries her face into Ko Tora's shoulder. "It was awful!" comes her muffled sobs. "Almost killed me it did. That hunk of gold is so heavy!"

Ko Tora pushes her away, holding her by the shoulders at arm's length. "Where is it?"

Sheffa rubs her eyes. "South of here, inside a volcano. It's Jexa's base."

"South?" says Ko Zola. "That's open desert. We had eyes watching there since the Capstone went missing. We'd have seen you moving it there."

Sheffa shakes her head. "You was lookin' in the wrong place. Jexa got a whole legion of Ori slaves no one knows about. They been building her a network of tunnels since the day we showed up on this planet. Oh, you should see how they live! It's worse than death, it must be. Worse than the Dark itself. You have to save them!"

Ko Tora wipes the tears from Sheffa's cheeks. "We will, sweet child. We shall save them all. Now, tell us about Jexa's defenses there."

"All the Watchers is gathered there now. One thousand of 'em at least. They use the tunnels to travel without drawing attention."

"How deep are these tunnels?" asks an Ori leader.

Sheffa hugs herself. "They's deep. So deep ya forget the sun's light even exists, but ya sweat in blistering heat like you's walkin' on its surface." To bolster her claim, Sheffa shows us blisters covering the soles of her feet. "The floor even glows red in some places."

"They're near the mantle," the Ori says to Ko Zola, who nods in agreement.

I slip in beside Ko Tora, so I have a clear view of Sheffa's expression when I ask my question. "How did you escape a stronghold guarded by a thousand Watchers?"

She meets my stare without flinching. "They was doin' attack drills over the desert. Jexa only left a few dozen to watch the skies, so I escaped through a tunnel."

"Why did no Ori join you? They could have dug their way to freedom long ago."

"They don't know anythin' better. They was born in darkness, and that's how they live. I tried tellin' em Jexa is evil, but they think it's all madness above ground. They think she's some god that protects them from the chaos. They do her bidding without question."

"How did you know where to find us?" I say, prodding her story for more holes. Sheffa had been taken before the fighting even started, long before we flocked to the pyramids. She'd fallen into captivity before we even knew that Jexa took the Capstone.

"I heard the Watchers talkin' about the 'traitors' gatherin' at the gate. She's a feared of ya. Doesn't think she can get here. I heard the words from her own mouth."

"Jexa discussing strategy in front of slaves?" I say with a glance at Ko Tora. "We should assume anything Sheffa heard was something Jexa wanted us to hear."

The senior Elders for the Ori and Fori, Ko Zola and Ko Rantha, each nod their agreement.

Ko Tora ignores me. "It was very brave of you to bring us this information," she says to Sheffa. She then hands Sheffa off to her warriors. "See to her ailments and make sure she gets lots of water. Then find her a suitable weapon, something light that doesn't take much effort to swing."

Sheffa's eyes grow wide with fear.

"Your fight is not yet over," Ko Tora tells her, almost sternly. "You're with us in this until the end, whether you like it or not."

As the Fori lead Sheffa away, I turn my back to her to face Ko Tora. "Jexa let her escape."

"That may be," says Ko Tora, "or it may be not. Either way, we outnumber the Watchers ten to one. We must take this opportunity to seize the Capstone for ourselves."

"Numbers count for less when you march upon the enemy's stronghold," I point out. "That's Jexa's fortress. She knows it better than any of us."

"Which is why she won't see it coming. Right?" Ko Tora looks to her fellow Elders. Zola and Rantha reluctantly offer fledgling nods of agreement. "We have a chance to strike at the Capstone. And we have the element of surprise."

"We'll never get it to safety," Ko Zola says, hugging herself.

"We have a dust maiden among us." Ko Tora looks to me. "We need not move that block a hair's width."

"You'd send me on a suicide mission," I say. The first pulse I send into that gold would blow me to pieces, and she knows it.

Ko Tora opens her mouth to speak, but Ko Rantha cuts her off.

"There might be another way," the Fori Elder says. "The young fugitive said the Capstone is kept inside a volcano. All we have to do is knock it down into the magma, then collapse the whole cone on top of it for good measure."

"There's no certainty the magma will melt the Capstone," Ko Zola says. "It's not your average gold. Its formation is held tight by sacred bonds, designed to withstand any form of destruction—natural or otherwise. So long as there's a possibility the Ori slaves can recover it, we shall live forever under threat."

"Why bother with the Capstone at all?" says Ko Rantha. "It's only half the equation to open a portal."

"A gate can be rebuilt or repaired," Ko Zola says. "The Capstone cannot. Besides, look at this thing." She leans back, sizing up the stone mountain and its two hundred stone courses. "With roughly two and a half million blocks, Nya would have to destroy four hundred and thirty blocks a minute to level the Gate before the Alignment. That's almost seven blocks a second, every second, between now and the New Moon. And that's assuming Jexa waits until the last minute to attack."

"But to damage it beyond function?" asks Ko Rantha.

"A damaged gate can be repaired," informs Ko Zola. "Besides, there are other gates, surely. Backups should disaster befall the main gate in Giza."

My breath catches. I'd not considered that possibility. "Could the Magister not arrive through one of those?"

"Not every gate is capable of interplanetary travel," says Ko Zola with a regretful shake of her head. "Some only have the power to transit between continents. Only three can leave Earth for the stars, and one is at Giza. But they will be spread far from each other, for preservation sake, and will therefore have different Alignments."

"So the only permanent measure to deny Jexa her goal is to destroy the Capstone," says Ko Rantha grimly. But a flash of hope brightens her eyes as she looks to me. "Ko Denia once told me of a master frequency that can destroy anything."

I've heard of this long-dead Ko Denia. She was the greatest Entropath to have ever lived. So great they called her 'Master Denia'. So great that the Watchers released her early from service, after only ten planets.

My breath catches. *Or did they?* Perhaps she grew too

strong, too fast, and became a threat. I'd sooner say her Final Gateway took her to the Dark rather than to our home.

"I fear not even Ko Skadia has cracked that code," I say, raising my wrists to show my marks. "And I am a good way off from her in terms of skill. For me to even attempt it would bring certain death."

"You sell yourself too short," says Ko Tora. "I heard how you destroyed their net during the first clash. How many were clutched in its hold? And not a single life lost, besides the tree it was anchored to. An impossible task, I've been told. You have more mastery of your abilities than you let on."

A few Fori and Ori watch me suspiciously, appraising me and my intentions.

My face and neck burn red hot. "I got lucky there."

"Perhaps with your life on the line, you'll be inspired to become lucky again," says Ko Tora. "With *all* of our lives on the line, perhaps the wisdom of your ancestors will shine through to guide you."

Thunder rumbles in the distance. Over the forest, lightning flashes across a wave of black clouds that sweep toward us.

"We better make up our minds soon," says Ko Rantha, instinctively fluttering the water beads from her wings. "The Aeri are coming in for round two. If you decide to go anywhere after that storm reaches here, it'll be on foot."

Ko Tora pounds a fist against her chest. "I'll lead a few hundred of our strongest flyers to scout out the volcano."

This is a terrible idea. "Even if Sheffa really did escape, we can't divide our forces," I say, trying to choke back my desperation. "Too many Fori and Ori took Jexa's pardon. Our greatest strength remains here, together at our fortifications."

I search the faces around me for Jaleera. I need her support and tactical wisdom in this matter. But her scarlet hair and bronze skin are nowhere in sight. Did she seek amnesty from Jexa as well?

"You give Jexa too much credit," says Ko Tora. "She can't defend the Capstone and launch an assault on the Gate at the same time. She'll expect us to hold up here and await her move."

"The Magister is coming in just a few days," I remind everyone.

"Even better," says Ko Tora. "Without the Capstone, Jexa can't call in reinforcements. She'll be of little threat before his arrival."

"And when he gets here, what then?" I say. "If it's Jexa who greets him at the gate because we sacrificed our position to hunt down the Capstone, and he asks her what happened? She'll pin the Consul's murder on us. That lie alone will condemn us, but the truth about the Capstone will be the end of us all. That's sacred stone. Destroying it will make us enemies of the Magister."

"Then we shall prevent his arrival altogether," says Ko Tora, her voice lower and more restrained.

This draws surprised looks from her elder counterparts, Ko Zola and Ko Rantha. I can tell she wishes to hold a private council with them over this, because now we speak of sedition against our supreme protector and authority.

"With enough dust maidens," Ko Tora says, "we can destroy this gate in good time. It'll be another thirteen years before any of the other two gates is in Alignment for his arrival, more than enough time to find and destroy them. With cooperation from Nya's kin, we'll cut this planet off completely. On Gaia, Repenters outnumber the Watchers one hundred-to-one. I'll take those odds any day. By destroying the Great Pyramid to seal ourselves here, it will only be a matter of time before we wipe out Jexa's army."

"We'll be stuck here forever, though," says a concerned Ori.

Ko Tora gives her a sympathetic look, though I see the sarcasm in it. "Would it be so bad, little clay digger? What's the difference between this planet and the next? Because make no mistake, that is our fate under Jexa. She dangles the promise of returning home before us, but it will forever remain out of reach."

Some younger Fori exchange wary looks.

"Don't believe me?" says Ko Tora. "Ko Zola, tell the good Fori here how long you've served *The Light Ones*."

"Ninety-nine times!" shouts an Ori follower. "This is her last planet."

Ko Zola gives a regretful shake of her head. "Four hundred and twenty-two lifetimes," she reveals.

I give the Ori Elder an incredulous look. She must have misspoken. How could the Magister let that happen?

"And after which gate crossing were you to see your home?" says Ko Tora.

"Was the same as the rest of you: one hundred." She rubs the black band on her forearm. "They stopped marking me a long time ago."

Her words leave me speechless. It seems the Magister has less oversight than I believed. Is it possible the Watchers could keep something like that from him? This also begs the question: who's to say the Pact even says one hundred planets? What if that's only to give us hope, the illusion of a bright future?

The Fori shift nervously, overwhelming terror rife in many eyes.

Ko Tora continues. "Ko Rantha, how long have you tended trees for the Watchers?"

"Five hundred and sixty planets I've seen," Rantha replies, raising two arms that are each black from wrist to shoulder. "It's true about the marks. They shuffle us around to different Hives or planets so no one figures it out."

"The Watchers, for all their renown in assessing ecosystems," adds Ko Zola, "did not foresee the decline in our population when they separated us from our mates. And when they started killing us for punishment, with no means of replacement..." She gives a solemn shake of her head. "If they sent us home, the Magister would notice a decline in his workforce. Their tyranny has upset the balance in so many ways. So, so many ways."

"And if they suspect you'll reveal their dirty secret?" asks Ko Tora.

"They wipe your mind clean and start you over."

I hear my own gasp as a distant echo. My head swirls. That can't be. That would mean at some point I could have completed my hundred-planet-Penance already.

Questions and possibilities shake me. Did I refuse to keep up the farce and they sent me back through the cycle? If what they claim is true, I could have served my hundred planets a hundred times over, in an endless cycle of servitude. Penance served and then restarted. Is that why I'm so fed up with it?

Ko Tora gives a satisfied nod and looks to her followers. "So now you see: our only chance to ever have a home is to make one for ourselves. That means cutting this planet off from the network and overthrowing the Watchers stationed here. The only way to do that is to destroy the Gate and its Key." She raises her sword. "Who's with me?"

Shouts and spear tips rise in the breaking light. Some of the faces seem uncertain at first, but as the cheering grows, so does their confidence. Reluctance turns to conviction, which scrunches their faces into anger.

"Stop!" I shout, throwing both my hands into the air.

They ignore me and chant on, hefting their spears high.

"You're all fools!" I say.

This gets their attention. The mob is in no mood for insults.

Nearly nine thousand pairs of eyes fall on me. Some furious, others curious. A good enough mix to sway the crowd.

"It's true," I say. "We outnumber the Watchers by many times. But Jexa is a Lord of War. If she's managed to divide us when we were at our strongest, she will continue to do so long after we're stranded here, until we are all destroyed."

Ko Tora points an angry finger at me. "She's afraid!"

The way she speaks with her hands, with such flare... I see what she's doing. She's been doing it since the night they arrived to our bonfire after the first battle, flashing her thick bands in a constant reminder. Appealing to the Hive mind. *See my Marks*, she says. *Hear my wisdom.* An Elder's word is sacred, more precious than air itself. I notice the eyes of a few flick my way, to size up my wrists. They can't help being obvious about it. Even in regular conversation, I've noticed if someone makes a claim, the first thing someone does is examine their stripes. My thin black bands do more talking to their programmed minds than my words ever could.

I clench my fists and feel my cheeks burning. "I am not afraid. I'm thinking about the future. What you do will bring irreversible consequences."

"It's too late for that, dust maiden. Where was your consideration for consequences when you stopped the Watchers from killing those apes? Did you think of the consequences when you trapped Jexa's fighters in a cave?"

My fists throb with rage. I can see from the nodding heads around me that Ko Tora has already split our force too greatly. At least half will follow her.

"But the daughter of Klora is right about one thing," says Ko Tora. "The Capstone will be well defended, so we'll need everyone we can muster for the raid. If any remain here, you do so to little effect. If we all fall on that volcano, the rest of you will not stand a chance here without us."

A shining truth comes to light in my mind. The plan to seal off the gate here forever requires one thing that I control.

"You're forgetting something, Ko Tora," I say, loud enough for all to hear. "To destroy the Capstone you need a willing dust maiden. I am the only one committed to our cause. And I refuse to do your bidding."

I try hard to contain my gloating smile. Then I try to contain my curious frown when a sly grin stretches across Ko Tora's face.

"Will you do it for the sake of your precious humans?" she says. "I've heard about your infatuation with them. They make pretty pets, I'll admit. But I'll not shed a tear to burn them out of their hiding place. How long do you think they'll last in the open when the Watchers come to pick them off?"

My breath catches. A few Fori join me in surprise and despair. Ko Rantha clutches her chest and says, "The trees... You wouldn't."

Ko Tora spreads her hands in resignation. "That is up to the daughter of Klora. I leave their fate in her hands. A simple lightning strike is all it would take to set ablaze their sanctuary." Ko Tora expands her wings to remind us of her power to command the thunder and the rain, and how many forest fires start from lightning strikes. She says to me, "If you destroy the Capstone, I'll see they live long and happy lives. They'll flourish in these lands under my rule."

Ko Tora's loyal enforcers position themselves on the pyramid steps above. Others crowd around some senior Fori in an intimidating manner, to keep silent any who may seem poised to speak out.

"But if you disobey me now, I will make sure they turn to dust and ash like everything else you've ever touched."

Fury boils in my belly, steams in my chest, and brings tears to my eyes. "You're no better than Jexa," I say, my voice cracking.

Ko Tora looks off into the distance and narrows her eyes in thought, as if evaluating my claim. She nods faintly. "One thing you can't deny about the Marshal, she knows how to get her way." She addresses her loyal soldiers and nods back toward me. "Bring her with us."

My heart thumps and my legs tighten like springs, ready to launch me into flight. Ko Tora has lost it.

Watching her followers' hesitation nervously, I raise my fists, which inspires more reluctance. They know what these hands of mine can do.

Their reservation loosens when my mighty hands start

shaking before me. They also suspect what I know deep inside my heart—that I'd never be able to harm one of my own.

I bend my knees and prepare to launch into the air, but someone bear hugs me from behind, pinning my wings to my back.

"When the time comes," says Ko Tora, "I know you will do what's right."

"Let go of me!" I shout. The arms constrict around me and stifle my heaving chest.

Ko Tora's muffled voice breaks through the commotion. "Bind her hands to her sides," she orders, "palms to skin. We can't have her wasting that talent on foiling our plan."

"Stop fighting, Nya," says one of my assailants as she forces my arms to my side, so that my left palm presses against my hip.

"I'm sorry," says another as she huffs to straighten my other arm to my side. "Please, just relax."

They act as if they care about me. They'd have me believe we were still friends, even as they coil wet vine around my torso, cinching my arms tight and my hands even tighter to my body, so that the only vibration I can send is to myself. The anger of betrayal swells in me.

I spot Kassini through the crowd, both hands gripping her axe handle. I'm tempted to summon her to my rescue, but I see in her eyes that she knows what I realize. If she helps me, she too will end up a captive or worse, dead. Ko Tora's enforcers shoot threatening glares at her and anyone else who appears poised to save me.

"Ko Zola," says Ko Tora, "have your Ori search the surrounding area for Jexa's tunnels."

"No!" I shout. Further divide what force remains at the pyramids? It's folly. *"Ko Zola, don't do it! You need to watch the pyramid!"* That's what I want to say, but the sudden pressure around my chest chokes me off, so that when I move my mouth nothing comes out.

They ratchet the vine around me tighter. I have so many colorful words to spit at them, but my heaving is restricted by my bonds, which suffocate me.

The coil tightens around my chest.

Anger turns to panic. I can't breathe! Someone points this out as black spots bloom across my vision, but it's too late. I fall into darkness.

CHAPTER 25

DEKA

When your race is teetering on the edge of extinction, every birthday becomes a big deal. It's a chance for your tribe to celebrate one more defiance against a promised demise.

This fourteenth celebration of mine will be one to remember. Not just for myself, but for all of humanity. Later generations will speak of how, on this day, my people broke down long-held barriers and made an ally of an enemy. All while traveling to give our tribe the greatest gift of all: freedom. And it all came without spilling a single drop of blood. My mother's methods will no longer be the ways of a fool. Science and progress will once again bring happiness to my kind, and humanity will once again smile in sunshine.

But this vindication is still a way off. For now, I'll be happy with the gifts and the pleasantries. Even Marlok doesn't deny me my day.

He claps me on the shoulder and sits on the log beside me. "You must think you're pretty special, getting a fire for your birthday."

I smile at the warmth cast from the crackling flames on my face. The smell of burning wood stirs a sense of nostalgia in me, though it must be wired into my genes, because I know it's been a long time since humanity had the luxury of wood to burn.

"A gift we all seem to be enjoying," I say, looking at nearly a dozen of my tribe's warriors seated around the fire in the twilight.

"Mali told me about your birthday gift competitions," Marlok says. "You set the bar pretty high with those goggles. Should have saved those for a later year. How did you do better than that since then? She never told me."

I crack a smile and recall Mali's last five birthdays. Marlok is right. I'd set the bar too high, and was forced to get more creative with gifts the following years. That meant moving away from material things. Like, for her fourteenth birthday, I snuck her out on my boat under a sky full of stars, to a cove where glowing algae had invaded the entire inner harbor and the stream running inland. The bloom was so thick that the surrounding hills glowed purple. But, even now, I dare not risk ruining the mood by telling Marlok I'd defied him back then by sneaking her out on the water.

"I think Mali kept it a secret for a reason," I tell Marlok, and offer him a sly grin.

He frowns at me, then looks up to the treetops.

"You celebrate the day you were born?" asks Mora. She crawls up from behind and squeezes in to sit between Marlok and me. "Why?"

"Because life is a gift," I say, "to be treasured. Each breath is a miracle."

Marlok doesn't look convinced, nor does the Ori.

"Well," says Huxley from across the fire, "you'll have a hard time beating Mali's gift this year."

It's only now that I notice Huxley has joined us at the bonfire, and that Mali is nowhere in sight.

"Where is she?" I say.

"It's a secret." Huxley lowers his gaze to sharpen a stick with his knife, but this doesn't hide the envy in his eyes.

I stand and look around, scanning the trees for Mali's surprise. It's been a while since we had our fight, when she stormed off. Huxley wouldn't just leave her after being assigned to watch her, so she must be near. What's she working on?

Marlok rises beside me, concern on his face. The serenity that had graced his eyes since Mora introduced him to the Mycelium is swiftly replaced by alarm. He sizes up our group, as if breaking from a trance. "Hux, where's Mali?"

"I told you, it's a—"

Marlok pounces over the fire and grabs Huxley by the shoulders. He gives him a shake and says, "I'm not playing around! Where in the hell is my sister?"

Huxley spreads his arms in surrender. "Fine! Don't tell her I told you."

Marlok bares his teeth and growls with impatience.

Huxley points to his rear. "She wanted to give Deka a birthday feast. One we'll all remember. She spotted tracks leading that way, so—"

"She went hunting," I say, almost in disbelief. "I told you to watch her!"

"She what?" Mora jumps to her feet. Not even the dirt smeared across her face can conceal the blanching of her cheeks. They're as white as the rolling surf. "You were warned!"

"I tried to go with her," Huxley explains, suddenly realizing his error. "But she shooed me off. She always shoos me off, even here. You know how she can be."

Our Ori guardians scatter in the direction of Huxley's indication, the group fanning wide like pellets from a shotgun blast.

Their reaction inspires a sense of dread in me as I join the pursuit. Marlok scrambles for his weapon, but can't find it. He snatches Huxley's crossbow and is close behind, while the others grab their weapons and race out to either side of me. Marlok is much faster and emerges ahead of us humans, but he slides to a stop when a shriek rises from beyond the trees ahead.

Cold sweat slicks my skin. That's Mali's cry. I've heard it before, when she played a joke on me in the tunnels of our home. Our familiar, predictable sanctuary.

This gets my legs pumping faster than ever before. I barely give myself enough clearance to round the trees, instead bumping into sturdy trunks in my straight-on dash. They stand firm and send me stumbling, but I hardly let up in my sprint.

The Ori's shorter legs do not hinder them in the least. They move faster than our fastest runner and reach Mali first. When I arrive at a clearing, three of them are wrestling a thrashing Mali on the ground. Mora leans over them while shouting instructions on how to immobilize her.

"Grab her legs!" Mora says.

Marlok aims his crossbow at the three Ori on top of Mali.

"Let her go!" Marlok orders. His crossbow shakes in his

hands. I've never seen him so rattled, and I fear he may accidentally loose an arrow.

The Ori pinning Mali to the ground freeze and then straighten to give Marlok curious looks. Stepping forward, I see their captive isn't Mali at all. It's one of those tree-tending folk that resemble Nya in almost every feature. *Fori*, she'd called them.

This Fori thrusts her hips upwards in an attempt to break free of the three Ori holding her. "Murderer!" she cries, her throat tight with sorrow and rage.

I follow her line of sight to a beast on its side. A male deer. I've seen the crown of antlers in mother's books. A crossbow bolt protrudes straight up from its still neck, and a blank stare suggests the animal is dead.

Wheezing draws my attention to my rear, to where Mali lies amongst the ferns. I'd overlooked her when I caught sight of the Ori wrestling the Fori.

Marlok shoves past me and drops to his knees by her side.

My whole body goes numb. I drift toward Mali in a daze. Lying on her back, she's staring at the sky, her eyes wide in pain and shock, her mouth open to draw breath that comes only in shrill gasps. When I step around Marlok, I see a wooden stake driven up under her right ribcage.

I kneel beside her and take her hand, but my own is so numb that I don't feel her skin against mine.

"M-Mali," I say.

Her eyes fall on me and her chest heaves higher, trying to inhale, but the surrounding air ignores her summons. It's her body's last attempt to save itself. She falls still and the pain in her eyes freezes to fear.

"Go get the medicine," Marlok tells me.

I stare at her lifeless body in disbelief. "She's—"

Marlok shoves me onto my back and presses a knife to my throat. "She's not! Now go get the medicine. Use your precious words to save her."

Mother's book on anatomy and physiology never interested me much, but I've read enough to know the severity of this wound. As a warrior, Marlok knows this too.

He clenches his teeth and tightens his grip, but neither act can hold back the tears in his eyes. They spatter on my cheeks and mix with my own.

He stands and marches to Mora and her Ori. They step back defensively, rightfully wary of his emotional state.

"Where is it?" he says, scanning the ground with both arms out wide, a knife in each hand. "Where is that creature?"

"We let her go," Mora says.

"You what?!"

Marlok looms over Mora threateningly, and though he's more than twice her height, Mora stands her ground.

"That Fori was defending an innocent deer. Your sister had no right to take his life. If you and your kin care to join her, make a move. You'll never make it out of this forest alive."

Marlok leans back and hurls a blood-curdling scream at the sky. He pulls his hair out in clumps.

This all happens in a blur around me. All I can do is watch her unnatural stillness, a quietness that sucks out all the warmth from my heart, leaving my blood cold and my chest hollow. This can't be my friend. My eyes play tricks on me. Or she is in a state of shock, frozen, and soon she'll snap out of it.

I lay on my side next to Mali and try pulling her shoulders square with mine, like we used to do when the northern drafts blew down the caverns of our sanctuary. The days of innocence we shared before she became a warrior were far too few. That was when the only warmth she needed came from me and not from the blood of her enemy. But now her body is stiff, and she won't move. So I curl into her side and try to keep her warm, in case she changes her mind and decides to come back with a second wind.

Please, Mali, come back. It is the last birthday gift I'll ever ask for.

CHAPTER 26
NYA

They must have given me a sedative, because when I wake, the battle at Jexa's stronghold is well underway.

My vision is blurry, but I can make out a black cone rising from gray wasteland three leagues away. I blink a few times to focus. A ringing sound grows loud in my ears.

"Get her up!" comes a muffled voice. "They're almost in!"

"Go easy!" replies a calmer voice at my side. Her pale arm waves away the source of the first voice. "If Ko Tora wanted her ready so early, she'd have let me give her the hype plant when I suggested."

"Look! There's the signal! Quick, give her another dose of the hype!"

A finger slides into my mouth and rubs cool jelly across my inner cheek.

I'm not sure if it's the stimulating plant medicine, or having someone's dirty finger in my mouth, but suddenly I'm vaulting upright with a surge of energy and disgust. My heart thumps fast and my vision sharpens.

"Welcome back," says the first voice. She grabs my arm to help me up, my movements made stiff and heavy by the plates of curved steel strapped to me. Someone had the forethought to put on my armor. Couldn't have anything happen to me en route to my demise. But it was done in haste and fits me awkwardly, straps done too tight in some spots and too loose in others. "Come on, girl. Ko Tora needs you. Can you fly?"

I wobble on my feet and wipe the thick crust from my eyes. Can I fly? I can hardly stand. How long was I out?

I blink a few times to focus on the volcano. Its dark slopes stand sharp against a cloudless blue sky, where black flecks swirl and clash like quarreling flies, with a few falling to the ground.

"Jexa?" I say, my voice hoarse as words crawl up my dry throat. "Watchers?"

"Our scouts saw them training in the south. Hurry, there isn't much time."

As my vision sharpens, I see much of what Sheffa had said appears to be true. Squadrons of Fori fly in arrowheads in pursuit of the stronghold's lone defenders—mostly Aeri and a few dozen Watchers—who are effectively separated by the Fori flying in the formations that Jaleera taught them.

I breathe a sigh of relief. Jexa really didn't expect us to do something so rash as attacking her stronghold after so many of our fighters had abandoned us. Now I feel silly for having doubted this plan and for putting up such a fuss. But it's not too late. I can dump the Capstone into the lava to buy us time. At least then it can be recovered at some point. Nothing of this world can unravel its sacred bonds. And if Jexa claims the gate before the Alignment, and somehow disables it to deny the Magister's arrival, we can somehow, some day, find a way to recover the gate key from the volcanic depths and locate a backup gate to send a signal to the Magister.

Yes, it's all clear to me now. I will not make myself an enemy of the Magister by destroying what is not mine to destroy. So far I have done nothing wrong by his laws. Even my acts against the Watchers were in defense of the *sapiens*. I will happily explain myself for that. But to stand trial for destroying sacred artifacts? Not a chance.

My wings buzz and lift my feet from the ground. Flying is easier than walking, so I get to it by speeding toward the volcano. Depending on where the Capstone is, I should be able to destroy its support and drop it down into the fiery earth. We can worry about how to retrieve it later, once we've neutralized the Watcher army.

But the closer I and my escort of twelve fly toward Jexa's base, the more winged bodies I see lying motionless on the ground. Many litter the volcano slope ahead. It's a wretched sight, with the occasional twitching wing revealing those who need help, so I keep my eyes locked on a glowing orange slit in the flared-out base of the mountain.

It's not an easy task to fly straight. The grogginess of the sedative lingers and hits me in waves. A few times I slam into my wing-mates flanking me.

We arrive at the entrance unchallenged. Hot wind blows out from the tunnel, where five of Ko Tora's warriors wave me inside. Heat blasts my face and blows back my hair as I follow them through the passage, heat from the same source that provides the orange glow that lights our way. My skin feels like it's about to slough from my bones and reduce me to a puddle, while the heat intensifies my grogginess.

Ringing steel echoes from high inside the cone. Ko Tora greets me inside the entrance, where a ledge surrounds an orange lake of swirling lava. The Aeri Elder's face is black with soot, which makes her smile unnaturally white when she sees me.

She points to the center of the lake. "There it is!"

She's right. On a platform held by chains anchored to the walls, suspended only thirty feet above the scalding lake below, sits a thirty-foot-tall pyramidion. Waves of orange light ripple across its polished surface.

"Don't worry, Nya," she yells over the clamor of the battle above, "you're stronger than you think. You can destroy the Capstone — I believe in you. Everyone here does. All that sacred bond stuff is just a lie to deter you. Do what you were born to do this one last time, then we'll all be friends and forget about what brought us here. Now, follow me."

Behind her, an Aeri falls and hits the lava with a splat. She wails and writhes as she sinks in the boiling liquid, her feathered wings bursting into flames.

"Are you with me, Nya?"

I snap my attention from the Aeri and give Ko Tora a few eager nods. She raises her sword and shouts, "To victory!"

I leap from the ledge. My wings flutter instinctively, but I only need them for steering as the thermal pressure from below lifts me across the molten lake. I reach the platform of suspended rock with little effort and land behind Ko Tora.

"Hurry," she says, "destroy the Capstone before word reaches Jexa."

Right. I must work quickly before Jexa returns from her training.

Ko Tora looks straight up and shouts orders to her warriors fighting above, directing them to scatter a cluster of Aeri regrouping in a crevice.

I make my way to the nearest chain. I just need to unfasten one of the four to tip the Capstone into the lava. With a boost from the thermal pressure below, a last-second warning is all Ko Tora will need to take flight.

I kneel beside the anchor point and touch the chain, feeling its frequency, determining what disruptive vibration will shatter its bonds. But... wait.

A realization stops me. *Training?* The grogginess clears from my mind. *Why does Jexa need to run her Watchers through drills?* They've fought lifetimes alongside each other. Flying in formation is their nature as sure as it is with migrating birds. Same with an eagle attacking prey. They don't need training. Each is a born killing machine.

"Nya, what are you doing?" says Ko Tora, her eyes wide and wild.

I stand and march to the Capstone. My hand trembles as I reach out to touch its surface. Pushing a fingertip to the hot metal, instead of the warm shimmer of gold, I'm met with a dense, muted sensation. It takes only the whisper of a vibration to send the pyramidion slumping into a mound of dust. Its avalanching slope buries me to my knees.

I turn to catch Ko Tora's horrified expression.

"It's lead!" I shout. My words echo up the hollow cone, loud enough that I hope they spew out the top and reach the Great Pyramid, to warn its meager defense force.

But I am a fool to hold such hopes. Yet even so, on this mountain, I am the least fool of all. And everyone watching me buried to my knees in dust knows it.

Ko Tora's jaw hangs slack. She shakes her head in disbelief.

I stomp out of the counterfeit Capstone's remains and step toe to toe with her. "It was lead, you idiot!"

I raise my hand as if to smack her and, to my surprise, she throws up both arms and turns her head away.

The sight of her trembling gives me pause. Does she actually think I'd dust her? I must appear somewhat unhinged for her to believe I'd ever harm a Ko Elder. Though, if an Elder ever deserved it, it'd be Ko Tora. Her wisdom is measured only by the numbers that follow her.

I lower my hand. "This is—"

The platform sways under me, its chains rattling. Rocks rain down and splash into the lava below.

And so the snare tightens, no doubt the work of Jexa's Ori slaves Sheffa had told us about. Superior in their craft they must be to collapse an entire volcano on command.

Ko Tora snaps out of her stupor. "The mountain is coming down! Everyone, out!"

The chain anchors explode from the walls. As the platform drops from under me, my wings buzz fast as a hummingbird's to lift me above the fountains of lava splashing from below.

Ko Tora zips straight for the entrance, risking falling debris from above and lava splash from below. She disappears into the exit just before it collapses.

Rocks pelt me from above. A boulder slams my shoulder

and drops me, so I raise my hands to shield myself. Panic already has them surging with a wild frequency. I close my eyes and fly straight upward, trying to ignore the screams of those falling around me, rising and pushing through shock waves. I don't dust all the rocks, just the bigger ones, until I burst free of the collapsing volcano and up into the sky.

My upward flight slows as gravity seems to shift. The caving mass of earth creates a suction that drags me down with it, so I fly sidelong, blind in a storm of ash and dust. It's so disorienting that I think I'm flying at an upward angle until I crash onto rocky ground. Here I bury my face into my arms as a tsunami of dirt and volcanic ash washes over me. As the blanket of debris grows thicker, I try to slow my breathing, but soot clogs my nose and dust fills my lungs.

After the wave passes, I sit up and shake the ash from my wings, but I find breathing no easier. In fact, I can hardly see farther than my own outstretched hand.

I fly straight up into the air to avoid suffocating. It takes a rise of one hundred feet to clear the dust. The cloud is still thickest where the volcano was, but it cannot hide what is left in its place. A sunken pit thrice the size of the volcano's base now reaches deep into the earth. It descends into darkness as far as I can see, but I feel as if my spirit has sunk even lower than the lowest depths of that pit. Jexa's Ori slaves are masters of destruction in their own right, using their skills to the opposite effect of Mora's kind.

I hover for a long while, watching a few survivors rise above the cloud. Less than one hundred. We've lost the bulk of our fighting force within seconds. How many thousand had followed their foolish leader here?

Ko Tora hovers half a league away from me. "Back to the pyramids!" she orders.

Many are already flying hard north.

"Wait!" shouts another voice from below. Kassini rises up to meet Ko Tora. "Listen!" She points to the pit, where I now see the edge had been bored out in a perfect circle.

I cock my ear toward the hole and hear shouts rising from the darkness.

"Help us!" shout voices, thousands of them.

"We'll need them at the pyramids," says Kassini, wide-eyed and breathless.

"We don't have time!" says Ko Tora, and her wild eyes warn she is on the verge of unraveling. "We need to race the Watchers to the gate."

"Jexa is probably already at the pyramids with the real Capstone," I say, trying hard to keep a lid on my rage. Further rattling Ko Tora will serve none of us well.

"It's too early," Ko Tora says, turning her back to the hole and the voices rising from it. "The Alignment is still three days away."

"She doesn't need to be on time!" Anger swells in my chest and up my throat, heating my words. How could she have not figured this out by now? "The Alignment is only for the Magister's arrival. Jexa plans to open a portal to every world that hosts a Watcher army."

"Can she really do that?" asks Kassini. "I thought only a Consul could open a gate."

"*Anyone* can open a gate," I point out. "Only the Consul can do it safely. Jexa may open a portal to anywhere. Another planet, the void of space, a sizzling gas cloud, a *Black Hole!* If she's allowed to activate the gate, she could collapse the whole Universe in on itself."

"It will take time for her to do that," says Ko Tora, her eyes wide and wild. "Many gates to open, to many planets, to summon the Black Tide. We can still stop her. We can retake the pyramid."

"We built up the defenses there and then abandoned them," I remind her. "If she takes the pyramid, she can hold it from us for as long as she wants. Look at us. We might have hundreds lost down there, and thousands more scattered, gone for the trees with no looking back."

"So we need our numbers back," says Kassini, nodding eagerly as she reinforces her point. "As many as we can get. And there are many more below who have plenty of cause to fight Jexa."

"The Ori slaves," says another Fori, noting the pit's perfectly round edge.

By now, a crowd has gathered around us, the buzz of excited wings clearing pockets of floating ash.

Ko Tora's expression sets. "You're right. We shall not return empty-handed."

It takes great effort to keep myself from throttling her. Is she really trying to make this sound like a victory?

"Everyone, split into search teams," says Ko Tora. "Let's go guide them back into the light."

She flies down into the pit with two dozen surviving raiders behind her. I'm lingering in the rear, but I stop at the hole entrance. Heat rises from below and tousles my hair, blasting me like a furnace. Cold sweat covers my body.

Looking into that great abyss feels like staring into the Dark itself. Already Ko Tora and her party have disappeared.

Swallowed whole. If something happens, if the walls collapse or if we get lost in the labyrinth of lightless caverns, no one would ever know what happened to us.

"Where are you?" rises a shout.

"I can't see the surface!" comes another. "It's too dark!"

The shouting fades…"This way!" growing fainter with each second…"I can't see!"…until…nothing.

It's so silent I hear the dust settle around me.

Then it hits me like a battering ram, knocking the wind from my lungs. What if this is another stage to Jexa's plan? The real trap? To lure us into a Dark crafted of earth and stone on our own free will would be the ultimate stroke of genius. Her *coup de grace*. And the fools dove headfirst into it!

Well, this is one suicide mission Ko Tora will not drag me into. I won't do it. They may have cost us this war, but they will not take my life with it. I am not ashamed to declare my fear of the dark and all its forms.

I rise away from the hole and fly hard toward the green line of forest tracing the northern horizon. I tear at the straps fastening my armor, flinging the plates free, lightening my load so I can make greater haste.

Somehow, the farther I fly from the pit, the louder the voices of its captives follow me.

"Save me, Nya!"

"Don't leave us!"

"Where are you going? Please, come back!"

"Coward! Get back here!"

"We need you!"

I cover my ears and scream for them to stop, but it doesn't

work. When I close my eyes all I see is their faces screaming at me in the dark.

"Get out of my head!" I shout.

They ignore my demand and continue, pleading for my help.

When I open my eyes, it's just in time to see the rough bark of a tree. I slam into it at top speed, and the impact puts a sudden end to my madness.

CHAPTER 27

NYA

If my desperation to distance myself from that pit wasn't obvious enough, all one needed to do was look at my wings. Even after slamming into that tree and rendering myself unconscious, my wings kept me flying in a state of subconscious navigation, so that when I wake, I'm buzzing over the treetops, still traveling northbound.

The collision seemed to have knocked the voices from my head, at least. Now a loud ringing is all I can hear. I'm abundantly grateful for this. At least now I can think.

Having stared into Jexa's makeshift Dark has left me with a new view on life. I could have been lost down there, but I'm not. I'm still free and alive. Every breath I take is a blessing. I have a future, however short it may be, and I will cherish every heartbeat from this second forward. I will no longer fret over distant lovers, nor shall I lament the future of my race. In doing so, my standard for joy has decreased dramatically.

That whack on the head also made clear what I must do. I will round up survivors, starting with Mora and her Ori.

They'll dig out a marvelous sanctuary, where we will live with Deka and his folk, all of us, deep within Gaia. The Fori will devise a way to grow vegetation down there. They've succeeded in this on the dark side of tidally locked moons. They will do it underground here, as well. With any luck, the Black Tide will miss us. When Jexa's army of darkness moves on to the next planet, and they nebulize Earth, we shall remain safe underground, in our fabricated paradise. And perhaps some day, after many years, we shall resurface to begin life anew.

I smile and even allow a laugh, though I'll admit this laughter does sound a bit crazed. But these are crazy times. To endure, one must become a little mad. I've been adapting to planets for ten lifetimes. This is simply an adjustment of a different kind. Besides, this seemed to have been my fate all along, trapped on a foreign planet, never to return home. At least, it's the kindest one I can hope for at this point. I'd resisted every other option, yet this one kicks my heart into a hopeful dance. And even if this wasn't my destiny, I shall make it so.

My optimism, however, evaporates when I reach the *sapien* hideout. I feel the gloom long before Mora races out to meet me. It's thick with emotion, like fog over my heart.

"It's not a good time," she warns.

That's an understatement if there ever was one, though I'm surprised to hear she's referring to Deka. Against her urging, I order her to take me to him. I find him and Marlok carrying a body wrapped in fabric through the forest toward the sea.

"It was a rogue Fori," Mora says. "A deserter from the pyramids. She told us about Jexa's offer. Is it true?"

I nod, but I don't notice her reaction. All I can see is Deka carrying a corpse that belonged to his friend.

"They're taking her body home," Mora tells me. "They don't belong here."

That last part Mora said is true, which makes her first claim impossible with their current technology. They certainly do not belong here, but they cannot take her body home. Not to her true home, anyway. Because Deka's ancestors were not born on this planet.

I look up through the canopy, to the bulging seam of stars in the night sky. The first *sapiens* came from somewhere out there. I've seen artwork on other planets that bear near identical resemblance to Deka. These images rise more clearly from the depths of my memories every time I see one of these *sapiens*. And how am I so sure those other races have not originated here? Well, the premature oxidation of their bodies is evidence enough of that. The original *sapiens* must have evolved elsewhere, on a planet more in harmony with their physical make-up. Of that I have no doubt.

Watching Deka struggle with Marlok to carry the girl's body, I'm trying to understand why they'd waste so much energy relocating it. This collection of organic molecules is just a vessel. A container that no longer holds the spark that once gave it life. It will do better nurturing the forest, becoming one with this planet.

I approach. "Deka..."

His shoulders hunch at the sound of my voice. He sets the girl's remains down, forcing Marlok to do the same. When Deka turns, his teeth are clenched and his face is twisted in animal rage to the point that I hardly recognize him. He points a condemning finger at me and says, "You stay away from us."

I place a hand over my heart and recoil. "I—"

"You did this," he growls. "I'll not have your curse harm another one of my kind, you foul creature."

His tone shocks me. This is not the Deka I know.

"This wasn't my fault."

Deka's face twitches and his expression softens. Tears glaze his eyes, and I see it's disappointment that tames his anger. "You said we'd be safe here. You *promised*. You said your people would watch over us and they didn't. Now Mali is dead. Our kind don't come back from death like you do. This is final." His lips quiver as he draws in a shuddering breath. In a flash, his rage returns in full. "Are you hearing me? It's permanent! She's gone! Forever!"

He stares at me expectantly, awaiting a response, but I struggle to find the words.

"I—I'm...I'm sorry," is all I can say. The words sound foreign leaving my mouth, so much that I'm not sure I've ever said them before. But it's true. I am sorry. Everyone I've ever tried to help ends up worse than when I started. Why haven't I learned this yet? I should have stuck to what I'm good at and left these poor folk alone. Oh, Mother of Light! How many more races have I unknowingly done this to? How many more will suffer in my quest for satisfaction?

"You're all demons in disguise," he says, and his words are laced with pure hate.

I take a step forward. "Deka, you—"

He raises his crossbow and aims it at my belly. "I curse the day I ever set eyes on you."

These words pierce deeper than any arrow ever could.

Tears well in my eyes, and it takes everything in me to keep them from spilling over. I see now more than ever that I should have stuck to what nature made me, but it's not too late. I can't bring his dead friend back, but I can give Deka's colony a bright future.

He gives me a disgusted shake of his head, then he and Marlok pick up the corpse and continue to carry it toward the sea.

I do not know where a *sapien* spark goes when it leaves its body, but I take comfort in knowing hers can't be in a worse place than the dark underground where she'd spent most of her life.

To Mora, I say, "Keep an eye on them. See them safe from the forest, then you may do as you please."

"Where are you going?"

I look down at my hands. "I was made for one thing. I now see how to use that ability for good."

"What will you do?"

"I will destroy the gate beyond repair. Neither the Magister nor the Black Tide will see this planet so long as I'm alive."

"You'll go alone? What if the Watchers are already there? And even if they aren't, word will spread quickly."

"Then I'll finally give Jexa what she's been looking for." I wipe tears from my eyes. "I will meet her at the gate, my mother's spear in hand, and do my best to buy us time. With any luck, I can distract her long enough to allow the Magister's arrival. If that's what it comes to."

Mora's eyes widen in alarm. "Even if the Watchers don't swarm you, a one-on-one with Jexa would end in..." She catches herself before she says anything to insult me or my abilities.

"She has waited so long for this encounter," I say, "she will not be able to resist the theatrics. Even if I arrive late, and she's about to set the Capstone onto the apex, she will ensure all eyes are on us. I'll make a grand display of words for all to witness. An exchange that will echo through the ages, will be Jexa's hope. A moment to solidify her supreme authority over all resistance."

Mora's eyes glaze with the deepest sorrow. "I don't suppose there's anything I can say to stop you."

I shake my head.

She wipes her eyes and clears her throat. "We'll escort the humans from the forest. You have my word. When they're gone, I'll head for the pyramids." She cocks her head with a sniffly laugh. "I will say, this isn't the worst idea you've ever come up with."

Laughter is what escapes my mouth. Ridiculous laugher.

"Goodbye, Mora."

With that, I rise into an eastward flight, back toward the Great Pyramid of Giza. I will destroy that sacred structure block by block, level by level. By choosing the right stones, I may even save myself a lot of effort and topple it. Sure, it's millions of blocks placed strategically to withstand the trials of time and disaster, but it's not impossible. Though my lack of enthusiasm and practice for my work has left me the weakest dust maiden on Earth, it's never too late to strive for greatness. And what better project to learn on. If this works, I'll be a legend among my kind.

And if Jexa interrupts me in my work? Or if she's already there with the Capstone? Then I can still buy us time until the Magister's arrival, by offering her what she wants more than even the Black Tide.

A duel with the spawn of Klora.

When you're racing toward your death, you gain a new appreciation for things you never gave much thought to before. Like the ocean. I've never really given these massive bodies of water the credit they deserve. Yet I've never been to a planet without one, which leads me to believe life cannot exist without them.

On this day, I follow the coast to draw in as much of the salty air as I can. No sunlight sparkles off the water to my left, but the gray sky at this hour rivals the most beautiful sunshine to grace my memory. The trees to my right pulsate with life in the misty air. I swear I hear every one of their leaves rustle in greeting as I pass. At the border of death, I have never felt so connected to life.

This splendid flight doesn't last long. I'm not even halfway to the pyramids when I become too heavy for my own wings. This fatigue hits fast and drags me down until I'm crashing onto the rocky shore, where I roll short of the water line. On the ground, with my wings clasped around my chest and belly for warmth, I notice a thick film of water covering them, which certainly didn't help. That alone would bring me down.

The exertion of the past few days has my body feeling as if every cell has turned to stone. I can't even flip over onto my back. Not that it would matter, anyway. With the mist now turning to rain, I'm not going anywhere any time soon. All I can do is lie on my belly as the tide creeps toward me. I have given more than I had to give, and it wasn't enough. I have pushed my limits too far for too long. Or this could be the hype plant wearing off. Perhaps it only temporarily overpowered the sedative, which I suspect they'd given way too much of. Whatever the cause, it does not matter.

Deka's harsh words ring loud in my head. *Foul creature,* he called me. Did he really mean that? Yes, I think he did. His tone left little room for interpretation. Fortunately I'm too tired to dwell on it.

The swish of the rising tide soothes me. My eyelids slide down easily and disobey my orders to rise again. What's the point, anyway? I let sleep take me. I am so tired. I have been for so long.

This is one darkness I go into without protest.

When my eyelids seal shut, I realize I may not wake up, and I would consider that a mercy. I've heard stories of Servants being worked to death, and now I myself know the feeling. This is the most peaceful ending I could ever hope for.

***

It's well past midnight when I wake. Somehow I'd slept through the rise and retreat of the tide, because I'm soaked with salt water from head to toe. I'm about to close my eyes to resume my slumber, but a familiar feeling tingles my spine.

I'm being watched. I know this feeling too well. I sit up and turn to see Jaleera sitting cross-legged on a rock shelf beside me. She stares wistfully at a glittering column of silver light on the water, sunlight reflected by the sliver of a crescent moon.

"Where were you?" I say. My voice comes out hoarse and barely audible.

"Recruiting Ko Skadia." Jaleera turns her face to reveal a fresh scar from the top of her newly-clipped ear, to the corner of her mouth. A gash across her shoulder shows where someone almost cleaved her arm off. "No easy task, I assure you. Together we set two more of your sisters free. They're gone to round up the rest. They'll be less guarded, but they're scattered far and wide."

I sit up all the way and wipe sand from my eyes. "How many?"

"Jexa executed those she thought might join the rebellion early on. Now, thirty at best."

I perk up, hope surging through me. "That's enough to destroy the gate."

"A noble endeavor," Jaleera says, "but I'm afraid that's no longer an option. Jexa began her attack on the pyramid while you were raiding her stronghold. She overran the defenses and is raising the Capstone as we speak."

My shoulders slump. "Then it's over."

Jaleera lowers her head. All the answer I need.

"Ko Tora?" I say.

"Only one of her scouts managed to escape the abyss. Left her wits down there, they say. The rest are lost in a maze of tunnels. Thousands, gone."

My eyes swell with tears for every one of them. Yes, even for Ko Tora. No one deserves such a horrendous fate. Not even the Elder who led them there.

"Jexa has created a Dark of her own inside the planet's

crust," says Jaleera, confirming what I already knew. "A hole so deep and absent of light that, once you are lost, there is no coming back. Mind separates from body. Madness fills the void."

I shiver at the thought. That could have been me down there.

"You shouldn't have left us the way you did," I say, trying to spark fire into my voice, but it only comes out damp. "You should have told us where you were going."

"I didn't want you to rely on your sisters joining the fight. They are heavily guarded. I got lucky freeing Ko Skadia. And even still, they may not make a difference."

Her words and excuses fade to the back of my mind. "Ko Tora and the others... at the pyramids... they'd have listened to you," I say, almost in a murmur, "Now they are lost. We have lost."

"I have seen enough battles to know that you are right." Jaleera rises with a spear in one hand, a round shield in the other. Barely covering her from waist to shoulder, the silver plate is comically small. "But I will go make a stand anyway. I will die as I have lived. At least now I know what I'm fighting for."

If the Watcher who drove a spear through my mother's back is expecting an emotional farewell from me, she is in for a disappointment.

"You know how I always find you, Nya?"

I say nothing. It doesn't matter now. Soon nothing will matter.

"Your light shines bright wherever you go," Jaleera says. "Even the darkest dark cannot dim that spark of yours. That is the greatest truth my kind have kept from your people."

I frown up at her. She looks away.

"Watching you grow has been my only joy," she says. It must be the way she has her head turned that chokes her voice. "You were the light in my darkness."

I want to laugh. Does Jaleera really expect me to believe she has a heart? But no laughter comes from me. And though I have little love for the monster that betrayed my mother, I take no comfort in the fate she has assigned herself.

"Did we ever have a chance?" I say.

"Jexa knows too well the danger of a united enemy. If it wasn't the counterfeit Capstone trick, she'd have found another way to divide you."

"So you knew we were doomed from the start? And you gave me that push to fight anyway?"

"We had to try, Nya. Do you know what will happen if Jexa opens that portal out of Alignment? She may unleash any manner of disaster upon this planet—a solar storm or noxious gas cloud, the vacuum of empty space, or who knows whatever else. That's why the Consuls are so important. Only they can see through the fabric of space-time. They keep the coherence. When you reach through space, you also reach through time. And when you reach through time, there's no telling what you'll pull out, nor what consequences you'll sow. Their training takes eons. To carve the path through chaos and establish a stable connection between gates requires the greatest mastery of mind over matter. And even for those properly trained, doing so still requires the correct Alignment. That part is imperative."

I'm glad I'm too worn out to process all this horrendous news. It's nice to be numb to it. I pray this apathy remains when Jexa opens the gate, and I hope that whatever manner of devastation she invites here makes a quick end of us all.

"You were right," Jaleera says, "we should have stayed together. All of us. I should never have left, and you shouldn't have lied about trying to recruit your sisters." Her voice flares with anger, but she steadies herself. "Anyway, this is no time for blame or regret. My hour has come. Farewell, Evening Star."

I say nothing as Jaleera flies away, only slap a rock with my hand. It bursts into shards, which land in a nearby tide pool. Bioluminescent algae glow purple where the rocks sink. *Sea sparkle.* I envy such an existence. To be beautiful and ignorant of your impending demise must be so blissful.

If only we'd stayed together. If only... No, that way of thinking is for fools. I cannot change what has already passed. Jexa will set the Capstone soon and the only force that can stop her is lost. They are lost, and I am glad I am not among them in that abyss.

I am not among them.

They are lost and I am not among them.

I stare into the tide pool, its water so calm. An eyelash falls from my eye and lands on the surface. A tiny purple flash responds to this change in its environment. It's hardly noticeable and lasts only a second, but it's enough to give rise to the flicker of an idea. No, not an idea. *Madness.*

I poke the surface. My disturbance sends glowing ripples spreading outward. I laugh and hear the madness in my voice. I latch onto it. Reel it in. I embrace the insanity, for I shall need every bit of it I can handle.

I will bring light to the darkness.

CHAPTER 28

DEKA

Mali once told me a true warrior never grows old. If dying young is what makes a warrior great, then she's earned her place among the finest. It didn't matter how many words Marlok recited from his holy book. It didn't matter how many times I begged her to stop playing dead.

Still, though she has long turned cold, part of me refuses to accept the finality of it. She is Mali. She has been a part of my existence for as long as I can remember. Without her, what am I? She can't be gone.

Shrouding her in a sail doesn't help. Not seeing her lifeless body feeds the fantasy that she'll come back. That it's not *her* who is wrapped tight in this gray canvas that I carry through the dark forest. That she'll jump out from a nearby tree and tackle me to wrestle her goggles from around my neck.

I steal a look up at the swaying treetops. For all its beauty, this is no paradise for us. Our place is in the colorless abyss, where we must endure the punishment for the faults of our ancestors.

We reach the shore and set Mali on the sand. We do so gently, as if she might complain about our rough handling. Everyone seems to breathe easier here in the open, without those giant wooden sentinels looming over us.

It's about midnight, and I wonder if the slim crescent moon reflects enough sunlight for our enemy to roam above.

"We have about five hours before we'll need to find cover again," I say. Five hours when the enemy will be less likely to roam the skies without the sun fueling their flight. This knowledge I gained from Nya, and I should be thankful for it, but gratitude may lead to a measure of forgiveness. That I cannot do. Yet...this refusal conjures a measure of guilt in me.

I shake my head and scold myself for allowing such a feeling. That demon deserved every venomous word I spit at her. Not only did she lead us here knowing the dangers of this world, but she even tricked us into thinking it was safe.

While Huxley and the others drag our boats from the tree line, I scan the sea for danger. A glittering wedge of moonlight obscures a large area over the water surface, so I pull Mali's goggles up over my eyes. A smudge across the left lens darkens my view, but I dare not remove it. I'll make this voyage home half blind before I wipe away any sign that Mali once lived. That the body at my feet once moved and breathed and wore these goggles to shield her seeing eyes from the sun, and at one point those now-stiff fingers wiped a fly from this lens.

Mora follows us onto the beach. "You should leave her remains here with us."

I shudder at her voice. All of Nya's kind should leave us alone. Can't they see we grieve because of one of them? I shoot her a rueful glare, yet she remains insensitive.

"Her body will do more good nurturing the soil," the Ori leader says.

The ice caps will cover the poles again before I leave what's left of my friend in this fool's paradise. Besides, we'll have our own soil to nurture now. At least for a little while. Hopefully the colony has filled every piece of scavenged plastic with rainwater. Mali's sacrifice will not be in vain. She will enrich the soil, which in turn will give us food that will fill our bellies. I will thank her for every bite. I'll remind Marlok to ensure everyone else pays her the same respect.

Huxley and the gang lay our two boats at the water line. Waves splash the polymer hulls.

He takes a drink of water from a clear jar, then passes it to Marlok.

"Is that all we have?" I say.

Marlok takes stock of our belongings and shrugs. In our hurry to leave the forest, we forgot to refill our drinking water. I can see he's too distressed to give this oversight the weight it deserves, but we'll not make it far with what we've got. We can't count on a storm to top us up like on our voyage here.

Marlok orders Huxley to go get the water jars we'd left behind.

"No way am I going back there," Hux says.

"I'll do it," I say. The thought of depending on something from that forest for our survival makes me ill, so it's best I just get it over with.

Without the weight of Mali's body burdening me, I'm able to reach our abandoned camp in good time. At least, I think this is where we'd held up. There are the black coals from my birthday fire, and the logs arranged in a circle for seats, but the jars we'd kept our medicine and water in are nowhere to be seen. Perhaps the Ori took them as souvenirs. If so, I need to get them back.

Whispering catches my attention. I creep close to a large tree, the one Nya had me climb, around which some Ori argue.

"Even if she destroys the gate, we'll still have the Watchers to fight."

"Assuming Nya even goes through with it. What did she take those jars for?"

I clench my jaw and ball my hands into fists. In another act of treachery, Nya has stolen our water containers. Does she think that will keep us from going home? Or is she counting on us to attempt the return voyage without them? Either way, she'll end up killing us all without spilling a single drop of blood.

"She didn't say why she needed the jars," an Ori says, "but she'll wreck the pyramid if it guarantees a victory over Jexa."

"Even if it means killing herself?"

"No one really knows that's what'll happen."

"Sure it will. I saw it once. An Entropath tried dusting an archway, only, she had no idea it was laced with sacred lonsdaleite. She blew apart right in front of me."

A long silence ensues.

My jaw goes slack and my heart slides up into my throat. Nya is going to sacrifice herself for us? And the last words I said to her...

Something I never thought possible happens on the walk back to the beach: I return with a heart heavier than when I'd left. Under the light of this same moon that glitters off the sea, I have cherished two people in ways that all the words in my mother's books could never describe. Today I lost one when she sought out a present for me. Now, another goes to certain death to offer me an even greater gift.

In my absence, Marlok and Huxley have laid Mali in the main boat with her crossbow on her chest. Words from our last argument stab at my heart: "*So you continue to walk the coward's path.*"

I grab her weapon and drop it into the boat that she and I had both taken here, then drag my small vessel away from the others.

"What are you doing?" says Marlok. The rage in his eyes is suppressed only by a measure of surprise.

"I'm going to the pyramids."

"The hell you are!"

"Mali knew what she risked by coming here," I say. "And if she could speak right now, she'd call you all cowards for turning away from this fight."

Marlok's upper lip curls in animal rage. Huxley glances between me and Marlok, shifting nervously.

My next words may be my last if I'm not careful, but I risk more by backing down. "By abandoning this cause, you offer her the greatest of disrespects. You'd say the quest she died pursuing is not worthy of your sweat and blood. You all know that if you or me or every single one of us died out here, she'd honor us by carrying on to the bitterest end. *Better to die fighting than hiding*...that's what she believed. And make no mistake, when you return home to our colony, that's what you'll be doing. *Hiding*. Even if you fire a few arrows into the sky, all you'll be doing is playing *hide-and-seek*. It's time to stop playing."

My fists clench so tight at my sides that my knuckles crack. "You all rush out to face death on our home soil, hoping your blood in the sand will buy yourself glory and our people a little more time. If that's what you consider victory, then you'll find no better arena than at the pyramids. There you will face every demon that has hunted our kind. There you'll find the only fight that will ever bring us freedom." I raise Mali's crossbow. "If it is death that awaits us, let us die as the hunters, not the hunted. Let us give that *Jexa* a fight she will never forget."

Marlok crosses his arms and appraises me with a mix of scrutiny and wonder. I'd spent my whole life shunning the warrior spirit, but now it is not only I who goes forth. Mali's spirit lives on with every beat of my heart, and she was a warrior until her last breath. Her fight will live on through me. Because now, I've seen that there is a time for caution, a time to think and evaluate—and there is a time for action, to be bold and courageous and put it all on the line.

Now is that time.

Marlok lowers his fists to his sides. But instead of reprisal, a faint smile lifts the corner of his mouth.

"We will return home victorious over our enemy," he says with a nod, "or we shall not return at all."

I couldn't have put it better myself.

"Well, in that case," says Mora, always eager to intrude on a sensitive moment, "you'll be wanting these."

She offers us tunics of silver. Only, as I take one in my hands, I notice this steel garment bends. It's too soft to be armor, yet, other than providing a bit of warmth, how will a shirt serve us on this daring mission?

"Bark spider silk," Mora explains. "It's the strongest

natural material we've come across on this planet. We didn't have enough to outfit all of our own fighters, so none dared wear it. Solidarity...or something like that. But there's enough for all of you, so it's yours now."

I slide the shirt on. It hangs loose, so Mora steps behind me and quickly reworks the material, jerking and jarring around my waist and under my arms, until it hugs me perfectly. Her three workers fit the rest of our warriors with this silky armor.

I notice Marlok staring at Mali's wrapped remains.

"We should bury her here," I say, sizing up the tall trees. "It's a peaceful place." *Even though it killed her.* But it's better than the battlegrounds to the east, or our desolate caverns to the west. Not like we'd have time to bring her home, anyway.

Marlok gives a faint nod of approval. I know he'd put up more resistance to my suggestion under different circumstances, but even in his grief he knows that our current situation leaves us with no better choice.

"We'll prepare her a grave," Mora says, then motions for two of her Ori to get digging in the tree line. She joins Marlok in looking at his sister's body. "Soon she'll be one with her Mother. What remains of her will break down until what was once dead reforms into life anew. She'll emerge from the cold earth a sprout, and once again she will feel the sun's warmth. She'll grow tall into a tree that will stand strong against even the fiercest winds, and..."

Marlok raises a hand to silence her. Mora trails off, then turns her attention to me.

"You'll travel by sea?" she says.

"Does the Nile still run inland?" I recall the river from

old maps, but much has changed since their use. It may have dried up for all I know.

"It passes less than a league to the east," she replies. "You can tell by the dry bed it's a trickle of what it was, but it's enough to get us to the Giza plateau. But..." she bites her lip, "it runs *into* the sea, not *from* it—south to the north."

"So we'll have to fight the current," Marlok says.

"Won't be much of a current," Mora says, "I can assure you that. Can you fit a few wee ones like us in your water craft? We're fairly light. Plus, I think we'll make fair paddlers."

"You can ride with me," I say. We'll need every hand we can muster to reach the pyramids in time, and even that may not be enough.

CHAPTER 29

NYA

The empty jars from the *sapien* camp come in handy. I buzz around a meadow gathering fireflies into the glass containers, but I'm catching more than just glowing insects. The jars that I've already filled with *sea sparkle* should provide more than enough light for my crazy endeavor.

Curious eyes watch me from the trees surrounding the meadow. Many have no doubt seen me before, in battle or at the pyramids, before they abandoned our cause. I no longer blame them for that. Fear is a powerful master of the mind, as I've seen myself. But soon there will be nowhere for them to hide.

Surely they wonder why I now play in a meadow so far from the fight.

I fill a jar with fireflies so that it glows neon green, then set it with a pile of jugs full of octopus bacteria. I'd ordered my Nixy cousins to retrieve me some before coming here. Having sensed a disturbance on the surface, even from their watery depths, they had messengers linger near the coast in wait for news. When I'd told them all that was happening, they were swift to fulfill my request.

In the night, the glowing light reaches every tree around the meadow, illuminating the faces of a dozen Fori watching me. It's a big enough audience.

"By now many of you have heard of our failure," I say. "But our fight is not yet over. I need your help to rebuild our ranks, so we can stop Jexa from seating the Capstone."

Some recoil. Others break straight into retreat, leaving only rustling leaves and shaking branches in their place.

"I'm not asking you to fight," I say, wishing I'd chosen my previous words better. "We have enough fighters. I just need your help retrieving them."

A few step out into the open.

Sheffa emerges at the forefront. "I ain't a coward, Nya. I was at the pyramids when Jexa attacked, and I held my ground for as long as I could. The Watchers and the Aeri... they overrunned us so fast. You can't expect to beat them."

"If Jexa opens the portal at the wrong time, there will be nowhere safe for you to hide." I proceed to enlighten them on the many manners of destruction Jexa may invite into this world with a misaligned gate opening. "So you see, your only chance is to help me."

I hold up a jar of purple *sea sparkle*. "Come with me to the edge of darkness, and help me find our warrior sparks. Then you may go back to hiding under whatever rock gives you comfort."

The gathered Fori exchange wary looks.

"I cannot do this without you," I say. "If we do not stand together now, we are all doomed to fall."

Sheffa approaches and kneels beside my pile of glowing

containers. She picks up a jar of fireflies and watches the floating green orbs absently for a long time.

Finally, she nods. "We got no idea what'll happen if we follow you, Nya, but Jexa misaligning the gate will bring us to a worse end. You've made that clear enough." She stands suddenly, clutching the jar tight to her belly. "I'll follow you to the edge of that dark. Just tell me what ya need."

Word of my folly spreads quickly. Hundreds of Fori gather around Jexa's Black Hole to watch. Many are eager to help. They fashion a tether of vine and hemp that stretches for miles, with many flying off to farther woodlands for more material to weave should I require greater range.

Working among them, swiftly and silently, is Jinny. When our eyes meet and she realizes I've spotted her, her cheeks glow red with shame and she whizzes away in search of more material.

I fasten the tether end around my ankle, securing it with a quadruple knot. But, standing on the rim of this perfectly round hole, not even a million knots would make me feel secure enough. My heart thunders and feels like it may explode from my belly. I shake a jar of sea sparkle to produce a purple glow.

Sheffa sets a basket of the remaining light jars at my feet. She must see the fear in my eyes, because she places a comforting hand on my shoulder. "We ain't goin' anywhere till you get back with all them lost ones."

I force a smile. "Well, then, let's not keep them waiting any longer."

I slide my spear through the handles that loop across the top of the basket of jars, then tie the spear horizontally across my waist.

Like jumping into cold water, I waste no time delaying and dive headfirst into darkness. It envelops me before I can allow regret to dissuade me. A layer of blasting heat greets me for the first few seconds, then fades to a still chill.

My wings flutter instinctively to slow my descent. The jars dangling from my waist clink and come to life with light. They reveal my own body and nothing but impenetrable darkness around me. I drift slowly, falling ever into oblivion... falling...falling...falling...until my tether tightens and jerks me to a stop. I cringe at the clinking jars.

A distant voice echoes from above, telling me to wait. So distant. When I look up, I see only a faint circle of light the size of my thumbnail.

I shake a jar of sea sparkle and take comfort in its glow. As I wait for the Fori to weave more line, I feel the darkness below pull on me. Gravity is heavier here, I swear it. Or maybe it's something else.

Before I can think more on it, I'm falling again. I clutch the jar of glowing algae to my chest and use my wings to control my fall, allowing some slack in the line above me.

Twice more I jerk to a stop, dangling in darkness, then fall again until something other than a shortage of rope stops me.

My feet hit solid ground and I scream at the unexpected sensation. The floor is sloped and I struggle to find my footing. It's useless. I slam onto my butt with a crash, literally, as glass shatters all around me.

I slap both hands over my mouth to stifle a scream. *Why does everything I touch have to break?!*

My muffled moaning travels out into the dark around me and comes shouting back louder, screaming words I thought I'd only thought. *"Why does everything I touch have to break?!"*

"Why does everything I touch have to break?!"

I hear those words several more times as echoes fade into the far reaches of the abyss.

Sitting amongst a pile of broken glass, I lose control of my breathing as purple streams of glowing bacteria carve a trail over stone ground into the darkness below. Above me, specks of whirling green light grow smaller in the dark until it swallows the fireflies altogether.

This can't be happening. Not a single jar has survived my clumsy landing. I can't stay down here without my light sources. *I have to go back!*

I spring to my feet and grab the safety line. I'm about to fly upward when voices echo from the abyss behind me. I squeeze the mended vine to my chest and listen.

Only my own thundering heart and rapid breathing grace this void. Were those voices in my mind?

When I bend my knees again to take flight, a shriek almost sends me rocketing upward. But I lock my knees and keep my feet planted on the cool rock.

Soft purple light glows from behind me, illuminating a perfectly bored hole in the wall ahead, the outer edges framed in a violet radiance. My shuddering shadow stands to the left of the passage. I turn to see the glowing bacteria has pooled in a dip where another tunnel slopes upward, casting its biological brilliance around this cavernous intersection.

Grabbing a few pieces of broken glass, I rush to scoop the glowing liquid into them. But even the biggest shard can't hold enough to produce much light, and any movement sends what's there spilling over the jagged edges.

Panic rises in me again. There's no way to harness this light I've brought, no way to bring it with me.

A voice echoes through the dark. It speaks my name. Or does it?

Yes. It's Jaleera's voice, rising from the depths of my memory. *"You were the light in my darkness,"* she says.

That's it!

Without another thought, I'm on my back, rolling in the glowing wetness, shivering as it coats my skin. When I stand, I hold my purple hands before me. I wriggle my glowing fingers and smile.

I am the light in the darkness.

I step forward into the black tunnel. Faint purple light pushes back the void ahead, revealing rugged rock walls that form a rounded tunnel. I push on, relieved to see the dark retreat from me. Empowered, even.

I pick up my pace, trotting fearlessly toward the retreating dark, until I emerge into a grand gallery. The hollowed cavern is about one hundred feet in diameter. In the walls along its circumference are round patches of blackness, each another passageway. Each another way to get lost.

"Hello!" I shout. My voice echoes down into the dozens of voids. "Ko Tora? Anyone?"

"HELLO! . . . KO TORA? . . . ANYONE?" are the deafening responses. They blast back so loud I'm forced to cover my ears. Then, nothing.

Perhaps they split up and lost their way. In the pitch

black it would be impossible to find the exit tunnel. It looks identical to the rest. So much that I'd not know it myself if not for the vine rope attached to my ankle.

"Hello! It's Nya! Come to my voice!"

Again, my own voice responds. This time it is not alone.

Footsteps patter in the darkness.

"Shhhhh!"

At a tunnel entrance to my left, a Fori crouches and looks above warily. As I approach, she recoils back into darkness.

"Wait!" I say. "Where are you going? I'm not going to hurt you."

"I know," the Fori whispers.

When I reach the tunnel mouth, I find her quivering in an alcove. She puts a finger to her lips. "You must be quiet, or it will hear you."

"What will hear me?"

She peeks around me for a look into the gallery. "Couldn't see, but it was just here. It ran away just before you showed up." She shoos me away. "Now get away from me, you're drawing too much attention to us. Find somewhere safe and hope it doesn't find you."

A scratching sound echoes from above. Pebbles fall to the ground in the chamber center.

My heart pounds and feels like it's rising into my throat. I grip my mother's spear tight and aim its tip upward.

But wait...

I lower my weapon and turn to my Fori friend. "You said it was just down here, but it left just before I arrived?"

She hugs herself and nods.

"Was it moving fast? As if it was running away?"

She frowns, contemplating.

I drop my spear and march to the center of the gallery. No doubt many watch me from the tunnels in fear, but I see something they do not. What must a creature that dwells in darkness fear? What it does not know, of course. *Light.*

I stop walking at a pile of fallen pebbles and set my wings to work. Gasps arise from all around as I float toward the ceiling. Below, many of my kin emerge from their hiding spots to watch me fly to my death.

Turning my attention above, I see the rough cavern roof come into view, and from the darkest recess two red eyes watching me.

I gasp and my wings freeze in fear, dropping me about ten feet. I stop at a hover and keep my eyes locked on the two red dots above. They dart back and forth.

I know this feeling. I've seen it in dwellers of the forest as well, when they feel cornered. Normally I'd leave such a creature alone, but I am not here to calm beasts of the dark.

I zoom up and snatch it with both hands. The furry creature squirms and squeals in my hold, but it cannot escape, for it is small enough to fit well within my two hands. In my violet glow I see it is a rodent with brown fur and chattering teeth. It's terrified.

When I return to the ground with my new pet, hundreds of figures emerge from the caves. Some hang back, but dozens boldly approach as if they'd known all along.

"It seems the darkness made a monster out of you," I say to the quivering rodent while stroking its soft fur.

My Fori cousins watch nervously, so I offer the nearest a closer look. "See, it is nothing to fear."

"Except that we're lost!" someone says.

Many huddle close to me for the comfort of my light.

"You *were* lost," I say with a victorious smile. I untie the rope from my ankle and hold it above my head. "This leads all the way to surface, where many of our—"

The commotion of scrambling feet drowns out my last words. I'm left in the dust of their retreat as they race down the exit tunnel toward the access pit, following my vine to freedom. Our lifeline jerks in my hold as they clamor for it in the dark of the tunnel.

Soon I'm alone with my new friend. I set him down and hurry in pursuit of my kin.

Back above ground, I'm greeted by a surprising sight. Hundreds of my recovered Fori friends sit along the rim of the pit, their feet dangling over darkness and their laughter descending into its depths. Some can't seem to believe how far they'd been lost. Nor how easy it was to vanquish their fears with just the tiniest bit of light.

"Didn't see any Ori slaves down there," Kassini tells me. "But I reckon we're four thousand Fori here."

"Jexa has the Ori moving the Capstone," I say.

Over the eastern horizon, red clouds announce the sun's approach.

Ko Tora flies overhead. "Back to the pyramids!" she shouts, stifling the celebration. "There's still time!"

I look north, to the pre-dawn sky. The portal is not yet open.

My heart beats with hope as I size up the sliver of a crescent moon setting to the west, so slim it's hardly noticeable. The next night will bring with it the New Moon — the proper Alignment. If we can delay Jexa from seating the Capstone until that time, the Magister will take care of the rest.

CHAPTER 30

NYA

We are a rabble when we leave Jexa's pit of darkness. In the crimson light of the rising sun, flying over desert, we form into cohorts. It's a real mess. Some of The Returned need more time to recover their wits. And the brilliant glare from the sun peeking over the horizon doesn't help. But by the time we reach the forest's southern border, our force of four thousand manages to at least reorganize into their original squadrons.

Ko Tora tries ordering the whole lot into an extended line, in which she is the center piece, but the collective Hive has a new queen.

I try lingering in the rear, to offer an elder the opportunity to take their place up forward — to foster a sense of comfort and normality among the Fori in our fateful flight — but the rear keeps shifting behind to place me in front, so that I find myself at the point of a ragged arrowhead formation. Eventually Ko Tora gives up and falls in at my left wing.

I can't resist. I order Kassini, who flies at my right wing, to maintain course alongside Ko Tora while I peel upward to take in the marvelous sight. It does not disappoint. Never in all my life have I been filled with such awe.

In the red sky, a grand arrowhead composed of smaller formations of Fori squadrons stretches out beneath me as far as I can see, soaring high above the forest. Here we are, trespassing boldly through Watcher and Aeri domain, far from the safety of the trees below.

My heart flutters with pride. The Watchers' Reckoning is upon them.

We stop for a rest and to prepare our weapons in the heart of the forest. The squadrons take care to maintain their positions on the ground, so that all it takes is an order to take flight and we're back in our massive arrowhead — four thousand strong. Our pace picks up with the rising sun. It's mid-morning when the dreaded moment happens.

A flash of light in the distance blinds me. A few heartbeats later brings a *BOOM*, and with it comes a shock wave that blows back my hair.

My forward flight wanes to a hover. I brave a look ahead to where, over the sacred pyramid grounds, a bulb of white light pulsates in the sky. A stem of translucent energy connects the portal to its power source beneath the pyramids.

Suddenly I realize I'm alone in the sky. The forest canopy below shakes as everyone takes cover, instinctively hiding inside trees. As if bits of wood will save them from universal annihilation.

I hold fast in my position in the sky. If that portal opened out of alignment we'd already be dead.

A few of my followers realize this and rush to join me.

"Fall into your cohorts!" I shout. It's my first official

command as Rebel Marshal, but those still in the trees rise as if they'd been listening to me all their lives.

I fly hard ahead and hope my warriors join me. Curiosity moves my wings faster than fear ever could. Clearly there was a method to Jexa's madness. The chances of aligning a gate by fluke are astronomically small. Which could actually mean... There's a chance she did not open it at all.

The energy concentrated through the top of the pyramid makes it too hard to see if the Capstone is in place. That would be a clear indication that it was Jexa who opened the gate. But if the pointed gate key of gold were absent from atop the Great Pyramid, then that would mean a gate was opened from elsewhere. Only one person would concern themselves enough with the affairs of Earth to open a gate here uninvited.

The Magister. Our savior. The Protector of Light and Life.

My heart swells in my throat. Could it be? Has he learned of the Consul's demise and come to restore order?

As we draw closer to that translucent ball that had once deposited us all onto this planet, I find myself drifting down toward the treetops. Everyone follows suit until we breach the canopy. We maintain our speed, slowing only to weave around trees, until the very edge of the forest comes into view, where the trees give way to open ground.

I stop at the outer row of trees and survey the Great Pyramid. The stem—a pulse of energy funneled straight up from the Capstone to feed the portal—cannot be seen due to a swirling mass of black dots that circles all three pyramids. More of these black dots fall from the portal above and join the rotating mass that skirts the Anomaly's border—Watchers from every corner of the Universe, all responding to Jexa's call to arms.

Wails of despair rise all around me. They vibrate through my core and shatter my heart into a trillion pieces. The sobs that follow make my hair stand on end. Any hope we had dissipates with these cries of defeat as my followers fall into each other's embraces for comfort. Beside me, Kassini rests her brow on her axehead and sobs away unabashedly.

But we are not too late. The tornado of black dots before us is only the tip of the spear, the first drops of rain from the coming storm. We can stop this flood before the dam breaks wide open. I can still unseat the Capstone. I just need to reach the upper tier. If I break enough of the right blocks, I can shift the pyramid enough to slide the gate key from its mount.

I look to my immediate surroundings and see that at least I still have an army. Though, I notice something I didn't before: a clear division among our ranks.

Those who had followed Ko Tora down into the abyss gather atop the canopy and shun the Fori who helped save them. I hear the whispers. *Cowards*, they call them. I could call them *fools* right back, but I know as well as anyone what name-calling can do to a person. Division must be avoided now more than ever.

I see the lower Fori, among them Jinny, watching those who've faced the darkness. I know the look in their eyes, that feeling of unworthiness. They want to fight, but they're scared. Their own kind call them cowards and they believe it. They don't realize it's only what you think of yourself that matters. The only time someone else's opinion about you counts is if you let it. If I'd listened to every cruel slur said about me, I'd be dead from despair by now.

I slide from my branch and glide down to join them.

"We'll be needing your help out there," I say.

A few shirk back, some retreating behind tree trunks.

"Up there right now, The Returned are worried you won't join us. They're worried because they know we can't do it without you. They'd still be lost in Jexa's dark if not for you."

"So why are they risking ending up in the real Dark?" says Sheffa. "We still have a chance to run and hide. Might be they won't find us."

"Because they learned something down below." I think back to the rodent, who, in the smothering darkness, made himself a demon to the unsuspecting "When you face something you fear head on, you see it's just something you didn't understand." I must, however, acknowledge that not all that lurks in the dark is benign. "And if it really is dangerous, and you understand how it can hurt you, then you can show that danger the respect it deserves. Then you're in control of whether it hurts you or not."

Jinny drifts closer. "But the real Dar-D-Dark . . . You're not afraid of it?"

"The Dark?" I say, playing with the word in my head. Truly analyzing it for the first time in my life. "No, I do not fear it."

"Even the *darkest* Dark?" presses Jinny, incredulous, perhaps thinking I've missed her meaning.

"Especially the darkest Dark," I tell her, and she recoils. I see in her eyes she thinks me mad, and rightfully so, so I must explain. "What is darkness but the absence of light? And the *darkest dark?"* I squeeze her shoulder. "Well, then your spark shall glow all the brighter in that void. And in this world, even a single spark can start a wildfire. Such infernos have wiped clean entire planets. You've seen it, how the tiniest spark can ignite such an unstoppable force."

I cast my gaze across my gathered cousins, many of whom know they are not fighters but refuse to sit back and weaken the numbers of their rising kin. Yet uncertainty still plagues their eyes.

"But there are no single sparks here," I say. "Should any of us fall on this day, we shall all fall together, four thousand sparks who let their light shine bright against the darkness of a tyrant. Each of us will go into the Dark bright as a raging firestorm, and from our glow the darkness shall retreat. Our arrival in the Dark will be a flash as big and bright as the moment of Creation itself, and from our fire the darkness shall retreat."

Captivated eyes watch me, ears twitching as they absorb my every word.

"Our story will spread across the galaxies," I say, "to the ears of the desperate and oppressed. And when they cry out in defiance, using our names as their own rally call to freedom...when our acts here fan the flames of rebellion in their hearts, then so too shall our sparks glow all the brighter. The Dark shall hear of our deeds and retreat from our light. Wherever we go as one, darkness shall die. Death to us is death to Darkness."

"Death to us is death to Darkness," a few murmur.

A massive shadow darkens the faces watching me. Heads tilt skyward. I follow their stricken stares to a swarm of black dots bearing down on us like a meteor shower of terror. Steel from a thousand conquered planets glint at the forward edge of this veil of darkness, weapons wielded by the enemy of all that is good and light.

"So many," Jinny says in awe, forgetting herself.

"Fear not the Dark, sisters," I say. This is the biggest army any Watcher has ever commanded, and it is that which allows me to believe my own words. For one thing is clear now: "It is the Dark that fears you."

Jinny's gaze meets mine briefly, and when it shifts back to our enemy in the sky beyond, there is something different about her stare. Something that once was there is now missing... I can't quite place exactly what, because it's only faint at first.

Then, when her eyes narrow and her lips twist in anger, I see it—all the scenes playing in her mind, memories she'd had to swallow down and bury in the darkness within her. The faces of her dead Fori sisters, murdered for not working hard enough when already worked half to death...

The memory of every time a Watcher whipped her bloody...

Living her entire life in fear, constantly shaking at the sight of those two-winged devils who wreak terror upon our kind...

She's thinking of endless lifetimes of servitude for simply being born with the wrong set of genes...

And when her jaw clenches and she bares her teeth, I know she could be thinking of nothing other than the time a Watcher took a hammer to her leg, smashing every bone so bad she'd never walk right again.

A growl rises from deep within her. Behind it is all the anger and hate she'd had to suppress for lifetimes of injustices boiling from her darkest depths, steaming in her chest and up her throat until it blasts out her mouth with all the force of a volcanic eruption.

She raises her axe and unleashes the fiercest battle cry I ever did hear. It's so loud and intense that her axehead nearly shakes loose from its handle, and the scream rattles me so deep that I almost fall back from my perch.

Then she leaps into the sky without looking back. And she is far from alone.

Everyone in sight rises from the forest like sparks from a wildfire, every one of them screaming and howling, many a heart proudly hammering away its final beats. Better to die in a moment of defiance than to live an eternity in servitude.

Remarkably, our fighters fall into perfect formations as we rise into the sky to meet our enemy—two hundred arrowheads making up a jagged line. And try as I might, I cannot catch up to Jinny to take the point. This is her moment. And what a moment it is. If it turns out to be her last, it will be the most glorious of any Fori who'd ever lived.

Being much faster flyers, the Aeri make up the Black Tide's forward ranks, with the main Watcher force following some distance behind. Jinny flies straight at their middle with her axe heaved back and ready to swing.

The Aeri before her slow their flight. By their stricken stares, something behind us gives them pause.

When I steal a look over my shoulder, I see we are more than the four thousand recovered from Jexa's dark, or even the ten thousand who had rallied at the pyramids. Behind, all the way to the west as far as I can see, a tidal wave of winged figures rises into the sky. It had started nearest us, with the swell now halfway to the horizon, so far back they are black specks against the midday sky. Thousands of forest folk who'd sat out the fight until Jexa opened the gate finally see we were not crazed warmongers.

This massive upheaval brings feathered flyers, too. Murders of crows and lone eagles join the surge, with sparrows and hummingbirds in the mix, as if they know the consequences that shall accompany our defeat.

I turn back in time to see Jinny ram into the Aeri forward line. She disappears through the front rank in an explosion of grey feathers.

Holding my spear horizontally before me, I infuse the shaft with my highest frequency, put my head down, and brace for impact. I am about to cross a line I've never thought possible. I'm about to use my ability to dust the living.

A sudden brunt and locking of my elbows tells me when I've made contact. I keep my head down and plow through, leaving behind clouds of sizzling dust until I punch out through the rear rank.

A stream of Fori slip through the clear corridor in my wake and emerge behind the Aeri, although getting behind our feather-winged cousins isn't necessary to get the better of them.

The Aeri wield Watcher weapons awkwardly, fumbling them in the havoc of battle as we smash apart their lines. They break easily against the raving mad swarm that has risen from the darkness of oppression, those pushed too hard for too long who finally lost their civil sense. They're a nice warm-up for our squadrons as their high-flying egos shatter against our grit.

I swing my spear wide and catch several Aeri in their flight. My vibrations are perfect. Each body explodes into a hundred trillion particles, adding to a cloud of sizzling dust that grows around me. The Aeri quickly lose interest in me, so I hover in place shouting orders for our straying squadrons to return to the larger formation, because diving across the open sky toward the melee are the Watchers. And they are a different story.

Their diamond formations slip into the battle without much of a clash. Yet their presence is immediately felt when Fori drop like flies to the desert ground. Most of my falling kin don't try to stop their fall, suggesting they've suffered fatal wounds by the passing enemy. The Watchers avoid our armored Fori at first, trimming our ranks swiftly and silently. And then comes the clatter and screech of steel.

The Watchers zoom about in their formations of four and cut up even our tightest groups with an elegance gained only from lifetimes of practice. But we need not defeat them. Only break through.

Amid the hurricane of buzzing wings and glinting steel, I see Jexa has left only a dozen Watchers atop the pyramid to guard the Capstone. It's tempting, and though I see many openings, I cannot abandon the fight up here. We match the Watcher numbers, but we're outmaneuvered in flight and skill. The Watchers also lack the fear that had broken the Aeri.

A Watcher alpha leads her diamond formation into a downward swoop toward me. I sweep left, leaving my spear across her path, and turn her swinging sword to dust with a well-timed pulse. Her squadron bursts apart like atoms from a broken molecule, each seeking an easier target.

My satisfaction lasts only a few heartbeats. Looking down, my heart sinks. Fori litter the sand below, with more dropping in a steady shower for their final rest. The wounded scream for help. A few Watchers fall with them, but it seems by mere luck that a small group of Fori are able to isolate and slay one.

In the sky, we are too scattered.

I study the Watcher tactics. They aren't trying to wipe us out in droves, merely attacking targets of opportunity. Then I see why.

Over the pyramid's apex, from the shimmering white bulb in the blue sky, clusters of winged figures now fall in the hundreds. Watchers from who knows what worlds, eager to answer Jexa's call for reinforcements.

But they are muddled when they arrive. They glide away from the pyramids, disoriented and confused, swinging wildly at the air with no targets near. Jexa is forced to abandon her front line of defense to round them up. Something I see she'd not been expecting by her frustrated shouting.

A Fori flies straight into me. When we hit, she spins and tries to take my head off with her axe. I catch her wrist and stop her mid-swing. When her frazzled eyes see me, she gasps and offers me an apologetic look.

"Grab hold of my leg and don't let go," I tell her.

She grabs my ankle, and when I set off, she holds on for dear life. I fly in search of lone Fori and, seeing my intent, the Fori dangling from my leg uses her free hand to snatch one of her sisters flying in our direction. The line on my left leg grows by one.

I weave through the fray, picking up stray Fori and adding them as links to my left and right leg. Each Fori grips an ankle in one hand, a weapon in the other. Soon the chain streaming from each of my legs are dozens long. But I feel the weight of them in my knees and hips. Any more and a jarring move may pull my joints apart.

I look over my left shoulder, to the first Fori in the line. "Keep up. I can't pull the whole chain. Pass it on."

The first Fori on my right also hears the order and, like the sister to her left, relays the message down the line. A sudden jolt forward tells me when those in the rear have received it, loud and clear. Rather than pulling, I'm now being pushed forward. All I need do is steer, which does take considerable effort and is not as responsive with all the force behind me.

I lead my ragtag squadron north, picking up more Fori as we fly. They cling to this formation for dear life as I steer us left, away from the pyramids, to avoid the Anomaly. I bring us back around, swerving in a figure eight to gather more of our flyers. The wide turns stretch our lines and sling sections apart, but our agile flyers spring swiftly back into formation, like elastic. In my first pass we have grown large enough that the smaller Watcher squadrons scatter at the sight of us.

When I've rounded a company of nearly a thousand, I shout: "Break off! Keep it tight. Nice and tight!"

As a clustering swarm, we begin hunting the bigger Watcher formations. They flee from us like frightened prey, scattering far and wide, which infuriates me.

"Stand your ground!" I shout at them, tauntingly.

Then I see it's not us they're escaping.

"Nya!"

I whirl around and see Ko Tora lingering in the rear. She points toward the Great Pyramid, where a colossal arrowhead of Jexa's newly-arrived Watchers sweeps toward our clustered lines.

The sight almost drops me from the sky. That arrowhead, led by Jexa herself, must be five thousand strong!

Every Watcher around us scatters. They can't get away fast enough, and for good reason. Flying down at a forty-five degree angle, Jexa's second wave will drive us right into the ground. Even with numerous stray Fori flying up to reinforce my group, the arrowhead sweeping toward us outnumber us five to one.

We don't have the luxury of fleeing, for our enemy have too much momentum and will catch us easily, and in retreat we'll make easy targets. Our only hope is to break them up.

I turn to square myself with Jexa and shout, "Wedge!"

Sloppy lines form back at angles to my left and right, with Fori sliding in behind me to fill in the space between both battle wings. Too many cram into the middle, which forces the sides of our wedge to flare out into a bulging triangle. This creates a blunted point, but there's no time to sharpen our formation. Jexa is so close I can see the vertical slits in her eyes dilating—a few quick breaths away.

Time slows. The sound of my heart thuds lazily in my ears. *Thud...thud... ...Thud...thud...*

Spear tips glitter in my peripheral vision as they reach forward from behind me in slow motion, while a few shafts extend over my shoulders from the Fori to my rear, aiming their spears to meet the coming attack. I hold mine out in front and aim the tip between Jexa's eyes.

She lines her spear with my belly and bares her teeth.

My spear shaft rattles with a vibration I cannot control. If it were made from a material any lesser than whatever this metal of my homeworld is, it would have burst into dust by now.

Screams and howls of defiance rise up from behind me. Locking eyes with Jexa, I scream so loud my throat feels raw. It's a steady yell, because I dare not let up before Jexa hits us in a few quick heartbeats.

Jexa lacks my commitment to our stare-down. Just before slamming into us, something calls her attention upward and to her right. Her eyes flash wide in alarm, and she shields her face while dropping from formation.

Half a blink later, a cluster of stray Fori rain down like a meteor shower upon the Watcher wedge at a forty-five degree angle. The loose formation punches through Jexa's arrowhead with flashes of blinding light. Only, they can't be Fori, because when they emerge underneath unscathed, each swerves upward and hits the Watcher ranks from below. Some blast through and rise above Jexa's wedge, but most remain in the thick of the hoard, where Jexa's neat ranks bust apart in flashes of light.

The howling that had risen behind me in anticipation settles. As my army watches this counterattack in awe, I hear familiar sounds rise from within the Watcher wedge—steel and flesh exploding to dust.

"Dust maidens!" shouts someone from my rear.

My heart leaps into a joyful dance.

I'd love to see the look on Jexa's face as she rises with her back to me, watching my Entropath siblings tear through her grand arrowhead. Her ranks shatter from within with bursts of golden light, but it's the demise of the rear line that's most impressive. Flying in from the side, a pair of dust maidens pull a long chain tight and sweep sideways through that widest rank, each of them infusing it with a resonant vibration in perfect harmony, their resonance building off each other's. A rolling flash obliterates a quarter of the Watcher line before the rest scatter.

Jexa has seen enough. She points her spear at a lone dust maiden at the fringe and shouts, "After them! Kill them all!"

This is when I'm hit by the surprise of a lifetime. Rather than follow Jexa's order, the Watchers hesitate. Instead, they allow these solo flyers to move freely, with a good many actually retreating.

I spot the leader of our mighty allies wreaking havoc in the middle of the broken arrowhead. She wears an antler crown of black diamond and, like her followers, a thick band of black paint covers her eyes, with swirling runes marking her arms. Two Watchers join shields and take a dive at her. She swings her golden hammer—yellow enlaced with white— and when it hits the platinum plates, both shields and their bearers explode backwards into a stream of atomic particles and sizzling light.

I watch in amazement as my scattered Entropath sisters smash Watchers to dust with their blunted weapons. Pride swells in me as our enemy fall into diamond formations and flee. A few of Jexa's fearless even cry out in terror. Imagine that...Watchers, actually afraid! In the thick of the Watcher storm, the dust maidens don't bother to even stay in pairs. They veer away on their own, chasing Watchers, and any who come near are quickly frightened away with a swing of their weapons.

But not all are so lucky. A few Watchers manage to grab hold of a dust maiden and slit her throat. My blood goes cold as she falls to the ground.

I point my spear at the battle and shout, "Reinforce the dust maidens!"

Wind from a thousand sets of wings tousles my hair as my Fori warriors rush to rejoin the fight. Each dust maiden quickly gains a following. They whiz about fearlessly, smashing apart shields and weapons, leaving Watchers defenseless against the Fori blades that follow.

It's too much for our enemy. They fall back in droves toward the Great Pyramid, landing with little grace at the edge of the Anomaly. Many are too hurt to make the run to the moat, and the sight of Watchers carrying their wounded brings a smile to my face.

"A beautiful sight, isn't it," comes a voice from behind.

To my left, Ko Skadia appears in my peripheral. Her crown of black antlers sparkles in the sunlight.

Normally my elder's presence would unsettle me, for she wields the force and temper of a hurricane. Here, I smile in greeting.

She frowns in return. "I must say, Nya, I'm offended it took you so long to invite us to your rebellion."

"I knew you'd hear the chaos and come rushing in," is my response, and I'm surprised at the lightness in my voice. "Heard you had some help ditching your watchful wardens."

Ko Skadia smirks. "*Jaleera*, is it? How refreshing to see a Watcher as committed to her duty as you. Truly inspiring. Just don't tell me you started all this to avoid a hard day's work. I'd be devastated."

I force back my laughter, nearly erupting with it. *Could you imagine?* The darkness of her humor reminds me why we're not allowed to mingle. Already I feel emboldened by her presence. Even with such a brief interaction, I feel like a whole different person.

She returns her attention to the ground, where hundreds of Watchers scramble toward the pyramid. A quick survey of the sky reveals it now belongs to us, with only a few unlucky Watchers cut off from the retreat.

But our fight is far from over. From the portal, more Watchers fall in clumps. For all I know, millions to billions more are on their way.

"We need to close the gate before enough arrive to take back the sky," I say.

Ko Skadia nods toward the enemy regrouping before the Great Pyramid, in front of the moat bridge. "You ever dust Watcher bones?" my Elder asks.

Come to think of it, I haven't. So I shake my head.

Ko Skadia gives me a devious grin and says, "Well, lucky you. The Marshal of Watchers will make a fine start."

CHAPTER 31

NYA

I time my descent so I touch down before the foot of the causeway. Many Fori land with me, but the dust maidens arrive with less grace. They're encountering the Anomaly for the first time since our hazy arrival on this planet, so many crash into the sand. Those who manage to land on their feet end up stumbling, but the Fori rush to help them. Ko Skadia shoves Sheffa away when she tries to help her up.

To our rear, hundreds of Ori race from the forest to join us. Good. We'll need every one of them, because standing on the bridge crossing the moat ahead, is Jexa. Her spear shaft glows bright with the many sparks she captured during the battle over the pyramid. But it is not the souls of the dead that raise my caution.

Several thousand Watchers line up before the moat to either side of the causeway. I see Bercidia the Butcher standing tall in the line to my left, and recognize a few others who, by name alone, inspire fear among my people. Jexa has held back her best fighters to guard the Great Pyramid, and their pride no doubt prevents them from using the water trench for defense. They adopt wide fighting stances, each with a javelin cocked back and ready to launch from one hand, and a shorter melee weapon held in front with the other. The Butcher appears to be the only four-armed Watcher in attendance, and likely known to exist, and for this rarity I am thankful. Her four blades flash as she scrapes them against each other to sharpen their edges. I pity whoever must square off with her first.

Kassini falls in to my left, with Jinny limping in to take up my right wing. Each wears Aeri feathers in her hair as trophies, with Jinny's sticking out through the ears of her blue helmet. And as is with the many Fori rushing up to join us, the orange blood of our allies-turned-enemies is smeared in two-finger streaks across their cheeks.

Jinny bends to grab a platinum short sword from the sand, gives it a test swing, then smiles proudly as she shows me her new weapon. Her smile levels, however, when her eyes meet mine.

The weight of a hard ring sits gently atop my head. I reach up to feel the smooth antlers of Ko Skadia's black headdress.

"The Krown of Klora," she says from behind me.

A tingling energy blasts my scalp and shoots down my spine.

"I think it fits you better," Ko Skadia says as she steps up beside me. She looks to Jinny. "Wouldn't you say?"

Jinny's cheeks rise with a prideful smile. Tears glisten her eyes as she gives me an approving nod.

"Now," Ko Skadia says, pointing her hammer at the Great Pyramid, "let's go finish what your mother started."

My heart swells with each beat, pumping strength out to

my toes and to my fingertips, infusing each atom of my being with all the violent energy of a lightning strike. I lock eyes with Jexa standing on the causeway ahead. With Kassini to my right, Jinny to my left, and Ko Skadia at my rear, I step up onto the elevated walkway and begin my march toward the Watcher net. I walk confidently, knowing the last time our enemy saw this crown on my mother, it did not have the backing of a united army behind it.

Sand swishes to both sides of the causeway as my force flares out into a wedge. The Watchers standing before the moat follow the advancing rebels with their spear tips. Hisses rise from the line as they rock back and forth. My skin prickles when we cross into their range.

Jexa spreads her arms wide in welcome. "Well, isn't this nice. A day of reunions."

I stop and check behind me to ensure we have the numbers in tight formation to storm the bridge. We must be two thousand strong in the wedge, with thousands of Ori stretched out in an extended line to face the Watchers before the moat. Ori banners of red and black stream in the breeze over their front rank. We are enough.

I grip my mother's spear and narrow my eyes on Jexa standing alone before the bridge. Having just witnessed the devastation my Entropath kin inflicted upon flesh and bone, I know the Marshal risks more by dueling with me. One clean hit with a well-timed pulse of high frequency will secure my victory. Anywhere on her body will do. And even if she blocks it with her spear, the shock may disarm her. My previous attempt had failed because I'd not expected to hit diamond. Let's see about now.

I set my feet marching forward, but a hand grabs my shoulder to halt my advance.

Jaleera steps up beside me. "Leave Jexa to me," she says. Her expression is stolid, but I see something in her eyes that, until today, I'd thought impossible for a Watcher. It's the look of fear.

She raises her hand to offer me a sparkling ruby. When I accept it, I'm immediately greeted by a familiar energy. The unique frequency takes me back to the day that changed my life. The day that led us all to this, when I'd first set eyes on Deka.

"Feed it to the energy stream," Jaleera says. "Then close the gate."

I spin the red diamond in my fingers to give it a better appraisal. When I'd tossed it into the sea, I thought that would be the last I'd ever see of it. Why has Jaleera gone through the trouble to recover this seemingly random stone? Perhaps it's an enchanted instrument, crafted to choke the portal... Or it automatically opens a gateway to the Magister... Or it's explosive destruction in the energy stream might dislodge the Capstone.

"There's no time to explain," Jaleera says, breaking me from my trance. "You must do as I say."

Her gaze locks onto Jexa, but her words are meant for me. "What are you going to do?" she asks. It's in the tone of an Elder ensuring I understand my task before we part ways.

"Deliver this to the energy stream, then close the gate."

"Good girl. You have enough of your sisters here to do the job safely."

Should have enough, I want to clarify. Breaking sacred chains is no exact science to those of our level, even Ko

Skadia. Only the makers who'd set them truly know what it will take to undo their work, and they are long gone.

"You have to be quick, Nya," Jaleera adds, and I realize she's stalling, "no messing about."

"I got it." My teeth are clenched so tight my temples ache.

I'm not sure if it's to stall more, but Jaleera kneels next to Jinny and whispers in her ear. Jinny's nostrils flare and her eyes widen as she listens to Jaleera while watching me. She swallows hard and accepts Jaleera's round shield absently, and when Jaleera stands, Jinny's expression hardens. She straightens the blue skull helmet on her head and stares up at the Capstone.

Without further ado, Jaleera marches up the causeway toward Jexa.

I let her go without protest. If anyone on our side has the skill to out-parry the Watcher Marshal, it's the one who has served lifetimes as her right hand.

Jexa narrows her eyes on Jaleera and smiles. "Traitor, you make things too easy. I thought I'd have to hunt you down."

Jaleera veers to the right edge of the causeway. Jexa moves to meet her, leaving the bridge wide open. Several Watchers clamber up from the line and form two ranks across the bridge.

Ko Skadia leans over my shoulder from behind and whispers, "Let's make dust of them." Though we are not physically touching, I sense her whole body vibrating. All of my sisters are charged, ready to blast away anything in our path.

As Jexa and Jaleera draw closer, we all watch to see who will make the first move.

Jaleera starts with a leaping thrust of her spear—

I break into a sprint.

Jexa bats Jaleera's attack away and springs into a spinning back kick. Her foot hits Jaleera's chest and sends her flying off the side of the causeway. Jexa leaps down after her as I race past.

As Jexa and Jaleera wrestle for top position on the ground, I focus on the line of Watchers blocking the bridge. They stand twenty across and two ranks deep. Those in front unsling shields from their backs and hold them in front. Each rectangle of gold locks into place with those to either side, fitting neatly like a puzzle that forms a wall from ground to neck. They duck their heads and brace for impact.

I don't slow even the slightest. Instead, the slapping of several hundred feet on the stone walkway behind emboldens me to run harder, so that when I ram the center shield with my shoulder, it nearly knocks me unconscious. I'd bounce back if not for the wall of bodies slamming me from behind.

The shield wall slides back against the initial impact, but quickly steadies. The Watchers plant firm and don't give up another inch.

Ko Skadia presses her hammerhead into the shield over my shoulder and sends through a steady vibration. The rattling makes my teeth chatter and vision blur. Several of my sisters join in, holding their weapons to the shields and blasting the golden wall with vibrations. Normally a mighty swing would bust this wall apart, but our tight quarters does not allow for it.

The shields of gold hold up admirably against our disruptive frequencies. The bones behind them, however, not so much. I swear I hear the snap of a forearm before the nearest golden plate tips away from me. The shield-bearer falls under her shield, and I'm forced through the opening by a stampeding mass of Fori, Ori, and Entropaths, everyone howling like raving lunatics. The flood of rebels forces the other shield-bearers over the bridge and into the moat.

I sprint on toward the wooden stakes at the pyramid's bottom level. A few swipes of my spear and Ko Skadia's hammer clear our way to the head-height stones. When I touch the ancient blocks, a fuzzy feeling spreads through my body. It comes from the pulsating energy that surges from the planet's core to fuel the open gate above, from which Watchers still fall in groups of a dozen or more. Jexa's call stretches far and wide.

I step back to get a running start at my climb, but the weight of my whole army shoves me forward and squishes me against the stone. Everyone's backs are to me and the pyramid, suggesting the Watcher lines have followed us across the bridge.

Jinny weaves through the rabble to join me.

"Only one way to go," she says, looking up the two hundred stone courses.

To our right, a junior dust maiden climbs up onto the bottom level. Doria's protege, the one I spied dusting the towers after I knocked the head off the Sphinx. A spear zips from the crowd's outer edge and cuts her nearly in half at the belly.

As I watch my sister roll down into the crowd, Jinny drops and crawls through the chaos of feet and legs. She returns a moment later dragging a shield and straps it to my back. It's a large, rectangular plate of gold that covers me from crown to heels. While I adjust the arm straps to fit my shoulders, she hefts Jaleera's shield to her shoulder and kneels, then invites me to use it as a step.

I lift a foot onto the curved plate, and Jinny pushes me up to the first level, where I lie on my belly and cling to whatever hold I can find. The rumbling pyramid threatens to shake me off and sends a vibration through me that makes my whole body feel as if it's made of fur.

Jinny's fingers claw at the edge for purchase, so I reach down and pull her up to join me. She follows my lead by staying low.

From this vantage point it's clear we're in trouble. The Watchers form a semi-circular snare around our entire force, which tightens against the pyramid base as they hack and slash at our outer edges. Our rebels on the fringe, desperate to escape the onslaught, shove their way toward the pyramid, leaving themselves exposed while cramming everyone too tight to fight. Anyone climbing up now must stay on their bellies, or they'll eat a flying spear. Even now, projectiles ricochet off the shield arched across my back. A few Fori manage to scramble up and then scoot to flank the perimeter, trying to drop outside the snare, but they make easy targets for Watcher spears.

We're right where they want us.

"Protect the flanks!" Jinny yells. She rises to a knee and points her sword at an inward bulge in the snare to our left, nearest the pyramid base, where the Watchers are having great success against the Fori there.

"Protect the flanks!" someone else shouts, but the order dissipates before actually reaching the outer edges.

Jinny screams directions, pointing to thin spots in the Watcher enclosure for our troops to break through and relieve the pressure, but her words are lost to the screams and ringing steel.

Several spears should have skewered her by now, but even those aimed dead at her shield never make contact. Instead, they curve away at the last second and smack the second course blocks behind her. Jaleera's shield must have diamagnetic properties. Jinny is unaware of its deflective effect, however, as she nearly pulls her hair out in frustration while watching the butchery below.

Then her crazed eyes and frustrated expression set. Her whole body relaxes, as if she's just accepted some fated news she'd been denying. She stands tall and forces a smile, but it's the saddest smile I've ever seen.

"Thank you, Nya," she says, "for letting me fight by your side."

"You're not done yet," I say from my belly. "I need you to help me reach the Capstone."

She shakes her head and backs away. "I can't climb as fast as you. I'll only slow you down."

"*No!*" When I reach out to grab her, a zooming spear smacks the face of the second level between us. I close my eyes to shield them from the chipped stone, and when I open them again I see Jinny has backed beyond my reach.

"Goodbye, Nya," she says. "It was an honor."

I'm on my feet in half a blink despite the bulky shield weighing me down. I lunge to grab Jinny, but she turns and leaps before I can snag her. All I can do is watch in horror as she lands in the rabble nearest the outer edge, right next to the Watchers who jab and swipe their spears without mercy.

Frustration and fear swirl like a tornado inside me. The only feeling that could rival it is the pity I feel when a

Watcher on the outer edge to my left raises an axe high in both hands, and swings it down into the skull of a helpless Fori. The Watchers in line beside her stab and jab with their spears as she wrenches the blade free, adding to the widening berm of slain Fori.

She raises the axe again for another swing, only, this time her whole body keels over with the blade, disappearing under the chaos of jabbing spears.

Jinny steps over the body with her round shield held over her head, swinging wide with the short sword in her other hand. It takes the Watchers squeezing the perimeter a moment to realize she's there, and by then she's already cut down five at the legs in her outward drive.

I watch her movements in awe. This is a fight where Jinny's size is actually an advantage. At Watchers' stomach level, the round shield she holds over her head is at too awkward a height. They try stabbing under it, but their packed ranks restrict their movements. She easily deflects the jabs, some of which she redirects into Watcher legs. They resort to slamming their sword pommels onto the shield, but the deflective field softens each blow. These frequent impacts knock her around, but they don't slow her sword swinging. Not in the least. She slashes wildly side to side, relentless in her assault. Watchers clear away, stretching the noose in this one tiny spot.

Some Ori see Jinny's technique and gather shields from the fallen enemy. They rush to add more pressure to the outward bulge, and their shorter stature is even harder for the Watchers to defend against. A few Ori teams hold back and use single shields as hand catapults, launching Fori and Ori through the air and onto unsuspecting Watchers. The blitz from above and below is too much for our enemy in this one spot, and soon the net bursts wide open.

"Jinny, you little devil," I say with a relieved smile.

The Watcher ring disintegrates all around the perimeter as both sides mingle into melee. I've lost sight of Jinny in the chaos, but I don't have time to find her.

I climb onto the pyramid's second course, then crawl to my knees to scale the third level. And onward and upward I go.

Climbing with the shield is a real chore. Not only does the weight add to my burden, but its size makes it hard for me to bend my legs to climb up over the ledges. I'm gasping by the time I conquer the tenth course. Even breathing at rest is no easy task while being forced to remain on my belly with the heavy shield pressing down on me. And I still have over two hundred levels to go! But I dare not shed my protection.

When I get moving again, a blow to my back shoves me against the next course wall. My shield deflects the spear into the stone beside me. Another hits with a deafening clang. I'm right in their red zone. I need to get higher, and fast.

The fresh memory of Jinny rises to fight off my dismay. Her daring deeds are enough to keep me going, but a new motivation appears before me. About thirty levels above, Ko Skadia is making good progress in her climb up the pyramid steps. She's above spear-launching range and has just shed her shield two levels below, which allows her to scramble up much faster than I.

She stops and presses a hand to the stone to assess the pyramid's frequency. The right hit with her hammer might knock the Capstone free, closing the portal. But if she goes too hard, she may damage the gate, perhaps beyond repair.

My heart hammers with urgency. We can do whatever we want to the Capstone—the Magister doesn't need it to come here—but he needs this gate in good form to open his own portal to here. If we close Jexa's portal, but destroy our gate in the process, we'll strand ourselves on this pyramid surrounded by Watchers with no way out. No one to save us. We need the Magister now more than ever. We need only to close the portal, to allow him to open his own way here. Besides, I must honor Jaleera's command. Before closing the gate, I must feed the diamond in my grip to the energy stream.

Ko Skadia thankfully determines she's not yet reached the right position to unfurl her havoc. She clambers up another two courses, but then stops for a rest. Climbing is no easy task for any of us. As winged creatures, we've had little incentive in our evolution to put our legs through such trials. Right now my thighs are burning fiercely, but I must seize this chance to catch up to my Entropath Elder. So up I climb.

I make it ten more levels before I'm due for another rest. Here I risk a look below and catch sight of Jexa. She stands alone on the moat bridge watching our climb with great intensity. Jaleera's body lies sprawled in the sand beside the causeway, her own dagger buried to the hilt in her heart. Judging by the distance between her body and where her head now rests, she denied Jexa the chance to claim her spark. And Jexa did not take this well, lopping off her head with terrible force.

I shudder. But this is no time to mourn my mother's killer.

A closer look now reveals Jexa's gaze is actually fixated on the portal above. She doesn't seem worried about us at all.

She's more interested in what may come through that gate, which inspires me to climb faster. Whatever she's expecting can't be good.

It turns out that Jinny had found me the perfect shield. Its curved face deflects spears much better than that on the back of the sister to my left, who is three levels above me. A spear slams square in the center of her back with a *THUNK!* She sprawls onto her belly and doesn't get up.

"Doria!" I shout. Although only three stone courses separate us, she will take time to reach, so I must let her know I'm coming.

She lifts her head to look at me. "My back," she cries, her face twisted in pain, "I think it's broken!"

All spears now focus on me—*TINK! PING! DING!* Each strike feels like a kick to the back and sends a deafening ring through my head, yet no spear lands dead on, which so far spares me the agony Doria now endures. I have my hero Jinny to thank for that.

"Keep your head down!" I tell Doria. "I'm coming!"

She rests her face on her arms while I scramble up onto the next course. Spears smack the stone around me as I crawl along the level below Doria. When I'm underneath her, I reach up to grab her hand. She gives mine a squeeze, but as I'm crawling up to join her she violently yanks her hand from my grasp.

That's what I think, anyway, until I see her rising into the sky. Her scream sends electrified terror through me. The wide feathered wings flapping from her back look like they could be her own, but I know better.

An Aeri carries Doria by her shield away from the pyramid, then drops her. Doria shrieks until she lands in the middle of the fight at the pyramid base, where she disappears amongst the chaos of swinging limbs.

Wind blows my hair and alerts me to my own impending doom. Without looking, I turn and thrust my spear outward with one hand, the other gripping Jaleera's diamond tight. I'm so enraged that my spear tip barely pierces the Aeri's skin when she explodes in a flash of light. Her death does nothing to calm my fury.

I turn and plunge my spear into the Aeri who'd dropped Doria, sending a mild, steady vibration down the shaft and into her chest. She beats her wings, desperate to fly backward from me, stretching the spring in my spear shaft. I lean back with all my weight, the shield adding extra leverage for me.

"Aeri traitor!" Rage amplifies my frequency, sending the Aeri into convulsions. Her limbs twist and bones snap. She drops to the stone course below me, writhing at the end of my spear, revealing two more swooping in from behind her. "Cowardice scum!"

I shoot a wicked pulse down my spear. The Aeri at the other end bursts apart, spraying me with blood and other bodily matter. The two flying in stop suddenly in their flight, watching the body parts of their sister fly off in every direction.

My spear tremors with a violent frequency as I point the bloody tip at them. "Who's next?" I growl.

The two exchange rattled looks, then shake their heads before flying off.

I scan the sky for more and see ten flying in from the direction of the forest. The closest swoops in for Ko Skadia, who is now fifty tiers above me.

"Ko Skadia!" I shout. "Behind you!"

My Elder doesn't even look. She just swings her hammer backward, hard and wide. Her Aeri attacker disappears in a flash, but she was not alone. The two who'd just abandoned me swoop in before Ko Skadia can redirect her weapon. One kicks her against the wall and knocks the hammer from her hand. The other snatches up the weapon and flings it down into the moat.

Ko Skadia swings her fists at the Aeri, but it's not enough to deter them. They both attack at once, each driving a spear into my Elder's chest.

"I'll skewer you both!" I shout.

To my surprise, my threat actually seems to deter them. They fly out to meet their flock, pointing to me and issuing words of warning.

"We've done enough," their leader shouts to the others, noting Ko Skadia's limp body as the closest rebel to the Capstone by a good distance. They fly back toward the forest.

With the Aeri off my back for now, I resume my ascent with fervor, promising not to stop until I reach the apex. I'm halfway to Ko Skadia when a familiar voice stops me dead.

"Oh, *Nyaaaa!*"

I turn to see Bercidia the Butcher marching toward the base level, all four arms wielding blades that mow down any who stand in her way. She minces Ori and Fori without taking her eyes off me and climbs onto the bottom level with her four arms.

At eight feet tall, she springs effortlessly up the levels two at a time.

I have no chance to out-climb her, so I kneel and point my spear at her face.

She stops five courses below me, where she slides her four

blades against each other to sharpen their edges. "I'm gonna eat you alive," she says, "then pick my teeth with your bones."

I hold my spear tight to keep it steady, but it's no use. My hands shake so bad at the sight of those four blades that my spear tip rattles.

A voice rises from the battle below: *"BUTCHERRR!"*

Bercidia turns and, when she sees it's Jinny calling her out, she laughs and turns back to me.

"Everyone, look!" shouts Kassini from the melee. She points her axe at Bercidia and says, "The Butcher is scared of a little runt!"

Then Kassini bursts out laughing. Jinny shoots Kassini an angry look, but it's only brief. She nods and shouts, "Yeah, Butcher, you better run!"

Anger flashes in Bercidia's eyes. To a Watcher, fear from their Servants is everything, so to have one laugh at you must be the greatest humiliation. She stares straight ahead, through the stone block a few feet before her face, seething, seeming to forget all about me as fury consumes her.

The Butcher leaps down into the crowd, and everyone between her and Jinny trip over each other to clear the space between them. Any who remain are diced up by the Butcher's wild swinging as she advances—Fori and Ori and Watchers alike. But the beast has eyes for only one in her midst, and may the stars bless that heart of hers, Jinny only allows four steps backward before stopping herself. But there's no hiding the terror on her face, and when she checks all around her, I'm sure she's looking for a way to disappear into the crowd. I'd not fault her for that. It's exactly what she should do.

But no. Taking stock of Bercidia's four blades, her

expression sets and she drops her shield to pick up a second sword. To even the odds, Kassini falls in beside her with an axe in each hand. When Bercidia stomps forward, both raise their weapons and rush in to meet her.

I can't watch. Instead, I honor the time they bought me by climbing. All I can do is hope Jaleera's diamond works some actual magic when I introduce it to the portal.

From the hundredth level I look to the Capstone above. Though I'm halfway up, it still sits so high, higher than most mountains.

That doesn't matter. If someone small enough to be called 'runt' their whole life just single-handedly broke the Watcher offense and turned the whole tide of battle, and then faced down one of the most ruthless Watchers to have ever lived, then I can climb a mountain of stone.

Oh, Jinny. I can't avoid it any longer. I look back to see Bercidia holding her up by her four limbs. Kassini lies in pieces at her feet, but Jinny's agonized expression suggests she'd met the easier fate of the pair.

Bercidia's four arms pull outward, stretching Jinny by her limbs in four directions. Jinny's head falls back as she looks to the sky, her mouth open wide to yell, but nothing comes out. The Butcher turns slowly with Jinny held high, displaying her for all to see.

"All hail the *HERO* of Giza!" bellows Bercidia in mockery.

For a second, every muscle in The Butcher's upper body flexes against the tension of Jinny's body, which gives way with a sickening release. She flings Jinny's remains away and sets her eyes back on me.

My body shudders with hot rage, boiling from deep down

in my core. Pressure builds inside my chest, swelling in my throat, searing up through my cheeks, and squeezes a single black tear from my eye. It lands on the stone between my knees, where it vibrates to the rumbling pyramid's rhythm.

I ball my hands into fists, feel another surge of pressure build inside my chest, rise up my neck to my face, and out squeezes another black drop from my eye. It spatters on the stone and flutters in place, resonating with the frequency of the pyramid—of the Earth itself—revealed to me through complex geometric patterns.

Another teardrop splashes on top of the others.

Waves of energy ripple outward, pulsating with Earth's ancient rhythm, Tears of Harmony vibrating in unison, showing me the sacred secrets of this structure.

I punch the nearest stone with all my might. An explosion of dust blasts my face, but it doesn't ease my anger. Not in the slightest. In fact, it makes it worse while at the same time feeling good.

So. Damn. Good.

I punch again, pulverizing the rock and those to either side of it. As I punch in a wide hook with one hand, followed by a sharp uppercut from the other, clearing away blocks with mighty strokes, I finally experience the satisfaction my kin derive from such destruction.

I continue punching, turning block after block into dust, chipping away at the great intergalactic gateway, driving my way into the pyramid with hooks and jabs and uppercuts, burrowing away from the flying spears and those wretched Aeri.

Rage fuels my fists, infusing my strikes with meteoric might, so that my glowing, unstoppable, volatile, explosive knuckles and what lies within their reach are the only things that matter.

The deeper blocks are softer. That, or I'm growing stronger with each swing, because I'm forced to step farther after each punch to reach the next block. At first it was only a short shuffle. Now, it takes two full strides. And then three.

My left hand packs more of a punch than my right, reinforced by the diamond ball clenched in my fist.

Each strike sends a wave of pleasure back through me. This thrill keeps my fists swinging in search of greater satisfaction, which I find with each bursting block. Euphoria builds inside me until my eyes roll back and my whole body tingles. This indescribable pleasure swells in me like a pressure that I feel is leading to something I've never felt before, an explosion the likes of which is beyond my experience. It's like that feeling you get when you're about to sneeze. There's a release coming and you know there's some strange satisfaction that will come with it. I'm not sure what will happen, but I pound my way toward it without reservation.

I vibrate uncontrollably, punching madly in search of that release, until I blast apart one block that—for a whole heartbeat—chokes the flow of energy to the portal. The pyramid goes silent, and the absence of the pyramid's vibration leaves my body feeling heavy and dense. I'd grown accustomed to the rumble, compensating for it, so I feel momentarily unsteady without it. Almost dizzy. The pressure inside me begins to settle.

My breath catches. *No! I don't want it to stop!*

When the rumbling resumes, I punch another block and feel an even longer pause. In the sky above, the translucent stem disappears briefly, and the spherical portal starts to fade until the energy stream returns.

Hope flares in me when, in the distance, Jexa's voice screams, "Get her! Stop her, now!"

I hammer away with my fists, laughing into the dust that blasts my face. Jexa's reaction confirms that I actually have a chance at closing the portal by chipping away at its base. Any moment I'll destroy this gate beyond function or send the Capstone sliding down to the ground. Reaching the apex on my own is not an option. That much has been made clear to me.

I punch so hard my left fist collapses in on itself. I don't need to look to know the diamond ball has turned to dust in my palm.

A rush of energy consumes me. Not even diamond can withstand my might. *I. Am. Unstoppable.*

My inward digging comes to a halt when two hands grab the shield strapped to my back. I twist to the side, but another set of hands grabs my arms to prevent me from wiggling free. When they pull me into the open I see it is not actually *they*, but one, four-armed freak.

Bercidia lifts me high and slams me onto my back. The impact blasts the air from my lungs with a cloud of dust, and my shield renders me like a turtle on its back. The Butcher is quick to grab my wrists with her upper arms, pinning them above my head while her lower hands clamp around my neck.

My eyes bulge at the pressure, made worse by the force of my thundering heart. Bercidia clenches her pointed teeth and leans in, black drool streaming down from her bottom lip.

I kick wildly but hit nothing other than stone and air.

Black spots bloom across my vision. I'm going to die any second.

I'm going to die!

This threat makes my panicked heart pound even harder and faster, which in turn burns up more oxygen and accelerates my suffocation.

I stop kicking involuntarily, and I feel my whole body seize up. Even my eyelids. This automatic response, of appearing dead, may have evolved as a defense mechanism with my ancestors, because it seems to work.

Bercidia jerks her head back to look up. She loosens her grip and sits up straight, as if to embrace an incoming attack. I remain perfectly still, my paralyzed body committed to the deception despite my desperation to breathe, a subconscious mechanism designed to fool my attacker into abandoning me, until the beast turns her head to the side. That's when I see an arrow through her right eye. She lumbers sideways and tumbles down to the course below.

The spell releases with a wheeze and a howling gasp as I suck as much air down my windpipe as I can, but even my struggle to breathe can't wrangle in my curiosity. I recognized the craftsmanship of that arrow, with its stiff polymer shaft and thin plastic fletching.

Two more arrows rain down upon an Aeri swooping straight for me. She crashes into the pyramid below in an explosion of feathers. Then a spear zips sidelong into an unsuspecting Aeri, and the impact not only stops her in flight, but the force folds her in half and sends her backward.

I look up for the origin of the arrows and can hardly believe my eyes.

Kneeling about thirty levels above, reloading a crossbow,

is Deka's war leader—Marlok. Deka crouches at his side and shoots a bolt at a banking Aeri. He misses, but the Aeri darts away and doesn't look like she's in a hurry to return.

Tears blur my eyes. I'm quick to wipe them away, determined not to miss a split second of this unexpected arrival. For a moment all I can do is watch Deka line up another Aeri target and loose an arrow while, all around him, a dozen *sapien* warriors emerge from the pyramid's rear side and spread across the levels above me. They had somehow crept up the back end unnoticed.

Deka! I try screaming his name, but my throat feels crushed. I struggle to loosen the straps binding my shoulders to the shield, the curved plate keeping me on my back like a turtle on its shell. But my body is still stiff and slow to respond. My fingers tingle and tremble as sensation returns to them, so I fumble with the fasteners as chaos builds around me.

Some *sapiens* shoot arrows at the Aeri, while others rush down the levels and swipe at the Watchers climbing up. I marvel at how swiftly they move up and down the courses while swinging their spears with skill and grace. It appears effortless compared to our struggle. And that's not the only surprise Deka's people bring to the fight.

A Watcher spear flies up and hits Huxley square in the chest. The force knocks the big boy back against the next stone level, and, as he falls onto his side, the platinum spear bounces free and clatters onto the stone beside him.

That strike should have cut even a beast like Huxley in half, which is why my jaw goes slack when he crawls to his knees with a loud groan. He feels his chest in shock, and when he smooths his shirt I see the sheen of bark spider silk.

A quick assessment reveals all twelve *sapiens* wearing this armor.

Huxley's astonished gaze drifts a few levels down, to the Watcher who'd launched the spear. When their eyes meet, a crazed smile flashes across the *sapien*'s face. It's enough to send the unarmed Watcher running sidelong toward the corner in hopes of escaping around to the other side. But she can't outrun this big *sapien* up here. He grabs the spear and chases her down in no time. But rather than use the weapon, he slams her head against the stone wall three times before flinging her all the way to the ground.

The numbness and tingling in my limbs persist, so I roll to my side and onto my knees, then grab the ledge above me to stand, the shield stiff and cumbersome on my back.

A few levels above, in his search for a target, Deka spots me. His face lights up with a smile, and he wastes no time sliding down the tiers toward me. I wave for him to stop, which he does, then I point hard at the Capstone. Deka whistles to Marlok, who'd just taken out three Watchers with a running sweep of his spear. When the leader's attention is directed to the Capstone and its twelve guards, Marlok is quick to lead a mad charge upward.

I watch the *sapien* attack in amazement. They climb with such ease. Though I suppose this should be expected of a species reliant entirely on their legs for mobility. Jexa's guards below the Capstone carry only spears and shields, so they're easily pushed to the other sides by *sapien* crossbow bolts.

When I resume my climb, it's with much less grace but with far more enthusiasm than before. Deka ignores my order to hold his position and slides down to meet me. I welcome his approach. After everyone I just lost, I want nothing more than to hold him tight, if only for a second.

We're three courses away when I run out of steam. Deka eagerly jumps down to close the remaining distance, but he stops suddenly, two levels above me. He unslings his crossbow and fumbles to load it. In the reflection of his round goggle lenses I see myself and a set of feathered wings flare out to either side of me.

The shield on my back becomes light. Its straps pull up into my armpits as I'm picked clean off the pyramid. Suddenly the levels are small steps shrinking under my hanging feet.

"Nya!" calls Deka's voice. It seems so far away.

I reach up to feel along the shield edge in search of the Aeri's fingers, but she'd chosen her latching points carefully. Though, do I really want to break her grip? Under my dangling feet, the warriors fighting on the ground are mere dots. The Great Pyramid itself looks like an ant hill with rival colonies fighting their way to the top.

"You'll make a pretty splat down there," says my Aeri captor with a grunt. She flaps her wings harder, lifting me higher.

Staying in her hold only promises a worse outcome for me, so I close my eyes and allow my arms to slide down through the shield straps. At this angle it requires a bit of shimmying to free myself, and when I do, it's with instant regret. My wings buzz instinctively, but it's no use. Instincts won't save me here. I fall straight toward the ground and there's nothing I can do to stop it.

CHAPTER 32
NYA

My hope during the ninety-foot plummet is that my vibrating body will shatter the walkway beneath me and soften my landing. It's a futile hope, one born of desperation. Luckily my wings react instinctively as fierce survival instincts take over. It's not enough to take flight in the gravitational force of the Anomaly, but it slows my drop like a half-open parachute. Hopefully it's enough to keep me from going *splat* on the ground.

When my feet hit the causeway, the first thing to give way is my left leg, which breaks with a sickening *crack*. I fall onto my side, and the sound of my snapping bones gives rise to a wave of nausea that swells from my belly to my throat like a surging tsunami.

Then the pain hits. It's an explosion that blasts away any control I had over my faculties. Pain so intense it blinds me.

I scream so loud and so unnaturally that I hardly recognize the horrendous noise as my own. My fingers claw at the stone beneath me, nails gouging lines into the surface as my arms instinctively retract toward my chest.

I lower my cheek to the stone and scream again, blowing dust up into my eyes and sucking more in as I inhale. It's worse than anything I've ever felt and in this moment I'd do anything to make it end. Stacking my arms before me, I bury my head into my forearms to drown out the world.

A weapon clatters onto the walkway ahead. It rolls straight toward me from the pyramid and slows to a stop nearby. When I look up, I see my mother's spear lying a short crawl away, just out of arm's reach. Just as intended by the person who'd rolled it there.

Standing on the bridge fifty feet away, between me and the Great Pyramid, is Jexa. Suddenly the pain in my leg is nothing as my heart swells in my throat.

I'm not ready to die.

Jexa drapes her spear across her shoulders and saunters toward me. I swear her weapon glows four times brighter than the last time I saw it, revealing she has captured many a brave spark in this battle. I am not ready to join them.

"Do you hear it, Nya?" she says in her stroll toward me. "The Dark is calling for you."

I shiver. The *sapiens* were right. Some of my kind *are* demons. Evil incarnate. This creature coming to finish me has spread terror across a thousand planets, sending untold races into extinction.

My body shakes with something other than pain: Fury. Ignoring the sharp throbbing in my leg, I push myself up to sit on my side. I'll not be slaughtered like a wounded animal. Most certainly not by the beast that used pack tactics in single combat to slay my mother.

Yet, when I try to stand, crippling pain blasts through my entire body.

Footsteps patter the walkway behind me. I look over my shoulder to see Mora as she arrives at my side. She jumps in front of me with a sword in hand, the blade shaking as she holds it toward Jexa.

Jexa stops. A smirk slides across her face. "I admire your bravery. Drop the dagger and I'll cut off only one of your hands."

Mora takes a step back and almost trips over me. When she glances down at me, her eyes are rife with terror.

"Run," I tell her. It takes all my strength not to cling to her legs and hold her back like an anchor.

Mora glances at the forest behind, where many of her Ori have rallied to protect the wounded Fori. She knows what I know. Everyone here today has learned this final lesson, once and for all. Fighting Jexa has only one outcome.

Mora's eyes set on me and her expression hardens. "We'll face the Dark together."

She widens her stance and grips her hilt with both hands.

Jexa gives a satisfied nod and approaches, her smile widening and eyes darkening with each step.

Mora shifts nervously from side to side. This is not a warrior's stance, yet she'll die a more noble death than me.

I search the ground for a weapon within reach. The only one in sight is my mother's spear, which seems statistically impossible considering the armed mob that had rushed through here when Jaleera clashed with Jexa. It's as if Jexa had taken the time to clear the causeway of any dropped weapons, leaving only my mother's spear for me to fight her with. *How sentimental of her.* But I'll not reach it before she arrives. She's only twenty paces away.

I inhale deeply to hold back the tears threatening to

cascade from my eyes. I am a child facing a monster. How many beats of my racing heart remain?

"Your sparks will make fine additions to my collection," Jexa says, lengthening her strides.

She's almost within swinging distance of Mora, her right arm tensing for the strike that will end my protector's life—another spark lost to the gloom in my name—when a shadow falls over us.

I look to the Sun to see a black curve push across it, like a finger nail scraping out the light. A solar eclipse.

Of course. The Alignment.

The moon slides across the sun unnaturally fast. The whole world feels like it's moving in fast-forward motion. In the growing shadow, the battle moves in a blur. No one else seems to notice, other than Jexa. She looks above, her head cocked, taking in this new development with sincere curiosity.

A purple cloud shoots from the portal, diagonally through the sky, swirling like a cosmic tornado, crackling and hissing, vaporizing any Watcher in its path. It spreads and mixes with Earth's thin clouds.

Every hair on my body stands on end as lightning shoots off in every direction. Aeri feathers explode. A group of Fori are launched from the pyramid, their recent position replaced by a black scorch mark.

"The gate is becoming unstable," says Mora.

A boulder gets lodged into the energy stream, halfway down to the Capstone. Ice vaporizes from its surface. *A comet.*

A jolt of upward energy from the pyramid blasts it apart. Shards of rock pelt me.

The sky darkens further as the moon covers half the sun.

The ground shakes. Sparks burst from the portal, followed closely by black smoke. Wails of despair cry out from beyond the cosmic veil.

What is happening?

Mora gasps. I return my attention to the causeway at the same time as Jexa, to see a fourth member join our party.

Somehow this new arrival had glided in from the side and spins gracefully to a stop at the causeway edge. Sparse light from the eclipsed sun traces the ragged edges of her four translucent wings, marking her for one of ours. Another fool to accompany us into darkness.

Mora steps back but doesn't catch herself this time. She trips over my bad leg and lands behind me, but even my instinctual reaction to pain remains silent in my awe.

The newcomer is unarmed and within range of Jexa's spear, yet, much to my bewilderment, Jexa not only cuts her advance short, but takes a few steps back. It's as if Mora and I have completely disappeared as the Marshal's wide eyes appraise this new obstacle from head to toe. Her serious expression suggests this new barrier is one truly worthy of respect. Then Jexa's lips curl into a devious grin.

"It's about time you showed up," says the Marshal of Watchers. She backs away to offer her new opponent an opening to take up my mother's spear.

As I lean forward for a look at this brave fool's face, she glances over her shoulder and, in the eclipse's twilight, gives Mora a look that could command legions. I struggle to recognize this warrior, but I'm sure I've not seen her before. Her brown shoulder-length hair is tied back, with a strand hanging over her ink-black eyes. A half-hoop nose ring hangs from her septum, its two tips dangling over her lips. Purple paint swirls up her body, glowing faintly over a base of black paint, from her toes to her neck, behind her ears, and traces her face in a pattern that looks familiar to me.

Mora grabs me under my shoulders and helps me to my feet. The pain in my leg is but a distant echo as all my focus locks onto the imminent duel. My savior steps to Mother's spear, kicks it up with her foot, and snatches it from the air without taking her eyes off Jexa.

"Come," Mora urges. Her arms fasten around my waist as she pulls me from the walkway to bypass the two combatants. Jexa doesn't even spare us a glance when we pass behind her.

"The Capstone," Mora says, dragging me along, "there isn't much time."

As my savior advances toward Jexa, I realize Mora is right. It's only a matter of time before this newcomer is another spark in Jexa's spear shaft. And though the *sapiens* have taken the pyramid's upper levels, they are having trouble dislodging the gate key. The upward energy stream still surges strong and steady, fueling the bulbous gate above.

I stumble along with Mora, biting my lip at the pain in my leg until I taste the tang of blood. The pyramid steps seem an impossible stretch away, but getting there will be the easy part. The Capstone seems to pierce the sky, resting upon numerous courses of stacked stone that I've already found a challenge to climb even with two good legs. My kind have never attempted such a feat. What winged species would?

At least the *sapiens* have a firm hold on the upper levels. Here, they are wardens of the battle. They have claimed this ant hill for their own. For now.

I can't resist looking back, and I do so just in time to see the clash. Jexa, who had kept her spear resting casually across her shoulders, plants one foot forward, squaring her hips to the side, to stand side-on with her opponent, and slides her spear straight across her shoulders, her right hand shooting the shaft out over her left shoulder. Her opponent bats it away with a thunderous crack. Jexa uses this momentum to swing her spear wide around her back, returning to her front, so that the weapon comes at her opponent's left side in a wide arc. My savior barely raises her spear in time to block it.

Though Jexa's attack was met with great skill, her opponent seems shaken as she stumbles to the side and almost falls from the elevated walkway. She regains her footing and presses an attack with a leaping thrust of my mother's spear, pushing Jexa back. It's a risky move made riskier by the use of her wings flapping to gain an extra foot of height, which leaves her chest exposed to counter-attack.

Jexa, however, relinquishes the opportunity to exploit the exposure. Instead, she deflects the spear and shuffles back. When she ducks and spins away from a swipe at her head, I see concern on her face. She respects this opponent.

Before I know it, we've reach the pyramid, where Mora sits me on the bottom level. The battle has moved halfway up the pyramid steps, with everyone racing toward the Capstone. A few dead and wounded roll to the ground around us.

Two Ori menders join us and set to work fixing my leg. Soon the sharp stabbing turns to a dull throb.

I watch the duel on the walkway ahead, mesmerized. This newcomer handles my mother's spear with such elegance. Her footwork is fluid, stepping forward and backward like a dance while spinning the spear around her back and shooting it forward from her hip, so that even with a few repeated shots like this, Jexa struggles to predict where the spear tip will reach until it's almost too late.

This smooth style of fighting differs greatly from the choppy hacks and slashes taught by Jaleera. How has this fighter remained in our ranks so long without drawing attention to herself? She couldn't have.

"Who is that, Mora?" I ask. "I've not seen her before."

Something about Mora's grave stare, and the way she stops directing the work on my leg, draws my attention away from the fight.

"Yes, you have," she tells me.

Before she can elaborate, a wounded Fori on the step to my right jumps to her feet despite her battered leg. She points her axe at the duel. "Look! It's Klora!"

My heart skips a few beats.

"It can't be!" shouts a voice from above.

Everything around me blurs. The only thing I see is the figure between Jexa and me, how her feet step confidently as she defends and attacks with my mother's—no, *her* spear—with a finesse beyond anything I've ever seen.

How is this possible? It isn't. That fall must have jarred my sense loose. Unless...

I lean back to take in the portal above, where Jexa's warriors pour onto this planet from distant worlds. Then down to the crater halfway up the pyramid, where I'd gone Berserk until The Butcher stopped me.

"It *is* Klora!" says the skeptical Fori from above. "Back from the dead!"

Of course! I'm on my feet without any regard for my broken leg. I laugh in crazed delight as I watch my mother in amazement. My *mother!* But she is not back from the dead as they claim.

I hold my left hand up to examine the palm that pulverized Jaleera's precious red diamond. *Feed this to the energy stream,* she'd told me. At the time I had no idea why, and I'd been too occupied to ponder much upon it. But now it's clear to me why.

To release its contents.

My heart bursts with elation. It seems Jaleera had acquired her own means of quantum containment before Klora's rebellion. By stabbing my mother in the back with the knife she'd given me, she also saved her from Jexa's spear, or from getting snared by the soul recycler, claiming Mother's spark for herself. Which she saved until now. The portal must be able to dissolve the container, or extract its contents. Only...

Jaleera didn't account for me wailing on the pyramid face halfway up. Lucky for us, I'd pounded my way deep enough to access the edge of the energy stream inside. Perhaps it was that which had dissolved the diamond in my grasp, releasing the essence from within. And there she is, my own mother, right before my eyes!

The clamor of battle on the pyramid above fades. Steady strikes of steel on diamond ring loud from the causeway, each contact sending a vibration through Jexa's spear that knocks loose a handful of sparks.

The stories are true. Klora is as good as the legends claim. Better, even.

But here she is at a disadvantage. She is fighting a better version of Jexa, one that has spent lifetimes meditating over their first battle and devising proper counter-moves.

This doesn't faze Klora. She presses the attack with short jabs and narrow slashes, driving Jexa backward. The smacking of shafts and the ringing of spear tips rattles my nerves. Mother drives Jexa back down the causeway until Jexa deciphers her pattern and timing. In a flash Jexa blocks a swipe and pins Mother's spear tip to the ground with her own, then jumps into a spinning back kick. Her rear leg stretches wide and hits Mother's chest with a force that lifts her off her feet.

A crushing weight leaves me breathless as I watch my mother fly through the air and land onto her back. Her spear bounces behind her and then rolls across the stone.

Jexa sweeps her spear tip at Mother on the ground. Klora rolls backward and handsprings onto her feet in time to avoid the blade, which slices off a strand of her brown hair. Hair just like mine.

Klora somersaults her way back to her spear and, while upside down in mid-cartwheel, she grabs the center of the shaft. Then she's on the attack again, spear shafts ringing and steel tips singing. Grunting rises louder from both fighters as they tire, but the tightness in my own chest has loosened and allows for easier breathing as my confidence in Mother grows.

I'm vaguely aware of the Ori tending my shattered leg. The pain is mostly numb, with only an intense throbbing reminding me of my recent brush with death. My mother's deathly dance with Jexa is all I care about. From the crowd gathering to either side of the causeway, I'm not alone in my fixation.

All up the pyramid, every Watcher and Servant has put their quarrel on hold to watch the infamous duel replay.

As the parrying progresses, Klora finds her rhythm and drives Jexa back with unpredictable swings and straight shots with her spear. Jexa stumbles in her retreat, barely able to raise her spear to block the relentless jabs.

Growing up, I'd never been proud when they called me Klora's daughter. For that, I was a fool. Those who followed her in rebellion were anything but. She is magnificent.

Mora's fingernails dig into my knee. I spare her a glance and see she is frowning, shifting nervously while watching the portal above us more than the duel. Now I see the Watchers are not the only species to have heard Jexa's call. Four-winged Servants fall through the gate with them. Then I see what Mora is watching for.

A Watcher swoops from the spherical gate, red hair rippling like silk flames in the wind as she glides toward the causeway. Lifetimes younger, Jaleera is still a jealous contender eager to earn her place as Jexa's right hand.

My heart stops dead for a few beats. Jexa's use of the portal... *It must have disrupted linear time.* I can see by her alarm at Jaleera's approach that she had not intended for this, for it was Jaleera who robbed her of her previous opportunity to slay my mother. A good lesson in why the Consuls are so important when opening a gate. When you reach across space, you also rummage through time, for both are intimately entwined. But I suspect this time rift is complements of Jaleera's quantum diamond imprisonment. I can only guess, but perhaps when she trapped my mother's spark in there, she also sealed in an essence of that timeline. Upon its release through the pyramid, the gate opened a portal to that specific point in space-time. And because

Jaleera's spark has recently departed this world, that opened a void for her time-breach here.

I vault to my feet, but the Ori hold me back. "Mother!" I shout.

Klora's feet slide to a stop as she breaks her attack. She glances over her shoulder at me, and for the longest moment our eyes meet. I can't help but smile. Though she'd never suspect I am her infant daughter, I see the dark fury in her eyes soften. A moment of peace in the eyes of a hurricane.

I shatter our reunion by pointing to Jaleera swooping down at her. She spots the intruder and breaks her spear shaft over her knee. She wields a half in each hand, ready to meet Jaleera when she lands on the side closest to the pyramid.

Klora stands with an opponent to her right and left. Holding half a spear toward each of them, she waits for her enemies to attack.

Jexa jumps in with a jab. Klora deflects it with the pointed end of her spear. When Jaleera takes a stab at her back, she blocks it with the blunt end.

Both Jexa and Jaleera come in hard from both sides, and Klora meets their weapons with a confidence that suggests she may be able to glimpse a second or two into the future. In fact, she makes fools of both supreme Watchers, batting away their weapons and landing kicks that knock them off balance and sends them staggering.

In a blur, Klora takes a swing with both shaft halves to knock young Jaleera's spear from her hands. She then turns to meet Jexa's swipe, sending her into a spin, and she even lands a smack across her back with the blunt end of her spear. As Jexa stumbles to regain her footing and Jaleera lunges in to recover her spear, mother leaps into a scissor kick that hits Jaleera in the chest and knocks her back. She raises her spear tip over Jaleera, but doesn't follow through. Instead, she kicks Jaleera's spear off the causeway and rushes at Jexa.

My mother has many chances like this to strike down Jaleera, but she restrains herself. She doesn't think Jaleera will actually take her out. She believes friendship triumphs over ambition with her. That Jaleera is a warrior of honor. If my mother ever was a fool about anything, it was underestimating Jaleera's ambition.

A swing at her belly from Jexa forces Klora to spring backward while doubling over, narrowly avoiding the swipe. From her bent position she punches the ground at Jexa's feet, while simultaneously raising her rear leg to sweep Jaleera's forward leg up and around to send her stumbling to the side.

The causeway under Jexa collapses from the shock wave delivered by my mother's fist. Jexa sinks to her waist in a pit of rubble. Mother turns to Jaleera and rushes with both halves of her spear, swinging furiously from every angle, her face twisted in a grimace of anger and regret.

Jaleera blocks and shuffles backward while timing Mother's movements. She manages to get a few swipes in to counter and halt her retreat, but it's not near enough to stop Klora's momentum. She front kicks Jaleera to create space between them, then launches into a forward spin that ends in her driving her spear tip into Jaleera's collar bone.

Mother screams in anger and frustration. It's the only noise I've ever heard from her mouth, and it sends a chill through me.

Jaleera's knees haven't hit the ground before Klora circles behind her to face Jexa. As Jexa climbs onto the causeway,

Mother adopts a wide stance, the blunt end of her spear held before her as she beckons Jexa to attack.

Jexa comes at her with a whirlwind of slashes and jabs, which Klora blocks and deflects in a backward parry with one arm held behind her back. It's a fine display of skill and confidence, but it's not enough. Jexa is too fast, coming from too many angles for one stub of a weapon to defend against. In one swift movement, Jexa bats Mother's spear away and keeps twirling backward until she drives her spear's bottom tip into Mother's belly.

"No!" I scream.

As my mother falls to her knees, I hobble down the causeway with Mora's dagger.

Jexa wrenches her blade free and holds it vertically over Mother's chest, preparing to add her spark to the collection in her spear. Tears well in my eyes, because I'm not fast enough to stop it.

When Jexa sees me coming, her eyes light up. She crouches beside Klora and points to me. By the softening of my mother's eyes, Jexa is telling her who I am. And the sorrow suggests that Jexa is telling her what she's going to do to me.

I'm halfway across the causeway when Jexa heaves up on her weapon for its final plunge. Tears blur my vision. I can't bear to watch this, but I can't look away.

Klora keeps her eyes on me, all the fight in her replaced by the warmth of a mother's love. The blackness in her eyes drains, her green irises rising from the inky depths as they turn to white. As Jexa drives her spear down, I smile at Mother in the hope that it's the last thing she ever sees.

But Jexa's spear does not reach its destination. A shriek

tears through the air, freezing her downward plunge. The piercing wail is loud enough to shred my eardrums, and covering my ears with both hands does nothing to save them. All I can do is fall to the ground like everyone else. I see Ori burrow into the sand and crawl in a panic underground. The only one not affected like this is Jexa, who drops her spear and stares up at the portal.

A hurricane of nausea whirls inside my gut. Bile burns up my throat as I come to a sickening realization. The gate didn't align with the duel between Jexa and my mother. It went a little farther back, to a time before Klora stole away her prized pet.

Another shriek blasts through the portal. It rattles my spark, paralyzes my mind, and locks my muscles stiff.

Jexa's soul-eating sky serpent has heard her call. And, like a dutiful pet, it is on its way to destroy all of her enemies. And this time, Klora is in no shape to stop it.

CHAPTER 33

NYA

It's hard to imagine a creature like Jexa ever loving something, but I swear that's what now lightens the darkness in her eyes as she watches the portal above. And as she drops to her knees with outstretched arms, it becomes clear who owns who. A master speaks from the past, and a servant throws out her arms and shouts, "I'm here! Come to me!"

The sight of Jexa's vulnerability to this thing stirs my belly. These heaven-shaking wails warp her into a trance, her composure shattered by a dark love song. The patterns come in vibrant waves, an infernal rhythm of intricate design I feel with every screech. It hits me like a shiver down my spine that does not leave, just seizes me like a mighty claw upon my neck and shoulders. These are not the yowlings of a mindless beast. An intelligent evil issues commands from across time, instructing its servants to bring it back into existence with a knowledge known only to a few beings across the Universe.

A ground-shaking shriek tears through the air and rattles me to my core, infusing me with a sense of awe and dread.

I cover my ears and close my eyes in a futile effort to block it out.

Dark tendrils weave through my mind, offering a calm reprieve should I simply welcome its assimilation into my being. In return, it will grant me a power beyond my comprehension. I need only to submit.

I take deep breaths to calm myself. *I must resist!*

My nerve endings ignite with searing pain. Every fibrous strand feels like its on fire. The portal above glows red and throbs like the pressure inside my head, vibration upon vibration in amplified arcs, an invasive, primal resonance that cannot be tamed.

"Why do you resist it, Nya?"

The foreign yet familiar voice stops me. Stops my heart. I hear myself gasp into a void. I turn to see the source, and I nearly spring to my feet with joy.

There's no one else around. Just the two of us, my fated mate and I, alone for the first time ever. My heart swells as I see my other side staring back at me, his green eyes shining bright with my own reflection.

"Join him, Nya," he says, his eyes soft and pleading. An imploring smile brightens his face. "Help him in his task, and he will reward us better than the Magister ever could."

His voice calms me, but his words ring hollow inside, stirring confusion. "Do his bidding?"

"He'll let us be together. He'd never tear us apart like the Magister. What cruelty to inflict upon us. We were so young. Our best years gone, replaced by suffering."

I crawl to my feet and limp up to him, close enough to touch, but I restrain myself. I look deep into his eyes. Instead of the fire that warms my heart, I see black nothingness. "You're not real," I say.

"I can be whatever you want me to be."

Is this how you seduced Jexa? Reached into the depths of her mind, found the desire most sacred to her?

My heart clenches, but this is far from the worst heartache I've felt today.

"Be gone," I say.

His mouth curls into a wicked grin. He gives me a gracious bow, and in a blink he is gone as commanded.

I now stand on the causeway before the bridge, outside the moat, close enough to reach my mother if I'm fast, but I cannot take another step in that direction. My destiny waits to my rear.

A louder shriek rips through the air, whipping a vibration of terror through my heart. Even the Watchers stare at the sky in fear. Well, the newly-arrived reinforcements do, anyway. Those originally stationed to Earth with Jexa drop to their knees and lower their heads in tribute to their god—the being whose wicked desires swayed them from their path—the darkness that shrouded their hearts, corrupting their good nature as benevolent Wardens of the Pact.

I narrow my eyes on the portal and clench my fists. It cannot come here. The monster and its master can never be reunited, no matter what it costs me. I must keep them separated, in past and present, where my mother can kill one and we can continue our fight against the other with some semblance of hope.

I must destroy the Capstone.

If I don't, Jexa will not rest until her spear shaft glows bright with the light of every spark that blasted outward from the birth of time. The innocent will forever remain in her grasp until the day she decides to toss that weapon into the Dark with all its imprisoned souls.

A blast of half shriek, half growl, shakes the ground. The bulbous portal swells. Wings and scales appear through the wavy walls of energy, like a dragon trying to break free from the confines of a translucent egg.

This time, I do not tremble. I allow the invasive energy to roll through me, to resonate and empower.

I understand why my mother abandoned me after my birth to fight Jexa. She did it for the love of me and every other innocent being that could not defend itself. But I am a child no more. I am my mother's daughter, and I will carry on her legacy, even if it means I share her fate.

I limp back toward the pyramid. In my retreat, I can't resist a look back over my shoulder, to my mother lying motionless at Jexa's feet, her chest rising and falling lightly.

Jexa's attention falls to me. By the alarm in her eyes, she sees my intent as I hobble on a broken leg. She bends and picks up her spear, and though I try moving faster, I know she will beat me in a race. If not on the causeway, then up the many stone levels that stand between me and the gate key.

A bolt whizzes over my shoulder toward Jexa's heart. She bats it away with her spear.

Suddenly my feet lift from the ground as Deka heaves me over his shoulder. I want to shout out in relief as he lowers his crossbow and carries me toward the Great Pyramid, but I save my energy.

Even with the burden of my weight, he is fast. Plus, when I look up from my slumped position over his back, I do so just in time to see my mother stab Jexa in the calf.

Jexa doesn't allow even a whisper of pain. She just falls backward, arms flailing, where she rolls with my mother on the ground.

I look away from the scuffle. There is no time to worry about Klora. She's already proven that she can handle herself. There is something greater that requires my attention.

Jexa's beloved must be an abominably large beast. The portal above pulsates, dilating and constricting as the serpent tries crossing the bridge between timelines. With each outward throb, the portal's crystalline perimeter retains a bit of its stretch, slowly growing with each pulse. Like a baby eager to escape the womb, the beast pushes hard to enter our world.

Deka sets me onto the pyramid's bottom tier. He stops to catch his breath and winces when he looks above. I join him in surveying our climb. It's a far trek up once. But to do it up and down, and then up again... he must be exhausted. Yet if that's the case, he doesn't let it show. He grabs me under my armpits to lift me.

"I can climb," I say, dreading to be more of a burden to him.

I stand and lean against the face of the second stone tier. Before I begin my ascent, I steal a look back down the causeway, where Jexa holds her spear upright in both hands, the tip buried deep in my mother's chest, the shaft glowing bright as she siphons Mother's spark.

I close my eyes and climb up onto the pyramid's second course. Now is not the time to mourn someone I'd thought dead my whole life. My eyes remain closed as I climb. It's all I can do to keep the hot pain in my leg from weighing me down. To see how far remains would only work against me.

THWAP!

I jolt, and a hand pats my shoulder.

"It's okay," Deka says. "I'm here."

"That noise?" It was too close.

"My crossbow."

"Is she coming?"

"Yes."

By the shudder in his voice, I know Jexa is closing on us.

"Keep climbing," he says.

I hear the creaking of polymer as Deka reloads his crossbow.

THWAP! Another whistling bolt fades through the air.

I try to block out everything and keep climbing, trusting that Deka is watching over me. The climb seems to go on forever, but I dare not stop.

Hands and feet patter on the stone beside me. "Almost there," comes Sheffa's voice. "Race to the top?"

I allow a half-hearted laugh.

As I climb higher, the loosing of arrows and bolts becomes more frequent. Feet scuff and weapons clatter off stone above. I can travel blind like this no more. I open my eyes to see a *sapien* shoot a bolt out into the sky, and I follow his line of fire to a swerving Aeri who narrowly avoids the projectile.

I look up to see we're barely halfway to the Capstone, and I huff a sigh of frustration. Still so far to go. So, so far. And worse than the distance is the swarm of Watchers between me and the apex. They scramble and clash with scatterings of Ori and Fori in their rise to the high ground.

A gasp draws my attention to the crossbowman who'd just shot at the Aeri a moment ago. He aims over my shoulder, eyes wide in fright at whatever approaches from behind me. He lowers his weapon as two arms hook under my shoulders. The horrible, familiar feeling of being lifted from the pyramid, accompanied by the pounding of feathered wings in my periphery, sends me into a panic.

I writhe and kick, desperate to free myself before I'm lifted too high like before. It's the worst feeling ever, helplessly dangling over a bloody battlefield, knowing you'll be dropped to a shattered mess at any second.

"Easy!" grunts my captor in my ear. Her voice is familiar, and stokes more anger than fear.

"Ko Tora?!"

"That's me," she grunts, "here to save the day."

About time. I'm too winded and relieved to say it out loud.

Her mighty wings beat in a concerted effort, elevating us with each downward flap, rising high and then dropping slightly until a double beat gets us rising again—one to stop the drop, another to gain another few feet of elevation. Her violent huffing in my ear reveals the incredible effort to bear me, the strain testing all of her resolve.

"Whatever you do," she grumbles, "you better be quick about it."

Below, two Aeri have each taken an end of Jexa's spear and are struggling to hoist her by the vertical shaft. Four more Aeri have acquired Watcher shields and form one great shield before the rising trio, blocking the crossbow bolts raining down.

Before I know it, Ko Tora is dumping me onto the stone course twelve levels below the Capstone. "Just a quick rest," she says, gasping.

"I'm out!" shouts Deka. He flings his crossbow at Jexa's rising entourage from twelve courses below me. It bounces off a shield and tumbles below.

Such a far way down.

I swallow hard and return my attention above. A few *sapiens* loose arrows from Fori-crafted quivers and bows scavenged during the climb. Six of them have gathered three courses below the Capstone, where they can hold a tighter perimeter.

"I'm out!" shouts Marlok.

"Me too!"

A shiver prickles my spine despite the heat and exertion. Jexa now rises unopposed. Deka and his fighters should have saved a few bolts for a close quarters encounter.

"Incoming!"

That word shoots terror through me. To my left, two Aeri dive straight for us.

Ko Tora hurls her short sword into the first Aeri. The blade lodges into her shoulder and sends her crashing into stone below. The second, seeing Ko Tora and myself now unarmed, swoops in with enough speed to throw us from the pyramid, which she certainly would if not for Ko Tora.

My Aeri companion leaps out and collides with her sister in a ruffle of feathers. They tumble toward the ground in uncontrolled flight.

Deka scrambles up toward us, eager to either join me or find safety among his kin below the Capstone. They crouch with spears and await the climbing swarm of Watchers, thousands strong now—their ranks replenished by the portal. The Black Tide rises steadily to drown us. But Jexa's serpent has choked off the gateway and has prevented more from coming.

I do not know what will happen to Deka and the survivors after I destroy the Capstone. If the Watchers continue to assail them on the high ground, how long could they expect to last? *Longer than facing that serpent*, I know that much. Besides, I cannot worry about that right now.

Sheffa and a few Fori crouch among the *sapien* defenders. She pats my back as I crawl through their perimeter, then gives me a boost up to the next level.

I collapse above the upper defense line to catch my breath, two tiers below the Capstone. This brief rest is not a luxury we can afford.

A head-splitting screech rattles whatever nerve of mine remains. My skull feels like it's cracked in half like an egg, my brain frying like yolk. Above, the portal glows red and bulges downward toward me. Through its wavy surface I see fangs—two rows atop and two below—hinging wide and snapping, and a golden eye with a great vertical slit.

I clamber up the last two tiers and throw myself onto the Capstone. Or, at least I try. The rising energy column pushes me up so that I don't even touch it on first try. The upward force blasts my hair and threatens to rip every strand from my scalp. Opening my eyes is not an option. I press downward, fighting against the current, but it's like wading through a flood. I push harder, my skin pulling tighter to my bones the lower I go, until I make contact.

The Capstone is almost too cold to touch, and the typical shimmer of gold is overwhelmed by a hurricane of frequencies surging through the stream, like a waterfall blasting through a funnel.

As if destroying the Capstone wasn't a mighty task on its own... It's impossible to pin down its natural resonance amid the cloak of chaos. All I can do is feel it out. Cast out a line and see what comes back.

The moderate vibration I send to test its molecular bonds produces the strangest sensation: my own vibration shuddering back. But it's not like the electrocution response I've felt with dense metals in the past, instead more a synchronous rebound, weaving through my body's atomic structure, threatening to dissolve me if I dare apply more energy.

My heart quivers. *So this is what the end feels like.*

I amplify the frequency and send a stronger counter-force. This is met with what feels like static charge. Something other than gold lies within. I try again, but the harder I push, the harder the Capstone pushes back, as if I've hit a wall. I send a jolt in deep and get one right back, like electricity. This feeling I know and dread.

My heart sinks. *Diamond.* The Capstone is made with a diamond core. Even if I destroy the softer outer layer of sacred gold without sapping all my energy or dissolving myself, the force required to destroy the diamond core will produce the rebound of a thousand lightning strikes. What a way to die, getting zapped into a hundred trillion sizzling particles in front of everyone.

I can't do it.

A roar drowns out the clamor. Above, two nostrils bulge through the gate's rounded side.

It's all the reminder I need. Jexa is trying to bring a beast back from death by disrupting space-time. If this is possible, then my task is no stretch. I can kill again what my mother

has already killed. Yes, I can and I will. For I am Nya
—*Destroyer of Worlds!*

I press with all my might and send the highest frequency I've ever produced. Knives stab my entire body in response. It takes all my might to keep from withering as glass grows inside my veins, spreading from my fingers to my toes, splitting me apart from the inside. My spine stiffens as my head falls back to stare at the sky, but I see nothing. Terrible pain blinds me, like razors flaying the tips of every nerve.

Waves of agonizing palpitations assail my heart, interrupted only by excruciating constrictions that nearly drive me to my knees. My arms tremble before me. I wonder which will give out first: the beat of my heart, or the strength of my bones?

My hands go numb, like when they fall asleep from lack of circulation. The numbness spreads up my arms... to my chest and up my face to my scalp, and down my legs... all the way down... everything down to my toes falling asleep until I am weightless. Relaxed. It's so peaceful...

"Nya!" The voice is distant. Maybe a memory.

I'm so sleepy. It's time to rest, I think. Just for a bit, to gather my strength and... and what? What was I doing? It doesn't matter. Whatever it is can wait. I just need me a good sleep.

Heaviness weighs on my back and squeezes my chest. No, *squeeze* isn't the right word. This is a hug. Someone is hugging me from behind.

For some forgotten reason I'm not supposed to open my eyes, but I risk opening them anyway.

At first I think my vision is blurry—that's why my arms appear loose as snowflakes rising from snow-covered ground, like a snowfall in reverse—until I look to the arms holding me. The detail of the brown skin is so sharp and vivid, down to the finest hair.

Deka clings to my back and buries his face into my neck, where he starts heaving. With him stabilizing me like this, the snow settles back upon my bones. My arms sharpen as my bonds regroup and solidify. I'd been shuddering so fiercely, violently rattled by tremendous force, that my body had become a blur.

The excruciating tightness in my heart loosens. I can breathe again, suddenly aware that I'd been unable to.

I remember why I'm here, what I am doing. And I must do it fast, because although Deka has grounded me, absorbing some of the rebounding energy that assails me, he has only bought us a bit of time. Already his arms are blurring from the severe tremors, his body unaccustomed to these forces. Not like mine. His bones will burst and his heart will falter at any second.

I want to shake him off my back, to free him from this doom, but removing my hands will reset the Capstone's bonds. I've made too much progress to give it up. Already the energy stream rising before me has weakened enough for me to keep my eyes open. I can see through to the other side, where a black figure grows larger through the milky haze.

Jexa!

She lands on the Capstone opposite me. Only... it's not Jexa. It's Ko Skadia! She's leaking from two gaping wounds in her chest, and it takes ten Fori to keep her upright.

She slams both hands onto the Capstone and immediately I feel the strain of my own effort ease. The cold knives withdraw, and the glass inside me melts into warm fluid. This, however, is no time for a breather, so I pour my freed energy into the diamond to further weaken its bonds. My hands are numb but I get this phantom sensation that they are playing with wet sand. The Capstone is softening. *We're doing it!*

I feel the internal chains stretch and strain to maintain their bonds, particles desperate to stick together. I ease off and feel the chains spring back like elastic. Keeping them stretched requires that I maintain at least this frequency. To my surprise, this isn't hard. In fact, I'm able to amplify it, which further stretches the bonds, separating particles at the atomic level.

My rejoice fades with Ko Skadia's body. Literally. She is a blur, almost see-through. When I look at Deka's arms around me and my own, I see the same effect, though not so severe. Ko Skadia's wounds have rendered her too weak to endure this strain. She is fading much faster than I. Her head sags and elbows lean against the sloped Capstone face.

Marlok must have noticed the effect of Deka's technique on me, because he latches onto Ko Skadia's back. Immediately the color returns to her face. Her dazed eyes widen with awareness. I feel the surge of her output and match its frequency to produce a compounding resonance. We are almost there, but *almost* is not good enough. I feel Deka and I start to fade again, like falling asleep. It's actually not so bad. Despite the havoc around us, it's peaceful.

Suddenly Deka grows heavier on my back. Impossible. He should be coming undone like me, sharing my fate.

Commotion across the energy stream draws my attention to Ko Skadia. Marlok is no longer alone in grounding her.

Several *sapiens* and Fori grab her arms and pile onto Marlok's back to share the load.

No amount of numbness can tame the goosebumps rising on my skin. Has there ever been a more inspiring sight?

Not everyone is here to help, however. In the sky behind Ko Skadia, two Aeri lift Jexa by her spear. They rise high above the pyramid and then dive toward us at alarming speed. Both Aeri release their ends of the vertical spear and send Jexa gliding down toward us. Towards *me!*

A hand clamps my forearm. In the corner of my eye, I see Sheffa convulsing as she reaches behind with her free hand in search of another anchor. Mora is quick to grab it from the level below, where a mix of Fori and Ori and *sapiens* hug her.

My heart pounds with a force of light and warmth that only the instant of Creation could rival. Everyone around this Capstone have enlisted themselves to share my doom, and this sacrifice stirs an energy deep within me, a light glowing with an intensity I never thought possible.

I smile as I shed tears of joy. *Could this be it?*

My whole body relaxes into a state of bliss as I align with the elusive frequency that has taunted all of my kind with the promise of infinite power. The foundational frequency for whatever must be done in the name of good, the sacred harmonic revealed only to the master in pursuit of the purest intent. The key to cracking any code. The force able to overcome any obstacle. A cosmic power that I've felt in brief flutters throughout my life...

It is the feeling I get when I think of my fated mate, the feeling so similar to that which stirred in me when Deka's eyes met mine for the first time. It is the look my mother gave me as she lay dying at Jexa's feet, when she sacrificed her immortal being to buy me a sliver more time. And the feeling that drove me Berserk when I saw my friends torn to pieces as they gave their lives to save mine.

My heart thumps with this master frequency, spreading its warm resonance to my chest, where it whirls like a hundred million butterflies, fluttering with gentle vibrations down my arms to my palms.

I blast this boundless energy through my fingertips and into the gold before me.

Jexa glides over Ko Skadia, through the energy stream, and drives her spear through my chest at the instant I feel the Capstone explode. The last thing I see is white light.

We are dust.

EPILOGUE

The dark is brighter than I'd been expecting. Heavier, too. It's almost enough to smother me.

When I raise a hand to shield my eyes from the glare, I'm surprised to have a hand at all. And it feels as if I'm forcing my way through a great heap of dust.

A grainy substance invades my eyes. I rub them, but it makes the gritty feeling worse.

I wiggle my toes and feel fine particles slide between them. I slide my feet around, encountering a silky layer of warmth above my legs and cold below.

When I lift my head and sit up, the weight slides to either side of me. Sand.

My head swirls and it takes all my effort to remain upright. I feel like retching so bad I gag and clap a hand over my mouth.

"There she is!" rises a voice from behind me.

I turn to see Sheffa standing atop a grassy bluff. Deka rushes up from the far slope to join her, then races down the sandy side toward me.

As if remembering a dream, I recall Jexa plunging her spear into me. I feel my chest and belly for a wound, but my hand glides smoothly over my skin and finds nothing out of the ordinary. How can this be?

Deka slides to a stop beside me and wraps me in his arms.

"Jexa..." I say, though I can hardly breathe in his embrace. "She stabbed me with her spear."

Deka holds me at arm's length to examine my chest, then smiles. "She tried," he says.

Of course. If Jexa succeeded, Deka and I would be skewered together, because he'd been clinging to my back. A quick look over him confirms this hasn't happened.

"She went right through you!" Sheffa exclaims, her eyes wide in disbelief. "Wouldn't a believed it if I didn't see it wiff me own eyes. You was like a ghost. We all was."

"And Jexa?" I say, looking to the sky warily.

Sheffa hugs herself and looks to her feet.

I accept Deka's help to stand and scan our surroundings. The Capstone must have exploded in spectacular fashion, because the blast had thrown me beyond sight of the pyramids. All I see is ocean to my right and a wall of grassy dunes to my left. The landing alone should have shattered my body, yet none of my bones feel broken. I flex my fingers. No pain.

I need a better look from high ground, so I race up the dunes, where my eyes struggle to accept a strange sight.

Nearby, to the east, surf rolls at the edge of a glittering ocean. In its retreat, it leaves a smooth expanse of silvery wet sand, like polished platinum. In the water beyond is an island of arched rock. To the west, even closer, a forest of white branches supports a canopy of glittering purple leaves.

Three dozen familiar faces join me on the bluff—Fori, Ori, and *sapien*.

"Where are the pyramids?" I say. I squint upward in search of Watchers, but see only fluffy pink clouds in a lavender sky.

"They's gone," Sheffa says.

"They are not gone," says Marlok, squeezing the silver shaft of a Watcher spear. He squints suspiciously at the forest. "They are exactly where we left them."

My breath catches. Deka's war leader is right. The light from the glowing star that fosters life on this planet feels different on my skin. It glows with less intensity than that of Gaia's Sun.

So, we didn't turn to dust after all. Somehow we got sucked into the energy stream and spit out here.

I survey the violet forest. Such scenery is nothing new to me, but I can tell by the glaze over Deka's eyes that he is awestruck. These shades of purple are new to him.

I look to the powder blue disk glowing in the lavender sky. "What star is that?"

The Fori and Ori gathered around us exchange unknowing looks and shrug.

So none of us has been here before. This is not a planet we've revived.

I scan the area for artificial structures. Nothing but sand bluffs, trees, and the sound of rolling surf from a glittering sea greet my senses. "Where's the gateway?" I ask.

This draws even more confused looks.

I crouch and hug my knees, trying to keep my concern from showing on my face. Without the information encoded into the markings inscribed on portal gates, we'll have to wait until night to survey the stars to determine our position.

Yet, what good will that do us without a gate? We'd be trapped here without one. It must be nearby.

"Come!" beckons a distant voice. "This way!"

A second group appears on a dune between us and the forest. Platinum sand slides beneath them and gives the dune the appearance of melting steel.

After my days on Earth, it's taking some time for my eyes to adjust to this planet's color spectrum. I notice Deka blinking and rubbing his eyes a lot, like he's thinking there's something wrong with them.

We join the group of Fori atop the large dune. Down the far slope, Ori and *sapiens* splash in a purple oasis. Their playful laughter rises loud. For a mono-planetary species, Deka's folk accept this change of environment remarkably quick. The transit must have muddled their minds.

Of all these strange happenings, perhaps the strangest is Ko Skadia, who is building a sandcastle at the oasis edge. Imagine, an Entropath Elder, *building* something. I slide down to join her.

"Ko Skadia, where are we?"

She smiles and scoops water onto dry sand, then sets about forming it into a turret.

Mora wades out of the water. "You're wasting your time. She's here in body, but I've not gotten any more than a stupid smile from her."

"Do you know how this happened?"

Mora looks to the sky. "Not even our wisest Elders know all the Universe's secrets. But we are here nonetheless. Only those who sacrificed themselves on the Capstone ended up on this planet. For all we can say, this is some sort of reward from a benevolent force."

"Or a curse," I add, but I'm quick to cover my mouth with both hands. Best not to whisper dreadful possibilities into this mysterious Universe.

None of my companions offer me even the slightest look of scorn. Instead, Mora smacks me on the shoulder. "Relax, Nya. It's not often our kind slip through the grid like this." She shakes her head at the sky. "If I had to guess, the connection became unstable and the gate shot us to a random place. It could be worse. At least here is a lot safer than where we were."

"Until the Watchers track us down," says Sheffa.

"They'd never know where to look." Mora scoops sand between both hands and lifts it for all to see. "There are as many planets as there are grains of sand on every planet in this Universe."

Deka shakes his head. "Impossible."

"Not impossible," I tell him. "*Infinity.*"

He frowns at this word and looks to the sand at his feet.

"It'd be an impossible shot in the dark to find us," assures Mora. "We should make ourselves comfortable. If a portal dumped us on a planet with no gate, this will be where we spend our remaining days."

"No gate?" I say. "How is that possible?"

Mora shrugs. "None among us is a Consul. Who's to say you need one on both planets to make a connection? Might be no one does it because you'd have no way back. If that's true, it would be the same for the Watchers. They'd not risk a pursuit on a one-way trip."

I look around, my heart swelling with panic. A gate is an

obvious presence that cannot be missed. Whatever our means of arrival, it must have been near here, because the humans could not make it far by foot. Which means there very well might not be a gate after all.

Tears well in my eyes. "If there's no gate, then..."

Deka locks eyes on me and, picking up on my distress, a flood of panic washes away his wonder. "There's no way back? My people... with all those Watchers... they'll be slaughtered!"

He falls to his knees and begins to hyperventilate. I latch onto his back in the same way he did to me on the pyramid, and I use my breathing to steady his.

"Don't worry, Deka," I whisper in his ear. "The Magister probably arrived after we shut the gate. He'll sort out the Watchers."

Mora shifts uncomfortably. I give her a warning look to keep her concerns to herself, for she knows what I do. When the Magister sees the carnage at Giza, the sacred gate littered with dead Watchers, unsanctioned rebellion will be his first conclusion. A few dead humans in the mix would suggest an alliance against his divine design. And just like that, Servants and humans would fall from his grace.

It's best not to dwell on that worst-case scenario though, not when we don't even know where we are.

"We'll find you a way home," I say to Deka, "and we'll save your people. I swear it."

Deka's breathing slows and falls into rhythm with mine. His hands reach up to where mine are clasped over his chest, and together we stare out to sea.

"We'll split into teams," I say, "to search for this planet's gate and its Capstone to unlock it. Then—"

"Easy," says Mora with a gentle squeeze of my shoulder. "We just fought the biggest battle in the history of our race. We need time to catch our breath and rest."

This is true. Looking around, even the *sapiens* don't seem in much of a hurry to find the gate. A few still play in the oasis with the Ori and Fori. Their laughter puts me on edge. I scan the sky, expecting a Watcher party to come swooping in to break up the fun. We have rules. Daylight is work time.

Marlok crouches beside Ko Skadia and helps build her sand castle. She doesn't acknowledge his presence, but smiles at the water canal he digs around her battlements, as if it appeared there by magic. Part of me envies her wondrous ignorance.

But no. There is work to do. My mother's spark now belongs to Jexa, along with many others who'd sacrificed themselves at the pyramids. For the same reasons that Deka cannot abandon his people, I dare not forget about mine.

Our fight on Earth is not yet over.

To Be Continued...

BOOKS BY JR DEVOE

Onero's Hunt

The Dark Monarch Series
Prequel: The Light Ones
Book 1: Dust
Book 2: Ashes
Book 3: Sparks

ACKNOWLEDGMENTS

This book has gone through countless revisions, each one I believed would be the last. Through it all, my parents, Julie and James Devoe, have been a constant pillar of support. They painstakingly checked every "final" draft for errors and were always patient with me, even when I thought I'd finally finished. I owe them endless gratitude for their enthusiastic proofreading and unwavering belief in me.

This second edition has also greatly benefited from the guidance of Mica Scotti Kole, who asked the tough questions that pushed me to enhance this story. A special thank you goes to Maciek, who let me know when I finally got it right.

I was fortunate to also have many friends help me out along this journey to publication. Colleen House, for giving me that push to go to the Big Apple and pitch my stories to the world back in 2017. And Paul Bailey, for always checking in on me as I slumped over his kitchen table in varying degrees of despair while trying to make the words go.

To my brother Mitchell, who inspired Deka's most admirable qualities.

Thank you to my beta readers who offered varying levels of contribution at various stages of development: Nikki Boccelli and Leslie Arambula.

A special mention goes out to Brigid Devoe, for everything from impromptu author photo shoots during rain storms, to helping me decide which combination of words would best summarize my story, and for entertaining my numerous late night ramblings about my failures, worries, and minor successes.

And to Tony, for always being there to cheer me on and whose visits provided the necessary distractions that pulled me away when writing the first draft of this book had become too hard on the head.

And for Leon Devoe, for showing me the light back when I'd be staring into darkness for too long.

Many aspiring authors have to face not only doubt from themselves, but also from their family and friends. As evidenced by the paragraphs above, I am not among those writers. Everyone in my life has offered me unwavering support in my pursuit of this dream, and for that I am eternally grateful.

ABOUT THE AUTHOR

J. R. Devoe grew up on Cape Breton Island, Nova Scotia, in the town of Sydney Mines. He has since traveled to six continents, including Antarctica in 2013 to research elements of his debut novel, *Onero's Hunt*.

In 2014, he pedaled a bicycle across Canada to raise money for WaterAid Canada, a charity that provides clean drinking water and sanitation services to developing countries. In 2016, he pedaled a bicycle across New Zealand for the sheer joy of it.

J. R. Devoe currently works as a professional seafarer, where his voyages continue to inspire his writing and fuel his passion for exploration.